Legend Press Ltd, The Old Fire Station,
140 Tabernacle Street, London, EC2A 4SD
info@legend-paperbooks.co.uk | www.legendpress.co.uk

Contents © Kat Gordon 2015

Print ISBN 978-1-7850798-6-3
Ebook ISBN 978-1-7850798-7-0
Set in Times. Printed in the United Kingdom by Clays Ltd.
Cover design by Simon Levy www.simonlevyassociates.co.uk

Kat Gordon was born in London in 1984. She attended Camden School for Girls, read English at Somerville College, Oxford, and received a distinction in her creative writing masters from Royal Holloway.

In between, Kat has been a gymnastics coach, a theatre usher, a piano accompanist, a nanny, a researcher and worked at *Time Out*. She has spent a lot of time travelling, primarily in Africa.

Kat lives in London with her boyfriend and their terrifying cat, Maggie.

Follow Kat @katgordon1984

This book is dedicated to
Janet and Alex Gordon,
and to Tom Feltham, with thanks.

PART ONE

Heart

One

It's nine o'clock in the morning when the phone call comes through.

"Miss Park?"

"Yes?"

"This is Marylebone Heart Hospital. I'm afraid your father has had a heart attack."

For a moment I don't understand. I'm still in bed, under the covers, head and one arm out in the open.

"He was brought in here at six this morning. We'll be moving him to coronary care shortly, where you'll be able to visit him. He's still under, though."

"Right." I feel I should say more. "Please let me know if there's any change in his condition."

"Of course."

I hang up.

I lie back in my bed. My brain feels like it's out of sync with the rest of me. I try to think about the last time I spoke to my father; it was five years ago. I can see him before me, white-faced, the nurse's arm around his chest as she propelled him out of the room. I wonder whether this heart attack was already lurking offstage, biding its time. I know that heart problems can build up over a long period, treacherous plaque mushrooming on the inner walls of the coronary artery. When

I was a baby, my father gave me a plastic simulacrum of a heart to play with. It was meant for medical students, but I used it to chew on when my teeth were coming through.

Years later, when I was alone in the house on rainy afternoons, I would read his medical journals. I became obsessed with the heart, its unpredictability. I can still recite the facts: ... *damage to the heart restricts the flow of oxygenated blood usually pumped out of the left ventricle. This causes left ventricular failure and fluid accumulation in the lungs; it's at this point that the sufferer will feel a shortness of breath. Patients may also feel weak, light-headed, nauseous; experience sweating and palpitations.* Approximately half of all heart-attack patients have experienced warning symptoms such as chest pain at some point prior to the actual attack.

My ears are ringing now. I plug them with my fingers, trying to push the sound back into my brain. I can't imagine how it must feel, the realisation that your heart is failing you, when for so many years you forgot that it was even there, ticking away like a little death-clock. All my muscles start to curl up just thinking about it. I couldn't have stopped it, I tell myself, but there's a heavy feeling in the room, like when you're a kid and you've done something bad and you're waiting to be found out.

I drag myself out of bed to throw up in the sink that stands in the corner of the bedroom. My hands shake when I run the taps to clear away the mess. I cross the room to the window. *We don't swim in your toilet, so don't piss in our pool* – my cousin, Starr, taped that sign to the glass.

I force the window open and stick my head out into the fresh air. Below me a cyclist screeches to a stop, drops his bike and runs into the building two doors down, his hair slick with sweat. The traffic is heavy and the air is already thick and sultry. Shop workers stand in their doorways, fanning themselves. Behind them, JXL curls out of the radio – the remix of Elvis Presley's 'A Little Less Conversation'. It's been number one in the charts for a month this summer. It's

2002, the year of the King's big comeback.

I feel sick again; I haven't been in a hospital for five years either.

My flat is in a converted Victorian house on Essex Road, N1. It's supposed to be a prestigious postcode, but the ground floor of our building and the one next door is taken up with a funeral parlour, hence the cheap rent. They do transporting, embalming, flower arrangements, the works. When I first moved in I was freaked by all the coffins I saw being carried in and out, but now I'm used to it. Below me is another flat, I share a toilet on the half-landing with him. Mine is the attic – two medium-sized rooms, a bedroom with sink, a kitchen with shower. It's not much – it's peeling and yellow and recently there's been a strange damp smell that sometimes means I wake up wheezing. I took it because it was close to work, and I have a weakness for badly-fitting wooden floorboards and windowpanes that let in cold air. I blame my grandmother.

Now, though, for the first time since I moved in five months ago, I wish the place felt more like home.

I pad into the kitchen and fill the kettle, checking my reflection in my cracked, bear-shaped hand mirror while it boils. My hair is dirty and there's yesterday's makeup smeared around my face; I don't necessarily want to go to the hospital, but I can imagine what my grandmother would say if I turned up like this – 'The poor man's got a weak heart, do you want him to die of fright?'

I shower, scrubbing myself hard. I drink a coffee while it's steaming and sort through the post, drumming my fingers on the kitchen table, impatient for the caffeine to kick in.

My uniform is draped across the back of a chair, waiting to be put on. It's a tight turquoise-and-purple mini dress like waitresses used to wear in American diners in the fifties. My name is stitched into it over the left breast, so male customers can gawp at my chest and get away with it.

Maybe I should let my boss know about my situation, but

the more time that passes, the more I feel I don't have to go and sit by my father's bedside – there's a reason we haven't kept in touch.

I get dressed in the kitchen, trying to iron out the creases with my hands. I can hear the golf coming in waves through the paper-thin wall separating me from my neighbour. I wonder what my mother would say to try to convince me to go, although if she were here we probably wouldn't be in this mess in the first place. She was always able to talk me out of being angry when I was younger. She'd say something like, 'This is the only point in your life you can go to the post office in a Batgirl outfit. Don't waste it on getting upset.'

She was the one who bought me the Batgirl outfit too, a reward for being brave after I fell out of a tree in our garden when I was five. I don't remember the fall; I remember my father picking me up off the lawn and carrying me inside. He laid me down on the sofa and started prodding me gently. I was completely still, but I winced when he took my head in his hands and examined my eyebrow. I could feel something warm start to meander down my face, and when I blinked my eyelashes felt sticky.

"You're bleeding a bit," he told me. "Do you know how bleeding happens?"

"How?"

"It means you've severed tiny blood vessels near the surface of the skin. When you do that, the blood comes out of the body, and we call that loss 'bleeding'."

"Okay," I said.

"Good girl," he said, and helped me up.

"Is it serious?" my mother asked.

"She'll need stitches, but she'll be fine."

We sat in the hospital waiting room for an hour; the bright lights and squeaky plastic floor and coughing patients made me shrink back into my chair. My mother held my hand the whole time. On the way home she rode in the back with me, showing me all her scars.

"This one is from my first cat," she said, showing me a white line running down the inside of her right arm. "And this one is from chickenpox." She pointed to a circle next to her left eye.

"You obviously ignored your doctor and scratched it," my father said, from the front seat.

"If only I'd known you back then, Edward," my mother said.

She was smiling. I looked at my father's eyes in the rear-view mirror and saw the skin crease around them, like he was smiling too.

"What's that one?" I asked, putting my finger on the little cross on her chin.

"That was from when your mother was saving the world," my father said.

"I fell over at a CND demonstration," she said, "and cut myself. It was when you were a tiny baby, and I was going to take you along in a sling, like in those photos I showed you, but thank God I didn't, or I might have squashed you."

"Where was I?" I asked.

"At home with Daddy," she said. "It was the first time I was away from you."

"Yes," my father said. "I seem to remember you cried all night."

* * *

I'm feeling the caffeine buzz now – my heart is pumping a little too fast and my ears are choked-up with its clamouring. *Lub-dub, lub-dub.* I wonder if I'm going to throw up again.

My mobile rings, it's Starr. "Thank God you picked up, have you heard?"

"Yeah, the hospital just called."

"Are you there?"

I light a cigarette. "Not yet."

"Are you on your way?"

"Not yet."

"Hon, what are you waiting for?"

I make my hand into a fist, and consider it. Roughly speaking, it is the size of my heart; my father taught me that. "I have to call work."

"So call them."

"I will."

"When?"

"Now."

"This is a really big fucking deal. You're the only one he has left, apart from Mum and Aunt G... You *have* to go."

I pretend not to hear her. "Where *are* you? It's a really bad line."

"I'm in Spain, remember, with Riccardo. I wish I could fly back but we're in the middle of fucking nowhere – flights once every ten days or something, and we've just missed one. Give Uncle Edward my love."

"Alright."

"You are *going*, aren't you?"

"Get off my back, Starr. I don't know yet. It's not like we're that close, is it?"

I hang up. I'm not ready to face my past quite yet, no matter how bad Starr makes me feel.

I sit on the edge of the bed, working up the will to put on my socks and shoes – black flats that won't pinch after an eight-hour shift. My feet have always been big with knobbly toes, like monkeys'. When I was a kid I used them to pick things up and carry them around – pens, rubber bands, coins. I wonder if my father remembers it.

If he dies now...

I pick up the phone again and call my boss to tell him I won't be in today. "It's a family emergency," I say.

"You can't expect me to believe that," he says. "That's the oldest trick in the book."

"Well this time it's true."

He makes a disgusted noise down the receiver. "I see right through you, missy," he says. "You've got a hangover again."

I start to say something, but he cuts me off. "I don't really care. If you're not in usual time on Wednesday, you can forget about coming in for good."

I bang the telephone down. If I had the guts or the money I'd quit in a flash.

"And do what?" Starr asked me once. I pretended I hadn't thought about it.

So work isn't an obstacle anymore. I don't want to see my father, but I can't pretend I don't know about it. If I hadn't picked up the phone this morning, I could get on with my daily routine. But I did pick up the phone. 'You were raised to know the right thing to do,' my grandmother would say. 'If you don't go now, it'll be because of your own pig-headedness.'

"You win," I tell her. "But I'm only going for you."

I throw on some non-work clothes and grab my cigarettes, keys, and phone and leave the flat, locking the door behind me. I walk to Islington Green, running the last few yards to catch the number 30 pulling in at the stop. It's only when I'm on it that I realise my aunts might be at the hospital too. The doors are still open, and I almost get off again, but something inside me puts its foot down – no more wavering. My grandmother's influence again, probably. I sit by the window and watch as the bus sails past sunbathers on the green, then Pizza Express and William Hill and the new Thai restaurant, with potted bamboo and stone buddhas outside. Pedestrians amble alongside us in the heat, flip-flops slapping against the pavement, and Brazilian flags still hang from second and third-floor flat windows, mementoes of their fifth World Cup win back in June.

I don't want to see any of them – my place among the family was always a little uncertain – but especially not Aunt Vivienne. She's my father's younger sister, Starr's mum, and I remember her being tall and glamorous and fierce. When I knew her, she had short, dark hair that licked each ear. "To look like Cyd Charisse," she said. In 1974 and 1975, a

13

twenty-two-year-old Vivienne had appeared, scantily clad, in several films with titles like: *Vampira*, *The Arabian Nights* and *Supervixens*.

She might not show up though – she has a bad track record of attending funerals at least. And as far as I could tell, when I was a kid, Aunt Vivienne didn't seem to notice my father much; maybe they haven't seen each other recently either. Starr said, once, that after I left my father basically turned into a recluse, but Starr exaggerates.

* * *

When we were children I thought Starr was the coolest person I knew. She wore glitter eye-shadow that suited her name, and could balance whole stacks of books on her head while walking round the living-room. Sometimes we'd visit them in their Primrose Hill flat and she would show us. She said that Aunt Vivienne made her practise every night so she'd have the right posture for modelling or acting.

"You know, I went a whole year without buying myself a single drink," Aunt Vivienne said once, smoking a cigarette and crossing her legs. "*Everyone* took me out to dinner. I went along with it of course, but I knew they just wanted to see if I'd get my tits out."

Me and Starr, playing quietly under the kitchen table, giggled to ourselves at the t-word.

"You should have come with me sometimes, Evie," Aunt Vivienne said to my mother. "You're very cute, you know. Not exactly right for the roles I got, but you could definitely have played a young country *ingénue*. That would have been right up your street, wouldn't it?"

Under the table I saw my mother's hands tighten in her lap.

"Right," Aunt Vivienne said, her face appearing suddenly. "Get out you two. Don't think I don't know you're snooping around down there."

We crawled out and I went to stand next to my mother.

Aunt Vivienne watched me. I watched her back. Aunt Vivienne never dressed the same as other women on the street – she looked more like the people from black and white films – and now she was wearing white trousers that flared at the bottom, and a white silk shirt. I could see through her top to her purple bra, and I wondered if she still needed to show people her tits.

My mother was wearing her red tea dress and her blonde hair big and wavy. When she'd come down for breakfast that morning my father had pretended to think she was Farrah Fawcett, although I thought she was much prettier. She put her arm around me and buried her face in my hair, speaking into it. "What are you up to?"

"Playing with dolls."

"That sounds nice," she said, and nuzzled my ear.

Starr was standing near the door. Aunt Vivienne crushed her cigarette out in the saucer in front of her and turned in her seat. "Starr, go to your room. And take your cousin with you. Can't I ever have an adult conversation around here?"

"Come on," Starr said when we were in the hallway. "Let's go to Mum's bedroom and try on makeup."

"Okay," I said. I thought Starr was very brave after the way Aunt Vivienne had just looked at her.

Aunt Vivienne had a whole row of lipsticks and pots of cream and brushes.

"The blusher's in here," Starr said, pulling open the top drawer of the dresser. She was wearing shiny silver leggings with gold spots on them, and a pink t-shirt with two elephants kissing. I stuck my hands in the pockets of my denim shorts and wished I looked as exciting as her.

"Oh, it's the left one." Starr struggled to close the open drawer. "Help me."

We tried pushing it together.

"You have to jiggle it," Starr said. "Quietly, or she'll hear us." She mimed drawing a line across her throat. I giggled.

"There's something stuck at the back," Starr said, reaching

into the drawer and pulling out sheets of writing paper, bills and photos. "Take these. We have to shove everything down."

I looked at the photo on the top of the stack Starr had given me. It looked like a birthday shot; there was cake on a table in the front and, standing slightly behind it, Aunt Vivienne and my mother, wearing party hats. My mother had an arm around Vivienne's waist. There was another face in the frame as well, all blurry. It looked like a man with dark hair, no one I'd ever seen before. Both my mother and Aunt Vivienne were looking at him, and Aunt Vivienne was reaching out a hand like she was trying to catch hold of his arm.

"Who's that?"

"Where?"

"Here."

We heard someone go into the bathroom next door and water running.

"Give them to me," Starr said, grabbing the stack and piling it back in the drawer. We scuttled out of Aunt Vivienne's bedroom and into Starr's. My mother put her head around the door as soon as we'd sat down. Her eyes looked red around the rims, like she had a cold.

"It's time to go, Tallie," she said.

Starr gave me a look and put her finger on her lips. We giggled again.

✳ ✳ ✳

I get off at Harley Street and make my way through Marylebone, past women with expensive hair drinking coffee, down wide, sunlit streets with 'doctor' written in front of the parking spaces, and quiet pockets of residential mews and small, peaceful parks. After the grey and brown of my road, it feels like the whole area has been splashed in colour – red brick, green trees and silver Mercedes. I wonder if I'll run into Toby; he used to live nearby, although I think he was closer to Edgware Road.

A young mother comes into view with a toddler in tow.

She's carrying too many bags and feeding bottles and a ball under one arm. The toddler is red-faced, and one tug away from a screaming fit. The woman looks tearful. I look away.

My mother – Evelyn – was wonderful with children, everyone said so. She used to stop and coo at babies whenever we went for walks together and they always smiled at her. She used to bake proper cakes for my birthdays, elaborate ones in the shapes of cartoon characters, with butter-cream icing, and she would stay up all night sewing costumes for me when I was invited to fancy-dress parties. She could do lots of different voices when she was reading stories aloud at bed-time. She smelled like vanilla, and sang low and sweetly.

I have all these memories at least. She's there in my head. It's in the real world that I've lost her – I haven't smelt her perfume since I was ten, or seen the strands of hair that used to build up in her hairbrush. I can't remember how it felt to touch her when she was still warm and soft from a bath. And what was she like when she wasn't with me? What was she like as a person? I think about my mother all the time.

Two

My father isn't in Coronary Care. When I ask at Reception I'm told he's been moved to Floor One. My father's worked here at the heart hospital all my life and I know what's on Floor One: Intensive Care.

"I'm afraid the heart attack, and the heart rhythm he went into, were very severe," a pretty nurse is telling me. "He had to be anaesthetised to let it recover."

Nurse Slattery, her badge says. She's very gentle with me, but she doesn't smile. I used to want to be a nurse. I wonder how I'd break the news if it was me in her place, if I could be as calm.

"Thanks."

"He's still under. You can sit with him if you want."

I make it to the doorway of his ward before I feel my chest begin to tighten. I pull up short and flex and unflex my fingers; they feel cold, like all the blood has rushed elsewhere. I tuck them into my armpits. It's okay, I tell myself. No one even knows you're here. You can go home without explaining yourself to anyone. My feet start to move instinctively, I'm halfway down the corridor in the other direction when I hear someone calling my name. I lift my face up to see Gillian, my father's older sister, coming out of the lift.

I stop. She hurries up to me and puts her bags on the

floor – she's been to Harvey Nichols – and kisses me on both cheeks. She smells of lavender, she's wearing navy linen trousers and a stripy top and her hair in a tight, blonde bun, just as I remember it.

Her eyes are shiny, like she's holding back tears. "How are you, darling?"

"I'm fine."

"I went to call you earlier," she says. "But then I realised I don't have a number for you. I didn't even know if you were in the country – I was so worried no one would be able to reach you. How long has it been? Five years?"

She's skirting the issue, letting me know my disappearance has been noticed, but not asking for a reason.

"The hospital called me," I say.

Now that I think about it, I realise Starr must have given them my number. My father certainly doesn't have it.

She hasn't taken her eyes off my face yet. "Have you seen him?"

"No."

"Come on then."

We walk to my father's room and Aunt Gillian goes straight in. I hover, half-in, half-out.

"Edward," I hear her say. She sounds choked.

My father looks terrible. His whole face is grey. I didn't know people could be this colour and still be alive. I look away, at the floor; there are scuff marks by the bed, as if it's been moved rapidly at some point.

"He's unconscious," I say.

Aunt Gillian is stroking his hair.

"They had to anaesthetise him to let his heart recover," I say. "They'll probably keep him under for a while."

"Yes," she says. "They said on the phone they'd done a PCI." She looks at me, then back down to my father. "We sound like pretty cold fish, don't we?"

"We sound like him," I say. My father is a heart surgeon, and when I was a little girl this terminology was as familiar

19

to me as my nursery rhymes. Perhaps even more so – I can't remember anything beyond the second line of 'Oranges and Lemons'.

It's when Aunt Gillian turns to face me that I realise I'm humming the tune. "Sorry," I say. I come and stand beside my aunt.

"Don't be," she says. "You're under a lot of stress." She guides me into a bedside chair. It's almost too close to my father to bear. I can smell his aftershave, dark and woody, mingling with antiseptic and rubber. He must have already finished his morning routine when he had the heart attack; he always got up early. I find myself looking at his ear, checking for the tell-tale crease, Frank's sign, named after Dr Sanders T. Frank. Frank's sign is a diagonal earlobe crease, extending from the hard pointy bit at the front, covering the ear-hole, across the lobe to the rear edge of the visible part of the ear. Growing up, I was fascinated by the idea that this little rumple of skin could anticipate heart disease. You find it especially on elderly people. My father doesn't have it.

"He's still so young," Aunt Gillian says, like she's reading my mind.

She's kind of right. He's fifty-four, but he looks much older than I remember – maybe it's the illness. He's the same, but he's changed. His hair seems finer, and I can see a dusting of grey in the blond, like the time my mother's camera had metal shavings on the lens and everything came out speckled with silver. There are a few hairs that have started to creep out of his ears and nose. His moustache and eyebrows are bushier, too, and there's a deeper 'V' at the cleft between neck and collarbone, where he must have lost weight. His hands are lying palm-down on either side of his body, but even at rest they're wrinkled. He's not wearing an oxygen mask – part of me wishes his face was covered up more.

I'm here now, Dad. I didn't want to see you again, but I came anyway. So now what?

Someone taps at the door and comes in. It's the pretty

nurse from before. I watch as she takes my father's pulse and examines his respiratory pattern. She opens his eyelids one after the other, and looks at his pupils. Then she turns his head from side to side, keeping the eyelids open.

"What does that show?" I ask.

"We call it the doll's eye test," she says, laying his head gently back down on the pillow. "If the eyes move in the opposite direction to the rotation of the head, it means his brainstem is intact."

"Like a doll," Aunt Gillian says, vaguely. I can tell the presence of someone official is making her feel better; she's stopped fidgeting and she's watching the nurse like she's going to perform some kind of miracle.

"Exactly," the nurse says, smiling encouragingly. "He's doing really well. He should be out of here in no time at all."

By which point I'll be long gone.

"The doctor's already seen him today, but he's around if you have any questions?"

"We're fine," I say. There's nothing quite like a man in a position of care and responsibility to set my teeth on edge, actually, Nurse.

She straightens his pillow, writes a few sentences on her clipboard and leaves, her shoes squeaking on the floor.

"They're very good here," Aunt Gillian says.

"Yeah," I say.

***

When I was six I was in a ballet performance, dancing the part of a flower girl in something our ballet teacher had written herself. My mother had stitched pink and gold flowers onto my wraparound skirt, but I was in a bad mood because I wanted to wear a tutu, like the older girls, or carry a basket, like Jennifer Allen. I was already jealous of Jennifer Allen because this was 1987, and my favourite TV character, even more than Batgirl, was Penny, Inspector Gadget's niece, who also had blonde hair that her mother tied up in pigtails.

"Look at that pout," my mother said, helping me into my tights.

"You have what is called a 'readable face', Tallie," my father said. He tapped my nose and I tried to hide a smile. "Shall we go?"

My mother straightened up. "Let me just get my camera."

The phone rang while we were waiting for her; I could hear my father put on his doctor's voice, and got a heavy feeling in my tummy.

My mother came downstairs. "Where's Daddy?"

He came back into the kitchen with his doctor's bag. He always said that he could run a hospital from his bag, and usually I loved it, loved the instruments he took out to show me. "I'm afraid I've got to go see a patient around the corner, Tallulah, so I might not be back in time for the show. I'm sorry – I did want to see you."

"Mummies *and* Daddies are supposed to come," I told him, sticking my lower lip out.

My father shook his head. "I have to go. It's very sad, she's the same age as you but she's been extremely ill. Maybe I can bring you a treat home instead."

I could feel my face get hot, like it did whenever my father talked to me about other little children who needed him.

"Never mind," my mother said. "You can come to the next show."

"There isn't going to *be* another show," I said. "Belinda said so."

"Who's Belinda?"

"The ballet teacher," my mother said. "Come on, we're going to be late if we don't hurry."

My father was asleep in front of the TV when we got home. We tiptoed past the open door and into the kitchen. My mother made me baked beans and potato smiley faces, and I ate in my ballet costume. I never wanted to take it off.

"You'll have to get undressed to have a bath," my mother said, picking bits of fluff out of my hair.

22

"I don't want a bath."

"Ever again?"

"Never ever."

"What if you start to smell?"

I chewed a smiley face. "I won't."

"Well in that case, there's nothing to worry about," my mother said. She pointed to my plate. "I'm hungry."

"So?"

"Will you let me eat something of yours?"

"Like what?" I asked, giggling; I knew what was coming.

"Like… *this* finger." She opened her mouth and grabbed my hand, lifting it up towards her face.

"No," I squealed. "You can't eat that."

"No? What about your elbow?" She cupped her hand underneath my elbow and put her teeth very lightly on it, pretending to chew. It tickled and I laughed, trying to wriggle away.

"Hello girls." My father appeared in the doorway. "How was it?"

"She was a star," my mother said. "How was your patient?"

"Absolutely fine."

"Good."

He yawned. He must have forgotten my treat, I thought, and I looked at the table rather than at him. He'd forgotten to get me a treat when he missed my birthday party at the swimming pool as well, when I'd had chickenpox, when I'd been singing at the school summer fair, and when I'd been left at school for two hours because my mother was at the dentist and he was meant to be picking me up. The teacher in charge of the afterschool playgroup was very nice and let me eat toast and jam with her in the office, while all the other children took turns on the scooters outside. But even she was worried when it was five-thirty and he still wasn't there. She'd locked up and stood outside with me, checking her watch, and I couldn't stop the hot tears from spilling out.

"Would you like a cup of tea?" my mother asked.

"Yes, that would be nice."

My mother closed the door of the living-room after taking my father his cup, so we wouldn't disturb him, and we read together in the kitchen.

"Are all Daddies always tired?"

"Only if they work too hard," she said

"Does Daddy work too hard?"

My mother stroked my hair. "He works very hard," she said. "But he's very important. And he's trying to look after me and you."

"I can look after you," I told her, because she looked sad. "When Daddy's working."

"I think it's meant to be the other way around," she said, and kissed my forehead.

✳✳✳

"Goodness," Aunt Gillian sighs, bringing me back to the present.

This tightness of chest, this hotness behind my eyes, is exactly the way I remember it from another hospital vigil. I can't tell if the aching feeling inside is for now, or for that memory. "Do you think we can open a window?" I ask Aunt Gillian.

It's a perfect day outside. Late summer, brilliant blue sky. We're far enough away from Marylebone High Street that the traffic is muffled, but we know that life is going on out there. There's a jug of water – presumably for relatives – on a table at the end of the bed, and ripples sparkle in it whenever we stir. I feel like this moment is made of glass.

"Perhaps we should wait and ask someone," Aunt Gillian says. She pulls another chair up alongside the bed and starts stroking my father's hair again.

We sit in silence.

Silence never bothered me. There are people in the café who have to talk all the time, but I was an only child with a busy parent. My mother and I developed our own sign-language for those mornings when he was trying to rest. The days got longer, and I spent more time outside: climbing, building, jumping. My mother would open the door that led to the garden and sit down in the kitchen, I would wrap my legs around the tree branch, one finger drawing a circle in the air – "I'm going to roll over and hang upside down."

I could bear being upside down for two minutes. I liked the feel of the rough bark digging into my legs as I gripped the branch, liked stretching my fingers out towards the ground, liked feeling the strain of my stomach muscles as I pulled myself back upright. My mother would press her hand to her cheek and open her mouth in a perfect "O" – "I'm impressed," – then press her hand to her heart – "I love you".

Aunt Gillian is talking – she seems to be trying a different tack. "You must come round to the new house," she's saying. "We're still in Knightsbridge, but a smaller place now. We moved after Georgia got married. Of course, you didn't come to the wedding… " She fixes me with another wet-eyed stare. "She would have loved it if you were there – we all would have."

"I'm sorry," I say, feeling like someone's punched me in the gut. I didn't know cousin Georgia had got married, she's only twenty-two as well. Starr can't possibly have forgotten to tell me. Maybe she thought I'd be jealous since I couldn't even manage a secondary-school crush on Toby without screwing it up. I try to push all thoughts of him away.

Apparently the groom is much older than Georgia, but very rich and very nice. I nod fuzzily. The dizziness has returned and I'm starting to get hungry.

"Are you alright, love?" Gillian puts her hand on my arm. "You look faint."

"I haven't eaten today," I say.

She beams. "I was just about to meet Paul at the steakhouse." Paul is her third husband. "Why don't you come and join us? It'll take your mind off things." She glances away from my father, who's so still he could be made of wax. Aunt

Gillian is a great believer in minds being elsewhere.

Lunch with Gillian and Paul will probably be a disaster, I think, but I really want a steak now. I allow myself to be hustled to the restaurant, where Paul greets me without mentioning that we've never met. He might not be able to tell one cousin from another – Paul is Gillian's oldest husband yet. He looks and smells like leather. "I see the stock market's taken another nose-dive," he says.

We don't mention my father. We talk about Paul's indigestion and their upcoming holiday in Majorca. Paul shows me a wad of Euros, fanning them out so I can admire them properly. I remember the fuss everyone made last year about introducing a single European currency; the notes don't seem particularly complicated to me. "You wouldn't believe the difference it's made," Paul says. "Bloody pesetas, and francs and lira – that was the bloody worst."

"Paul travels a lot," Aunt Gillian says.

I eat my steak quickly. Gillian is drinking red wine and she's a little flushed by the time we finish. Paul makes his excuses after the main course, although I think I see him eyeing the cheese selection wistfully. Aunt Gillian always puts her husbands on a strict no-dairy regime.

"No rest for the wicked, eh?" he says.

"You must be very busy then," I say. He guffaws, but Gillian gives me a look.

After Paul leaves she brings up Georgia's wedding again. "She looked so beautiful you know," she says. "We bought this *beautiful* ivory-coloured gown. And a cream, diamond-studded crown."

"Sounds nice."

Gillian fishes in her handbag. "I have some photos. You must see them, since you couldn't be there. Now where are they?" She rummages some more, then makes a little triumphant sound and pulls out a pocket-sized, leather-bound photo album. I lean in, and feel my eyes pop. Cousin Georgia has changed since I last saw her. She used to be chubby and placid. Aunt Gillian said it was the result of quitting her swimming training, but we all knew it was because Georgia ate hunks of butter by themselves.

The Georgia in the photos before me is slim and fresh, with large brown eyes and a vibrantly scarlet shade of lipstick. I think she looks beautiful. Beautiful and lost.

"You two look so alike now, dear," Aunt Gillian is saying. "One would think you were sisters." She's always had active hands when she talks, and now she flutters them in my direction. She's slightly drunk though, and her glass of wine gets knocked over and starts to bleed onto the album. "Oh," she says. "Oh, how *silly* of me." She fusses with napkins, mopping the wine from the photo of Georgia (alone with her bouquet in a garden setting), and makes faces of distress. She is berating herself, under her breath and very fast. Instinctively I put my hand on her arm. She stops muttering and mopping and looks up; we're both surprised. I take my hand away.

"Well," she says. "Well, I think I'm going to have dessert. Perhaps the sticky toffee pudding. How about you, Tallulah?"

Three

In the beginning, you are two separate entities – spermatozoon, and ovum. When the two cells come together, the ovum is fertilised. You (fertilised-egg-you) leave the fallopian tube, pass through the utero-tubal junction and embed yourself into the endometrium – the lining of the uterus. You need nourishment, sustenance, and foetus-you does not take in oxygen or nutrients the same way you will outside the womb; your lungs remain unused for the gestation period. Instead you get everything you need from the placenta and the umbilical cord. During pregnancy, your mother's heart rate will increase by as much as twenty percent to produce thirty to fifty percent more blood flow for you. This blood is carried from the placenta by the umbilical vein, which connects with veins within you. Oxygenated blood is collected in the left atrium of your heart; from here it flows into the left ventricle, is pumped through the aorta and travels around your body. Some of this blood will return to the placenta, where waste products such as carbon dioxide will leave you and enter your mother's circulation. This is part of what is called the 'communication' between foetus and mother.

Even before I was born, therefore, my mother's heart and mine were working for the same purpose.

✳ ✳ ✳

Like me, my mother had been an only child, and sometimes she worried I would get lonely.

"Were *you* lonely?" I asked her.

"Not always." She was mending my dungarees as I stood in them, kneeling in front of me, holding up buttons to see which was the right one. I was wearing a short-sleeved check shirt underneath the dungarees, my favourite shirt from the age of seven to ten. She had a flowery dress on, and she was wearing her tortoiseshell reading glasses for the first time, which must have made it 1989. "It would still have been nice to have a little sister, or a brother to run around with."

"What about your mum and dad? Did you play with them?"

She held up a big pearly button with brown rings around the holes. "What about this one? Do you like it?"

"Yes."

"They were quite old when they had me," she said, biting off the thread. "They used to call me their little surprise."

"And you didn't have *any* other family?"

"No. And my parents died when I was sixteen, so then I was an orphan."

She'd made a mistake, I thought – orphans were children, like Annie, or Sophie in *The BFG*.

"Hold still," she said. "You'll get stabbed if you keep on wriggling."

"Are you lonely now?"

"Not now," she said. "I have you and Daddy now, don't I?"

"When did you meet Daddy?"

"When I was twenty-one."

"How did you meet?"

"At an ice-rink." She patted my bottom. "There – all sewn on."

"I want to hear about you and Daddy."

My mother started packing her sewing kit away. "I was

29

there with a friend," she said. "And she fell over. She couldn't get up, and then your father suddenly appeared and said he was a doctor. It was all very romantic."

I went and stood on her feet and she walked us across the room, wrapping her arms around me to keep me upright.

"What was wrong with your friend?" I asked.

"He said her ankle was twisted, so we sat in the bar for the rest of the night with him and his friend." She kissed the top of my head. "He had a moustache back then, and a big hat, and I thought he looked like a blond Omar Sharif."

"Who's that?"

"An actor I used to have a crush on."

"What happened to your friend?"

"She ended up going out with the other boy," my mother said. "And then she moved back to Wales and we lost touch."

"And you and Daddy got married?"

"Not straight away."

"But you stayed together forever?"

She smiled, but she lifted me off her feet and started tidying up, shuffling my drawings together. "That's nice," she said, turning the top one to me. "Is it Snow White and the seven dwarves?"

"It's me and my cousins," I said. "I wrote it at the bottom."

"I see it now."

"Anyway, *I'm* not lonely," I said. "I've got Starr and Georgia."

"And Michael and James."

Because my mother was so worried about me being lonely we saw a lot of my cousins. We all lived in London, but usually, when the weather got hot, we would visit our grandmother out in Shropshire.

Our grandmother was terrifying – she towered over us, all bones and dark eyes. Her fingertips were yellow after years of smoking and she smelled like lavender with an undercurrent of mushrooms. She walked four miles every day; she didn't believe in being ill. She never spoke to us, unless it was to tell us off, and she cleared her throat all the time, making a sound like 'hruh'. If she wasn't there, James said, going to hers would be great. I agreed, the house seemed like a castle to me, with a gardener and a cook, a lake, and stables – although, sadly for us grandchildren, no horses. My grandfather had been the rider and within a week of his death, she'd sold them all off to the farmer two fields away.

Most of the house, my mother told me, had been built in the Victorian period, but little extensions had been added over the years so that from the outside it looked like a puzzle with the pieces jammed together in any order. There was a long, tree-lined drive leading up to it that twisted and turned and suddenly opened out onto a clearing and the house and a silver glint of the lake in the garden beyond. The windows on the ground floor were the biggest, at least three times as tall as me; the first floor windows led on to a little balcony that ran along the front of the house and the second floor windows were small, where the ceilings were lower. The outside of the house was a pale yellow colour, like it was made of sand, and the roof was covered with grey tiles.

There was an older wing, made of small, grey stones, to the left of the house. It slanted upwards like a church, and it was the only part of the original Tudor house left after a fire destroyed the building in the nineteenth century. My grandmother had a painting of the house in flames that she hung in the entrance hall. When I was older, I asked her why she kept it; she said it was a reminder that our family had been through disaster and come out the other side.

The Tudor wing was where I slept, in a yellow room that faced the walled garden at the side of the house. I was separated from the others by a short, uneven corridor, and a thick, wooden-beamed doorway. My parents' room was just beyond the doorway; it was rear-facing with a view of the lake, but I liked my sloping ceiling, and the latticed window high up in the wall. I had to climb onto a chair to see out of it, which was forbidden because the chairs at my grandmother's were all at least a hundred years old, or so she said.

One visit we were having milk and malt-loaf in the kitchen when a rabbit limped up and collapsed against the open French door. Its eyes were glassy and it had red all over its fur, like something had taken great bites out of it. Aunt Gillian shrieked when she saw it.

Michael stooped to pick it up. "It's hurt," he said.

"Michael, *don't touch it*," Aunt Gillian said. "Get the gardener," but my grandmother snorted and strode over.

"Let me see that," she said, and Michael held it out to her. She looked it over quickly then put her hands on it and twisted the neck until we all heard the snap.

"Foxes," she said. "Or dogs. Nothing else we could do." She took the body and went out into the garden. Next to me, I heard Georgia whimper softly, and Michael turned away from us, white-faced.

That night I had a nightmare about a ghost being in the room with me, and stumbled down the corridor to my mother. My father steered me back to my own bed and tucked me in again. "There are no such things as ghosts," he said, but he sat at the end of my bed until I fell asleep again.

We spent most of our time by the lake, seeing who could skim stones furthest across the water, launching paper sailing boats that Michael taught us to make, or eating cold chicken or cheese and pickle sandwiches that we had to sneak from the kitchen. The grown-ups stayed indoors, playing cards and arguing, especially Aunt Gillian and Aunt Vivienne. My father usually sat apart from the others, reading a newspaper. Sometimes he'd save the cartoons for me, especially ones about Alex, the businessman in a pinstripe suit and his friend Clive and wife, Penny. I wasn't always sure I understood what was going on, but I liked how hopeless Clive was.

Our grandmother sat apart too, watching everyone from her special armchair. There was another, matching armchair that Starr told us had been our grandfather's while he was alive, but no one ever sat in it. The grown-ups never talked about our grandfather either. Michael, who was eleven at that point, said our family was a matriarchal society, like elephants, and men weren't important, although one time when me and Georgia were on a food raid we heard Aunt Vivienne and our grandmother in the hallway fighting about one. They didn't mention his name, and Aunt Vivienne seemed pretty angry by the end.

"You just want me to be a fucking doormat, say please and thank you and kiss their feet."

"No one forces you to come down and see everyone, Vivienne."

"And look what happens when I'm not here."

There was a pause.

"I know you're strong, my girl, but sometimes circumstances are stronger."

"Don't be ridiculous, Mother. Just because *you* failed to stop it doesn't mean it was inevitable."

There was another pause, then, "You're a cold person and no mistake," my grandmother said, and her voice was even more terrifying than normal.

We heard footsteps start in our direction. Georgia, her hand deep in the biscuit tin, looked at me with widened eyes. We slipped out of the kitchen and back to the others. Without agreeing on it, neither of us said anything about the conversation.

✳ ✳ ✳

At four a.m. I give up trying to sleep and drag my duvet into the kitchen to watch TV. I'm addicted to it in the way my mother was to afternoon plays. She used to talk about the characters as if they were real. I used to come home from school and find her in the kitchen with the radio on, eyes wide and hands paused mid-action: chopping a tomato, scrubbing the table, feeding the cat. I guess she liked the company. My mother didn't work. She'd been a waitress, like me, when she met my father at the ice-rink.

33

Later that morning my eyeballs feel like someone's pushing them back into their sockets. Aunt Gillian calls me as I'm sweeping up china shards from a bowl I smashed in the kitchen.

"Paul's gone to Glyndebourne," she says. "To see *The Magic Flute*. I don't like Mozart all that much, although I know you're not meant to say that. *Madame Butterfly* is really more my cup of tea."

"Aunt Gillian… "

"Anyway," she continues. "I just thought it might be nice if you could come and keep me company for the day. Maybe we could go to the hospital together. That's if you don't have any plans? You're not working, are you?"

"No," I say, before I can stop myself.

"Oh good, maybe Georgia will join us. I doubt Vivienne will." She sniffs.

I meet Aunt Gillian at the bus stop by Hyde Park Corner; she's brought two teas and more photo albums.

We sit at the front of the top deck.

"Let's see which one this is," Aunt Gillian says, bringing out another slim black volume, with 'Memories' written in gold calligraphy on the bottom left corner. I cradle my cup in my hands, blowing on the liquid to cool it down. She licks her thumb and opens to the first page – I'm surprised to see a black and white photograph of Aunt Vivienne as a young girl. She's wearing a knitted jumper dress, long socks pulled up to her knees and t-bar sandals. Her hair is in two bunches on either side of her head, which is tilted away from the camera, though her eyes are definitely on it. She's laughing at something.

"She loved that dress," Aunt Gillian says. "The sixties died for Vivienne the day it unravelled past repair."

"I didn't think you two were close," I say.

Aunt Gillian's leaning over me, looking down at the photo and shaking her head. "She always was a hoity-toity little madam. Just like you when you were younger." She smiles at me. I'm not sure how to respond, so I take a sip of my tea.

"Do you remember my second husband, George?"

I remember George, a wheezy red-head who used to squeeze all the girl cousins inappropriately, until Starr complained. Aunt Gillian and Aunt Vivienne didn't speak to each other for a year after that. The last I heard of him, he was going to prison, although I'm not completely sure what for.

"He used to say you were going to grow up to be a real handful," Aunt Gillian tells me. "You certainly used to drive us all to distraction with that mangy old cat you carried around."

She's talking about Mr Tickles.

A week after my sixth Christmas, I found a cat in our garden. It had half an ear and one eye and clumps of fur missing; I wanted to adopt it straight away.

My mother was washing up when I ran in and tugged at her skirt. "There's a cat in the garden," I said breathlessly. "But I think he's hurt."

"Tallie," my mother sighed. "Are you sure he's hurt? Is he just lying down?"

The week before I had dragged her over to see a squirrel who walked funny, who was walking fine by the time she got there. And I was always scared that pigeons would get run over – they didn't seem to have ears to hear the cars coming. If I saw a pigeon in the road I would chase it off, flapping my arms at it.

"No, really hurt," I said. "Can we help him, pleeease?"

My mother was resistant at first to bringing an animal indoors, but she gave in when I showed her the frost on his coat.

"Can I name him?" I asked as my father wiped his wounds and sprayed them with antiseptic.

"What would you name him?" my father asked.

"Mr Tickles."

"That's a good choice." My father shone his penlight in Mr Tickles' ears and down his throat. "He seems pretty healthy, all things considered. Although we should probably take him to a vet."

"Don't get her hopes up, Edward," my mother said. She put her hands on my shoulders. "Tallie, this is someone else's kitty. See, he has a collar. We'll have to advertise in case anyone wants him back."

"But he ran away."

"Cats run away a lot," my mother said. "Don't get too attached to him. I don't want you to be upset about it if someone gets in touch."

We advertised in the local paper. I spent a month in fear every time the telephone rang, but no one came forward to claim him. It wasn't that surprising – the cat ate like a horse and smelt like an onion. From that moment on, wherever I went, Mr Tickles came too.

✳ ✳ ✳

Aunt Gillian is looking out of the window at the road ahead of us. I think I see water welling up in her eyes.

"We never really know what we have until it's gone, Tallulah," she says.

My father is no longer under anaesthetic, but the rhythm of his heart hasn't stabilised yet, and they want to keep him in Intensive Care.

He's asleep when we enter, his face still the colour of papier-mâché. Aunt Gillian and I pull chairs up next to the bed. She starts talking to him in a low voice. After a few minutes I realise she's singing. Some song I don't know – from their childhood, probably. I feel ridiculous, like I'm an imposter.

I think about what she said on the bus. I wonder who she was talking about. John, her first husband? George, my grandparents? Not my father, anyway, he's not gone yet. I catch myself trying to imagine my life without him; it's hard to see how it would be different, when we haven't spoken in so long. I can't see it being like when my mother died – if my father stopped breathing now, I don't think I would even cry.

"What was that?" I ask Gillian when she's finished.

"It's something our French nanny used to sing to get him to sleep," Aunt Gillian says, waving her hands. "It was from the region of France she grew up in."

"It was from France, period," a voice from the doorway says. "So it's probably all about adultery and fine wines."

Aunt Vivienne enters the room. She's wearing a black suit; the jacket is fitted and the skirt is pencil-style. Her hair is shoulder length and chestnut coloured – a dye job, but a good one. I tried to describe her to Toby once, but now I think I might have underplayed her old-Hollywood magnetism.

"Vivienne," Aunt Gillian says icily.

"Gillian," Aunt Vivienne drawls, eyebrow raised. "And *Tallulah*. The prodigal daughter returns." Maybe it's a good thing he never got to know my family, I think.

I can feel Aunt Gillian fuming next to me. "Why the hell are you dressed for a funeral?" she snaps.

I slip out while they're arguing and find a nearby nurse. She's not best pleased; she rushes in and I can hear her scolding from outside the room, "This is an *intensive care* unit. If you two want to continue whatever this fight is, then you're going to have to go outside to do it."

One of the aunts murmurs something.

"If you're finished, then you can stay. But one more word from you, and I'll have you out so fast, don't think I'm afraid of you" – that must be to Aunt Vivienne – "I have a duty to my patients you know."

I lean against the wall in the corridor. I've hardly smoked all day and my body is screaming for some nicotine. I close my eyes and concentrate on the buzz. While I still did ballet all the spinning made me feel dizzy and sick. I learnt to turn my focus inwards, and then I could shrink the dizziness to a tiny, manageable lump inside me. I try to do that now, but it's been a while. When I open my eyes I have to blink twice. I can see someone far off down the hall being very still – they look familiar. It takes me a few moments to realise it's my reflection. "You're cracking up," I say out loud, and a passing nurse gives me an odd look.

I walk to the lift and push the button, but it takes too long, so I find the stairs and jump down them two at a time.

Outside, I light my cigarette, disconcerted to see my hands shaking. I tell myself to get a grip, smoke two cigarettes in quick succession and go back inside.

It doesn't seem real, being here for any reason other than waiting for my father to finish his shift. My mother used to bring me after tea-time on a Thursday. She had a friend who ran an old book-binding shop and we'd go there for biscuits and orange squash first, then walk the ten minutes to the hospital, sometimes with my mother's friend, too. Her name was Vicky; she had dark, curly hair and lots of rings on her fingers. She was the only person who ever babysat me, and only once – my parents can't have gone out much. I guess most families have the grandparents around to help out with things like that, but my grandmother lived too far away, and her husband had died of a heart attack when my father was thirty-one. Not – as Starr once informed me – because my granny poisoned him, but because he drank like a fish right up until the day he keeled over.

I was jealous of other kids at primary school, who had all their grandparents left. My best friend Kathy lived next door to hers; she used to go across the front lawn every afternoon to have tea while her granny plaited her hair. When I was young, I thought my grandmother was so different to Kathy's granny, and to all grannies in books and TV shows, that she almost didn't count. It was my mother who first let me see my grandmother as a real person – not a figure of authority – on a fruit-picking trip.

My mother used to make all our jams and marmalades herself. She said her own mother had started doing it during the war years when there was rationing, and then she'd taught her daughter. Now she was going to continue the tradition by teaching me. I had a special stool to stand on, so I could reach the counter where all the fruits and glass jars were lined up neatly, freshly washed. I wasn't allowed to use the knife, so I stirred the pulpy messes in their pans. Every so often I would lick my finger then stick it in the bag of sugar.

In 1990 – the year I turned nine – we had an unusually late autumn that was still sunny in October, so my mother and I went blackberry picking. "They'll be extra big and juicy," she told me. "It'll be nice to choose the best ones for ourselves, won't it?"

I waited impatiently in the hallway while my mother searched for the pails.

"You have to wrap up nice and warm for me," she said, when she finally appeared. "I don't want you to catch a cold."

"I don't want to wear my scarf," I grumbled. "It's scratchy."

"Hmmm," my mother considered me for a moment, turned around and walked towards her bedroom. She came back holding her pink cashmere jumper, my favourite of hers. "What if you put this on underneath the scarf and coat?" she asked. "Then if the scarf feels scratchy you can just concentrate on how the jumper feels instead."

I stroked the cashmere. It was unbearably soft and feminine. "Okay," I said. She slipped it on over my outstretched arms and pulled it down; it felt like cream being poured over me. I rubbed my face with the sleeve. My mother handed me my coat and scarf and watched as I buttoned up. I was still wearing my red duffel coat with the hood from when I was seven. Back then I used to like to think I was Little Red Riding Hood. My mother would pretend to be the wolf and jump out of bed at me. Now that I was upstairs at school with the oldest kids, we didn't play that game anymore.

"Where are we going?" I wanted to know.

"Richmond Park woods."

We walked hand in hand. The air was cold enough to turn my nose and feet numb.

"How come I can see differently out of each eye?" I asked.

We were swinging our linked arms for warmth. My mother carried the pails in her other hand.

"What's the difference?" she asked.

"Things look more colourful out of my right eye than my left."

"Really?"

"Yes. And when I look at something then shut my left eye and look at it out of my right, then it looks the same, but when I shut my right eye and look at it out of my left then it moves a little bit, like I've moved my head, but I haven't."

"Well," my mother said. "That means your right eye is stronger than your left."

I thought about that for a while. "Does everyone have a stronger eye?"

"No," my mother said. "Not everyone."

"Is it good to have a stronger eye?"

My mother squeezed my hand. "There's nothing wrong with it," she said. "Your aunt Vivienne is short-sighted in one eye, even though she won't wear glasses. And your grandmother is blind in one eye."

"How come?"

"Something happened to her."

"What?"

My mother paused. "Someone hit her," she said eventually. "On the left side of her face. Her cornea was damaged and she never saw out of that eye again."

"What's a cornea?"

"It's the part of your eye that you can see."

"Who hit her?"

My mother stopped walking and put our pails down. She took her hand back from mine and rubbed it against her cheek, not looking at me. I waited for a minute, then asked her again.

"Your grandfather," she said, still not looking at me.

I tried to grasp this idea. "Why did he hit her?"

"They fought a lot. And your grandfather grew up in a

40

time when it was accepted that a man might hit his wife. He could be very respectable on the street, but what happened behind closed doors was his business."

"Oh."

She picked up the pails and we tramped on. The woods smelt like earth and cold air. The leaves underfoot weren't crunchy anymore, but stuck to the ground.

"Why did Grandma stay with him?"

My mother smiled at me. We stopped by a blackberry shrub and she picked some blackberries. She put one in her mouth. "Open up."

I opened my mouth obediently. She gently placed a berry on my tongue. I brought my teeth down and the juice was sweet, just right. Not like some blackberries, where it was so sharp it made my mouth sting.

My mother was picking more blackberries and tossing them into her pail. "I don't know," she said. "I imagine it's because there was nowhere for her to go. Things were harder for women back in the 1950s. And she loved him." She turned away then.

"How can you love someone who hits you?"

"Sometimes people are drawn to each other because they're both damaged by something that has happened to them," she said. "And sometimes, if you're damaged, then you can't see past it, and then you hurt the other person, or you expect the other person to hurt you."

"I don't understand what you just said," I said.

She sighed. "Sweetheart. It's absolutely wrong to hit someone, and most people know that. But sometimes you can love someone so much that even when you know they're wrong, even when they hurt you, you still go on loving them." She placed a pail in front of me.

"That's stupid," I said. "If someone hit me, I would stop loving them." I kicked my pail. It tipped over and rolled away.

My mother cupped my face in her hands. "It's not always simple," she said. "But you're clever and brave, and I'm so thankful for that. Every day." She kissed me on the forehead. "Now go pick up your pail."

∗ ∗ ∗

I buy a coffee from the café by the entrance and find a place to sit in one of the chairs that line the hallway.

Maybe I took in what she was saying more than I realised. Maybe I've even used it as an excuse.

If I had to describe myself, 'damaged' would probably make top of the list, and look at me now – best friend gone, a family of strangers and a dead-end job.

I rip off the top of the sugar packet with my teeth; my mother used to make a tear in the middle, my father opened them like a bag of crisps, but I use my teeth.

I tip the sugar into the liquid. I've forgotten to pick up a wooden stirrer, so I wait for it to cool then use my finger. No one gives me a second glance here – hospitals are like train stations, or hotels without the complimentary toiletries, an endless round of people turning up, staying, moving on. Everyone blends into the background unless they do something drastic. Or maybe I'm particularly good at being inconspicuous.

Maybe I never really tried to make my life any better because I assumed this was my lot. I wouldn't be the first Park to do that.

∗ ∗ ∗

I didn't see my grandmother until the following Easter. It was 1991 and I'd just had my tenth birthday. My parents decided to celebrate with the whole family in Shropshire; it was dark by the time we set out and I had a blanket to cover my legs. Mr Tickles was purring in his cage next to me. I watched the houses become fewer and farther between, until the only light came from lampposts along the central reservation, and occasional cars overtaking us. My mother peeled an orange and handed back the segments for me to eat. I fell asleep in the backseat, a Roald Dahl tape playing on the car stereo.

The next morning I woke up in my bed at my grandmother's. I didn't remember arriving the previous night. I shuffled along the corridor and down the stairs. My cousins were all in the kitchen, eating cereal.

"Tallie," Georgia said, when she saw me standing in the doorway. "We're having an Easter egg hunt." She patted the chair next to her. "Can we be on a team together?"

My mother and the gardener were responsible for the hunt, with paper clues scattered around the house and garden and a prize at the end of the trail. The prize was a pillowcase full of miniature chocolate eggs that we were supposed to divide equally between us, but later that afternoon James was sick, which made me think he'd managed to sneak more than everyone else.

I hadn't run into my grandmother much by that point, but on Easter Sunday I was made to take her a plate of hot cross buns that the cook had baked. She was asleep in the living-room, or at least I thought she was. It was a warm day so she'd rolled up the sleeves of her jumper, and her hands were clasped across her stomach; I noticed how the skin on her arms was still smooth like a younger woman's, and see-through, but her face was wrinkled like an old apple, especially around the mouth. She had a mole on her cheek, and I strained to see if there were hairs growing out of it, but I couldn't find any.

I lingered for a moment after balancing the plate on her knee, watching her breathing in and out. Her teeth made a sucking sound. I wondered if they were false, although my mother hadn't mentioned that on our fruit-picking trip. I tried to remember what her eye looked like, but I'd never been brave enough to look her directly in the face.

At the door to the living-room I turned around and caught her sitting bolt upright, her eyes wide open and looking at me. I fled.

The grown-ups were arguing less than usual that weekend

and, apart from my grandmother, we all ate together in the garden every night. Uncle George and my father carried the kitchen table outside and my mother strung lanterns up on the roof of the porch. The cook made potato salads, meat pies, and meringues, and put dishes of butter out with ice cubes nestled among the yellow pats to stop them from melting. A cake with candles was brought out for me and everyone sang happy birthday. Afterwards, Aunt Vivienne said how Aunt Gillian had always been the loudest singer, even if she was the most tone-deaf. Uncle George bellowed with laughter. Aunt Gillian's face flushed, but she just said, "I suppose you're right, Viv."

My mother put us to bed that night. Georgia and Starr brought their mattresses into my room and she read us a bedtime story. After she'd gone, Starr and I talked while Georgia snored gently in between us.

"You know I'm going to a new school soon, right?" she said.

"Yeah – I heard your mum say."

"She's enrolled me in a boarding school – all the Parks went to it, she says."

"Where is it?"

"Not that far from here."

"Are you going to come and see Grandma by yourself?"

Starr shuddered. "No way. She probably eats children when no one's watching."

I giggled.

"Where are you going to secondary?"

"I don't know," I said. "I haven't even finished Year Five. But I just want to go wherever my friends go."

"Oh," Starr said. "Well, you should think about boarding school. You get to be away from your parents – it's really grown up."

"I don't want to be away from my parents," I said.

Starr rolled over. "Yeah, I guess not," she said. "Anyway, I'm tired. Night night, Tallie."

"Don't let the bedbugs bite."

Starr snorted softly. "You can't say that when you go to secondary," she said.

✳ ✳ ✳

The next day after breakfast my grandmother suggested we go for a picnic. None of us grandchildren said anything.

"That'll be nice, won't it?" my mother said, smiling at me over the rim of her mug.

"We'll go to the field at the back of the garden," my grandmother said. "They've got horses – we can take them apples."

I looked at Michael, who raised and dropped his shoulders slightly.

"If we can pat the horses," I said.

Starr came and stood in front of me when I was putting my wellies on.

"I'm not coming," she said; she looked fed up. "Picnics are boring anyway."

"They're not," I said. I knew Starr didn't think they were either, and I was going to ask if she was okay, but then my mother called for me to help her pack the picnic basket.

Outside, my grandmother led the way and carried the blanket. She wore old people's clothes – a long tweed skirt and an old, cream woollen jumper whose arms she kept rolling up – but she walked very quickly and upright. Michael tramped behind her, a cricket bat under one arm. After him was Georgia, limping because of blue jelly shoes that were too small for her. She was wearing split-coloured cycling shorts – one leg lime green, the other hot pink – that I'd seen once in C&A. My father had refused to buy them; he said I'd thank him when I was older.

Behind Georgia and Michael, James carried the apples and sugar for the horses. My mother and I were at the back, holding the basket between us. I let it bang against my legs, not caring if it hurt because my mother seemed so happy. She had her hair up in a ponytail and it rose from side to side like a swing-boat when she turned her face to smile at me. She looked young and beautiful, I thought, and was I proud of her.

"What a lovely day," she said.

"What's Starr doing?"

"I think your aunt wanted some alone time with her," my mother said.

"Why?"

"Well… "

"Dad said she just didn't want Starr spending time with Grandma," James said, keeping his voice low so our grandmother couldn't hear.

"I'm sure that's not true, James," my mother murmured, but she didn't finish answering me.

We reached the wooden fence at the bottom of the garden. My grandmother swung her legs over the top and landed on the grass on the other side, then took the cricket things Michael was handing over. He jumped up to sit on the fence and held his arms out to Georgia, who let herself be picked up and dropped lightly into the field. Michael stood up, balancing on the top rung.

"Michael," my mother said. "Are you sure it's safe to do that?"

"I'm on the gymnastics team," he said, and walked to the nearest post and back without wobbling. He looked so confident and grown up that I stared at him; he was actually quite handsome, I thought, and then I was embarrassed to be noticing my cousin that way.

James looked annoyed. "I can do that too," he said. "You don't have to be on the gymnastics team to be able to walk."

"Bet you can't do *this*," Michael said, and somersaulted backwards off the fence. He landed off balance and had to take a step forward to stop himself from falling. "I learnt that last week."

"I'm sure it comes in handy," my grandmother said, raising an eyebrow.

"You're so *clever*, Mike," Georgia said, and Michael grinned. For a moment, I was jealous of how close she was to him, then James started climbing onto the top of the fence and my mother dropped the picnic basket and put her hand out to stop him.

"James, please," she said. "I wouldn't be able to face your mum if you got hurt."

"Michael did it," James said.

"Yeah, but I know what I'm doing," Michael said. "You'll probably break your neck."

"No I won't."

"Gymnastics is certainly less important than saving your neck," my grandmother said. "James, Tallulah and Evelyn, if you wouldn't mind climbing over the usual way."

James looked furious, but he climbed down carefully, and my mother and I joined everyone else, handing the basket to Georgia while we were trying to get over.

"I *can* do a somersault," James muttered, on the other side. "I've done one before."

My grandmother pinned him down with what I assumed was her good eye, and he turned a funny colour. When she started leading the way again, he hung back, looking sullen. Georgia tried to take his hand, but he shoved her away.

"Get lost, podgy," he said.

"That's not very nice, James," my mother said.

"It's Dad's nickname for me," Georgia said; her eyes were full of tears, and I prayed she wouldn't blink. Everyone knew once you blinked you were definitely going to cry.

"Do you want me to help you with the basket?" I asked her. "We can carry it like me and Mummy did."

"Yes, thank you," Georgia said. She smiled again and I felt ashamed of being jealous of her before.

"Thank you, darling," my mother said.

"Is anyone actually coming?" my grandmother called to us.

The field was mostly muddy; eventually my grandmother stopped and beckoned me and Georgia over to a dry patch.

"Unpack that here," she said.

We took the basket to the blanket, which she'd already laid out, and opened it. There were salmon-paste sandwiches, salad, jacket potatoes in their skins, Petits Filous, slices of cold chicken, Ribena and leftover cake from my birthday dinner.

We all tucked in. My mother shifted to make room for James on the blanket when he reached us, but he took a sandwich and went and sat facing away from everyone.

My grandmother asked Michael, loudly, what he was doing at the moment. He was going into fourth year, and he reeled off a list of subjects he'd be studying, mostly languages. "You must have got that ability from your father's side," she said, and he went quiet.

My mother broke the silence, saying school seemed like a long time ago to her; she'd stopped going when her parents passed away, which she said was a shame, as it was something else she lost. She sipped her wine and smiled at Michael, who was still being quiet.

My grandmother turned to Georgia who was still in primary, like me. "And what would you like to do?"

Georgia thought about it for a moment. "I'd like to be Mary in the Nativity play," she said. "Last time I was only a shepherd."

I thought my mother and grandmother were trying to hide smiles. I was hoping they wouldn't get around to asking me, but my grandmother swivelled her head in my direction.

"And you, Tallulah?"

"I'm the same year as Georgia."

"And would you like to be Mary?"

"No," I said. "I'd rather be a Wise Man and wear a beard."

"I see," my grandmother said.

My mother pulled me onto her lap and hugged me.

After we'd finished all the food, Michael tried to teach me and Georgia how to play cricket. Georgia was supposed to catch the ball when I hit it with the cricket bat, and throw it back to Michael, but she wasn't very good and spent most of her time trying to find it, instead. Michael said he wanted to practise his bowling, and threw the ball too fast for me to see it, until I threatened to throw it back at his head.

"Sorry," he said. "I'm not used to playing with little kids."

"Oh, you're so *grown up*," I said.

"Do you want me to teach you properly, or do you want to play a sissy game?"

"Forget it," I said, dropping the bat. "Cricket's boring anyway."

I made my way back to the picnic blanket and flopped down onto my belly. My mother and grandmother were sitting at the other end. I watched them over the hill of my forearms, screwing my eyes up so it looked like they were closed and I wasn't spying.

My grandmother looked very serious. "Nothing to forgive… " she said.

My mother put her glass down. I caught the last bit of her sentence, "… hard on you."

"I can't blame her," my grandmother said. "We saw him through different eyes."

My mother turned away as she was speaking, and the next thing I heard was my grandmother saying, "Whatever you do, Evelyn, don't blame yourself."

I felt something cold land on my neck and jumped up, yelling and brushing it off. James was laughing evilly, and when I looked at my fingers they were covered in slime. A fat, grey slug was curled up on the blanket where I'd just been.

"Your face," James said. "You were so scared."

"Was not."

"Were too."

"Was not."

"That's enough, children," my grandmother said.

"Were too," James said under his breath, and looked smug.

Later, we walked over to the corner of the field where the horses were grazing. My mother placed apple segments and sugar lumps on our palms, and taught us to feed them, keeping our hands flat and still. The horses' mouths tickled when they took the food and I squirmed inside, but didn't move, because my grandmother was watching me closely.

"Good girl," she said.

Four

"Excuse me."

I look up at the man in front of me; he has dirty silver hair and an even dirtier dark-green fleece. His shoes squeak on the hospital floor as he takes another step closer. Above us, a neon light flickers, on-then-off-then-on. All the lights along this corridor buzz quietly.

"Excuse me," he says again, "have you seen Marilyn?"

"No," I say. "Sorry."

His eyes look milky. "She went to see her sister last week," he says. Spit is forming at one corner of his mouth. "I'm getting worried because she hasn't called – she always calls to say goodnight to Jane." He wipes a hand across his face.

A middle-aged woman hurries down the corridor towards us. "Dad," she says; she has lipstick on her two front teeth. "You can't go wandering off like that." She takes her father's hand and he looks at her blankly.

"Are you Jane?" I ask.

"Has he been bothering you?" She shakes her father gently by the shoulder. He's looking off into space now.

"Jane's ten," he says.

"He's looking for your mum."

The woman rolls hers eyes. "She died about ten years ago," she says, kneeling down to tie her father's shoelace.

"We all miss Mum, don't we, Dad?"

"She's got lovely black hair," he says.

"Oh for crying out loud," the woman says. She's still kneeling in front of her father, and she takes his hand again and clasps it between her own. "What are we going to do with you?"

He looks down at her and smiles uncertainly. "Have you seen Marilyn?" he asks.

"Come on, Dad," she says. "Let's take you home."

"You need any help?" I ask.

"No thanks," she says. "Sorry for bothering you."

I watch them walk towards the exit; he's leaning on her shoulder. That'll never be us, will it, Dad? I wonder what Jane's father was like when she was growing up, for her to be so dedicated now.

You're absent from so many of my memories. I guess that's how I would have characterised you as a father, at least in the beginning. But if that's all you'd been, I'd probably have been okay with it. Plenty of doctors' children never see their parents, after all.

∗ ∗ ∗

It was May of the same year when the dark-haired man turned up. It was one of those weekend mornings where my father hadn't come home from work yet, and my mother made me waffles. She always made waffles in the spring, she said they reminded her of breakfast in Paris, where it was sunny enough to eat outdoors. She'd gone once, with a friend for a weekend, and it had stuck in her mind. That morning she sat across from me at the kitchen table and sipped coffee while I ate.

"*I* want to try some coffee," I said.

My mother raised her eyebrows and smiled at me.

"Please," I wheedled.

"Coffee's very bitter," my mother said. "And strong."

"But I'm strong too."

52

She pushed her mug towards me, handle-first. The first swallow was horrible. I blew on the liquid and pretended I was waiting for it to cool down. The doorbell rang. I jumped up to get it, my mother smiling as I ran out the kitchen.

The man at the door had very long eyelashes. He was wearing a t-shirt and jeans. My father never wore jeans, neither did any of the other men who came to the house.

"Hi there," the man said.

"Hi," I said.

The man was staring at me. I noticed one of my socks needed straightening. "Are your mummy and daddy home, Tallulah?" He was talking to the top of my head.

I ran back to the kitchen. My mother had taken the coffee back while I was gone.

"It's for you," I said.

She was in the hallway before I realised what was bothering me – he knew my name.

My mother stopped smiling when she reached the door.

"Evie," the man said, grinning. Something about him reminded me of next door's wolfhound.

My mother stood in the doorway. She kept the door open with one hand on the latch; I hid behind her and saw her knuckles go white. "What are you doing here?" she asked.

The man laughed, but it didn't sound like he found anything funny. "Come on, Evie," he said. "It's pretty cold out here."

My mother hesitated, then stood back to let him in. He stepped past her and stopped on the doormat, stamping his boots. "You're looking good," he said.

Her cheeks went pink. The man leant over to give her a kiss, but at the last minute she turned her head and he got a mouthful of hair.

I caught my mother's hand as she shut the door. "Who's he?" I whispered.

"I'm your Uncle Jack," the man said, looking straight at my mother. She always said my whispering voice needed more practice. He crouched down in front of me. "Aren't I, Evie?"

"Yes," my mother answered. She squeezed my hand hard. I remembered where I'd seen the man's face before – in the photo at Aunt Vivienne's house.

We all heard the key at the same moment. When my father walked through the door he found us frozen in our positions in the hallway.

I'd never seen my father go pale before.

"Eddie," – the man came forward to give my father a hug – "it's been too long."

They embraced quickly. It was over before I could goggle at the sight of my father hugging another man.

My father hung up his coat very carefully, as he always did. "Evelyn, could I have a word with you in the kitchen?"

My mother was twisting her ring. "Of course. Jack, could you wait here?"

Uncle Jack held up his hands and laughed again. "No problem guys. I'll just get acquainted with this one here."

"Tallulah has homework to do," my father said. "Tallulah – upstairs, now."

I climbed upstairs and walked along the corridor. When I heard my parents go into the kitchen and shut the door, I walked back and sat on the top step. Uncle Jack was leaning against the wall, scowling. He didn't see me at first, and when he did he blew his cheeks out and stuck his hands in his pockets. He didn't say anything.

"I don't like you very much," I said.

✳ ✳ ✳

Uncle Jack only came three or four times after that first visit, but the house always felt uneasy when he was there. He would go to my father's study with him and talk; they always closed the door. Once my father came out unexpectedly and caught me trying to listen in. "What were you doing?" he asked, frowning.

I thought he probably knew what I was doing. "I was trying to hear what you were saying," I said. I didn't know what to do with my hands, so I started scratching my head.

"Evelyn," my father called. My mother came out of the kitchen, wiping her hands on her skirt. Uncle Jack appeared behind my father.

"Perhaps you could find something for Tallulah to do," my father said to my mother. "Then she wouldn't have to eavesdrop to amuse herself."

"Edward," my mother said. "That's hardly fair."

He stared down at me again. "Do you have some sort of parasitic problem, Tallulah?"

"No." I dropped my hands down by my side, wondering why my father was clearly so irritated with me.

He turned and ushered Uncle Jack back into the study. I saw a smile on Uncle Jack's face, and I thought I heard him say: "Well at least you've brought *her* up to be honest, Eddie."

The next time Uncle Jack came to the house my mother turned off the cartoons I was watching and handed me an apron.

I didn't need a stool anymore. I stirred the jam with one hand and held a wineglass of water in the other, imagining I was Keith Floyd, and we were cooking on a fishing boat, like in his show. Mr Tickles was nudging at my feet. "Why does Uncle Jack have to come round?" I asked my mother.

She was taking the stones out of the plums. "He's your father's brother, Tallie." She kept her eyes on what her hands were doing.

"Is he really Daddy's brother?"

"Of course he is."

Uncle Jack didn't look like my father, I thought. My father was blond and heavy and blinked a lot. Uncle Jack was tall and dark and looked like he never blinked, even though his eyes were always moving.

"He doesn't act like a brother," I said. "Or an uncle. He never even brings me presents."

My mother looked sideways at me and smiled.

"Other peoples' uncles bring them presents," I pressed. "Charlotte's uncle buys her fudge, and she brings it into school. It's pretty good fudge."

"Do you want to take some of this jam into school?" my mother asked.

Mr Tickles meowed in front of his empty bowl.

"No." I turned back to the jam.

"Okay then," she said.

Mr Tickles made the rattling sound that passed for purring with him. I picked him up and hugged him.

"I've already fed him twice," my mother warned. "Don't be fooled."

"He can smell food," I said. "He doesn't want to miss out."

My mother picked up a plum and waved it in his face. "Trust me," she said. "You don't want this."

Mr Tickles eyed it eagerly.

My mother took a step back and put the plum down. "I think he might just eat it anyway," she said. "This cat... "

I scratched his ear. "It's just because it smells so good," I said.

"It does," Uncle Jack said from the doorway. "Plums always remind me of you, Evie."

I dropped Mr Tickles, who let out a yowl and left the room. My mother put a hand up to her face.

"Don't worry," Uncle Jack said to me. "I'm just returning my glass."

He walked around the table to the sink and put his glass down in it. When he walked back to the door he went the other way around; we had to squeeze together to let him past.

"See you later," he said to us. "Maybe I can have some of that jam when you've made it." He was looking at me, but my mother answered.

"Sorry, Jack, I'm only making enough for the three of us."

His smile slipped for a moment, then he shrugged and winked at me as he left.

"I've been sent to find you," Aunt Vivienne says, appearing before me in the hallway. "Gillian would have come, but she's staying with our comatose brother, in case he wakes up and suddenly needs mothering." She peels off her leather gloves; I wonder why she's kept them on until now. Probably in protest against the dingy, neglected air that seems to choke the building.

I gesture to the chair opposite me. She sits down.

"So you all but dropped off the family radar," she says. "What exactly have you been doing with yourself these past five years?"

"Nothing much," I say warily.

She arches an eyebrow again; it must be her trademark. "Darling, I do hate the way your generation seems to cultivate inactivity and boredom as if they're virtues," she says.

I blow my cheeks out. Aunt Gillian is probably right when she says that Vivienne could do with being taken down a peg or two. "Speaking for my generation," I say. "I think we prefer to call it *ennui*."

Aunt Vivienne inclines her head slightly in my direction. "I'm glad you haven't turned out so *nice*," she says. "I was afraid you would. Your mother was the nicest person I've ever met." She wrinkles her nose.

"Fortunately," I say, "the Park genes seem to have overcompensated slightly."

Aunt Vivienne appraises me again, and takes a hipflask from her handbag. "Fancy an Irish coffee?"

I push my cup towards her. She gives me a generous splash of whisky and stops a male orderly walking by to order a coffee.

He's confused. "We don't have table service here, Madam," he says. "But there's a café just over there… "

"I'm sorry," I say. "It's okay, I'll get it. Aunt Vivienne, I'll get it."

The orderly smiles gratefully at me and leaves.

"Thank you, darling," Aunt Vivienne says. She settles back further into her chair. "That's very sweet of you."

The café is small and smells like antiseptic and new paint. The boy on the till recognises me from my last order and tries to make conversation. "Caffeine addict, huh?"

I think of saying that this one isn't for me, but it's easier just to force a smile.

"I can spot a fellow coffee fiend a mile away," he says, ringing up two pounds fifty on his till. "I drink at least twenty cups a day."

"Mmm," I say. He's got blond facial hair, little tufts growing in patches on his chin and up his jawline. I wonder if Toby has a beard now – it would be dark if he did, like his hair. I think it would suit him.

The boy's still talking. "I probably should be dead by now," he says, "the amount of junk I put into my body."

"Sensitive," I say. "For someone who works in a hospital."

His mouth drops open and his face flushes red. "Shit, no, I didn't mean – I'm sorry, I hope I haven't offended you."

"Forget it," I say. I hand him a five pound note.

He scrabbles for change. "No, really. I didn't think… "

"It's fine," I say.

Vivienne's right – I'm not as nice as my mother. Or Georgia. I inwardly curse my cousin for not keeping her promise to Aunt Gillian and showing up. Georgia used to remind me of my mother, all soft and sweet-tempered. I couldn't be as good as her if I tried.

I bring Aunt Vivienne her coffee; she doesn't say thank you. We sit, not talking, looking at each other from time to time. I notice she has a scar, a very small one, slinking down her neck.

"This is the part people complain about I suppose – the waiting," Aunt Vivienne says, breaking into my thoughts. "I always wondered what could be worse than hearing bad news."

I shrug and inspect my coffee cup. "Maybe the anticipation is the worst part," I say.

"How polite," Aunt Vivienne says coolly. "Do you really believe that?" She cocks her head at me. I think how if they were birds, Aunt Vivienne would be an eagle. Aunt Gillian would be a hen.

"I can't speak from experience," I say. "Everyone I know has died suddenly."

I look at the ceiling, away from her. At least she's not trying to hug me.

"You remind me of him, you know," she says.

I'm still, blinking at the ceiling, not saying anything.

"I'm talking about your father."

I'm careful with my next words. "I wouldn't have said we were anything alike."

"Well, in what way are you different?"

I think of my father's love of silence, the careful way he buttered my toast when my mother was too ill to make breakfast. I think of how he changed after Uncle Jack turned up, his slight frown and his closed doors and his closed face; I think of the cards from grateful patients and families every Christmas. I shrug again. I don't think he ever opened up enough for me to know who he is, even before he stopped liking me.

"I'm going to find a bathroom," Aunt Vivienne says. "I'm sure it'll be as depressing as the rest of this place, but needs must."

I down my drink when she's gone; the alcohol leaves a tickling feeling in my throat. I wonder what my father told them. I'm sure he made it all out to be my fault. Knowing he's in the building with me makes me feel light-headed. He could wake up at any moment and Aunt Gillian would bring me forward, expecting us to hold hands. I rub my temples, but that seems to make my eyesight bad. Tiny black spots are creeping in from the far corners of both eyes.

I need to get outside, away from my family, especially

my father. I start walking towards the exit. If the roles were reversed, would anyone be there waiting at my side? Would my father? I dig my nails into the palms of my hands. Probably, just so he could let me know what a failure I was when I woke up.

I push my way out of the hospital into the heat and walk far enough away that I don't recognise the streets around me anymore.

"Screw him," I yell.

A couple, arms linked, hurry their steps to get away from me. I hear them giggling when they think they're at a safe distance. I'm officially a crazy person.

When I start running I don't stop; I don't look back.

* * *

Summer 1991 was languid, the hottest I could remember. Everywhere on the news people spoke of hosepipe bans, and ice-cream trucks running out of supplies, and pub gardens filling up, even during the daytime. We lazed in the garden on picnic rugs, or sat indoors in swimsuits with the curtains drawn. My mother made lemonade and I got browner and browner. Mr Tickles paused in his quest to eat everything in sight, and stretched out in the cool at the bottom of the stairs, where my father tripped over him all the time.

I was about to start my last year at primary school, and try-outs for the swimming team were that September. When we went up to my grandmother's, I spent most of my time in the lake with my cousins. It was also an excuse to avoid the grown-ups, which was something I wanted to do more than usual because on the second day of the visit, Uncle Jack had joined us.

We were all snoozing in the garden after lunch when we heard the doorbell. Aunt Gillian got up to answer it, strolling indoors with her giant, floppy sunhat in one hand.

A moment later we heard her scream.

"What the blazes?" Uncle George sat up.

Uncle Jack's voice wafted out to us. "Calm down, Gilly – didn't Eddie tell you I was back?"

The grown-ups all turned to look at my father, then Aunt Vivienne jumped up and ran across the lawn and the porch, banging the kitchen door open in her rush to get to the figures inside. "*Jack*," she screamed. "Is that you?"

They reappeared, Aunt Vivienne clutching Uncle Jack and Aunt Gillian walking behind them, looking bewildered. Aunt Vivienne was white, with red spots on her cheeks. "Mother, Jack's here," she said loudly.

My grandmother pursed her lips. "So I see," she said.

"How's my favourite girl?" Uncle Jack asked, breaking away from Aunt Vivienne and taking long strides towards his mother. Us grandchildren watched with open mouths as Uncle Jack reached her and suddenly hesitated – maybe he was put off by her expression.

Our grandmother let her gaze travel over him. "Still alive," she said finally, and turned her cheek up to be kissed. Uncle Jack leant down and gave her a quick peck, and I thought I saw his shoulders drop, like he'd been tensed up for something.

"Who *is* that?" James hissed.

"It's Uncle Jack," I said, pleased to know something the others didn't.

"Who's Uncle Jack?"

"He's Dad's brother, and your mum's, and yours."

"Where's he been?" Georgia asked.

"Dunno," I said.

"Bloody hell," Uncle George said to my father. "You could have warned us, Edward."

"I didn't know we were to be having the pleasure," my father said, his face expressionless.

"Jack never said anything," my mother said.

Aunt Vivienne wheeled around. "So *you* knew as well?" she demanded.

Aunt Gillian had been standing to one side, silently, and

now she stepped forwards. "Children – this is your Uncle Jack – he's been travelling and now he's home," she said. She smiled brightly. "Isn't that fun?"

"Why has no one ever talked about him before?" Michael asked.

"Haven't we?" Aunt Gillian said.

"I know him," Michael said.

Aunt Gillian shook her head. "No, Michael, you don't."

"I do," he said. "I remember him. He used to live with Starr and Aunt Vivienne. And… "

"With *me*?" Starr asked.

"Michael, it *doesn't matter*," Aunt Gillian said. "Why don't you all have a quick swim – it's getting very hot out here."

We started to move off and Aunt Gillian beckoned to Michael. "A quick word," she said. I thought I saw him give me a funny look before he followed her.

The atmosphere was strained for the rest of the visit. The first night, over pre-dinner drinks on the terrace, Aunt Gillian mentioned a party their neighbours were throwing because Nelson Mandela had been elected head of the ABC, or some other letters I couldn't hear properly. "They're artists, of course," she said. "But it sounds fun – they know some terribly important people."

"I'm not going," Uncle George said. "The man's a terrorist."

"I didn't know you were such a friend to ex-cons, Gilly," Uncle Jack said.

All the grown-ups went quiet, and Aunt Vivienne got angry with Aunt Gillian for some reason. I waited until we went in for dinner, then complained about Uncle Jack to my mother, saying that he was always around, until she told me to stop it, looking sad although I couldn't tell why.

I concentrated on the swimming instead. Georgia and the boys were already strong swimmers, but Starr had never been in the water because of her asthma. Sometimes, watching her, I wanted a cool blue inhaler of my own. Aunt Vivienne had bought her a white bikini, and she lay on her towel on the jetty, squealing whenever the boys splashed her.

"Come in with us, Starr," Georgia said once. "It's nice."

"No thanks," Starr said. She wore her sunglasses on the end of her nose, so she could look at us over the top of the lenses.

"But won't you be lonely out here while we're all having fun?" Georgia asked.

"You can't *have* fun with boys," Starr said, sitting up. "Not at this age anyway."

Term hadn't even started, but ever since Starr had been accepted at the boarding school, she'd been putting on airs. Georgia and I knew about the school, everyone did; kids there were famous for smoking, and for kissing before they were twelve. Whatever Starr was talking about, she probably knew more than us, or would do soon.

"What do you mean?" I asked. I hugged my knees to my chest, so did Georgia. Starr sat with her legs curling away from her, her body turned in our direction. I thought how flat her stomach looked like that, especially next to Georgia's rolls of flesh.

"Well," she said, lowering her voice. "Boys have this thing called *sperm*. It's like, swimming around in their bodies... "

"Where in their bodies?" I asked.

"In their blood, or something," Starr said, annoyed. "I wasn't listening in class. And it gives them these *urges*, which make them act funny in front of girls. That's why they pull girls' hair, and want to take your clothes off and stuff."

"Are you talking about... " Georgia started, her eyes round.

"*Sex*," Starr said in a stage whisper.

Georgia's eyes got rounder. I thought it sounded stupid.

"So Michael and James want to take our clothes off?" I asked. Georgia looked unhappy with this idea.

"No, they don't, because we're family," Starr said. "But all other boys do."

"I think that's bullshit," I said. It was the first time I'd used that word, although I'd heard Uncle Jack say it. It seemed grown up enough for this conversation. "No one wants to have sex now, we're too young, and it's too… " I searched for the right feeling, "disgusting."

Starr rolled her eyes at me. "Not everyone's as much of a baby as you, Tallulah," she said, draping herself back over the towel.

"Ten's not a baby."

Georgia drew her breath in sharply. "Starr, have you *had sex*?" she asked.

"I shouldn't say."

"Oh *come on*," I said. "You haven't had sex."

Michael and James appeared behind us, dripping water all over the jetty and laughing. "Of course she hasn't had sex," Michael hooted. "Look at her, she doesn't even have any tits. Who'd have her?"

Starr got up, haughtily, and started walking back towards the house. "I'm going to find your mother, Michael," she called over her shoulder.

Michael shrugged and grinned at us. "Stuck-up little princess," he said.

"Yeah, as if anyone's gonna want to have sex with *any* of you," James said. "You all look about seven."

I kicked him hard in the shin, he let out a shriek and started hopping around. Michael laughed so hard he stopped breathing.

"I don't want to grow up," Georgia said softly. "Mummy said I'm going to have to wear a bra, and bleed and stuff."

I wrapped my arms around my chest and glared at James, who was inspecting his shin. "I don't wanna grow up either," I said. "You're older and you suck."

"Whatever," he said. "Bet you can't do a dive bomb. Bet you're a crybaby – you look like one."

There was no way I was going to let the boys win. I sprinted down the jetty and launched myself into the air. I was going too fast. I didn't have time to bring both knees up into a tuck. One leg was still extended when I hit the water. The force of it brought my head forward, just as my knee jerked upwards. I opened my mouth to shout and swallowed water. I swallowed again and again, trying to get rid of the water in my mouth, my throat, until everything started to go red and I felt like someone was squeezing my chest. My body suddenly remembered how to swim and I climbed to the surface. The other three pulled me out of the lake. I could feel blood trickling down from my nose where the collision had taken place.

Georgia wanted to call for a grown-up. Michael and James hovered around me, inspecting the damage. "Does it hurt?" Michael was asking. "You smacked it pretty hard." He patted me on the back, the only physical contact he allowed since his voice had dropped. Standing next to him, I noticed how tall he was now, and how a faint line of hair kissed his upper lip.

"Oh, Tallie," Georgia said. She looked like she was going to cry.

"Does it feel broken?" James asked. "Can I touch it?"

"It's fine," I said. I touched it gingerly and felt a sharp pain. "It doesn't hurt. I'm just going to wash it."

I set off back to the house at a trot. I wanted to find my mother, but she wasn't reading in her bedroom where I'd last seen her. I checked the time – the grown-ups would be having tea in the front room now.

I heard a snatch of the conversation as I opened the door. "For God's sake, Vivienne," Aunt Gillian was saying. "*She* wasn't the one who broke your…"

"She did what she always did – nothing."

"I am *here*," my grandmother said. She nodded her head in my direction. "As is Tallulah."

They all turned at the same time towards me. I cupped my hand over my nose so they couldn't see the blood.

"Yes, Tallie?" my father said. He was balancing a teacup on one knee, and, as usual these days, he looked annoyed.

"Where's Mummy?" I asked.

"I can't hear you," he said. "Don't you know not to talk with your hand over your mouth? Come in properly, take your hand away and ask the question."

She obviously wasn't there. I moved my hand but ducked my head. "What were you saying just now? What got broken?"

Aunt Vivienne was closest to me. I'd felt her eyes on me and now I looked at her properly. Her face was tense. Something passed over it quickly when she caught my gaze. "Edward, darling, you're too uptight," she said. "Tallulah, I saw your mother go towards the rose garden, if that's who you were looking for."

I bobbed out gratefully and closed the door. As it shut I heard Aunt Vivienne say, "Tallulah is really quite pretty, Edward. You shouldn't let her run wild like that. Comb her hair once in a while, put her in a dress."

"Her mother does all that," my father said tersely.

"Well I think the problem is that she *doesn't* do all that," Aunt Vivienne said. "When I was in the flicks I had to look ravishing *every day*."

"You haven't been in a film for well over a decade," Aunt Gillian said.

"And you should really watch out for Georgia, you know, Gilly. She looks like she'll get your acne."

Aunt Vivienne laughed. No one else did. I hung around, hoping for some more comments on my appearance. I'd always felt too dark and skinny to be pretty. I wanted to look more like my mother: blonde and soft and round, with big green eyes. Not my brownish ones, under eyebrows that Starr said looked like caterpillars.

The aunts started arguing; it wasn't about me anymore, so I ran off.

The rose garden was inside the walled garden to the west of the house, separated from it by a gravelled pathway. I decided to wash my face before I went to find my mother. The blood had dried now, and the skin underneath felt raw and tight.

My bathroom was at the end of the corridor, all cold white squares. The toilet had an old-fashioned cistern high above the bowl, and a chain flush. When I was younger, I hadn't been able to reach the chain unless I climbed onto the toilet, which didn't have a lid, and several times I'd nearly fallen in.

I splashed my face now with cold water – the only kind we got at the house other than for two hours in the morning – and scrubbed it with an old, rough towel. My skin still felt raw, but at least I was all the same colour again.

Out of the lake, I'd been feeling colder and colder so I sprinted back to my room to put some clothes on. I found an old pair of ripped jeans and a yellow Aerosmith t-shirt. I was still in my Steve Tyler stage; I'd fallen in love with him on Top of the Pops and had made my mother buy me the *Pump* LP the day it came out. I would put it on in my room, draw the curtains and dance in my knickers and vest, practising my spinning and strutting. Sometimes she joined in, but she always said they'd gone downhill since the seventies.

Voices had been floating up towards me as I was getting dressed, but it was only when I was buttoning my flies that I started to pay attention to what they were saying, and who they belonged to. Uncle Jack and my mother were beneath my window in the rose garden. My mother was angry. She was shouting at Uncle Jack, and she never shouted. I dragged a chair over, as quietly as I could, and stood on it, fingers hooked into the diamonds of the lattice. They must have been just inside the garden, behind the high walls, because I couldn't see them.

"Don't you *dare* say anything," my mother was saying. "I won't – I *won't* let you come between us, you hear me?"

Uncle Jack said something in reply, quieter. I couldn't hear the words but his voice reminded me of the time the piano tuner had come to service the baby grand. I'd watched as he opened up the lid, and seen all the wires stretched out. 'Be careful there girly,' he'd said. 'If one of these snaps, it could take your arm off – they go right through the bone.'

I shivered.

"How can you say that?" my mother said. "You're not being fair, Jack. Do you think I don't feel guilty?"

Her voice made me feel hot and cold at the same time.

"But you managed to make quite a comfortable little nest for yourself, didn't you?" Uncle Jack said, louder now. "He probably couldn't believe his luck when you went back to him. Edward's not strong. He always did drool over you." His voice dropped again. "You took advantage of my brother, Evie, of both of us. That's not what nice girls do."

I was digging my fingers into the metal. There was a slap and an intake of breath then I heard the stones on the gravel walkway scattering and what sounded like two people struggling.

"Viv was right to warn me about you, Evie."

"Get *off*."

More gravel scattered. I ducked instinctively.

"Tea was served an hour ago, you two," another voice said loudly. It was Aunt Vivienne. I could hear her now, walking down the path between the house and the garden walls. I imagined her entering the garden, looking at my mother and Uncle Jack, that half-smile on her face.

"Tallulah's been looking for you, Evelyn," she said. "I told her you might be here, but it doesn't look like she's found you."

My mother said something I couldn't catch. I heard quick steps leaving the garden.

There was a silence from below. I pictured the other two facing each other, not blinking.

"You should leave it alone, Jacky boy," Aunt Vivienne said finally. "She's not your type, good little soul that she is."

Uncle Jack laughed colourlessly and said: "Poor Evie."

"I sent the girl out here after you two – I thought it'd be a nice surprise for her."

"Catty, Viv. You always did try to make trouble where there wasn't any."

"That wasn't quite the impression I got, darling."

"You know what I mean."

"Well, I can't help it. I can't *stand* how faultless she thinks she is."

"I need someone with a bit more edge then?" Uncle Jack asked.

"Exactly," Aunt Vivienne said. I heard the scratch of a match being lit and a deep breath.

"Someone dark and depraved like you?"

"You're perverted," Aunt Vivienne said evenly. "Let go of my wrist, my darling."

Uncle Jack laughed again, but he must have let go of Aunt Vivienne. I heard him sigh. "How can you even bear to be here?"

"It's my house too."

"Doesn't it give you nightmares?"

"No."

"I can't stand it," Uncle Jack said. "All this tea and politeness. And the bloody people – even the kid."

There was a pause. My lungs and throat felt like they were filling up with stale air. I'd stopped breathing.

"Don't let it get to you, Jack."

"Don't be stupid, Viv," Uncle Jack said. "This is my *life*."

"Yes it is," Aunt Vivienne said. "So fuck them. Now come inside and have tea. Gillian's such a bitch these days, I need an ally."

Their voices passed beneath my window, then were gone.

I climbed down from the chair as quietly as I could. I heard footsteps coming up the stairs; my mother was calling me. I opened the door and walked to the top of the staircase.

"There you are," she said, as if nothing had happened. "The boys said you'd hurt yourself. Do you want me to take a look?"

I shook my head. My mother watched me for a moment, then stretched her hand out. "Tallie," she started to say. "If anything's wrong, you know we can talk... "

"I'm fine," I mumbled.

I slipped past her and took the stairs two at a time, passing Starr at the bottom, who screwed up her face in disgust as I went by. "You know, Tallulah, you're going to have to start acting like a girl sometime," she said.

I made the V sign at her back and carried on running.

I sat inside a bush at the back of the garden with my knees drawn up to my chest, wishing I had Mr Tickles with me. I closed my eyes and imagined I could feel his wet nose wiping itself on my skin, his small furry head butting into me and pushing at my arms, trying to get past them and into my lap. This had been the first time I wasn't allowed to bring him to my grandmother's – my mother said he was too old for long journeys.

When I thought about my mother I got a knotted feeling in my stomach.

It was Georgia who found me. I was lying on my side, my knees still hugged against my ribcage.

"Tallie?" she said. I could see her anxious eyes peering in at me. "Tallie, are you alright? Everyone's been calling you for hours."

I crawled out of the bush and wiped myself down. Above us, the sun was sliding down a pink, waxy sky. We walked back to the house. My father was standing in the doorway frowning at me. "Dinner's cold," he said.

"Sorry."

"Go and wash," he said. "We're going to eat in five minutes, whether you're down or not."

Georgia came upstairs with me and laid out some clothes while I was washing. She sat on my bed and watched me get dressed, playing with her plait; it was nice to have the company. I wanted to be nice to her back, but I was full of my mother and Uncle Jack, and I could only think of one thing to say. "Your hair is really pretty."

"Thank you," Georgia said, going pink.

Dinner was almost silent. Aunt Vivienne ate with an

amused expression on her face. Uncle Jack drummed his fingers on the table. Starr asked me why I looked so pale and I said I had stomach ache.

"We can go home tomorrow if you're still not feeling well," my mother said. I could feel her trying to catch my attention, but I wouldn't look at her.

"Maybe it's the weather," Aunt Gillian said brightly. "It's still unbearably hot, isn't it?"

My father said nothing.

* * *

The next day I have seventeen missed calls listed on my phone. I go to work like nothing's happened. My boss still thinks the heart attack was an excuse – he narrows his eyes at me and asks if I've recovered, overly polite; I don't bother to try to correct him.

The café is small – there's space for ten tables and, at the far end of the room, a formica counter, with a cheap, plastic register, a tips jar and a basket of paper napkins. Behind the counter is the serving hatch to the kitchen, and above that, our menu, with pictures of the meal options, in case someone hasn't had a Full English Breakfast before, and wants to know what it is.

The walls are dirty off-white, with a green tile frieze running around them. The floor is lino, made to look like parquet. I don't know who thought that would be a good idea. As soon as I get in, my boss puts me on mopping duties with one of the other waitresses. It's nine a.m, so I've got about fifteen minutes before the second shift of regulars start to traipse in. I grip the handle harder than usual as I'm mopping, trying to concentrate on what's in front of me now, forget the last few days. I'm good at clearing my mind. I have these little tricks I developed after my mother died, trying to escape the strangeness that remained long after that day.

"Stop dawdling," my boss says.

He's leaning against the counter, inspecting me. He's

got a big mole on his chin that he sometimes covers with a plaster, and hair sprouting out of his ears. He wears the same colour scheme every day: off-white wife-beater, dark trousers, brown shoes. I wouldn't be surprised if they were actually the same clothes; he's the tightest person I know.

I finish mopping and collect my notepad. The café gets busy soon, and I'm on my feet all day except for a half-hour break at two, where I drink a carton of orange juice in the alley running alongside the building and smoke a couple of cigarettes. I take the second one slower, gradually building a haze around my head. Through it I watch a teenage boy run for the bus; he drops his minidisc player and I'm about to go pick it up for him when Sean, one of the chefs, comes out and sneaks a few puffs of my cigarette while I'm distracted.

"I'm giving up," he says.

"So give up."

"Get out of bed the wrong side this morning?" He passes it back. "Not that there's a right side in that dump you live in, Maggie." He started calling me that after Princess Margaret died earlier this year and I cried at her obituary. I was mostly crying because I felt like her life had been wasted, but he said, "I didn't know you were such a monarchist," and brought me a packet of tissues when the Queen Mother died seven weeks later.

He reaches over and wraps his hand around one of my shoulders now, digging his fingers in to massage me. I've slept with him a few times, nothing too emotional; he's a fun person to have around, but he's no Toby. I let him knead me for a moment or two then shrug him off. "My dump's fine," I say.

"It's uninhabitable."

"You've got health and safety on the brain."

He grins at me. "Good," he says. He pulls me in towards him and kisses my neck. I stand there, enjoying being blank for a while, then I reach up and bite his earlobe, gently.

"Crazy," he says, laughing down at me.

"Break's over," my boss calls to me. "Get your arse back in here now – they're waiting for you on table four."

"See you around," I say to Sean. I go back to waiting tables, wiping surfaces, yawning, blocking out my thoughts.

I clock off at five p.m, and check the rota on the wall: in again tomorrow.

"Shit," one of the other waitresses grumbles, "always work."

I pull a sympathetic face. Right now, though, I'd rather be at work than back at the hospital.

Another two waitresses arrive to take our place, and for a moment there's a babble of other languages, gossip exchanged - tongues clicking and shocked exclamations as jackets are taken off or shrugged on. Five of the waitresses live together in a freezing cold flat by Old Street roundabout. I went back there once after a late-night shift; all I remember is a bottle of vodka and a lot of empty takeaway cartons. The next morning I woke up with a killer hangover and near frostbite.

"Bye," I say to the knot of voices and shiny, dark hair.

"Tomorrow," someone says back, and I leave through the kitchen.

Back at home, I shower and take an aspirin. My fridge is cold and empty – like the flat – except for some coffee, milk, a few cans of beer, half a tin of baked beans, some squashed clementines and a Peperami stick. I pick at the cold beans and wash them down with milk.

I turn on the TV and watch the news for a while. The average price for a property in England and Wales has topped a hundred grand, a blonde reporter is saying, although properties in London are expected to cost double the national figure soon.

In the bedroom, my phone starts ringing; it's shrill and impatient. I let it go to voicemail. The news moves on to a grim forecast about pensions. I switch off the TV and wash up, taking my time over it, until there're no more distractions left. I might as well get this over with, I tell myself, and go to the bedroom to listen to the answer-machine message.

It's Aunt Gillian.

"Tallulah," she says. "I just wondered what happened to you yesterday. Vivienne said she came back from the bathroom and you'd disappeared. And I didn't see you at the hospital today, so thought I should give you a call. Let me know, dear."

I delete the message.

I turn the radio on for some background noise. Maybe the heart attack will change him, I think, reveal a softer side.

I run my finger along an invisible line in the air in front of me and recite out loud, "The prognosis post myocardial infarction will be influenced by a number of factors. If a mechanical complication such as papillary muscle or myocardial free wall rupture occurs, prognosis is considerably worsened."

Maybe my father will die, after all.

The phone rings again, shocking me into banging my elbow against the wall. I see Aunt Gillian's number flickering on and off the screen in luminescent green. Seven-thirty. I try to work out what time of day it is in the hospital schedule – end of daytime visiting hours, probably.

She doesn't leave another message. Nothing's happened, then. I rub my eyes, and my throbbing elbow. If only everything could stay exactly the same, in stasis. I know it can't though. I pull on some clean socks and shoes; if my past is catching up with me, I might as well find the one person from it I really want to see.

✳ ✳ ✳

We left the next morning. Uncle Jack hadn't been at breakfast, and I'd heard murmurs that his bed hadn't been slept in. Aunt Vivienne said loudly that he'd earned the right to have a little fun and my mother went pale. I clattered my spoon against my cereal bowl, saying I wanted to leave right away, hoping home would feel safer.

74

As we reached the gate at the end of the drive I saw a flash of dark. I turned around to look properly, straining against the seatbelt. Uncle Jack was standing just off the road, hands clasped behind his head, watching our car disappear.

The weather was still hot when we returned home from my grandmother's; tempers were even hotter. My parents barely spoke to each other, although my father must have said something to my mother about my appearance, because she started to sit me down after breakfast with a brush in her hand and a determined look on her face, but, however smooth and knot-free she got it, the next morning it would always be as matted as a bird's nest. She was gentle with me, but the tangles pulled at my scalp like burning little needles. Most of the time I would give in to the ordeal, but once I jerked my head away and stamped my foot, yelling in pure frustration, until she smacked my thigh with the back of the brush, something she'd never done before.

The smack stung for a few seconds; a red mark appeared then slowly faded. I stopped yelling and looked at the floor, playing with my sleeve. I could see my mother out of the corner of my eye, she looked exhausted. I went to her and laid my head on the cool of her shoulder; she wrapped her arms around me and kissed my face. I felt tears building behind my eyelids. "Do you have to brush it?" I asked. "It hurts."

"No, sweetheart," my mother said into my hair. "We don't have to brush it. We'll braid it before bed, then it shouldn't be so bad."

She gave me another kiss, then a pat on the bottom. "Go and play now, while I clear up the breakfast things."

"Can I go see Kathy?"

"Kathy's on holiday in France, remember?"

"Do you want to play cards then?"

"Not right now, Tallie."

I went outside. Mr Tickles wouldn't join me so I tramped up and down the lawn for hours, trying not to think too much about what I'd heard at my grandmother's and dragging a stick behind me to make little channels in the grass. When my father came home and caught me I thought he would tell me off, but he just asked where my mother was.

"In bed."

"How long has she been in there?"

"Since she cleared up the breakfast things."

"Is that true, Tallulah?"

"*Yes* – I've been bored all day."

"Well, another few hours won't kill you," my father said, and went indoors.

He came back downstairs before dinner and told me I had to be less of a nuisance for my mother from now until the end of the holidays.

"*I'm* not a nuisance," I said.

I went to find my mother. She was making the beds – something she normally did in the morning.

"Am I really a nuisance?"

I had to repeat myself, louder, before she looked over at me.

"Of course not," she said. "But I've been having headaches for a few days now, Tallie. I might have to lie down from time to time and you'll have to entertain yourself."

"Can I watch TV?"

"Ask your father," she said, not really looking at me. She still seemed tired, even after her lie-down.

"Was that you bellowing upstairs?" my father asked when I went down.

"I was trying to get Mummy's attention."

My father opened his mouth like he was going to say something, then closed it again. I played with my fingernails, trying to scrape out the dirt from the garden. "What's wrong with Mummy?"

"Nothing," my father said, but he didn't look at me either.

"Where's your bag?" I asked. "Maybe we could take her temperature."

"The bag isn't a toy, Tallulah."

"But… "

"There's nothing in the bag for your mother, and I don't want you messing around with it."

He went into his study and banged the door shut. I wanted to shout after him that I wouldn't mess around but he wouldn't believe me. Recently my father seemed to have forgotten that I'd stopped being an annoying baby. He'd always been away lots with work, but now he didn't want to spend time with me even when he was around.

Georgia came over to play the next afternoon and we built a den at the back of the garden, in the pine tree. We draped blankets over branches until there was a small, enclosed section at the foot of the trunk, just high enough for us to sit upright, and long enough for us to lie down. I dragged up the stack of shelves that were in the cellar, waiting for my mother to make them into a bookcase, and we laid them down as a floor.

"How shall we decorate it?" I asked Georgia, because she was the guest.

"With flowers," she said. "And ribbons."

We went around the garden pulling up daisies and buttercups and some of the more withered-looking roses and spent an hour or so winding them around the trunk and branches.

"Shall I make us a fire?" I suggested.

"How would you do that?"

"I don't really know," I said. "But the Famous Five managed it, and they seem kind of stupid."

"I'm not cold anyway," Georgia said. "Let's play shopping – I'll be the shopkeeper."

She got really into it and hunted out some tins from our cellar to stack in the corner of the den.

"These peaches are really good, madam," she said.

"Can I have two?"

"That's twenty pence."

By the time she left I'd bought tins of kidney beans, tomato soup, alphabetti-spaghetti, macaroni cheese and pineapple chunks.

"What did you need my tins for?" my mother asked.

"Pretending to be at the shops," I said.

"You girls are going to love being grown-ups," she said.

I entertained myself for the next few days, reading *Alice in Wonderland*. I liked to lie on my front on the lawn, my vest rolled up so I could feel the cold tickle of the grass on my stomach, my head cupped in one hand, one arm across the pages. Mr Tickles liked to lie on the book. Occasionally my mother would appear and ask me about the story.

"She's at the tea party," I said. "There's a mouse in the teapot."

"With the Mad Hatter and the March Hare?"

"Yes."

"Good," she said, and went away again.

That was the day my father came home early in the afternoon. I'd given up reading and I was sitting cross-legged on the floor in front of the TV when I heard his footsteps, and his key in the door. I turned *Danger Mouse* off quickly; my father didn't like me to watch too much TV.

He came into the living-room, slower than usual. "Where's your mother, Tallulah?" he asked.

"She's lying down upstairs again," I told him.

He put his hands over his face, almost like he'd forgotten I was there.

"Do you want me to wake her up?" I said. I thought if I asked him questions, maybe he would be distracted enough not to notice where I was.

He didn't seem to have heard me, so I repeated the question. My father took his hands away from his face and looked at me. His face seemed tired and old, older than he'd looked this morning. Something terrible must have happened, I thought, and I felt very sorry for him.

"Don't stare, Tallulah." He looked away. "Your Uncle Jack's disappeared, I'm afraid."

"Oh." But isn't that a good thing?

"I'd better go and tell your mother."

Five

The passage is open, but a sign on the reinforced metal door warns it's about to be closed for the night. I loiter on the stone steps that lead down to the triangular courtyard, one hand on the black rail, the other jammed into my pocket.

I've come to see Toby – Starr said he works here – but now I can feel my flight instinct kicking in. It's been five years since I saw him, too.

Daylight is purpling, and behind several windows there are lights on, spilling gold into the evening. To my left is the row of houses I've just walked past and a gravel path; in front of me are railings enclosing Gray's Inn lawn, the metal poles completely hidden by pink climbing roses and greenery. On the right is a white building with a few ornate balconies and venetian blinds down over most of the windows. His building is through an archway on the right. I looked it up a week or so ago, maybe I was already planning on finding him back then. I think about him nearly every day. I've tried to imagine how he would react to my boss, some of the odder customers. If something funny happens, it gives me a hollow feeling that I can't share it with him. If something bad happens – but that's why I'm here. I know he'll understand.

I stare at the grey, uneven paving slabs on the courtyard floor, then at my feet. If someone comes out and sees me here like this, there's no chance I won't look out-of-place. I inspect my outfit: black jeans with holes in the knees, white vest with polka dots and bright orange cardigan. I don't know why I didn't take the time to put on something nicer, smear on some eyeliner and rouge.

I guess the logical thing to do would be to go to his building, buzz on the door, or wait outside to see if he comes out. I could be waiting for a long time, though, or he could come out with someone else, not want to talk. After all, we didn't just lose touch gradually. I left pretty abruptly.

Or he might have forgotten me. Maybe I've built up our relationship in my head. Maybe he never felt the same way. Maybe it's weird I think about him so much.

I hear footsteps, and talking; I resist the urge to hide. A man and a woman come around the corner. They're both in smart suits, carrying briefcases, and both have shiny brown hair; I wonder if they're related. Or maybe they're dating.

They see me and smile. Or, at least, the man smiles, the woman looks like she's sizing me up.

"Working late?" he asks.

Tell them you're looking for a friend.

"Yeah," I say.

"You're not the first," he says. He climbs the steps to stand in front of me and gestures at the door. "After you."

"Thanks," I mumble.

They follow me out into the road I was just on. I could ask them now if they know Toby. I don't know how many people work in the Inn, they probably won't have heard of him.

"Have a nice evening," the man says.

"You too," I say, but he's already turning to the woman and asking how she's getting home.

I walk the long way around to get to the tube, making sure I don't bump into those two again. I feel like an idiot, standing on the escalator as it takes me underground. What was the point in coming all this way, then?

I wonder if Toby still has his shy smile, if he's developed

a slouch from sitting in front of a computer all day. Maybe he was never as good-looking as I thought; there weren't many guys to compare him to.

A gust of warm air hits me at Highbury & Islington, even though it's evening. I walk home quickly, my bag strap's rubbing against my neck and my feet hurt and I'm tired. I let myself in. My phone rings again, I check I'm not missing a call from Starr. If she was around, I wouldn't have gone to see Toby. I just need someone to talk to, I tell myself, but I know it's bullshit. Toby's the only person I've ever even *thought* of opening up to about my father.

At around eleven o'clock I go over to the open window and lean out. The sky is velvet-black and close with the heat. A cat prowls among the rubbish bins. A few drunk guys stagger past, one of them wraps himself around a lamppost and pretends to feel it up. His friends think it's hilarious. I pull my head back inside and draw the curtains.

✳✳✳

"Why *did* Uncle Jack leave?" I asked Aunt Gillian, a week after the news reached us. We were helping get her house ready for my mother's birthday party.

"He probably had to," Aunt Gillian said, mysteriously.

"Why?"

"I don't know. He could have been mixed up in things."

"What things?"

"Things – " Aunt Gillian said. She flapped her hands at me. "This isn't the time, Tallulah."

"What things?"

"Could you find your mother in the kitchen?" she asked. "Her birthday cake needs dusting with icing-sugar. I forgot to do it before."

Aunt Vivienne was setting up folding chairs next to us in the living-room. Georgia told me that she and Gillian had been fighting over having my mother's birthday party at Gillian's, and not at our house. Aunt Vivienne said Gillian was a control-freak; Gillian said she was only trying to help out. When I thought about it, I couldn't remember ever having a party for my mother. Usually we went to the cinema, and she and my father had a glass of wine when he got back from work. She didn't like to make a fuss, she said. And her birthday was in August, which meant that most people were on holiday anyway. Georgia also told me that my father had said this was a special occasion, to try to get her out of herself, but neither of us were sure exactly what that meant.

"What cake is it?" I asked.

"It's Victoria Sponge," Aunt Gillian said, looking down at a list in her hand.

"My mum hates Victoria Sponge."

Vivienne opened another folding chair, a little too forcefully. "See that, Gillian?" she said. "You don't always get it right."

Starr and Georgia, who had been polishing the cutlery, looked up, interested. Aunt Vivienne and Aunt Gillian were facing off above my head, hands on hips. Aunt Vivienne was wearing a tight-fitting black cocktail dress, with a long green ribbon tied around her bun. Aunt Gillian was wearing white trousers and a mustard-coloured sweater, and her face looked pink and hot.

"Well, I'm sorry, Tallulah, but most people don't," Aunt Gillian said, ignoring Vivienne's comment. "Most people love chocolate cake, but hate lemon. Or love lemon but hate carrot. Victoria Sponge is a compromise."

Outside, we could hear the whooping from James and Michael as they tried to bat a cricket ball into an open, upstairs window. They'd been excused from setting up because they were boys and would only get in the way.

"My mum hates it," I said again.

"It's Evelyn's fucking party, and she doesn't like Victoria fucking Sponge," Aunt Vivienne said. Starr looked embarrassed.

"I don't see why *you're* getting so involved, Vivienne,"

82

Aunt Gillian said. "Maybe you should just go outside for a bit. Have some air."

"Are you afraid I'll make a scene, Gilly?"

"I just don't know why you're getting so upset," Aunt Gillian said.

"Of course I'm upset," Aunt Vivienne hissed. "Jack's missing. *You* need to fucking react, Gillian, he's your brother too, I mean… " she tailed off, and smoothed her hair back from her face.

"Mum?" Starr said.

Aunt Vivienne swept out of the room.

The room got calmer after she left. Aunt Gillian shrugged her shoulders. "Perhaps it's best if you just help with the cake now, pet," she said.

I nearly ran into my father in the hallway. He was carrying a newspaper and looked like he was trying to escape. "Don't run indoors, Tallulah," he said automatically.

"Sorry," I said, trying to look responsible. Since Uncle Jack, I'd been careful not to get on my father's bad side, although I rarely succeeded. I carried on past him, walking quickly but carefully.

My mother was sitting in the kitchen, fresh coffee in front of her. She was wearing jeans and a cream top and that made me feel uneasy, because normally my mother dressed up for parties. She was tapping her wedding ring against the mug, making a dull clinking sound; that seemed unlike her too. I shook my head. This was my first grown-up birthday celebration, and so far it was shaping up to be a pretty strange afternoon.

"Aunt Gillian says you have to do the icing-sugar," I said, pointing at the cake in front of her.

My mother turned her face towards me. She had bright red spots on her cheeks, but besides these I'd never seen her face so grey. She took my hand with both of hers, and cupped it underneath her chin, kissing it absent-mindedly. I shifted my weight from one foot to the other. My mother held my hand loosely, her fingers hot from the coffee. A ladybird dropped from its flight path onto her shoulder and we watched it together with interest.

"Shall I get a leaf to put it on?" I asked her after a while.

She didn't act like she'd heard me, but when I made a move to go she pulled me in towards her and squeezed me hard. She nibbled on my ear, like she used to do when I was little. I let her, even though bending down made my back ache.

"I love you, Tallie," she said. "Everything's going to be alright."

On my way back to the living-room I stopped short; Aunt Vivienne was blocking the hallway, standing in front of the coat rack. As I was about to turn and tiptoe in the other direction, she reached out and took the sleeve of my mother's jacket in between her fingers, stroking it. She made a weird half-moan, half-whisper noise in her throat, which sounded like '*Jack*', then stood perfectly still, looking like she was in pain.

"Aunt Vivienne?" I said.

She wheeled around. "Were you spying on me?"

"No."

"Yes you were. How long have you been standing there?"

"I dunno."

"Bloody child," she said, then walked out of the front door.

The hours slipped by. People arrived, mostly strangers; they stopped to talk to me, and to eat the food that my mother and Aunt Gillian had laid out. I ate too; I was starving. Despite the fuss I'd made, Aunt Gillian's Victoria Sponge was perfect: warm, soft and buttery, with just a hint of lemon.

Halfway through the party, I took a cup of orange squash and drew myself into a corner. I flipped open a folding chair and sat down, crossing my legs on the seat until I remembered I was wearing a dress and was probably exposing my knickers.

The dress itself was bothering me, all lace and stiff underskirt. Aunt Gillian had loaned me one of Georgia's.

She'd also jammed me into a pair of Georgia's tight, polished shoes and they were making my feet hot. I envied Starr on the other side of the room, barefoot and in black stirrup leggings and a crop top. Even if Aunt Vivienne was crazy, she chose cool clothes for her daughter. I wanted to scream and rip mine off, but I sat quietly and sipped my juice. As I was draining the last drop, the front doorbell rang.

"I'll get it," Aunt Gillian called. She shimmied over the floor, air-kissing guests as she passed them. I caught Starr's eye across the room – she made a face and I grinned.

I heard the front door opening and then my grandmother's voice. "Gillian, I found someone to chauffeur me, so I didn't need a taxi after all." Then my grandmother appeared in the doorway, with a giant man I'd never seen before. Aunt Gillian was right behind them, looking flustered. "You didn't tell me you were bringing anyone, Mother."

"It's not a date, if that's what you're worried about," my grandmother said. She saw me and nodded in my direction. I gave her a shy wave.

"Mother… "

"Be quiet, Gillian," my grandmother said, and strode over to my mother. "Happy birthday, Evelyn."

"Thank you," my mother said.

"I brought you an old friend."

"Thank you," my mother said again, but I saw her shake a little.

Out of the corner of my eye, I saw Starr signalling me to follow her outside. I wanted to watch what was happening at the other end of the room, but she looked desperate.

"Have you seen my mum?" she hissed at me, when we were in the hallway.

"Not since before the party."

"Crap. She'll flip if she misses him."

"Misses who?"

"That new guy, who came in with Grandma."

"Who is he?"

"I can't remember his name, but he came to the flat once before. She was talking about him the other day. Can you help me find her?"

"Okay."

I spent five minutes walking around the house and garden but I couldn't see Aunt Vivienne. I came back and sat on the doorstep, and after a moment, the giant came out and sat down next to me. "Howdy," the giant said.

"Hey," I said.

He had long grey-streaked hair and he was wearing dirty brown boots. When he smiled I noticed that a few of his teeth were black. "You must be Tallulah," he said. "I'm Malkie." He put his hand out – a huge paw, with rough patches of yellow skin at the base and tip of each finger. I gave him my hand and he shook it solemnly. We let go and sat in silence. Malkie smelled like bonfire smoke. I liked just sitting and breathing him in.

"I haven't seen you around before," he said after a while. His voice was low, and soft, and when he said 'round', it sounded more like '*roond*'.

"I've never seen you either," I said.

"I've been looking out (*oot*) for you, though. Jacky used to talk about you, and I wanted to see for myself."

"See what?" I asked.

Malkie looked down at me, smiling. "You, sugar."

I stared at him.

"He seemed pretty taken with you," he said after a while. He crossed one leg over the other, letting the raised ankle rest on his knee. "I guess everyone should get to know their nieces."

I continued staring.

"Well?" Malkie said. He smiled encouragingly.

"I only saw him a couple of times," I said. "I don't really know him."

Malkie pulled a cigarette packet from his suit pocket. "Jacky isn't always good with people."

The sun came out and flooded the garden with light. Malkie leaned back and sucked sincerely on his cigarette. I took off my shoes and socks and stretched out my legs. Ivy and purple wisteria curled up the trellis on the front of the house, and filled my nose with the smell of summer. Aunt Gillian had placed a doormat in front of the doorstep. It was brown, with curly writing spelling out 'come in' to the visitor.

"Have you *seen* Uncle Jack?" I asked Malkie.

"Nope," he said, flicking some ash to the ground. "From what I hear no one's seen him for a few weeks. Your aunt's pretty mad about that."

"You mean Vivienne?"

He nodded and grinned. "She's a handful that one."

"Why's he disappeared?"

"Jacky was always pretty much a law unto himself." Malkie looked away and dragged on his cigarette again. "How's your mom enjoying her party? I haven't had much of a chance to speak to her."

"Do you know her as well?"

"Yeah, from a while back. Nice lady, your mom."

"No shit," I said.

Malkie gave me a sideways look, but didn't say anything. I warmed to him even more. "How do you know her?"

"Me, your Uncle Jacky and Vivienne were all friends first and then Vivienne introduced us to Evie – your mom."

"And you were good friends?"

"Pretty good, yeah."

"What about my grandma?"

"I have a lot of respect for your grandmother too."

"How did you know Aunt Vivienne and Uncle Jack?"

"Jacky was right about one thing – you ask a lot of questions."

I was silent for a moment. "Are you annoyed?"

"By you? Course not."

I sighed loudly, hoping to convey the depth of my feeling. "*I'm* annoyed," I said. "No one cares about me. I'm sick of it." I picked up a stone and threw it at Aunt Gillian's driveway, then curled my toes on the ground, gathering more ammunition into my feet.

"I see." Malkie stubbed out his cigarette. "Well, when I'm feeling frustrated I like to listen to music."

"Like what?"

"Classical, mostly."

"Boring." My father had a huge collection of classical tapes – all music and no words.

Malkie looked back at me, resting his chin on his shoulder. "Chopin's 'Funeral March'," he said after a pause. He grinned again. "They played it at JFK's funeral."

"Who's that?"

He shook his head. "Don't you know any history?" he teased. "Kennedy was the President of the USA. Before your time, of course."

"Oh," I said, trying to look like I knew what he was talking about.

"Jeez," Malkie said, rubbing his neck. "You never really know how old you are 'til everyone you've heard of is dead." He looked away.

"How old *are* you?"

Malkie grinned again. "I try not to think about that," he said. "How old are you?"

"Ten." I scratched at a bite on my leg. "How does it go?" I asked, "The Kennedy song."

"If I had a piano, I'd pick it out for you."

"You play the piano?" I was surprised. Malkie's hands didn't look like they could do anything delicate.

He pretended to swipe at me. "Yes I can play the piano, little lady," he said.

I stood up. "There's a music room downstairs," I said. "We can go down, no one will be there, and it's soundproofed." Aunt Gillian wanted her kids to be musical, but she didn't necessarily want to hear it.

I led Malkie back into the house, carrying my socks and

shoes in my hands. Malkie followed on his tiptoes along the parquet floor.

He whistled when he saw the piano, a black Steinway Grand. I pulled up the stool from the corner for him; it didn't seem like Georgia and James had been practising too hard.

Malkie sat down and ran his fingers lightly over the keys. I sat cross-legged on the wooden floor, my shoes and socks abandoned, my heart thumping in my chest. Malkie started to play. He closed his eyes and swayed slightly, rocking backwards and swelling forwards with the movement of the music. I drew my legs up and buried my face into my knees, using them to squeeze my eyes shut too. I had never played the piano, or heard anyone who was any good play in front of me, and it made me feel the closeness of the room, and the humming of my body and the air around us.

"That was so sad," I said, when the piece was over.

"Yeah," he agreed.

I looked down at my feet, my eyes welling up. Malkie must have seen them, because he swung his legs around and faced me. "You can let it all out, doll, I don't mind."

It was just as well – the tears were already spilling out onto my dress. Malkie gathered me up in his arms and sat me down in his lap. I was too big to sit like that with my mother, but I felt almost lost inside Malkie's giant hug. I waited until my shoulders had stopped heaving before I spoke.

"It's my mum's birthday and she's sad," I said.

"I'm sorry, doll. Do you know why she's sad?"

"No. But she got worse after Uncle Jack went away," I said. I sniffed and wiped snot off my face. Malkie offered me his sleeve.

"Is that so?"

"Yeah," I said. "But I know they're not friends anymore. I heard them arguing and my mum said Jack wasn't being fair, and Uncle Jack said she took advantage of my dad."

"Oh?"

"Why would he say that?"

Malkie looked uneasy. "I dunno," he muttered.

I punched my leg in frustration. "I don't like Uncle Jack," I said. "*I'm* not sad about him going away. I just want my mum to be normal, like before."

"Sometimes people are sad, doll. You just have to let it run its course."

"So do nothing?"

"Yep."

"That's stupid."

"Well that's my advice," he said. "You can take it or leave it."

"I'm gonna leave it."

Malkie chuckled. "You know your own mind, at least," he said.

Aunt Gillian swooped down on us when we emerged from the music room. "Tallie," she cried. "We've all been so worried about you."

"I was just downstairs with Malkie," I said, pulling my arm out of her grip. "He was playing the piano for me."

"You play the piano?" Aunt Gillian looked a little taken aback. My face burned.

Malkie inclined his head at her, and gave me a wink.

"Well, it was very nice of you to show Tallie," Aunt Gillian said. "But really, none of us knew where she was. Everyone's very upset."

"Who's upset?" I asked.

She ignored me. "Evelyn's… not strong at the moment," she said to Malkie. "And the children… "

James strutted out of the kitchen with the largest sandwich I'd ever seen. "Hi, Dolly," he said to me, spraying crumbs everywhere.

Aunt Gillian looked a little put out. "Dolly?"

"Dolly Parton," James said. He dug me in the ribs with his elbow, then remembered the last time and quickly sidestepped away. "It's a joke, Mum. 'Cos she's got no *tits*."

"James," Aunt Gillian said, looking shocked. "I can't believe I just heard that word come out of your mouth."

"Yeah, shut up, idiot," I said. I refrained from kicking him; I didn't want Malkie to see me lose my cool.

"I'm sorry, Gillian," Malkie said. "I didn't mean to cause any trouble."

"Well in that case you shouldn't be here at all," Uncle George said, suddenly behind Aunt Gillian and James and putting his hands on their shoulders.

Malkie narrowed his eyes. "I don't see how it's any of your business."

"It's my *house*, sonny. And I don't appreciate old skeletons forcing their way out of locked closets."

"Matilda invited me."

"Well, no one else wants you here."

"Why can't Malkie stay?" I said.

The sunlight falling through the hall window glinted off Uncle George's glasses, hiding his eyes. "Because, Tallulah," he said slowly. "Your aunt and I don't welcome thieves and drug addicts into our house. Especially not crack-heads who ruin people's lives. Why don't you just run on back to Canada, where you belong."

Malkie's bellow was like no sound I'd ever heard a human make. James' mouth fell open and Aunt Gillian whimpered. Turning towards Malkie, I saw him ball his hand into a fist and start advancing on Uncle George, then, "Mr Jones," my father said, appearing from the kitchen. I realised he must have been standing just out of sight, listening to our conversation. Malkie stopped and my father gestured towards the front door. "If you wouldn't mind stepping outside."

"Malkie," Aunt Gillian said, her voice trembling. "Malkie, please – we're just trying to think of the children."

Malkie glared at Uncle George and followed my father outside. Uncle George faced Aunt Gillian, wiping his forehead. "Did you see that?" he asked. "He was going to *hit me!*"

Aunt Gillian put her hand on his arm and shook her head quickly. She looked at me and James, then at someone behind us. I turned to see Michael with a strange expression on his face.

"Tallulah, James, you two run off and play now," she said. "Michael, can you make sure they stay upstairs for a bit?"

"We don't need looking after," James grumbled, but he followed his older brother and so did I.

Upstairs, James shut his bedroom door behind us, muffling the buzz of the party downstairs. We sat on the floor, leaning against his bed. Michael stood at the window, kicking his heels against the wall.

"Why was your dad hiding in the kitchen?" James said.

"Why was *your* dad so mean?"

"He's not our dad," Michael said, without looking at me.

I was surprised. Uncle George was Aunt Gillian's second husband, but my cousins never talked about it. Uncle John, Gillian's first husband, had died when I was one, and I'd never questioned how the children would feel about his replacement.

"Your stepdad then," I said. "What he said was horrible." I hadn't understood what he'd meant exactly, but I'd caught the tone. "What's a crack-head?"

Michael was ignoring us, fiddling with the cord that tied the curtain back, so I turned to James who shrugged. I felt angry. Malkie had been nice to me. I didn't understand why everyone was being rude to him.

"He called Malkie a thief, but he wasn't stealing – I was with him, he didn't touch anything."

"George doesn't like Uncle Jack or his friends," Michael said.

"Why?"

"He's a bad influence," James said. "Jack always has problems and we always have to pick up the pieces."

Michael snorted. "You're just repeating George word for word."

"What problems does Uncle Jack have?" I asked.

James gave me a funny look. "You can't actually be as

92

thick as you seem," he said pityingly.

I went to kick him, but he scrambled out of the way.

"Stop it, kids," Michael said, but I saw his grin.

I lay down; James stayed where he was, looking down at me. "You know, Tallie, if you don't change your behaviour, you're going to end up like Jack," he said.

"Like how?" I asked.

James muttered something under his breath.

"I can't hear you," I said. "But you better not be calling me names."

"Don't say anything," Michael warned from across the room.

"I won't. Tallie's too much of a baby, anyway, and she'd just tell her mum."

"I wouldn't," I said. "I don't tell her everything."

I was annoyed – I really didn't know anything about Uncle Jack, like I'd told Malkie, and no one seemed to want to tell me, either. Even James knew something.

"I'm bored of babysitting," Michael said after a while. "I'm going downstairs. Tallie, if he's annoying you have my permission to thump him."

"You can't give permission for that," James yelled.

"I'm your older brother – I can do what I want," Michael said. He walked over to us and cuffed James around the head. "Like that."

James tried to throw a punch but Michael blocked it easily and cuffed him again.

"Get lost," James shouted after the closed door, then turned to me. "I can beat him."

"In your dreams," I said. "So tell me about Uncle Jack."

"He was in prison."

"You're *lying*."

"Am not," James said, inspecting his nails.

"When was he in prison?"

"Until this year."

"What was he in for?"

James looked shifty. "I think drugs," he said.

"You don't know."

"I do – Dad said he was into drugs, so it must be drugs, right?"

My mouth felt dry. I thought of my mother at the kitchen table, ring finger clinking against her coffee mug, and wondered if she knew about Uncle Jack being in prison, and why she'd never told me if she did.

"He was selling drugs to people." James's voice was starting to make me feel sick. "You do that, you go to prison – it's as simple as that, and anyone who says different is just a hippy."

"Stop it."

"I can say whatever I want."

"My mum says it's society's fault if someone becomes a criminal."

James smirked. "That's just more proof she's going mental."

"What?"

"Everyone's been talking about it. They say your mum's cracking up."

I felt my stomach rush towards the floor. "Don't say that about my mum."

"Why not?"

"Shut up."

"I'm just telling you what they're saying."

I kicked his bed. "Don't talk about my mum like that." My voice was high and James started to look worried.

"Sorry, Tallie," he said. "I didn't think *you'd* go mental." He came over and tried to touch my arm. I scratched his face.

"Leave me *alone*," I yelled.

He backed away from me. "Sorry," he said again, looking even more frightened. He paused. "Can we make up?"

I stood there, waiting, until I could breathe again.

"Tallie," James whispered after a moment. "You won't say anything to anyone, will you?"

I wiped my eyes with the back of my hand, then my nose. He looked really scared and for a second I thought about telling.

"Tallie?"

"I'm not a grass."

James looked relieved. "Friends, okay?"

"Fine."

We went downstairs. Aunt Gillian shrieked when she saw the scratch on James' face, which was bleeding a little. "James. What happened to you?" she asked, mopping at him with a tissue.

James looked guilty again, and a little sick at the sight of the blood.

"I scratched him," I said. "We were fighting."

"*Tallulah*." Aunt Gillian straightened up and looked disapprovingly at me. "You've been *very* naughty today. Going off with strangers, and now *fighting*."

Uncle George, who was skulking behind her, muttered something like: "Blood will out."

I stared at him with what I hoped looked like hate. If Malkie could have come in just then and smashed Uncle George in half I would have clapped. I tried to imagine it happening. I imagined the piano wire snapping and taking Uncle George's head off, blood pouring from his neck and his body crumpling to the floor. I imagined kicking his head as it rolled towards me, or jumping on it until it was a pulpy mess beneath my feet.

"Believe me, young lady, you have no reason to be smirking like that," Aunt Gillian said.

I went home in disgrace.

Six

"You're late," my boss says when I turn up for the early-morning shift the next day.

"I know," I say. I'm already annoyed with myself for bottling out of finding Toby, and now I'm working my least favourite shift: six a.m until two p.m, with a half-hour for lunch. I'll have to deal with the truckers and builders in the morning, the vulgar comments and the blatant sexism, and the local office workers around midday, sexist in a subtler way. On the whole I prefer the builders.

I take the plates Sean is holding out to me, push my way through the kitchen doors and put them down in front of the two men on table three.

"Lovely," one of them says. He's got a scar running diagonally across his face, dissecting his mouth so it looks like he's talking out of one side of it.

"This isn't ours," the other one says. He's got a tattoo of a bluebird on his neck.

I check the order again – it's for table eight. "Okay," I say, scooping the plates back up.

"I don't mind," the first one says. "I'm fucking starving."

"I'll bring yours out soon," I say, and deliver the plates to the right table. Table eight don't say anything; they don't look up from their newspapers.

"Any sauces?" I ask. "Ketchup, mayonnaise, mustard?"

One of them grunts, probably a no. I go back behind the counter and refill the coffee pot. The bell goes off by the serving hatch and I take the plates out to table four, then table five, then table three.

"About bloody time," the first guy says.

"Don't mind him," the other one says, winking. When I turn around I feel a sting on my arse. I look back and he's leering at me. I pick up his fork and bend down towards him.

"If you do that again," I say, "I'll put this through your hand."

"Fucking hell."

"Calm down – he's only playing around," the first one says.

"I'm not," I say. I put the fork back on the table and give him my best Aunt Vivienne smile.

My boss is standing behind the counter; he beckons me over. "What the fuck's going on?" he hisses.

"Nothing."

"What were you doing with his fork?"

"Nothing."

"Where's my ketchup?" the guy from table eight yells.

"Pull yourself together," my boss says. "I dunno what your problem is today, but it better fucking disappear."

I take the ketchup over and settle the bill for tables four and five; I refill coffee mugs for table two and take table six's order. I clear surfaces and dry the cutlery that's just come out of the dishwasher with a teatowel. One of the guys on table three makes a signal with his hand and I take their bill over.

"Sorry about before," the first guy says. "He *was* only playing though, sweetheart."

"Eight pounds ten," I say.

"We don't wanna make any trouble – we come here all the time."

"You shouldn't eat so much fried food," I say. "It's bad for your heart."

"I know, I know," he says. "But the fags'll probably kill me first."

I take the tenner he's holding out and dig in the pockets of my apron for some change.

"Keep it, love."

"Thanks," I say, trying for a real smile this time.

I wipe the table down after them. I think about my father, and how healthily he ate, compared to this lot. Salads and fresh fruit juices, muesli for breakfast. It went downhill a little after my mother died; maybe he stopped altogether after I was out of the picture. Maybe he spent the last five years gorging himself. Toby used to be able to get through two dinners a night.

I vaguely hear the bell from the kitchen, but it doesn't register until my boss shouts my name across the café. "Are you bloody deaf?"

All the workers are laughing. I carry the plates over to table six. I try to avoid looking anyone in the eye. Halfway across the room I stumble and the contents of one of the plates slops all over the floor. My boss is fuming when I get back behind the counter. "That's coming out of your wages."

"I know."

"Go and clean it up."

I get the mop and some cheap blue kitchen roll and clean it up as best as I can. I take the new plate over when it's ready and put it down in front of the guy. "Sorry," I say. "Any sauces?"

"Let's not risk it, eh?" he says.

I try to rinse the mop out. My boss stands over me, watching. "I mean it, young lady. Don't think there isn't a queue of girls waiting to take your place. Fuck up again and you're out."

I think about the nurses pottering around my father the other day, wonder whether they enjoy their work. Maybe I'm being naïve, and no one does what they really want to do; maybe the nurses are all frustrated pop stars. I take the dirty dishes from table three into the kitchen and start loading the dishwasher.

∗∗∗

Sunday night after the party I lay awake for longer than usual, long enough to hear my parents come to bed, halfway through a conversation I didn't understand.

"So he actually accepted it?" my mother asked.

"Yes," my father said. "Why?"

"I just thought… "

"Thought what, Evelyn?"

"I thought it was going to get better."

"This *is* better. Surely you understood what a strain it was, the whole situation?"

"Of course, Edward. I was under the same strain."

"I'm glad to hear it."

"Excuse me?"

"Sometimes I got the impression that you welcomed… Never mind."

"What were you going to say?"

"It doesn't matter."

"*I* didn't know he was going to turn up."

"Hmm."

"How could I? He stopped speaking to me ten years ago."

"That's exactly my point."

"Edward."

"Yes?"

"Aren't you tired of all this?"

I heard the bedsprings creak, like someone had sat down, and then my father's voice, "Of course."

I didn't understand what 'all this' was, but it sounded serious. I thought about Uncle Jack standing in my grandmother's garden, watching us leave, and shook my head immediately, trying to make the picture go away.

"If Vivienne's giving you a hard time… " my father said.

"No more than usual."

He sounded impatient. "Why do you insist on dwelling on it then?"

"Don't be like that, Edward. What do you want me to do? Where are you *going*?"

"Out."

On Monday my mother didn't get out of bed. My father had gone to work early so I made porridge for myself. It was a little burnt, but I scraped the top off and fed it to Mr Tickles. I took some to my mother on a tray. I picked some orange flowers from the garden and took them up too. I couldn't find a vase, so I washed out a milk bottle and put them in that. My mother hadn't opened the curtains. I left the tray just inside the room, next to the door.

My father came home late that night, so I ran my bath and made myself and my mother a ham sandwich for dinner. He was working early the next morning too. I had an apple for breakfast.

I didn't run myself a bath that night. I watched TV until I heard my father's key in the lock. There was something exciting about running upstairs before he could see me and pretending to be asleep when he stopped at my door, although I was fully dressed beneath the sheets, trying to make my breathing come slow.

On Wednesday my father came home early. I was sitting in the kitchen when he walked in. I hadn't washed for two days and Mr Tickles was licking peanut butter off my fingers.

Aunt Gillian moved in on Thursday morning.

My father called at lunchtime; I knew he'd want to talk to Gillian, but I beat her to the phone.

"Where are you?" I asked him.

"I'm busy at the hospital," he said. "Can you put your aunt on the phone?"

"Why can't you take time off? Why does Aunt Gillian have to… " I didn't want to sound too rude. "Who's looking after Georgia?"

"Tallulah, I'm due in surgery in five minutes. Gillian's

going to take good care of you, don't worry, now let me speak to her."

I passed Aunt Gillian the phone and stomped upstairs.

Before Aunt Gillian arrived, I'd been cleaning up after myself, opening my parents' curtains and arranging things in their room, trying to make it seem as if my mother was getting up from time to time. With Aunt Gillian there I couldn't. Instead, I kept watch at the bottom of the stairs in case the bedroom door opened.

Aunt Gillian appeared next to me once, with lemonade and buttery biscuits.

"Tallie, does your mother – does she *look after* herself at the moment?" she asked, hovering over me.

I turned to face her. She lowered the plate and I took a biscuit.

"I mean, is she eating, and washing?"

"She's just tired," I said, biting into the biscuit. "She eats and washes." I didn't know whether she was washing, but she'd left most of the porridge and sandwiches I'd taken her.

"Oh, good," Aunt Gillian said. She looked relieved. "Your father didn't really leave any instructions about that. Oh, you know he's had to go to a conference?" She lowered the biscuit plate again, and handed me the lemonade.

I nodded, though I hadn't known.

"And how are you?"

I shrugged.

"It must be difficult, your mother being – *tired*."

I shrugged again. Aunt Gillian hovered for a moment then left. "Just give me a shout if there's anything you need," she said.

The next day, when Aunt Gillian was on the phone, I carried a sponge and a cake of soap upstairs to my mother's room. I could hear Aunt Gillian tutting below us. "George, you can't *imagine* what it's like here," she said. Then: "Yes. I mean, I can see how it got too much for him. You know how busy he always is."

There was a long pause. I tried to peer through the banisters and down the hallway to the kitchen, where Aunt Gillian was, the phone cord stretched tight as she moved around the room.

"She hasn't left their room since I arrived. Edward wouldn't say much about it, but I gather she hasn't been speaking to anyone. Poor Tallie, she's the one Edward was worried about. It makes me mad when mothers just abdicate all responsibility like this, it really does. It's just not *normal*, is it?"

I could hear a buzzing sound from the other end of the telephone.

"It's Jack, of course it is. I really wish he'd just stayed away, we were all doing fine. Is that Michael in the background? What's he doing? Put him on then."

Michael was evidently handed the phone, because her tone changed, and she started threatening not to let him go on a school skiing trip. I waited until her voice got even louder before I slipped into my mother's room.

My mother turned her head when I closed the door softly behind me. I crossed the room to the bed. She was lying on her side, curled up. The duvet was twisted around her legs and there were dark stains underneath her eyes.

"We have to wash you now," I said. "I told Aunt Gillian you were washing."

My mother didn't move, she watched me as I rubbed the soap hard with the sponge. It didn't foam up, but there was a white paste covering it after a few minutes. I put the soap down and looked at my mother. She was wearing a sleeveless cotton nightdress; I decided to start with her arms. The paste smeared onto her skin easily, but then it wouldn't come off.

"Wait a minute," I said.

I tiptoed out of the room and into the bathroom. I ran the tap and soaked the sponge. I came back to the bedroom and started wiping my mother off, but a lot of water was coming out of the sponge now, and the sheets got wet. My mother started shivering. I got the hairdryer and plugged that

102

in next to the bed and turned it on to maximum heat. My mother dried with white streaks running down her arms; the sheets wouldn't dry. If Aunt Gillian saw this, we'd both be in trouble. I bit my lip.

"Please get up," I whispered. "Please, please please."

She reached her hand out to me and I took it. She looked at me silently for a moment, then pulled me onto the bed with her and wrapped her arms around me. I was so relieved I started crying.

"Sshhh," my mother said. "It's alright, Tallie. Sweetheart. It's alright."

"Are you going to get up now?" I asked her.

She kissed my hair. "Yes, I'll get up," she said. We lay there in the wet bed for a while longer then my mother got up and rinsed her arms and put on a jumper and some makeup under her eyes. I sat on the toilet while she rubbed and painted her face and twisted her hair up in a knot. Aunt Gillian didn't say anything when my mother came downstairs; she offered to make tea for everyone and we sat in the kitchen with the garden doors open. Mr Tickles lay outside on the patio, washing his face.

"Lovely weather, isn't it," Aunt Gillian said. "I can't believe it's early September."

We agreed with her. I spooned some sugar into my tea; my mother watched me over the rim of her cup, but she didn't say anything.

"I suppose Tallie will be going to secondary school next year," Aunt Gillian said.

"Yes," my mother said. "Edward wanted her to go to boarding school, but I like to have her here with me." She smiled at me and I felt my body relax for the first time in weeks.

"Oh, but boarding school is so good for camaraderie," Aunt Gillian said. She was dipping a biscuit in her tea. "Vivienne and I went to boarding school and loved it, and Edward, and… "

My mother reached across the table and took a biscuit. "Your children aren't at boarding school are they?" she asked.

"No," Aunt Gillian said. "But then there are three of them, and Tallie's by herself. It's so nice to be surrounded by people of the same age, don't you think? And she could even go a year early, they have a middle school that starts from ten. It might give you and Edward some time… "

My mother sipped her tea. "Well, Tallie's staying here," she said. "There's a very good school around the corner, and Kathy, a friend from primary, will be going there. We did ask her whether she wanted to go away."

"I don't want to," I said quickly.

"You don't have to, sweetheart," my mother said.

We finished the tea. Aunt Gillian fussed around us with the washing up. "You've had a rough few weeks," she said. "Just let me do this, then I'll get on with the hoovering and then I can start dinner."

Now that I had my mother back I wanted Aunt Gillian gone. I tugged at my mother's sleeve when Gillian's back was turned. My mother took my hand in hers. "Gillian," she said. "I can't thank you enough. But surely your own family must be missing you. Why don't you go back to them now? Let me do the cleaning and dinner."

"Well," Aunt Gillian paused. "I promised Edward I'd stay."

"We'll be fine, won't we, Tallie?" my mother said.

I nodded, not too hard, in case Aunt Gillian was offended.

"Michael *is* acting up a little for poor George," Aunt Gillian said, untying her apron. "I think he might need a hand."

She called Uncle George, who came to pick her up. We walked her to the door, and I put her suitcase in the boot. Uncle George didn't get out of the car.

"I'll give you a ring tonight," Aunt Gillian said, kissing my mother on the cheek. "Edward will be back in a few days."

"Of course," my mother said.

Aunt Gillian hugged me and walked quickly to the car. She carried on waving from the passenger seat until it turned the corner. My mother smiled at me. "Alone at last," she said. "What would you like for dinner? Your choice."

"Sausages and mash," I said. "And mushy peas."

She put her arm around my shoulder. It smelt of soap still. "Sausages and mash and mushy peas it is," she said.

My father came home two days later. If he was surprised to see my mother up and Aunt Gillian gone, he didn't show it.

I stuck close to my mother over the next few days. We made brownies together, my mother's mother's recipe. She plaited my hair while I watched cartoons. We started *Alice Through the Looking-Glass*. We made orange ice-lollies, homemade popcorn, Mr Potato Heads, new cushion covers for the sofa, sock puppets, a soapbox car for my teddies and labels for the autumn jam. My mother spent hours on the phone to Aunt Gillian, who was still calling every day. I tried to teach Mr Tickles to shake paws, without any luck. If I caught my mother staring off into the distance at any point I'd creep away and come back loudly, stomping and yelling her name until she put her hands over her ears and laughed. "I'm right here," she said.

"*Now* can we play cards?"

"You know I love you, don't you, Tallulah?"

We sat down to play cards, but my heart continued to beat double-time all throughout the game.

✳ ✳ ✳

This time it's Aunt Vivienne who calls me. I'm sitting cross-legged in the middle of the bedroom after work, scraping an old coat of hot-pink nail varnish off with the end of a paperclip.

"Hello?"

"Darling," Aunt Vivienne says. "You mustn't be so melodramatic."

I almost laugh. I seem to remember some story about

Aunt Vivienne threatening to kill herself after Uncle Jack disappeared. I have an image of her smashing a wine glass against the sink and holding it to her throat, my father calmly telling her to put it down, Aunt Gillian squawking and flapping about in a panic. In my mind I see Aunt Vivienne laughing, her eyes shiny with alcohol, sliding down the kitchen counter and passing out on the floor, the jagged glass rolling out of her hand. I don't know where this picture came from; it's possible I was there.

"I'm not being melodramatic."

"I suppose running off seems perfectly rational then?"

"It's kind of normal in our family, wouldn't you say?"

She sighs down the line. "You children, always back-talking. Are you going to come see your father again or not? I have to report back to Gillian, you know."

"I'm not," I say. "I need to work – I need the money."

"How mercenary of you."

"We don't all have unlimited funds."

"Yes," she says drily. "I suppose you think you've earned the rights to them too?"

"I don't mean to be rude," I say, "but we haven't exactly been best buddies over the years. I don't know why you think I won't just hang up."

"You'll hurt my feelings."

"That's a good one."

"I'm not your enemy, Tallulah."

"No. You only bother to hate the people you know won't stand up to you."

She tuts at me.

"I need to go now," I say. I pick up the paperclip with my toes, raising my leg so I can admire the way they grip it still, after all these years without practising. "Tell Gillian you did your best."

"I've got a trick up my sleeve, my darling," she says, and rings off.

I wonder what she means by that – Starr can't be back

from holiday already. I miss her, but even she wouldn't be able to persuade me to go to the hospital again and sit by that bedside, listening to my aunts squabble while I wait for my father to open his eyes and say what exactly – my name? That he wants to rebuild our relationship?

"No fucking way," I say out loud to myself. 'You can't choose your family,' my grandmother used to say. She probably meant you had to accept them, but it works the other way too. You choose your friends, your lover, you choose whom to spend your time with. When I was a teenager, I spent a lot of time looking for an alternate father figure. I'm sure he would have chosen someone else as his daughter, too.

I leave the flat again late in the afternoon to try to get some fresh air. My skin feels sticky, like it always does after I've been in the café kitchen. I stop off at the newsagents on my way home; I buy cigarettes, a new lighter, some milk and tinned soup. The man behind the counter leers at my tits the whole time I'm counting change into his palm. I hold on to the last pound.

"Hey, you're short."

"This is for the show," I tell him. "You don't get to perv for free."

"You can't do that."

"I just did."

I push my way out of the shop and feel my phone begin to vibrate in my pocket. "What do you want?"

Starr's voice comes down the line, muffled, like she's speaking through cotton wool. "Have you been yet? How is he?"

"What? I can't hear you properly."

"Wait, you're on speakerphone… "

I can hear thumps and a crash, as if she's dropped it. Then a man's voice – Ricardo's I imagine – and a slap. "Get the fuck off me, I'm talking to my cousin."

"Come on baby, let me kiss your ass. You've got such a beautiful ass."

"I said I'm talking to my cousin." She comes back on the

line, a little breathless. "We're flying home in five days' time, a night flight."

"Hmm?"

"Tal – you there?"

"Okay." Hearing the two of them reminds me of Toby again, and I'm blushing like an idiot down the telephone.

"So I'll see you next Wednesday, right? Meet you at the Pizza Express on the corner of Baker Street at ten."

"Did your mum ask you to call?"

"I haven't spoken to her. Why?"

"No reason."

"She's there too? Jesus – bet she's winding all the nurses up."

"Uh-huh."

"But he's okay, right? Has there been any change?"

"Not that I know of," I say into the phone.

"What? Ric, get off… Tal, I have to go. See you soon. And don't let Mum throw her weight around."

If not Starr, what's Vivienne's trick? Is she here, watching me? I scuttle back to my flat, sleep for a few hours and wake up at seven-thirty. It's still bright and hot outside and I still feel grubby and washed-out. I sit at the kitchen table, smoking, with the window wide open and my feet on the sill. Maybe I'll have a cold shower. I don't want to think about anything particularly, I just want to feel normal again.

At five minutes past eight the buzzer goes. Our lock is stiff, and sometimes I have to let the downstairs neighbour in; I push the button without asking who it is. I can hear heavy footsteps all the way along the hall and up the staircase, but they don't stop at the floor below. Someone knocks on my door. I'm wearing the old, men's t-shirt and running shorts that I use as pyjamas. I open the door a crack and keep my body behind it.

The man must have taken a few steps back after knocking; he's leaning against the banister, and his hat is tipped down, so at first I don't see his face. I see his hands though. They're the same as before, still brown and hairy, with blunt fingertips and nicotine-coloured nails.

"Holy fuck," I say.

"Hey, doll," the figure says.

"Hi Malkie."

I open the door further and he steps forwards and envelops me in a hug. I'm stiff inside his arms and I can feel my heart going double-time. I can't believe this is happening. I can't believe they're all catching up with me at once. I bite my lip, take a gulp of air.

"Your aunt's all shook up about the way you upped and left, you know," Malkie says.

It takes a few swallows before I have enough saliva in my mouth to get it working properly. "Oh yeah?"

"Yeah. Now lemme look at you." He breaks into a grin, holding me at arm's length. "You're very pretty. Didn't I tell you you'd grow up pretty?"

"Maybe," I say. "You want a drink?"

"That would be a pleasure."

I stand back to let him pass. 'Pull yourself together,' my boss would say. 'Be normal.' I shake myself mentally and go to the fridge and peer inside. "I have some beers. You want a beer?"

"Sure."

I don't know how to talk to him now I'm not a kid anymore, and my flat feels suddenly strange, like it's new to me too. Letting in someone from my past, from outside, seems to highlight how closed my world has become recently.

"Sorry about the shittiness here."

"Doesn't bother me," he says, looking at the piles of stuff on surfaces and the stains on the walls and table.

"Sit down."

His giant legs fold beneath him and his crumpled jeans ride up over a larger belly than I remember. He smiles at me; that's the same as before, at least. I put two bottles down in front of him.

"I don't have an opener. Normally I just use the side of the table." I point to the scuff marks notched into the wood.

"That's okay." Malkie picks up a bottle and cracks it open in his mouth. "I've never had a bottle opener neither. Want me to do yours?"

"Yeah, thanks."

We drink in silence. After a while I start to notice the hum of the fridge, how soothing it is. Then it starts to remind me of the heart monitor attached to my father, back at the hospital.

"Jeez, it's good to see you again."

I turn the beer bottle slowly in my hands, not saying anything. I can feel my face pulling itself into some sort of grimace. I know what's coming next.

"Pity you gotta be so sulky though. Like I said, your aunt's worried, doll. Why'd you stop going to see your old man?"

"I mean this in the nicest possible way," I tell him. "But mind your own business."

Malkie purses his mouth, but he doesn't say anything.

"So when did you get back?" I ask him.

"Six months, a year, give or take."

"There's kind of a difference between them, you know."

"Smart too, huh?"

"Well, I can count."

He takes a mouthful of beer.

"And you didn't come and find me?" I ask.

"That why you're pissed at me?"

I rub my eyes. "I'm not *pissed*," I say. "I'm tired. It's good to see you too." I'm lying – I *am* mad at him, but I feel ashamed of it, almost. Malkie's so nice he makes you feel like a criminal for thinking bad things around him. And I've missed him.

"I came to see you a couple of months ago," he says. "But your pa said you weren't living with him anymore, and he didn't know where you were. He was kind of short with me, so I guess he wasn't too pleased that I was back. I been asking around and Vivienne's girl told me you were still in London,

110

but she wouldn't say where."

Nice of Starr to let me know.

"I *had* been writing," he says. "Cross my heart. Then my letters started getting sent back to me."

"Hmm," I say, but it feels good to know he'd kept his promise. "So what are you doing here now?"

"This morning Viv calls up, asks me to come and see you. Try to talk you into going back to the hospital." He fixes me with his gaze. "So, have I persuaded you yet?"

I take a sip of beer and shrug. We look at each other in silence for a moment.

"You keeping up with the music?" Malkie asks after a while.

"Not so much."

"You were good, doll."

"I don't have a piano."

"What you been up to, then?"

"I left school," I say. "I'm working as a waitress. Nothing, really."

He shakes his head again and stretches out, cracking his knuckles. "No wonder you had a fight with your old man."

I finish my beer and stand up, rinse my bottle out and put it on the draining board, keeping my back to Malkie. You have no idea, I want to tell him.

"I hate seeing you cut yourself off from everyone," I can hear him say.

"I haven't."

"It sure looks like it from here."

I turn around and stare at him. I can't believe he can't tell the truth by looking at me. I want to break something, scream, get his attention somehow. Something happened to me, Malkie. It wasn't my decision.

"Doll, I know that you're angry," he says. "But your pa's sick, and he's family. You gotta go see him. Reconcile yourselves."

"I don't want a reconciliation," I say. I know I sound

petulant, but I can't explain it to him. I could say I was betrayed, and he'd look at me with those sad, brown eyes and tell me that it's better to forgive – for me as well. But it's anger that keeps me going – that allows me to get up, to work and eat. And I've kept this secret for so long I can't physically force it out now.

"Look at it this way," Malkie says. "If you go, and he wakes up, and you talk – you'll never regret it. Even if you can't be friends after all." He stands up. "But if you don't go, and you never talk again... " He comes over to me, putting his hands on my shoulders. "You'll regret that, okay? Maybe not for a while, but it'll hit you some day."

I can feel myself wilting underneath the pressure of his arms; he's staring at me, making me blink. "Okay," I say. "I'll think about it." Maybe he's right, maybe I would regret it. It's hard to say anymore.

"Good," he says, and relaxes. He smiles at me. "I'd better be off. I'd like to come back and do this again though."

"Yeah, fine," I say. My flat is small and cold, and I know if he doesn't leave soon I'll try to make him stay, even offer to cook dinner tonight.

"See you later, princess."

He stoops and gives my forehead a kiss. I wait, hearing him clomping on his way out and the front door slam, then I run into the bedroom and throw the sash open. Malkie's a few metres down the road. "Hey," I call to him, waving. "Sorry for being a dick."

He looks back, waving too. "Hey yourself," he says. "Take care."

That night I heat up some soup and chain-smoke over the meal. Seeing Malkie has made my stomach tight, and I can't finish the food in front of me. I pour the soup down the sink and go into the bedroom, undress slowly and climb into my pyjamas.

How is it possible that Malkie's only the second real friend I've seen in years? How can this be my life?

It's still warm outside, even though it's past ten. I grab my cigarettes, a thin cardigan to wear over my pyjamas, and go outside. I sit on the doorstep, barefooted. My downstairs neighbour raps on his window and waves to me. He's wearing a white vest and big headphones; he does a quick burst of shadowboxing as I'm looking at him, maybe to impress me. I hold my cigarette up in a mock salute.

I know what went wrong, really. Or at least, I know where it started to go wrong.

Seven

We lived in Battersea: No.1 Kassala Road, the end furthest away from the park. All the houses on the street were the same – Victorian terraced buildings in red and brown brick, with small front gardens enclosed by box hedges, or white picket fences, or low walls. Every house had a bay window on the ground floor, a kitchen extension, a cellar and a loft conversion. The street ran north to south, so the houses were either east-facing, or west-facing. Ours was west-facing, so it got sun in the afternoon, when the day was hottest. There was another house to the right, and to the left there was a narrow strip of grass, leading to the back garden, that I called The Corridor. The Friday before I was meant to be going back to school I was in The Corridor, bouncing a ball against the kitchen wall. A shadow on the front lawn caught my eye. Malkie was standing at the gate.

"Hello, dollface," he said. "Your mom in?"

I ran to him, then stopped, not knowing whether he would want a hug or not. He was looking down at me with his mouth twitching. I scuffed my shoes in the grass, and he reached down and squeezed my shoulder. He was wearing a light brown jacket, checked shirt and faded blue jeans.

"She's inside," I said, and ran back to the house.

My mother came to the front door and beckoned Malkie

inside. I followed, slowly. Malkie stopped just inside the hallway. I stopped too, in the doorway. My mother paused; we all shuffled our feet.

"Would you like a drink?"

"A beer would be great."

"It's only twelve o'clock," I pointed out.

"Ignore her. Come into the kitchen," my mother suggested. "Tallie, go get Malkie a beer from the cellar."

I loved going to the cellar. I loved the coolness of the air, the smell of wet earth and walls, and the little chinks of light that struggled in through the tiny windows. My father had a stack of beers in the fridge down there, and a rack of wine that ran the length of the room.

Reaching in for a beer, I scraped my arm on the ice that had crystallised in the freezer compartment. When I pulled it out there was a trickle of blood running down from my elbow; a drop or two had fallen onto the ice and spread, pinkly.

On the way back to the kitchen I stopped halfway up the stairs, clutching the bottle to my chest; I could hear muffled voices speaking quickly.

"Why would I want to talk to him?"

"Sorry, Evie. I thought… "

"And don't bring him up while Tallulah's here."

"I won't."

"No, it's fine. I know you're only trying to do the right thing by your friend. I just *knew* he wouldn't stay away."

By the time I came back upstairs Malkie and my mother were facing each other over the table, Malkie was leaning towards her, his giant body spilling out of his chair. I washed my arm, opened Malkie's bottle for him and fetched a glass from the cupboard. I couldn't believe he was there, in our kitchen. He made everything seem smaller, especially my mother.

"How you doing, doll?" he asked.

"I'm good," I said. I pulled out a chair next to him, and sat, my face cupped in my hand, looking up at him. He smiled down at me. I smiled back.

"Would you like to have piano lessons?" he asked.

I was surprised. My mother looked surprised too.

"I could teach her," he said, turning back to my mother.

"It's a very kind offer," she murmured.

"Can I, then?" I said.

"I'll talk it over with Edward," she said. "We'd pay, of course."

"No you won't," Malkie said. "I like spending the time with her. Besides, she'll keep me out of trouble, won't you, Tallie?"

His large hand thumped me playfully on the back, taking my breath away. "Come on, Evie," he said. "It'll be like old times."

"When you two were friends?" I asked.

"Oh yes," she said. "When I was a lot younger, and a lot less wise."

I held my breath in case Malkie was offended, but now they were smiling at each other and I realised my mother was joking.

"We were the three amigos, plus one I guess," Malkie said.

"Oh… Yeah," I said, angry with him for bringing Uncle Jack into it.

My mother saw my face. "I think maybe we should get on with the chores," she said.

Malkie mussed my hair and pushed himself away from the table. "Well then, I'd better get," he said.

"Tallie, why don't you give Malkie some jam to take home?" my mother said.

"What's your favourite fruit?" I asked him.

"That depends," he said, rubbing his chin. "Do you do pineapple jam?"

I made a face. "Maybe I'll pick one out for you."

"Maybe you should," he agreed, grinning.

I stood in the pantry, gazing at the shelves. The jars were identical in the dark, but I knew which was which off by heart. I reached up and took one of the apricot jams down.

My father liked blackberry, my mother preferred plum, but apricot was the best, I thought.

Malkie took my present with a deep bow. He kissed my mother goodbye, and swung me up into his arms. "I'll say I tried," he said quietly, looking at my mother.

"He can come round this afternoon, if he wants," she said, like she was sad about something.

"Okay."

"Thanks for stopping by, Malkie."

He kissed the top of my head, then put me down. "Just let me know about the lessons," he said. "Bye, princess."

After he'd gone, my mother stood in the kitchen, holding on to the back of a chair. Something about her face made me not want to ask about who was going to be calling.

"Well," she said after a while. "That was a surprise."

"Are you going back to bed?" I asked. I came to stand next to her, and she put her arm around me.

"No," she said. "I wasn't expecting to see Malkie, that's all. He's from a different part of my life, and it can be a bit strange when he appears."

"Okay," I said. "Can I still have piano lessons?"

My mother squeezed me. "You like him?"

"Yeah."

"Me too," she said.

"Why doesn't Uncle George like him?"

"Well, Malkie can be a bit gruff," she said. "But he'd never hurt anyone."

I remembered Malkie's eyes at the party when Uncle George was being rude – he'd definitely hurt Uncle George if he got the chance.

"It's really just that Uncle George has a hard time believing that Malkie has changed," my mother said.

"Changed from what?"

"Well, sweetheart… He was in prison for a while. He hasn't had a very easy life, and he made a few mistakes. But he's a good person."

"Malkie was in prison?" I asked. Everything felt a little blurry, and I shook my mother's arm off. She turned to face me.

"What did he do?" I asked.

"He was involved in drugs."

"Like Uncle Jack? He was in prison too, wasn't he?"

She went white. "Who told you that?"

I didn't say anything, remembering my promise to James.

"Who *told* you?" my mother asked. She was angry, but I wouldn't speak. I shook my head.

"For God's sake," she said, turning away from me. "*Nothing* is sacred in this bloody family."

She hugged me when I started crying, and suddenly she wasn't angry anymore.

"I'm not mad at you," she said. "I'm not even mad at all really, it's just… " She shrugged her shoulders. "I'm disappointed in some of the grown-ups. Not with you."

My insides were hurting now; I'd never worried about being a disappointment before.

"And don't think badly of Malkie," she said. "I met him when he'd already realised his mistakes. So you see, it didn't matter to me that he'd done bad things in the past, as long as he tried to be good in the present." My mother blinked a couple of times and squeezed me harder. "And Tallulah, we're not going to mention this to your father, okay? It'll just be our little secret that Malkie came to see us."

I felt my stomach drop when she said that, and I turned away from her. "Okay."

Later that afternoon, about an hour or so after Malkie had left, I went downstairs, planning to help my mother in the kitchen. Halfway down I could hear her crying – chopping the carrots up and sobbing quietly.

"Mum?"

She turned around to face me, wiping her eyes quickly with the corner of her apron.

"Tallie, I thought you were upstairs."

I went to give her a hug, but she'd turned back to the chopping. "I was going to call you in a bit, you should be outdoors on a day like today."

I went back to The Corridor and sat propped up against the wall. Mr Tickles was sunning himself on top of the dustbin. I called him to me; he lifted his head and yawned, but didn't get up.

My mother came out after a while, wiping the backs of her hands on her cheeks. "Kathy got back yesterday, didn't she?"

I shrugged.

"I'm just going to the main road to buy some coconut milk," she said. "Why don't we call on Kathy and see if she wants to play?"

"I want to stay here."

"Well, it'll be easier for me to get on with dinner if I'm not worrying about how bored you are."

"I'm not bored."

"Come on, it'll be nice to have the company while I walk."

"Okay."

My mother got her purse and we walked the hundred yards up Brynmaer Road to Kathy's house. The pavement was littered with blossoms and the sun was golden on the windscreens of the parked cars; I put my hands over my eyes to stop myself from being blinded and my mother guided me, her hand on my shoulder squeezing me if there was an obstacle in the way, like we used to do when I was five.

She dropped me off at Kathy's house and promised to come and pick me up before dinner. "Be good now," she said, and dropped a kiss on my cheek. I threw my arms around her neck and breathed her in. She untangled herself, laughing, and went down the road and out of sight.

Kathy's garden had apple trees and a pond with bright orange fish in it. Kathy's mum collected gnomes, and put them around the pond with little fishing rods. I didn't like them, but Kathy had named them all and took a towel out to dry them if it'd been raining.

We practised our skipping that day, then tried to make a swing out of the skipping rope, a tree branch and a cushion. It wasn't very comfortable, but I sat on it anyway. When Kathy went inside to get a jumper, I stayed out, thinking about Aunt Vivienne at my mother's birthday party. Before leaving with my parents, I'd run across her in the hallway, tugging on Malkie's sleeve. She was asking about Uncle Jack.

"You really don't know where he's gone?"

"Nope."

"I thought he might come today."

"Doesn't look like it."

"I can't believe he just left – he'd tell me where he was going, I know he would."

"I came home one night and his stuff was all gone, just a bunch of cash to help with bills."

"Couldn't he stay for me?" She slumped against the wall. "I'd die for him, you know."

"No one's asking you to, Viv."

I thought about that especially. I didn't think I'd ever want to die for anyone, except maybe Mr Tickles.

Kathy stuck her head out of an upstairs window and called to me. "Mum says it's getting cold and you should have a jumper, too."

I climbed the stairs to her room. Kathy was very neat and all her jumpers were arranged by colour. I stood in front of them, trying to choose.

"Why don't you have the yellow? That's a summery colour." Kathy knew I was no good at choosing clothes.

"Okay, yellow." I pulled it on over my head and looked at myself in the mirror. It made me look pale, I thought, and it was baggy everywhere, like I was Kathy's younger sister.

"You don't have any boobies at all," Kathy said. "Have you got your period yet?"

"No," I said, embarrassed.

"I have," Kathy said. "I must be nearly ready to have a baby, you know."

I looked back at my reflection. Last week, I'd stood in front of the mirror in my bedroom, trying to look grown up. I'd put my hands on my hips, like I'd seen Aunt Vivienne do, and pushed one hip out, making a kissing shape with my mouth, and playing with my hair. I looked pretty good, I thought, until my father caught me. Now I felt like more of a child than ever.

"Are you okay?" Kathy asked. "You look weird."

I heard footsteps, then Kathy's mum was in the room, looking flustered. "Your mum's been gone a while, hasn't she?" she said. "Let me just give her a quick call, see what's happening. I've only just seen the time and we've got to get to a clarinet lesson soon."

I wandered into the garden with Kathy while she called my mother to come and pick me up. The clouds seemed to be moving too quickly, like someone had them on fast-forward. I lay face-down in the grass for a while; Kathy sat next to me, making a daisy chain. Her mum came out and spoke to me but she sounded muffled. I turned my head to look at her, and her face was creased up with worry.

"What did you say?" I asked.

"I said I can't get through to your house, love. It's been ringing for about ten minutes now."

"Oh."

"I think I'd better walk you home."

"Okay."

Kathy stood in the hallway with us while her mum decided on shoes and fingered things in her handbag. "Kathy, stay inside," she said. "I'll be five minutes at most."

"Okay," Kathy said, calmly. "See you later, Tallie."

I leaned my head against the wall. The patch inside the doorway was cool where it had been in the shade all day. Kathy's mum patted my back and I tore myself away from my little spot and followed her down the path.

The sounds are what I remember most when I think of that day – the shuffle of our feet as Kathy's mother walked me home, her gasp when we turned the corner and reached my street and my father came running towards us, his face white and his hands stained a pinkish colour. At the time, I just wondered what he was doing home so early. He kept saying something over and over again, but it wasn't until he shook me by the shoulders, making my brain rattle around inside my head, that I realised what it was he was trying to tell me. "Go inside. Go inside, Tallulah. Go inside and shut the door."

Mr Tickles scratching to be let out, and, as if from far away, someone screaming.

✳ ✳ ✳

I'm flicking ash all over myself. A breeze has started ballet-like movements in the trees up and down the street. I'm still sitting on my doorstep, smoking, watching a leaf play aimlessly on the pavement. It's green and juicy-looking, harder to blow around than the dry brown ones that will join it in a few weeks; it's a hopeful-looking leaf, I think, then a passing dog pees on it.

I stretch my legs and wrap my arms around myself; it's cooler now that the breeze has picked up. The elbows of my cardigan are wearing thin and I can see my skin through the material. If my mother were alive she'd have mended it herself, but she doesn't seem to have passed on the gene – my flat is full of broken things.

They buried my mother, killed by a speeding car a few steps from our front door, in a wooden box under six feet of earth. She'll suffocate, I wanted to say, but then she was in the ground and it didn't seem to matter anymore. They told me to be brave and carry on, my father especially. 'We'll have to learn to just be a two, now, Tallulah.' I didn't know how to say that everything had changed. Getting up was different, brushing my teeth, breakfast, playing with Mr Tickles. Only half an hour of the day used up and I was already so angry.

In the weeks following the hit-and-run, I started to have nightmares. Nightmares full of blood, rivers of it. They told us in the hospital that my mother had lost a lot of blood – they were going to try to give her a transfusion. The bleeding wouldn't stop, they said, then, eventually, it did.

The blood that my mother lost was the same blood that had nourished me while I was growing inside her, roughly seven inches below her heart. The blood stopped flowing when the heart stopped beating, and when they buried her all that remained of it was on the road outside our house, a dark purple stain, until a man from the council came and washed it away.

Thinking of this now makes me feel funny. My stomach hurts and I get a prickling sensation behind my eyes. I pull at a loose thread on my cardigan, twisting it around my finger until the tip of the digit goes white. A sudden wind dives at me when I stand up, whipping my hair back. It may have taken another family tragedy, but I think the cobwebs are finally starting to blow away.

PART TWO

Skin

Eight

Skin functions as a temperature regulator, insulator, the receptor for 'sensation', synthesiser of vitamin D, and protector of vitamin B folates. In humans it is made up of layer upon layer of tissue, and covered with hair follicles.

Skin is actually an organ – although this is not commonly known – and guards the underlying muscles, bones, ligaments and internal organs. It is, in fact, the largest organ of our integumentary system – namely, the one that protects the body from damage. When severely damaged, skin will attempt to heal by forming scar tissue (the name we give areas of fibrotic tissue that have replaced normal skin after an accident, after surgery, after disease). On a protein level, this new fibrotic tissue is the same as the tissue it has replaced. But on a structural level, there are marked differences. Instead of the 'basketweave' formation found in normal skin, you'll find the new tissue runs in a single direction.

The scar above my eyebrow will always be lighter than the skin around it. Even if no one else notices it, it'll always catch my eye, always mark me. Scars are a natural part of the healing process. But sweat glands and hair follicles will not grow back within scar tissue. It is more sensitive to sunlight. Scars are not regeneration. The new tissue is inferior to the old.

✳ ✳ ✳

The lift doors swish open; no one looks at me twice as I walk down the corridor, familiar by now. I stop at the doorway, knock, and take a few steps in. Aunt Gillian's sitting by the bed, knitting. I don't know whether she's more surprised or I am; her hair's down and she's wearing a frosting of pale, pink lipstick, and sunglasses pushed back into her hairline. She looks relaxed, happy. "Oh Tallulah," she says. "Come and sit next to me."

I come into the room properly and take the chair she's offering, on the far side of my father's bed.

"How are you feeling?" Aunt Gillian whispers, like she's trying not to let my father hear.

"Fine," I say. "How's everything here?"

"Much better now." She puts her knitting away into a wicker bag at her feet. "They say he might even wake up soon."

"Good," I say, lamely.

"It certainly is," she says, and smiles at me.

"I'm sorry," I say. "I mean, I'm sorry that... "

"Forget it," Aunt Gillian says, waving her hand. "You're entitled to be scared. We all were." She brushes a lock of hair away from my father's face. "But we're over the worst of it, at least."

He definitely looks healthier – golden, almost, then I realise it's probably the sunlight slanting across his face. He's breathing deeply; a ripple of air comes out of his mouth and tickles the moustache hairs closest by, so they lift a little as in a breeze. He's got a new mole on his neck. I didn't notice that the other day. I feel a knot inside my chest. If he were to open his eyes, he'd see a stranger, just like he's a stranger to me. But I guess nothing's changed, then.

I pour us some water, and we settle in for the wait. Malkie's right, even though I'm still uncomfortable here, still angry, I'd feel worse if I never came back.

128

Maybe you don't want to be alone forever then, I tell myself. Except for a few visits from Starr, from time to time. And I can't cherry-pick the family members I stay in touch with. It would be nice to see Georgia again, and Michael and James. But they'd never keep visits a secret from Aunt Gillian; even Starr's been nagging me for months to get in touch with my father. So it's nothing to do with Dad – it's the rest of the family I'm here for.

Aunt Vivienne arrives, carrying a bunch of grapes. They're purple and delicious-looking, nearly bursting out of their skins. "One must keep up the traditions of the sickbed, darling," she says to me. She's wearing a navy cape, with a fur collar, and a pillbox hat with netting. I try not to laugh. I suppose with Aunt Gillian becoming more casual, more unfussy, Aunt Vivienne is just readdressing the balance. I wonder whether these are clothes from her own wardrobe, or a favourite role. She looks fantastic either way.

Aunt Gillian gives a world-weary sigh and takes out the knitting again.

Aunt Vivienne strips off her outer layers and sits opposite me. From time to time I catch her looking in my direction; she's probably gloating over her little coup. I balance my elbow on the arm of my chair, and rest my head in my hand. I look at my father; when the nurse comes around, I look at her, at her quick, efficient hands. She repeats what they told Aunt Gillian this morning – he'll probably wake up soon. "He'll be nice and rested," she says. "But he might be a bit disorientated, nothing to worry about."

"Of course," I say.

I wonder whether my father will remember what happened between us. It might be easier if he doesn't. I don't know if I'll be able to hold my tongue, though. The nurse leaves, and I close my eyes. I'm vaguely aware of Aunt Gillian and Aunt Vivienne talking, then I drift off.

I dream about Toby, it doesn't look like Toby, but it's him. We're up a mountain, or maybe we're in a shopping mall, it keeps changing. He's angry with me, and I feel guilty because I know I did something wrong, I wasn't a very good friend to him, and I buy him a cookie from an old woman, and Toby throws it on the floor and says, '*That's* all you think it takes?', and then Aunt Vivienne's shaking my shoulder. "Tallulah," she's saying. "Wake up. Afternoon hours are over – we have to clear out until this evening."

"Where are we going?"

"Dinner."

"I'm not hungry."

"Look," Aunt Vivienne says, sitting down again. "Just come and keep us company." She looks me over. "You look like you could do with some food though."

This is rich, coming from her. Aunt Vivienne has never been more than a size eight.

"Where's Gillian?"

"Bathroom."

I look down at my father; his face looks even rosier than earlier. It's probably the most peaceful I've ever seen him.

Aunt Gillian appears too. "He's still asleep," she says, unnecessarily. She looks at me with a pained expression on her face. "You must be exhausted, poor thing," she says.

"Poor thing," Aunt Vivienne mutters mockingly.

"Where's Georgia?" I ask. "Wasn't she going to come down today?"

"She's not here, darling," Aunt Gillian says, again unnecessarily. Aunt Vivienne snorts. Aunt Gillian gives her a dirty look. "She couldn't make it down today, but hopefully tomorrow… " She looks away.

"What's wrong with her?" Aunt Vivienne asks.

"Oh, you know. Nothing. I'll let her tell you." She's practically beaming.

"Gillian, has the good husband got Georgia pregnant already?" Vivienne arches her eyebrow.

"Well, it's not really my place to say." Aunt Gillian says. She's radiating happiness now.

"Congratulations," I say, feeling sick. Georgia's gone forever, then.

"Gillian, a *grandma*," Aunt Vivienne coos, unkindly.

"I guess that makes you a great-aunt then," I say to her, taking some pleasure in her grimace.

"Well, let's go and celebrate," Aunt Gillian says, and stops. "Not celebrate, of course. Not until Edward's fully recovered. Oh, maybe we should save this… "

"No," I say, taking her by the elbow and steering her out of the room. "Any good news is welcome right now."

In the restaurant we order a bottle of wine and three pasta dishes. The waitress who brings the drink sidles away from our table quickly, the air between my aunts is palpably thicker than in the rest of the room.

"Georgia's a little young to be having kids, wouldn't you say?" Aunt Vivienne suggests. "How old is she again?"

"She's twenty-two, as you know," Aunt Gillian says icily.

Aunt Vivienne swirls the wine around in her glass. "How old is her husband?"

"Thirty-two."

"How are the boys?" I ask, hoping to distract the two of them.

Aunt Gillian lets out an exasperated sigh. "Michael lives in Brazil," she says. "He's running a bar out there – he went travelling a few years ago and met some local woman and never came back. James runs a used-car business from home. He buys them, does things to them then sells them on. I would say he's wasting his time but he's made quite a bit of money out of it."

She looks sad. I wonder whether these were the lives she planned for her children. I wonder whether my father planned for *my* future. I never told him about my nursing dream – would he have encouraged me in that?

I've started playing with my napkin, tearing it into strips.

"What does Georgia do now?" Aunt Vivienne asks.

"What?" Aunt Gillian asks; perhaps she's thinking about

131

James' car menagerie. "Well, she was – is – training to be a primary school teacher." She turns to face me. "She's wanted to work with children for ages, do you remember?"

"Not really," I say. "Maybe that was after we used to see each other."

"Yes, maybe," Aunt Gillian says. She smiles sadly at me. "We mustn't lose touch again, Tallie. Family's so important you know."

Please don't cry, I pray. Aunt Vivienne hisses quietly, but Gillian doesn't hear.

The waitress brings us our pasta and we eat absent-mindedly. I make myself chew slowly – I've suddenly realised how starving I am.

"Could you pass the pepper, please, Tallulah?" Aunt Vivienne's looking at me, hand outstretched. I give her the grinder. "Thank you," she says. She has perfect white teeth, I notice.

"You have really nice teeth," I say, and something about this stirs a memory.

Aunt Gillian's fork stops halfway to her mouth.

"Thank you," Aunt Vivienne says, tapping one. "They're not all real, you know?"

"Oh?" I know what I'm remembering now – Malkie telling me that my grandfather wasn't just violent towards my grandmother. I swallow, I can't believe that I ever forgot that, but I guess it got buried when I was caught up in my own misery.

"No," Aunt Vivienne's saying, and I feel a surge of pity for her. She butters a bread roll elegantly. I admire the way her wrist makes the little flicking motions. I can never spread butter; half the time the bread comes apart and sticks to my knife.

"Well anyway, dear. It's nice to have dinner like this, isn't it?" Aunt Gillian interrupts.

"Yeah," I say. "How's Paul?"

"Paul? Enjoying the opera, I hope."

"Is he coming here afterwards?"

"No, dear." Aunt Gillian shifts uneasily in her chair. "Hospitals aren't really his scene."

"Does he think he's getting to the age where they might be necessary?"

"Really, Vivienne. That was horrid."

"Please do accept my apologies."

Aunt Gillian sniffs, then pushes her chair back. "I'll be back in a minute," she says.

I give Aunt Vivienne a look when Gillian's gone. "That was pretty mean," I tell her.

"Was it?" Vivienne gives a little laugh, like we're co-conspirators, and I'm back to not feeling sorry for her anymore. "You've never lived with her, Tallulah. Not properly, anyway."

"She's just proud of her daughter. Why can't you let her be happy about it?"

"Happy has nothing to do with it, my dear."

"What?"

"Think about it," Aunt Vivienne says. "Gillian's just relieved her little Georgia's following an acceptable trajectory." She sneers. "Marrying her off at some ungodly age to a man practically old enough to be her father. It's hardly the romance of the century. She wanted to make sure her daughter didn't turn into a ruined woman, like me... Or you... "

Aunt Gillian appears behind her sister as Vivienne says, "We've been failed by our mothers, Tallulah. But at least no one will be able to say *Gillian* produced a bad seed."

"Viv... " Gillian says, looking at me.

Aunt Vivienne closes her mouth and bites her lip. Aunt Gillian's doing the same thing. So there are similarities after all.

My mother chewed her fingernails instead. She told me how *her* mother had put bitter aloes on her nails to make sure she wouldn't want to taste them. 'It was awful,' she'd told me. 'People use it as a laxative, so for the first few weeks I had stomach pains all the time.'

I feel my breath catch in my throat when I remember this. "Well, anyway," I say. I pull my wallet from my bag and fish out a twenty. "That should cover me."

"But we're not finished," Aunt Gillian says.

"For God's sake, Gillian," Aunt Vivienne murmurs. "Let's just pay the bill and go."

The waitress is only too eager to get rid of us. She brings us our change and I scrape back my chair. I can't bring myself to meet Aunt Vivienne's eye.

I want to know what exactly my mother did to make Vivienne dislike her so much. But at the same time I'm scared to find out.

∗ ∗ ∗

I was furious with my father, with myself, with the world, with the driver of the car for taking my mother away. I withdrew. I pretended not to hear my father when he called me for meals, or asked me questions. Eventually he gave up and we ate separately and in silence. I couldn't stop seeing my mother being loaded into the ambulance, covered in tubes and a mask and blankets. Paramedics' hands, holding me back as I tried to climb in after her – 'No, sweetheart, go with this lady here' – and Kathy's mother crying. Kathy, who'd been fetched from her house, in the back with me, saying it'll be alright. Following the stretcher into the hospital, and seeing my mother's arm falling out and dangling there, bumping around as the doctors ran with her to surgery. Then the waiting room and nurses stooping down to talk to me as I lay across three chairs, dry-eyed.

Then I'd see my father, pacing up and down, answering questions the police put to him, wringing his hands. "It's *my fault*," he shouted at one of them, the older one, who gave his partner a look. They put their pens away and straightened their faces.

"We'll come back later," the older one said to my father. "You've been very helpful."

I remembered Kathy's mother hugging my father, saying, "How were you to know she'd run out?"

"They were talking – I should have known, I *did* know."

"Drivers should be more *careful*."

"I *pushed her away*."

Then, finally, the white sheet, pulled up over her face, the shape of her body underneath it.

Kathy's dad had turned up halfway through the evening and driven her home, so she hadn't heard my father. "What do you think he meant?" she asked me, when I confided in her. "He must be talking about something else. He didn't *actually* push her into the road."

"How do you know?" I said.

We were brushing the manes of her My Little Pony set, arranged by colour and height. My one had a tangle in the hair somewhere that I wasn't managing to separate successfully with the little plastic brush. Kathy took the pony off me and starting working on the knot. I slumped backwards, propping my head up against her chest of drawers and letting my arms fall to my sides. I'd been feeling heavy all the time, like I was carrying something around inside me, and my eyes felt like they were tiny slits, although, apart from a slight pink rim around them, they looked normal in the mirror.

"Your dad wouldn't do that," Kathy said.

"Maybe he pushed her and she fell."

"My mum said it was an accident." Kathy put the brush down. "She said your mum just didn't see the car."

"But she wasn't there."

"She talked to the police."

"My mum wouldn't run out into the road," I said. "She always made me stand on the kerb and look both ways."

"Sometimes people forget to look both ways."

"My mum never forgot," I said. I was furious with Kathy for suggesting it; I wanted to throw her ponies out of the window. "It must be my dad's fault. He must have distracted her. Or pushed her."

"I don't think he pushed her."

"I don't *care* what you think," I shouted.

Kathy turned away and started brushing the pony again.

I felt ashamed of myself, but I couldn't say sorry. After a moment of silence I picked up a different pony and showed it to her. "This one's cool, I like the rainbows on her leg."

"*His* leg," Kathy said.

"Oh."

"He's one of my favourites," Kathy said after a while, and we went back to brushing.

It was weird to be let back into the house by Kathy's mum. The lights were off, but after she flicked the switch in the hallway my father came out of his study, blinking.

"Oh, Edward, you're home already. I'll just give you these back now," she said, putting my mum's old set of keys down on the hall table.

"Thank you for looking after Tallulah so often over this... period," my father said.

"Glad to help out. I'd better skedaddle though. Get dinner on for Ted and Kathy." She bent down and gave me a kiss on the forehead. "Tallie, you're welcome at ours any time, you know that, right?"

"Thank you," I said.

"Yes, thanks again," my father said. He shut the door after her. "Now, Tallulah, I think we should have a little chat." He laid his hand on the top of my head and for a moment I was so shocked at his touching me I didn't say anything.

"I miss your mother too, you know." He looked at my expression. "Of course I do. I've been trying to plan the funeral and... " he sighed. "It's very hard for all of us."

He didn't even look sad, I thought, just far away. His hand felt hot through my hair and I jerked it off. He stared at the front door, like he could see through it to the road.

"I didn't think it would be this hard," he said. "Maybe... "

Mr Tickles appeared, crying for food. My father frowned at him and then at me; his eyes looked less cloudy all of a sudden. "I'm going to need your co-operation, Tallulah. No more tantrums. We can all behave nicely to one other, at least." He walked back into his study and shut the door, leaving me in the hallway with my heart hammering, although I wasn't sure why.

∗ ∗ ∗

It was at the reception after my mother's funeral that I found out I was going to be joining Starr at boarding school, although not from Starr or Aunt Vivienne, who didn't even come to the funeral.

I was sitting in the boiler room, hiding from everyone, trying to make myself cry. I heard a creaking outside the door, then it opened and my grandmother looked in.

"Aren't you getting rather hot?"

"No."

"Suit yourself," she said, and closed the door again.

I waited a moment, then scrambled after her. She was sitting on the step opposite, looking straight at me.

I sat down next to her. "How did you know I was in there?"

"I saw you go in."

"Oh."

"A few people seem to be missing today," she said. "Don't you find it odd that your uncle and aunt couldn't make it to the funeral?"

"Uncle Jack isn't in the country."

"Is that what your father told you?"

I nodded.

My grandmother took a cigarette out of a gold case. "The trouble with stories," she said, pointing it at me, "is remembering what's been said to whom."

"What?"

She put the case away. "Your father wants to send you to boarding school," she said. "You'll go to middle school first

137

then transfer after a year."

I felt my heart flip inside my chest. "Why?"

"He thinks he's too busy to be able to take care of you properly, and you're too young to be spending all your time alone."

"I don't want to go."

"No one ever does," my grandmother said, grimly. "But they say they enjoy it afterwards – when they're older."

"Do I have to go?"

"That's up to your father."

"Why are you telling me?"

My grandmother looked at me. "I didn't think it was a good idea," she said. "But I guess we'll see."

Now the tears came easily enough. I ran upstairs and lay on my bed, face-down in the pillow, not wanting to see anyone.

It felt like hours before my father was standing at the door.

"Tallulah? Why are you lying here in the dark?"

I turned to face him. "Why are you sending me to boarding school?"

There was a pause. "I gather Mother told you, then."

I was silent.

"I'm sorry, Tallulah. It's the only solution I can think of."

I know it's your fault somehow. I know she's dead because of you.

"Fine," I said. "I don't want to stay here anyway."

In the light of the corridor behind him, I saw my father put his hands in his pockets and look at something on the ceiling. "I'll give you some time alone," he said. "It's been an emotional day for both of us."

I felt my whole body seething with hate. I tried to keep my voice steady when I spoke. "When am I going?"

"It's probably best if you start as soon as possible."

Eventually he left. I heard his shoes squeak as he went downstairs, then I turned to the wall and cried until my face was so swollen, Mr Tickles meowed in fright at the sight of it.

✳ ✳ ✳

Evening visiting hours over, we stand outside the main entrance. Around us, cafés and shops are closing up, everyone gathering up their belongings, ready to journey home.

"I suppose I'll see you both here tomorrow?" Aunt Vivienne says, patting her hair.

"Are you coming back then, Viv?" Aunt Gillian asks, frostily. "I thought you might be too busy for boring family affairs."

"*I* know how to stand by my family, Gillian," Aunt Vivienne says. "Well – until tomorrow." She gives me a curt nod and sashays away. Aunt Gillian looks disapproving, but she doesn't say anything.

"Are you getting the 74?" I ask.

"Oh yes, let's get it together," she says. "So much nicer to have a travelling companion."

It means getting two buses instead of one, but I guess I owe her some time together after running away before.

"Sure," I say. "Is Paul back soon?"

"Not for another night or two." She takes my arm. "But he spends most of his time at his club, anyway. Do you live alone?"

"Yep."

"And you don't get lonely?"

"Nope."

"Oh well, it must be me," Aunt Gillian says. "I was always a nervous child, apparently. Didn't like to be by myself for too long. I was so pleased when Mother said she'd had another little girl. Edward was a dear, but he was a boy, and not too into playing with dolls." She smiles at me. "But then Vivienne was quite horrid, and not at all the playmate I was expecting. I suppose we're not very well suited. And then Vivienne is so good at holding grudges… "

"What did you do to her?"

"Oh." Aunt Gillian shakes her head quickly. "*Everything*

139

I did was wrong."

The bus pulls up at the stop and Aunt Gillian lets go of me to climb aboard, and then we have to wait while she finds her change purse.

"I'm not used to getting public transport," she whispers to me as we sit down. "Georgia used to drive me around until she moved out."

"When did she move out?"

"Just before the wedding. It made it a little bittersweet, I suppose, letting go of her like that. But I knew she was going to be well taken care of, and that's what you want for your children." She must remember the conversation at dinner, because she changes the subject hastily. "Any romantic interest in your life, Tallulah?"

"Not so much."

"Well now, that must be temporary," she says, comfortingly. "You've turned into quite a beautiful young lady. I'm sure you'll find a nice young man soon." She pats my hand.

"It's okay," I tell her. "I'm not that bothered." That's a lie, Aunt Gillian, it's just that I pushed away the guy I was bothered about and now I'm too gutless to try to get back in touch with him.

"James hasn't found anyone either," Aunt Gillian says. "I wish he'd get himself a girlfriend and stop going out all hours of the night."

"Does he still live at home?"

"He's converted the rooms above the garage into a little flat. We hardly see him."

"Do you miss Michael?"

"Of course I do," she says, surprising me. For some reason I never thought the two of them were that close. "Michael turned out very like his father, in the end." She smiles, looking softer. "It's funny, I can't really see John in either of the other two at all. But then, I guess, children aren't always like their parents."

I catch the No.19 at Hyde Park Corner and I'm back home

an hour and half after I boarded the first bus. I'm hungry again – dinner with Gillian and Vivienne feels like ages ago, and I've been burning nervous energy all day. I start to peel a clementine, digging my nails into the orange skin. I like the smell of citrus that will stay under them until I next have a shower. I'm almost too tired to eat though; each day I get through without my father waking up leaves me drained and relieved at the same time. And at the same time, there's the knowledge at the back of my head that the longer he stays under, the less likely he is to ever come round.

If he dies, I'll be an orphan, like my mother was. Like my father is, like all of them are, now – Aunt Gillian, Aunt Vivienne, Uncle Jack.

I've lived like an orphan since I left home. I've been completely alone, not counting the others in the hostel, and it's never bothered me too much until now. Maybe Aunt Gillian's right when she says children aren't always like their parents, or Aunt Vivienne could be right instead, I could be more like my father than I realise. He spent his whole life with his brain switched on, researching, operating, in studies and hospital theatres. He didn't know how to relax with us when he came through the front door; we were probably harder work for him than his patients.

But how could I turn out like him when I tried so hard not to? I guess we both lost my mother, and it changed us, even if he was already drawing away from me before that day.

I eat the clementine. No point in worrying about my father until the hospital staff bring it up. I should be concerned instead that I tried to drop in unannounced on my best-friend-and-maybe-more the other day, after years of radio silence, and now I'm dreaming about him. Am I obsessing? He's been quietly nagging at me, I realise, ever since Starr told me that she ran into him recently. But he'd have every right to be angry as he was in my dream. So now what?

I throw away the peel and crawl into bed.

***

My father drove me to the school. I was in the passenger seat, the first time I'd been up at the front, and I nuzzled against the seatbelt, trying to catch the smell of my mother's soap, or her perfume, tracing patterns with my fingers on the glovebox, imagining they were her fingers.

The journey that day was the same as to my grandmother's. I could almost predict when we would change lanes, merge with the M1, when the signs for Watford would appear, then for Birmingham, then Shrewsbury. I stared out at the landscape as it altered gradually, first dusty fields and small villages, and later railways and hills – the green slopes streaked brown with beeches and sweet chestnuts – and market towns, until the houses turned from red brick to grey stone, and iron bridges sprang up over emerald rivers.

My father didn't look at me once during the whole journey. I snuck glances at his profile, trying to work out what he was thinking. Kathy's voice kept coming back to me, 'Sometimes people forget to look both ways.' My mother would never have run out into the road though, I told myself, because that would be dangerous and she would never put herself in danger in case something happened and then I wouldn't have her anymore.

I knew this. I knew it because I knew, for a fact, that my mother never, ever stopped thinking about me.

Kathy was probably right about my father not pushing her, or the police would already have arrested him. But why did he say it was his fault? Why wouldn't he look me in the eye? I tried to work it out while he was driving, and staring at the road, but he might as well have been made of glass.

We ignored the turn for the market town closest to my grandmother, and drove ten minutes in the other direction. The roads were emptier now, and once, turning a corner, we startled a flock of birds who took off flashing orange, brown and white.

"Those were wrynecks," my father said. It was the first time he'd spoken since we got in the car.

Eventually, he put the handbrake on and turned the engine off. "We're here."

The school was exactly as I had pictured boarding school to be: redbrick main buildings and dormitories, green walls in the canteen. The paths around the grounds were gravelled and kept in pristine condition; the gym and swimming pool were modern and tucked away at the back of the grounds, past the boys' dormitories and the playing fields.

My father came on the tour with me, walking a few steps behind. When we got around to the front of the building again, he got my suitcase out of the trunk and handed it to me.

"Be good," he said. "You can always telephone, of course."

"Mm-hmm."

The teacher showing us around smiled encouragingly at me. "You won't remember to after a while," she said. "Our students love it here."

My father checked his watch. "I'd better be off... Avoid the traffic. You have everything, don't you?"

I nodded.

He pulled out slowly. It was weird to see him turn left at the gate and disappear behind the wall, like that was the last time I'd see my old life, and for a moment I almost wanted him to turn around and drive back for me. He didn't. The teacher raised her eyebrows and gestured for me to follow her inside.

* * *

It was a bell that woke me on the first morning, ringing far off somewhere, and then voices much closer, the sounds of doors slamming and footsteps thundering up and down stairs. My bedroom at home was at the back of the house, overlooking the garden, and I was used to waking up to birds, or Mr Tickles yowling to be let in. At the weekends there was the whine of lawnmowers. And always noises in the kitchen directly below me – my mother running the taps or opening the fridge, humming to herself.

I propped myself up on one elbow and blinked away the film of sleep. I could see creamy-yellow walls, thick orange curtains and a brown carpet. There were three small windows and ivy grew like a green fringe on the outside walls, colouring the light that streamed in. There were five other beds, each with a bedside table and lamp. And four other girls, wrapped in towels, bare legs poking out underneath, hopping from one foot to the other like they were trying to keep warm. They seemed much louder than normal people, pushing each other and screaming. One of them saw me awake and nudged the girl nearest her.

"Are you Tallulah?" she asked. She looked older than the others. Her hair was long and perfectly straight, and she had dark blue nail polish on her toes. Two plump mounds spilled over the top of the towel. I'd never seen breasts that big on girls our age and I turned my face away, not wanting to be caught staring.

"Yeah."

"I'm Cressida. You can have my place next in the queue."

"Thanks," I said. I felt embarrassed in my Winnie the Pooh pyjamas, but I didn't want to take them off while everyone was watching. I rooted around in my suitcase for a towel.

The door to the bathroom opened and a girl scurried back in, wet red hair dripping around her shoulders.

"You go," Cressida said, and pushed me in the right direction.

The bathroom was freezing and smelt mossy. The plastic shower curtain clung to my limbs when I climbed in, and I hadn't brought any soap in with me, so I got myself damp all over and stepped out again, wrapped my towel around myself and went back into the dorm.

I changed quietly in the corner, trying not to draw attention to myself. The red-head sat on her bed, staring at the floor. Her skin was so pale it was almost see-through, except where

144

it was covered by freckles. I vaguely remembered her from the day before. I recognised one of the louder girls too, the one with the blondest hair and a turned-up nose, but I couldn't remember either of their names.

"You can sit with us at breakfast," Cressida called across the room to me. The red-head didn't look up.

The breakfast hall was in another building, one long room with a huge ceiling that sloped upwards towards the middle, and tiny, diamond-shaped tiles on the floor. The noise was terrifying; it felt like there were thousands of other children swarming around the room. They all seemed to know each other too. I gripped my tray harder, trying not to panic.

"All Johnston Housers sit here," Cressida said.

"What's Johnston Houser?"

"Johnston *House*. It's where we sleep," Cressida said. She tucked her hair behind her ear. "Daddy wanted me to be in Johnston. He said everyone else was nouveau riche."

Breakfast was seven-thirty until seven-fifty. We had to be in our form rooms by eight, the girls told me, or we got a Saturday with Ricky Dicks.

"What's that?"

"You have to stay in Saturday night with the Housemistress."

"She's not married," Cressida said. "But she calls herself Mrs Richard Dickson. Everyone knows she's a lesbian."

The other girls snickered. I didn't say anything. I'd met our Housemistress the day before. She wore lipstick, which had smeared itself into the wrinkles around her mouth. She'd patted me on the head and called me 'poor love'. I thought how, for a lesbian, she looked a lot like any other woman.

I caught a glimpse of Starr as we were leaving the hall and she gave me a wave. I turned my face away from her – if Starr and Aunt Vivienne couldn't be bothered to come to my mother's funeral, I didn't have to bother to be friends now.

"You know her?" Cressida asked me.

"She's my cousin."

"She's the year above us. That's *so* cool," Cressida said. The other girls nodded.

There were even more students in the main school building and I had a sudden urge to cry, although I didn't know if it was because everything was huge and unfamiliar or because it was sinking in that this was going to be my home from now on.

Cressida gave me a hug at my form room door. "We know about your mum," she said. She stood back and waited for me to say something.

"Yeah?" I muttered.

"You can be in our gang," Cressida said, and everyone nodded again. "We think you're really brave."

I didn't say anything. My stomach felt cold and I couldn't look at them.

The blonde girl opened the door for me. "Look after her," Cressida said, and the blonde girl put her arm around my waist and steered me in.

"Let's sit together," she said. "I'm Abi, remember?" She smiled at me and I noticed the whites of her eyes were slightly blue, just tinged that way, and she had a blonde moustache that caught the light.

We walked towards the back of the classroom, and she tossed her plait over her shoulder as we went. "I'm *so* glad you're here now. I was stuck in this form all by myself. Cressida tried to get the teachers to swap me, but they said they couldn't."

"What's wrong with the other kids?"

"Edith – the girl from our dorm – is really geeky." She lowered her voice. "Then there's these twins, brother and sister. They're day-schoolers and they always hold each other's hands." She giggled. "They have identical packed lunches too. Cressida says they probably share a bed at home, or something."

Abi kept talking and I zoned out. Slowly the other seats started to fill up, then the teacher arrived and made me come to the front and introduce myself.

"We didn't do this properly yesterday," she said. "But this is Tallulah, a new student. Tallulah, why don't you tell us something about yourself."

Abi smiled encouragingly at me; my mind went blank.

"Like what?" I asked.

"Like your favourite food. Where you live. Anything like that."

"I'm from London."

"Okay… That's good. Edith's from London too, aren't you Edith?"

"I'm from Kingston," Edith said.

"Anywhere near you?" the teacher asked.

"I don't know where that is," I said.

"Oh well, never mind." She smiled at me. She had big blue eyes and curly blonde hair tied up in a ponytail and away from a high forehead. She looked young, almost younger than Cressida. "I'm Miss Rochard. I'll be your form tutor for the next year or so, and my favourite colour is gold." She lowered her voice, "And Tallulah, if you need to talk to someone, you can come to me anytime."

I wiped my palms on my skirt. For some reason they were hot and sweaty.

"You can go and sit down now."

I slunk back to my place.

"Don't worry," Abi whispered. "I'll make sure she doesn't try to pair you up with Edith."

I closed my eyes and tried to shut everything out of my brain. Abi was still whispering next to me. I wished I was in my old school. I wished Kathy was next to me instead of Abi. I wished I had Mr Tickles to curl up on my feet tonight. I wished I could see my mother again.

✳ ✳ ✳

The word had spread at school about my mother, and, at first, girls brought me little offerings – lipstick, fizzy cola bottles, chewing gum. The boys ignored me, which was the nicest thing they could think of doing.

A couple of times I heard Starr call out my name when I was in the corridor between classes, but I always pretended I was busy talking to someone else. Once she was coming up the main staircase as I was going down, and I hid behind two girls who had their arms linked together; she didn't see me, and I felt victorious, but also disappointed in a weird way, like I'd actually wanted her to notice me after all.

My teachers were nice to me too. Miss Rochard was very friendly, although she made me feel uncomfortable – she was always taking my hand in hers, or squeezing my shoulder and saying positive things. I preferred my science teacher, who never bothered me. He had a big white moustache, and wore the same red jumper and green corduroy trousers every day. Then there was Mr Hicks, the head of art. The art studio always smelled like incense, which he burned in little holders. Sometimes during lessons he would give a student some money to run to the tuck shop and get us all chocolate. Mr Hicks was tall; he had good skin and dark hair and brown eyes, and all the female teachers laughed whenever he made a joke, especially Miss Rochard. Once, I saw them standing at the back of the assembly hall together, during a fire safety talk; Mr Hicks was leaning towards her, whispering into her ear and her eyes were even bigger than normal.

From the beginning I found it hard to keep up with lessons. I'd never learned French or German before and I didn't know the difference between a noun and a verb. Mostly I thought about my mother instead. I tried to remember what her favourite colour was, and I realised I'd never known. My favourite colours on her had been pink and peach. When I was younger she'd read a book to me called *Each, Peach, Pear, Plum*, and in my two-year-old mind the two of them had been mixed up, so that I thought my mother was made of fruit, like the flush of peach on her cheeks, or the plum colour she went when she was upset. If you peeled away a layer of her skin, I thought, she'd be sweet and firm underneath, like a peach itself. After the accident though, the few glimpses I'd caught of her had proven me wrong.

"*Ma mère est une professeur*," we chanted in French. "*Mon père est un avocat.*"

She was wearing dark blue the day she died, a sleeveless dress that always reminded me of sailors because it had a big white collar and a white anchor pattern.

"*Elle est professeur.*"

Somehow, when they buried her, she was wearing a green dress that I hadn't remembered seeing before. I wondered who'd chosen it. No one had asked me.

"*Il est avocat.*"

I thought about my father too, about whether he would send for me. Maybe he would suddenly change his mind and want me around. I didn't think he would.

Some teachers drew me aside to ask me if I was struggling during classes. They went through my homework patiently with me, explaining where I'd gone wrong.

"You really *are* paying attention, aren't you?" Miss Rochard said. "In all your lessons?"

"Yes," I lied.

I kept thinking about the accident, instead of listening in class. I wondered if she'd known about the car at the last second, if she'd seen the driver trying to brake, what she'd heard. And if my father hadn't pushed her, had he *not* saved her? Could he have stretched out a hand to pull her back to safety?

"*Was* it an accident?" I said, once, when I forgot where I was. Abi gave me a weird look, but nothing else happened.

I spoke to my father once in that first term. The Housemistress had to come and find me in my dorm room, so he'd been waiting for a while on the other end by the time I got to the telephone.

"I won't be able to be on much longer," he said.

"Sorry," I said. The Housemistress was hovering over me.

I turned away, blocking her with my back.

"No, it's not your fault." He cleared his throat.

I asked about Mr Tickles, clutching at something we could talk about. He asked about the weather and my teachers.

"They're fine."

"I'm sorry, but I'm going to have to go now – this was just a quick break. You're doing well in class?"

"I guess."

"Good. Well, I'm sure we'll speak soon."

"Okay."

"Bye Tallulah." He cleared his throat again. "All my love."

"That was quick," the Housemistress said, when I handed the receiver back to her.

I didn't want to go back up to the dorm room straight-away. It felt weird to hear my father use the word 'love'. I couldn't remember him using it for a while, with me *or* my mother. Now I wondered if he'd *ever* told us he loved us. Maybe he hadn't, and I only noticed after he got so grumpy. Maybe he didn't think of me as his daughter, and that's why he didn't love me. I didn't look anything like him, but I hadn't looked like my mother, either. I leaned my forehead against the cool of the staircase wall. Which part of me was her, and which part was him? It was hard to believe I'd come from either of them, that I'd grown inside her, even. And now I was left with whatever hidden part of my mother that was in me. Or did it die when she died?

Cressida and Abi tried to ask me about my mother, but it felt wrong to talk about her with them. Sometimes, I wondered if Cressida thought it was romantic that she'd died so young. "At least your mum will never get old and wrinkly," she said.

Cressida and the others talked all the time, about boys and lipstick and where they were going skiing over Christmas. I had nothing to add to those conversations. I still wasn't interested in boys, and the way girls fluttered their eyes at them, or found excuses to touch them seemed boring to me. Cressida was obsessed with one boy in particular, Toby

Gates, who was two years above us. I'd seen him around school. He had dark hair and green eyes and played rugby. Cressida wrote 'Cressida Gates' all over her school planner and drew up ideas for their wedding, which was going to have white doves and be on a Mexican beach. Cressida liked to plan things. She came up with a secret handshake we all had to practise too, and a password to gain entry to our secret meetings. She wanted to start a relief fund for starving children in Africa, which she said was the most important issue of our time. She said we should memorise facts about all the different countries in Africa and decide which one needed our help the most.

Abi had been bought an encyclopaedia for her birthday, and Cressida made us study it in turn, writing crib sheets on countries she picked for us. Mine were Egypt and Tanzania and Lesotho, which I assumed was pronounced Le-soth-oh. We had to give presentations on our countries and when all the presentations were given, we would vote for our favourite. Abi put a lot of effort into her presentation on Malawi, sticking photos and glitter onto coloured sheets of card, and drawing big red hearts in the margins. I voted for her.

"Are you *sure* you want to vote for Malawi?" Cressida asked me.

"Yeah."

She turned her face away pointedly. Cressida won with South Africa, and Abi threw her cards away. Even though everyone else had voted for her presentation, Cressida seemed put out. I waited to be told how we were going to help the children of South Africa, but in the end nothing happened.

✳ ✳ ✳

When I'd started at boarding school they'd made me go see the school counsellor, Dr Epstein. He had one long eyebrow hair, like an antennae. "Tell me what's bothering you the most," he said.

I tried to describe how out of control everything seemed,

151

but he misunderstood. He thought I was saying that my mother had protected me, and now I had to grow up too quickly. But no one was making me feel like I was growing up – not my father, not my teachers; even Cressida told me what to do.

I practised reading his handwriting upside down. After a few sessions I was able to make out the words *disturbed*.

"Are you sleeping?" he asked me.

I nodded.

I woke up every night, my face wet, although I had no tears during the day. A couple of times I'd tried to stay awake all night, because the worst was the morning, just after opening my eyes, before I realised where I was. Sometimes, for a split second, I didn't remember about my mother, or going to boarding school, and then I had a feeling like I'd been punched me in the gut when I saw the other girls, and knew everything again.

When I wasn't sleeping, everything went slowly, when the other girls' heavy breathing meant I couldn't turn a light on and read. My pyjamas and sheets felt sticky after all my tossing and turning, and the ticking of Edith's alarm clock, and the wind slapping the windows were so loud it made me think I'd go crazy.

I'd push my face into my pillow. My mother loved me – that thought was the one thing I could cling to. She used to surprise me after school with little presents that she'd found in junk shops. Little toys or books or trinkets for charm bracelets. Lying in bed, listening to the other girls breathing heavily, and the creak of their beds, I'd think about the times that my mother had stopped me at the front door to our house, her hands behind her back, saying that she'd found something very special for me. I wondered if I'd ever been grateful enough.

I was in pain all the time, but it was a slow pain I'd never felt before. My whole body ached, thinking about my mother. All I wanted was to feel her again, touch her. I wanted her skin pressing against my skin when she hugged me, or her chin resting on my hair. I wanted the pressure of her fingertips on my shoulder, as she held me back at a busy road when I wasn't looking where I was going. I wanted the coldness of her toes. She used to slip her feet underneath my bottom as I sat on the sofa, to warm them up, and I would wriggle away from her. It was these moments that I missed the most; my body was crying out for them. It was like a layer had fallen away from me and left me exposed.

The insomnia was taking its toll. I dragged myself to classes and sat there like a zombie. My head was pounding and my body felt like it was losing power. Everything my brain told it to do, it tried then gave up. I put my head down on my arms and closed my eyes.

Abi woke me up by jabbing a pen into my side. "You're snoring," she hissed.

Mr Hicks was standing over us, a half-smile on his face. "Tallulah, would you mind staying after class?" he said.

He made me stand at his desk while he sat. "I'm afraid I'm going to have to give you a detention," he said. He played with his pen, clicking the lid. "I can't let you get away with sleeping in my lessons, do you see that?"

"Yes."

"I'm sorry. Are you being kept up by girls in your dorm?"

"No."

"Well, you look exhausted. You must try to get some sleep. Have you been to the school nurse?"

"I'm seeing the counsellor."

"Well. We're all here for you, Tallulah." He tore off a slip of paper. "You'll have to spend tomorrow lunchtime in here with me, okay?"

"Okay."

I dragged myself back to my dorm. The girls weren't keeping me up, not directly. I didn't like Cressida; most of the time I didn't want to be around her, but I dreaded being completely alone. It was partly the idea of facing boarding school without anyone on my side that was keeping me up. But my novelty was starting to wear off and I wasn't sure if Cressida still thought I was interesting.

I played out confrontations in my head. I imagined myself telling Cressida what I really thought of her, challenging my father, asking him about the accident, why I had to be here. 'If you couldn't stop it happening, why couldn't you heal her? You're a doctor.' And Uncle Jack, too: 'Why did you come back? You made everything worse. And where are you now if you're not abroad?' In my head, I crushed the three of them with my anger.

Nine

Aunt Vivienne can't come in the next day after all. I sit with Aunt Gillian at my father's bedside while she continues knitting. I try not to look at him too often – he's so still I can almost forget he's there.

Aunt Gillian is making a jumper for the new baby. "It's a shame there were no more children after you, dear," she says. "I always thought our extended family might be bigger."

"I guess no one else really pulled their weight."

"Mm-hmm," Aunt Gillian says, looking guiltily at my father. She binds off the stitching, shakes the material out and inspects it critically. "Not really up to scratch," she says. "I can give that one to a charity shop, I suppose." She checks her watch. "Shall we get something to drink from the cafeteria?"

"Sure."

As we pass the nurse on duty, Aunt Gillian gives her a detailed account of where we're going, and how long we'll be.

"Georgia asked after you," she says, as we take the lift. "She'd love for you to go around sometime."

"That would be nice."

I get a coffee and Aunt Gillian has an Earl Grey tea. We sit at a table and drink.

"What's the age difference between all of you?" I ask her.

"Well now," Aunt Gillian says. "I'm a year older than

Edward, then Vivienne was another three and a half years after him, then Jack came along two years after that." She purses her mouth when she says his name; it looks almost automatic.

"So you're six and a half years older than Jack?"

"Yes," she says. "I suppose it meant I took on the role of second mother, as it were."

"When Grandma was busy?"

"When she was ill," Aunt Gillian says, vaguely.

"Who was the easiest to look after?"

"Oh, Edward. He was a darling."

"Was *he* close to the other two?"

She fidgets in front of me. "The best way to handle them was to get in their way as little as possible."

"So they weren't close? Even as kids?"

"Well, no."

We lapse into silence. I wonder why Jack approached my parents and not Vivienne, if he'd never been close to my father. There was another possibility, of course, but only one person could tell me everything. The other person was dead.

Everything changed after Uncle Jack came back; I wish my mother had had nothing to do with it.

I stand up. "I've got to make a phone call," I say.

In the corridor I punch in the number. It rings and rings on the other end; I feel sick. A mechanical voice comes on, telling me to leave a message. I start to speak, my voice shaky.

Then, halfway through, there's a click. "You alright, doll?" Malkie says. "How's your pop?"

"He's okay," I say. "He still hasn't woken up and it's been six days."

"Is that good or bad?"

"It's not good, but it's not bad yet."

"Mm-hmm. You sure you're okay?"

"Yeah."

"What can I do for you then?"

"Do you know where Uncle Jack is?"

There's a silence on the other end of the line.

"Malkie?"

"I'm here," he says; I can almost hear his brow furrowing. "Why d'you wanna know, doll? If it's okay for me to ask."

"I wanna talk to him."

He sighs. "He's not exactly in great shape."

"Does that mean you know where he is?"

✳ ✳ ✳

Autumn was well under way; the leaves that hadn't fallen were the colour of ripe aubergines or rust. Starr came and got me from the Junior Common Room and we walked around the grounds. Our breath rose from our mouths when we talked, like clouds of smoke. I wore a woollen hat with a pom-pom and wellington boots. Starr wore thick grey tights and a diamond-pattern cardigan over her uniform. She was chewing gum, something I knew was forbidden at school.

"They said you needed someone to talk to," she said. She wasn't looking at me at all, and I suddenly felt shy around her, instead of angry. "So... how you finding it?"

"It's okay."

"Making friends?"

I shrugged.

"Are you mad at me?"

"Why would I be mad at you?"

"I thought you were ignoring me... " She left it hanging there. When I shrugged again she spat her gum into her hand and pressed it quickly onto the underside of a windowsill we were passing. "So, we're fine, right? I'm sorry if you *are* mad at me, anyway."

"Fine."

"How's Uncle Edward?"

"Fine." I blew into my hands to keep them warm; he'd only called back once more, but I was at Prep and he hadn't left a message. I was pretty much convinced he didn't care about me at all. "How's your mum?"

"Yeah fine. She forgets about me, then feels guilty. Then she turns up here to take me out as a treat."

"What do you do?"

"Go to town, get a manicure. Sometimes she takes me to the cinema." She grimaced. "Normally she gets drunk. You're lucky your parents are normal... Uncle Edward's normal." Her cheeks were blotchy with red, and she put her hands up to fiddle with her hair, like she was trying to pretend she was busy. I thought of the conversation I'd had with Kathy and stayed silent. Starr would think I was crazy too.

"Did you know I'm on the tennis team? Maybe you could try out."

"Do you remember our tennis tournaments at Grandma's?" I said.

"Not really. We didn't even have real tennis balls there."

"Yeah," I said. "I guess not."

"Anyway," she said, looking at me for the first time, "you're really fine, right?"

"Yeah," I said. "I've gotta go to detention now."

"Okay," she said, looking relieved. "I'll come find you soon. And come to a practice, yeah?"

"Okay," I said.

For my detention, Mr Hicks got me sorting out the wax crayons into colour groups, and dipping paintbrushes into turpentine with him, while the radio played in the background. He made me laugh while I was working, singing the really high female-voice parts of songs, and cracking cheese-based jokes.

"Which cheese would you use to get a bear out of a tree?"

"I dunno."

"*Camembert.*"

"Is that a cheese?"

"You shock me, Tallulah, you really do."

It was almost like spending time with an older cousin, like Michael. Or like a father, who didn't hate me and was less tired and more fun. When I got up to leave, Mr Hicks helped me collect my things. "Don't keep falling asleep," he said. "You'll make me think my lessons are boring."

"They're not," I said. "They're pretty much the only interesting ones."

Mr Hicks laughed. "Thank you for the compliment."

"You're welcome," I mumbled.

He ruffled my hair, like I'd seen Michael do with Georgia, and I felt my cheeks get hot and prickly.

* * *

I can't stop thinking about what Malkie's up to. I imagine him picking up the phone, calling old friends, walking to an unknown part of London. Knocking on doors. I don't know what I want after that. What would I ask Uncle Jack? And do I really want the answers?

I can't take it back; don't think about it. Maybe nothing will come of it, anyway.

"What's happening now?" Aunt Gillian asks; another nurse has arrived.

"Nothing yet," the nurse says. "Just checking everyone's okay in here."

"Yep," I say.

"Good. I'll be back in a little while to move him."

"Move him where?" Aunt Gillian asks.

"Just onto his other side. Nothing to worry about."

She leaves. Aunt Gillian turns to me. "Why do they move him?"

"I dunno." I think I have an idea, but I don't know why she's looking to me for explanations, like she thinks my father will have passed down a genetic understanding of hospital procedures. It makes me feel weird – it's the fact that my father is part of the medical world that stops me getting into it. Or one of the things that stops me, anyway.

I get up and walk over to the window, looking out onto the red-and-white-brick of the buildings opposite, and the black of the railings on street level. A couple of girls stroll past, wicker bags swinging from their arms. Probably off to the park for a picnic. If things had been different, that could have been me and Edith. Or even me and Toby. 'Isn't it worth talking to him then?' my grandmother would say. She knew how I felt about him. 'I'm sure he misses you too.'

'I'm sure he's been able to replace me,' I argue with her. 'With someone who's not such a head-case.'

I don't want that to be true, but what do I expect? I didn't think about how it would feel for him when I'd gone, about how shitty it would be to be abandoned by the only person who knows all your problems, knows how vulnerable you are. I was a stupid kid who persuaded herself that he wouldn't care; that it was him who abandoned me.

'So go say you're sorry.'

I tip my chin upwards and take in the sky – less azure than the last few days, it reminds me of a shade called Carolina Blue. We used to have tubes of it in the art studio – light blue with a blush of silver, like the sea at sunset. I might even have some back at the flat. Years ago, I went on a splurge, buying stacks of different colours. It was after Toby bought me the paint brush set. I lugged everything back to school with me; I must have wanted him to see me using his present. I try to remember if I packed it all when I left, but I can't.

"Tallulah?" Aunt Gillian says. "Can you hold the wool for me, love?"

I go back to my chair and take the ball from her, still trying not to look too closely at the sleeping figure in front of us.

"Did you get through to whoever you were calling before?" she asks.

"Yep," I say. "Just work."

∗∗∗

Christmas was coming, and lessons started to wind down. Teachers wheeled old TVs on tall trolleys into our classrooms and we watched Christmas videos like *Miracle on 34th Street* and *Father Christmas Goes on Holiday*. For days after we watched *Home Alone*, all the boys went around saying "Keep the change, ya filthy animal" and making machine gun noises. It got dark so early it felt like our lessons were carrying on into the night; we wore slippers and dressing gowns to sit and do prep after dinner. The school choir sang carols at the train station and the shopping centre in town; our year were given elf costumes, and sent out with donation buckets. A few days later, I found a card in my pigeon-hole. Miss Rochard had written in gold glitter: *Dear Tallulah, This Christmas I wish for you to be happy. You're a very special girl and you deserve it! Merry Christmas, Annie (Miss) Rochard xxx*

Aunt Gillian picked me up to spend Christmas at hers then talked all the way home, while I stared out at other cars, other families.

Georgia was waiting by the window when we pulled into the driveway. I climbed out of the car, stretching my legs, and she opened the front door, letting light stream out of the house. "*Tallie*," she said. "Oh my God, I can't believe you're *here*."

Michael carried my stuff up to Georgia's bedroom. "Welcome to the madhouse," he said, and left.

I lay on the camp bed they'd made up for me. Georgia lay on her bed, facing me.

"Remember when we were at Grandma's, and we used to nap in the same bed?" she asked me. "Me, you and Starr?"

"Yeah."

"I can't believe we ever fit the three of us in a single."

"We were smaller."

"Do you see Starr much?"

"Sometimes."

"What's she like now?"

"Fine."

"Mummy always says 'poor Starr'," Georgia said. "But she's so pretty, and she has such a cool name. I always think she's going to do something cool when she's older."

"What's happening with Mr Tickles?" I asked.

"I think Uncle Edward's bringing him."

"Can he sleep in here?"

"I'll ask Mummy."

"Georgia, Tallulah," Aunt Gillian called. "Tea's ready."

There were sausage rolls, smoked salmon on crackers, mince pies, spiced star-shaped biscuits and mini stollen laid out on the table. All the lights were on; there was a vase of holly and ivy on the sideboard and one white wreath hung on the back of the kitchen door. Taps and the draining board shone. Aunt Gillian beamed. She'd obviously gone to a lot of trouble. "Help yourself," she said. "How's the bed for you, Tallulah?"

"Fine. Thank you."

"Mummy, can Mr Tickles sleep with us?" Georgia asked, and I felt a glow of affection for her.

"He doesn't have fleas or anything like that, does he dear?" Aunt Gillian said, unenthusiastically.

"No," I lied.

"Okay then. Now tuck in. I'm making chicken pie for tonight – do you like chicken, Tallulah?"

"Yes," I said.

"Good." She turned the oven on. "I thought I'd check now that Vivienne has become a vegetarian." She said 'vegetarian' like she'd say 'prostitute', or 'terrorist'. She dipped a brush into some egg yolks and painted the pie crust with it – quick, annoyed brushstrokes.

"Don't worry about Mummy," Georgia said in a low voice. "Her and Aunt Vivienne had a big fight about something again."

I chewed my sausage roll in silence.

"Can we have some apple juice please, Mummy?" Georgia asked.

"Of course." Aunt Gillian went to the fridge and took the carton out. She poured two glasses and brought them over to the table, all smiles again. "Did Georgia tell you she won a spelling competition recently? She came top of her age group in the county."

"Mummy, you're being embarrassing."

I took a sip of apple juice. "Congratulations," I said.

"What about you, Tallulah?" Aunt Gillian asked. "I remember how hard they work you at that school – the teachers used to say to me, 'If you had half as much brains as your younger brother, you'd be fine'." She smiled.

"I'm failing most of my subjects," I said. With two exceptions, my grades were Cs, Ds and below.

"Oh," Aunt Gillian said, looking embarrassed. "Well, you mustn't be discouraged, dear. Sometimes it takes a while to discover our strengths. Do you belong to any sports or social clubs?"

"No."

I looked straight at her, daring her to ask me another question. She stared back at me with her mouth open, then shut it, quickly, and put on a smile. "I'm sure you're too busy with friends." She checked her watch. "I'll just nip down to the cellar to get some wine."

"Don't worry about school," Georgia said to me, as soon as Aunt Gillian was out of the room. "I'm not as clever as Michael either."

I shrugged. "What did your mum and Aunt Vivienne fight about?"

"Mummy said Aunt Vivienne should have come to the funeral."

"What did Aunt Vivienne say?"

"She said Mummy always wanted to sweep everything under the rug."

"Were they talking about Uncle Jack?"

"Maybe," Georgia said. "Mummy did say when Aunt Vivienne had left that she was kidding herself if she thought Jack was coming back."

'The trouble with stories is remembering what's been said to whom.' The words quickly came back to me.

I had a sudden urge to see Malkie. I didn't want to tell Georgia that Jack might still be around, or that I thought my father might hold some blame for my mother's death, even if

163

it was only by *not* doing anything. But maybe Malkie would know; maybe he'd be able to explain everything. Like why he'd come by that afternoon, and why my mother had made me leave the house.

"I'm going to the loo," I said.

Upstairs, I rummaged among my clothes until I got to the photo of my mother I kept at the bottom of my bag. She was smiling, sitting with her knees pressed together, on some steps outside an open front door. It could have been the house she grew up in, the one she lived in with the grandparents I'd never known. I'd found the photo after she died, when my father was throwing out her things, rescuing it and her recipe book from the same box. It was hard to tell how old she was in the picture. Whenever I looked at it, I tried to find some similarity between us, but there was nothing on the surface.

I heard the front door open and male voices, feet stamping; it'd been snowing lightly since we got in. I went to the top of the stairs and crouched out of sight as Aunt Gillian came into the hallway to greet them.

"It's freezing, Mum," James said.

"How's our notorious guest?" Uncle George said.

"Not doing as well as we hoped." Aunt Gillian sounded worried. "She was actually quite difficult earlier. Edward said she wasn't exactly setting the school on fire at her Primary, and we thought maybe the boarding school would be a good influence on her, but she sounds like she's struggling... Of course, it's hard to tell how academic Evelyn was, because she had to leave school so early, but... "

"Boring. What's for dinner?" James asked. They went into the kitchen and I went back to the bedroom.

＊＊＊

My father was due late on Christmas Eve. We were already in our pyjamas, killing time until we could go to bed, and Georgia was fizzing with excitement; she kept hugging me and Michael and her stuffed dog, Humphrey. "I won't be able to sleep," she kept saying.

My heart skipped when I heard the doorbell, and then there he was, carrying Mr Tickles in the travelling cage. I let him hug me, quickly, then opened the cage and carefully lifted Mr Tickles out, kissing his ears and stroking his belly.

"I see Gillian got you here in one piece," my father said.

"Oh shush," Aunt Gillian said, taking his coat. "We had a lovely ride over, didn't we, Tallulah?"

"Yeah."

"Edward, would you like some mulled wine?"

"That would be nice."

She left us alone in the hall and Mr Tickles struggled out of my arms and padded after her. I inspected my feet, so it seemed like I had something to do.

"Ah. Are you looking forward to tomorrow then, Tallulah?" my father asked.

"Yeah."

"Good. It's nice of Gillian to let us take over the house, isn't it?"

I didn't understand what he meant. There were only two of us, and my father barely seemed to be there at all. I looked up, he looked back at me, but not like he really saw me. I didn't answer him, and after a moment he walked into the kitchen and I followed, confused. He rubbed his eyes a lot while Aunt Gillian fussed over him, heating up the soup she'd made us all for dinner earlier. He didn't ask me any more questions, or touch me again.

We half-watched TV, then went to our rooms. I climbed under my blanket and Mr Tickles sat on my pillow. He looked thinner and mangier than before and I wondered whether my father was feeding him properly.

Georgia tied her stocking onto the end of her bed, and mine onto the doorknob, then turned the main light off and climbed into bed. I could hear the grown-ups downstairs, the murmur of voices and the chink of glasses and Georgia a few feet away, her breathing getting slower and heavier.

I squeezed my eyes shut, but my brain was buzzing and I didn't fall asleep for hours.

Christmas morning was louder than at my house, and later to start, and we were only allowed to open one present each in the morning. Gillian's Christmas pudding was homemade, like my mother's, which she used to start making in February, but it was dry and there were too many pieces of fruit in it. We had to watch the Queen's speech after lunch, while everyone opened the rest of their presents and drew up lists of what they'd got. Michael and James argued over who had the best haul; I pulled a cracker with Georgia and won a wind-up musical toy that annoyed Uncle George no end. In the living-room, in front of the TV, my father sat upright, fingers drumming on the arm of his chair. I'd stared at him over my food earlier, trying to find signs of grief, or guilt, but he looked exactly the same as always. It made it worse that he'd known that I might struggle at boarding school, I thought, because it meant that he'd wanted me out of the way at any cost, even if it meant humiliation for me. Aunt Gillian's words rang in my head the whole time – 'Edward said she wasn't exactly setting the school on fire at her Primary.'

Around six o'clock I escaped to my bedroom. I took the photo of my mother out again and rubbed my thumb across it, over her face. "Merry Christmas," I said.

* * *

I got off to a bad start in 1992. My teachers were losing patience with me. Before, when I got homework or tests back, they wrote comments like *good effort*, or *come and see me and we'll go through it*. Now they wrote *I'm starting to get really worried, Tallulah.* I dreaded seeing the grades circled in red on the bottom of the page. I began forgetting to hand homework in on time, skipping classes and hiding in the toilets, or in the school nurse's waiting area.

"You must have really weak genes, or something," Cressida said. "To be ill all the time."

I didn't say anything. I wondered if maybe my mother had had a weak heart – I knew that was genetic. Maybe that was why *she'd* been ill all the time by the end; maybe that was why she hadn't survived.

"We're going to have to get in touch with your father," Miss Rochard told me, sadly. "I'm sorry, Tallulah, but your grades aren't improving at all. It's school policy."

"Please don't," I said. "I'll get better, I promise."

"Well I'm glad you're willing to work hard," Miss Rochard said, but she looked worried. Her hair was dirty and scraped back in a bun; she was chewing her nails too, and it wasn't the first time she'd worn the same outfit twice in a row. "Please try to concentrate," she said to me. "For me, please?"

"Okay."

"I trust you, Tallulah. And you can trust me too – I'm here for you."

"Okay."

A week later, Miss Rochard burst into tears during a sex-education class. The next day, Ms Conrad appeared; Miss Rochard had some personal problems, and they didn't know when she'd be coming back.

Ms Conrad had no time for daydreamers, she told me; either I learn to focus, or spend my lunchtimes going through the lessons by myself.

I glared at her as she walked back to her desk, mad at how smug she looked. Turning, she caught my eye and raised an eyebrow. "Isn't there something you should be getting on with, Tallulah?" she said.

I stared at the page in front of me, but my heart was pounding so hard that I could feel it in my skull. Please let me leave this school, I begged silently. Please let me go back to my old friends and live in my house and see Mr Tickles. I'll be nice to my father. If he lets me go back, it means he has nothing to hide, anyway.

"Tallulah?" Ms Conrad called. "I can't see your pen moving."

"Tallulah, write something," Abi whispered. "Or you'll get another detention."

I met up with Starr every week in my first year, but it wasn't until the summer term that she started talking to me properly. I was trying to blow on a grass stalk like a whistle; she was striding ahead. Starr was nearly a foot taller than me and she had breasts and a gang of friends who did whatever she wanted. I didn't see why Aunt Gillian called her 'poor Starr' either.

"Tallie, I'm sorry I haven't really seen you much," she said, stopping suddenly. "And I'm sorry I didn't come and see you when you first got here."

I threw the stalk away and pulled up another one. "You have your own friends. Whatever."

"It's just, Mum was always so weird about you guys. And then I felt guilty for not coming to the funeral... "

I stopped listening; I played with my stalk and thought about Aunt Vivienne that summer, how she'd drunk more than usual, laughing hysterically, linking arms with Uncle Jack, and the looks she'd given my mother as she was doing it.

Ten

My father was busy again over the summer holidays. Aunt Gillian and the cousins were off on a family holiday in Greece for two weeks, so I was sent to my grandmother's this time.

"They'll join you there in August for a bit," my father said. "And I'll come down when I can."

No one picked me up. I caught a bus from town and walked at the other end. The road to my grandmother's was almost a dirt track. I was dragging my suitcase behind me and by the time I arrived I was covered in dust.

I stopped at the bottom of the drive, partly to wriggle my fingers to try to get the blood flowing in them again, and partly to take stock of my surroundings. Looking around, I saw the trees were encroaching onto the path and the grass was high, almost halfway up my calves, and I wondered whether the gardener had left.

My grandmother must have been watching out for me, because the door was thrown open before I had a chance to knock. "Come in," she said, "and may I enquire what on earth is going on with your appearance?"

My hair was pulled back in a ponytail and held there with a rubber band; my fringe was long enough to cover my eyebrows and the tips of my eyelashes. My t-shirt was crumpled and, looking down at my feet, I realised I had odd socks on.

"I… " I started, but she was already walking off.

I followed her into the kitchen. This was the first time I'd been at the house by myself with her, but for some reason I wasn't afraid. A kettle was boiling on the stove; there were fresh chrysanthemums lying on the table, bound with blue string, and a cigarette smouldering in an ashtray on the floor by the open back doors, like she'd been smoking and looking out on the garden.

"Tea?" my grandmother asked. "I don't drink the stuff, but I know people do."

"No thanks."

"Your hair looks like you cut it yourself."

"I did."

My grandmother looked away, but I thought she was smiling.

I picked up my suitcase and lugged it up the stairs to my old room. I had a cold shower and changed into a new t-shirt. I tried to do something with my hair, but it was too matted, so I snapped the elastic band back around it and went downstairs. My grandmother was out in the garden, walking around the vegetable patch; it looked like she was squeezing tomatoes, checking them for firmness. "Tallulah," she called, "bring me the spray can from the windowsill."

I took it out to her, noticing how the sill itself was crumbling under its white paint. The sun was low in the sky, flashing at me through the leaves and branches of the oak trees that grew near the house. My grandmother didn't seem to notice it; she walked between the rows of tomatoes, spritzing them with whatever was in the can. The fat, red fruit, the deep green of the vine leaves, the golden light, the straw hat she was wearing; everything was so vivid and I felt a tug in my chest that my mother would never be able to look at anything as beautiful as this again.

The peace was beautiful too. Except for the birds, and my grandmother's soft tread, there was no noise at all. It was a relief after the confusion of living with hundreds of other kids.

My grandmother turned and walked back towards the house.

"Are you coming?" she called to me. And then, like she'd read my mind, "No point in catching a cold now you're free."

***

Before my father came to visit that summer I was left to my own devices, so I had time to roam my grandmother's house and garden. Everywhere I looked seemed to have been touched with neglect. The ornamental pond to the right of the lawns was covered with a fine sheen of algae, the rose garden was withering, the jetty was rotting, the lake clogged with reeds and, beyond the lake, the orchard of apple and cherry trees grew in rows of straggling, twisted wood. Only the vegetable patch near the house had survived. "What happened to the gardener?" I asked my grandmother.

"The National Trust stole him," she said, sourly.

Inside the house, the furniture was faring just as badly. Chesterfield sofas were spilling out their stuffing, wooden trunks were splintering, rugs were threadbare and curtains fell off the rods if you pulled too heavily on them. I wandered through the rooms, picking up fluff and dirt as I went, and thinking that my father couldn't have made our house more different to his old one if he'd tried.

***

In the hospital, Aunt Gillian's plumping up my father's pillow. I find myself wondering if it's greasy after being under his head for four days straight. My father would hate that, but maybe they already changed it.

"Open your eyes, Edward," Aunt Gillian murmurs. "We're all waiting for you." She looks around at me. "Might as well try," she says.

I force a smile. I want to say: No. I know you're worried, but he can't open his eyes 'til I've got all the answers. Not now I'm doing something about it.

A nurse comes into the room. "Time to move the patient," she says.

171

"Do you have to?" Aunt Gillian says. "I've just made him comfortable." She sticks her lower lip out, like an irritable child.

"I'm afraid I do, yes," the nurse says. "It's to prevent atelectasis and pneumonia, and bedsores."

"What's… " Aunt Gillian begins.

"Need some help?" I ask.

"Go on," she says. "But don't let the doctors know I roped you into it."

We turn my father onto one side. I feel like flinching when I touch him – his skin is so warm and yielding. I have to set my jaw and pretend he's someone else. The other two don't notice.

I can probably count on one hand the number of times there was physical contact between me and my father after I went to school. Much like the number of times he called me up. I suppose he called my grandmother about as often.

He called that summer, the night before he arrived, but just to let us know he'd be with us by late afternoon.

My grandmother waited for him downstairs, in front of the Wimbledon final. I lay on my stomach in the first-floor hallway, listening to the muted thwack of tennis balls and excitement from the crowds. When the crunch and spray of gravel came, I drew back from the top of the stairs. A key turned in the front door; I heard footsteps as my grandmother came out of the living-room. "Edward."

"Hello, Mother."

There was a small, dry, kissing sound.

"How are you?"

"Fine. How's Tallulah?"

"Delightful."

"Where is she?"

"I haven't got a clue."

"I distinctly remember asking you to keep an eye on her, Mother."

"Stop fussing, Edward. The girl's not as foolish as she looks."

I had to hold in a sneeze, and missed most of what my father said back.

"… damage. Hardly a candidate for your particular brand of attention."

"No need to be uncivil, Edward. Come and have a drink. That hideous man is going to win Wimbledon."

"Agassi?"

Her voice got louder. "I'm sure Tallulah will be along shortly to say hello."

I lingered on the top step for a while before going downstairs. My father and grandmother were in the living-room, sitting in their usual spots.

"Hello, Tallulah," my grandmother said, looking at me over the rim of her glass.

"Hi."

"How has your summer been so far?" my father asked.

I shrugged.

"I thought we could have a belated birthday celebration for you. Is there anything in particular you'd like to do?"

"Not really."

"We can ask Cook to make you a cake," my grandmother said.

"Don't worry about it," I said. "I don't want to do anything."

"You've got to do something," my father said, impatiently.

"Don't force her to celebrate if she doesn't want to, Edward," my grandmother said.

"You're not helping, Mother."

"Tallulah doesn't want to have a birthday party. Surely that's all there is to it."

"Tallulah is still a child."

"I'm going outside," I said.

I felt prickles of anger all over my skin as I crossed the lawn to the oak trees and started to climb one. The bark scratched the palms of my hands and my bare legs. I shimmied up to the lowest branch and sat there. I hated grown-ups and the world they ran. My father didn't care about me and none of my teachers cared about me, apart from Mr Hicks. They wanted me to fit in and pretend to be happy as if nothing had happened. Even Malkie hadn't bothered to come and see me. I lay back along the branch, steadying myself with my hands, and kicked my feet against the trunk of the tree. After a while my father came out and stood beneath me. "I'm sorry, Tallulah," he said. "I didn't mean to upset you."

I looked down at him.

"But these things are important," he said. "Evelyn's gone, but we can't give up."

"How *did* Mum die?" I asked, surprising myself.

My father shook his head. "I don't think that's an appropriate conversation to have right now."

"Why not?"

"Because you shouldn't dwell on these things."

"I should know," I said. I looked back up through the branches.

He sighed. "Your mother was hit by a car."

"But she wasn't dead straight away, was she?"

"No."

"So how did she actually die? Why couldn't you save her?"

He took a while to answer. I kept staring at the sky. "She died of an aneurysm, caused by trauma to the skull. There was nothing I could do."

"Was Uncle Jack there?"

My father's voice changed. "How did you know about that?" He took a step forward. "Had he come around before?"

"You answer me first."

We were silent for a moment, eyeing each other. I put my feet against the trunk and pushed hard. It didn't move, but the strain felt good. I could tell my father didn't want to talk too much about that day in case he revealed something. In my mind, he'd already slipped up by saying there was nothing he could do – my father had always been able to do something. That was why there had been so many missed parties, and dinners, and ballet performances. Because he was needed elsewhere – to save someone.

Eventually he put his hands in his pockets and sighed. "You don't have to have a birthday party if you don't want to," he said. "If there's nothing else, I'll go back inside."

I stand back from the bed. I have to stop myself from wiping my hands on my jeans.

"All good for another few hours," the nurse says to my father. They talk to him like he's listening, like Aunt Gillian does.

"Shouldn't he have woken up by now?" Aunt Gillian asks.

"Recovery times can be different," the nurse says, soothingly. She looks down at his chart and frowns slightly. "Although it has been nearly a week – we've rather lost track of time, here, haven't we?" She bends over my father. "Now, Dr Park. We're very busy and we need this bed." She winks at me. "I'll be back in a few hours to turn him again."

"How did he feel?" Aunt Gillian asks me when she's gone.

"What?"

"When you were moving him."

"Fine," I say. "Like a person."

"I keep worrying that he'll have gone. And no one will notice."

"That won't happen."

"You never know," she says. "You hear about patients being forgotten in hospitals all the time."

"We're here," I say.

Her face relaxes. "Yes," she says. "At least he has us."

That's more than he can say for me.

✳ ✳ ✳

I avoided my father for the next few days, making a point of getting up before him and spending all day in the oak tree, reading. And then he left and Aunt Gillian and Uncle George and the kids arrived, and Aunt Gillian tried to rope me into sorting out old boxes with her.

She found one full of my father's books on the top shelf of my wardrobe.

"Look how awful his handwriting was," she said, holding up a history exercise book. "Born to be a doctor."

A medical textbook caught my eye. I pulled it out of the box and flipped it open.

"Oh yes," Aunt Gillian said. "Our parents gave him that when he went to university." She put her hand up to pat her hair. "He was the only one of us to go, actually. Did you know that? Jack was going to, but didn't... " She looked around after mentioning his name, like it was going to make him appear.

I ran my finger down the contents page. The book seemed to cover every part of the body, every possible complication.

"Better move these somewhere less dusty," Aunt Gillian said.

I waited until I'd gone to my room that night before I put the textbook safely away in my suitcase. If I understood the medicine behind it, I told myself, I'd know for sure if my father was guilty or not. I didn't believe it was possible that he could save everyone else but not my mother. That couldn't be true.

My grandmother walked me to the bus station when it was time to go back to school. "Be good," she said, as I climbed onto the bus.

"Bye," I said, feeling strangely like crying.

I kept my head pressed against the window as the bus carried me further away from her, trying to think about the cold glass and nothing else. At the other end, I collected my suitcase from the luggage compartment and walked to school. I was the first back, apart from Edith, who came down to help me with my stuff.

"Thanks," I said, realising that I'd barely spoken to her before.

A couple of weeks later we were filing into assembly, and

a girl with a cherry-pink headband stuck her foot out and sent Edith crashing to the floor. A few students in my form stopped, unsure, but quickly started walking again, picking their way around her. I saw Cressida and the others already sitting down, crane their necks to see who'd fallen. Cressida mouthed the word 'Edith' and all of them started to laugh.

I stopped beside Edith and offered her my hand; her cheeks were dark red.

"Get into your seats, girls," our new form tutor hissed behind us. I felt a flash of anger at her, and everyone else. Edith walked in front of me, her hands dangling at her sides. We passed Cressida, and she said something that made Edith bring her hand up to her face like she'd been slapped. I gave Cressida a cool stare. Her eyes slid away from mine after a moment and she looked uncomfortable.

We were learning about the dangers of drugs that term. Abi was in the States, so I was paired with Edith.

"I wasn't listening last lesson," I told her.

"I know it," she said; her head was bent down a couple of inches away from the desk and her hair had fallen over her face like a curtain. "Don't you care about your grades?"

"Do you?"

"My parents would kill me if I got a 'C'."

"My dad wouldn't," I said. "We hardly talk."

I could see her wince out of the corner of my eye; she must have remembered my mother's accident.

Our teacher set us a quiz. Edith got every question right and we won book vouchers worth five pounds each.

"You can have mine," I said to her that evening.

"Okay," she said.

I was starting to realise that she was easier to be around than Cressida, who I avoided even more now. I spent most of my time in the library, poring over my father's book. I was sure I'd find something that could have saved my mother. I started off reading the section about skull fractures, depressed and linear, and then the one on aneurysms. I couldn't really understand more than a few sentences, and reading about the brain made my own thump behind my eyes, reminding me it was there. Maybe aneurysms were genetic. Maybe I would fall and bump my head and die, like my mother had done. I flicked through the pages until I got to the lungs, then the heart. I liked the way the lungs looked like two birdcages; I liked the heart. Unlike its cartoon-shape, it was square-ish and smooth, without the sharp point at the bottom, although there was still a vague arch at the top. I drew doodles on my planner; my heart came out messy and stumpy-looking, with both vena cavas sawn off to give a cross-section.

"That's gross," Cressida said when she saw the pictures. "What's your problem, Tallulah?" She tossed her hair and stared at me, her eyes were cold and flat.

My social decline happened almost overnight. Suddenly, whoever I sat next to would find some excuse to move elsewhere, until finally I was placed in the middle of the front row, by myself. I spent lunchtimes alone too, listening to other kids snigger about me. I knew Cressida was making up rumours. I didn't know what she was saying, but I hoped it wasn't about sharing a bed with my twin brother.

I had a growth spurt and shot up almost a foot higher than anyone else in the year, even the boys. I felt gangly and ridiculous. I was given braces; when they took the braces off they gave me a retainer to wear and said I would need it for the rest of my life. I threw it into a bin on the way back to school.

My father was barely in touch. I didn't really want to talk to him, either. I couldn't prove that the accident was his fault, even with what he'd said to the police, or that he should have done anything different after my mother had been hit. But I knew all about *our* relationship.

At least with all the reading I'd picked something up about biology. We started a module on the human body, and I was getting B's, and, one time, a B+. Now that I was off bounds, the only person willing to be my lab partner was Edith. She liked maths and brussels sprouts, I found out, and didn't like art. She wore a necklace with a St Christopher pendant that her great aunt had given to her because epilepsy ran in their family, and he was the patron saint of epileptics.

Edith's father was a banker and her mother was an interior decorator. She had a younger brother, who she hated with a passion, and a girl-gerbil called Zorro who she loved.

"I've got a cat called Mr Tickles," I said. "But I haven't seen him for ages."

Edith started tagging along with me wherever I went. At first, Cressida made snide comments whenever we walked past, but after a while, she went silent. I'd almost forgotten about her by summer term, until we came back into the dorm after a Friday Prep and she was sitting on her bed, looking pissed off. "Do me a favour," she said, when we walked in, "and just hang out somewhere else, yeah?"

"Why don't you?" I asked. "We sleep here too, remember?"

"I'm grounded," she said, giving me a dirty look. "The Housemistress found my cigarettes. Someone must have grassed me up."

"It wasn't me, I swear," Edith said.

"Was it you?" Cressida asked me.

"Nope." I shrugged. "Maybe one of your sheep stabbed you in the back."

"It *was* you, wasn't it?" she said, flushing. "I can tell."

"Why would I bother?"

"You're jealous."

"Unlikely."

"Come on, Tal," Edith said. "Let's go downstairs."

I could feel a bubble of anger inside me that wasn't all about Cressida and her stupid long legs and big tits. If I'd never been sent here I wouldn't be in this situation now, I thought; if my mother had never run out in the road that day, I wouldn't have a huge hole inside me.

"No," I said. "I want to stay here."

"You're jealous that people like me," Cressida said. "'Cos

179

I'm not a weirdo or a lesbian."

"Shut. Up."

"It's not your fault really," Cressida said. "You don't have any female role models now your mum's dead. Of course you're gonna dress badly and… "

I grabbed a handful of her hair and tugged it until I felt it ripping out of her scalp. She was screaming *"Fucking bitch,"* at the top of her lungs and swinging at me. I dodged her arm, but then she was trying to kick me, and one of them landed. I let go of her hair and got behind her, twisting her arm back.

"You crazy fucking bitch," she screamed. "You're in *so* much trouble."

"Whatever," I said, panting.

The Housemistress was called. I was put on toilet duty for a week.

"See what happens when you try to touch me, lesbian?" Cressida said.

"You want me to break your nose?" I asked.

She backed away from me, covering her face with her hands. "You're perfect for Edith," she said. "You're both freaks."

I took a step towards her and she fled. If I acted unstable, I realised, people would be more likely to leave me alone.

After that I was definitely stuck with Edith. Starr wasn't too happy about it – she cornered me on the back staircase a few days later and told me I was turning myself into a social pariah. "It's fine that you beat up Cressida," she said. "She's a little snot. But don't be such a weirdo with everyone else – they're not all bad."

I shrugged.

"I can't protect you, you know."

"Please just leave me alone."

"Tal… "

"Just fuck off, Starr."

"Fine," she said. "You get your wish."

***

In 1993, someone called Bill Clinton became the President of the United States, getting everyone excited, even in Britain. I wondered briefly what Malkie thought of it, but that just made me sad that I'd never see him again.

Over the next year and a bit, more and more things that I didn't understand seemed to happen in the world. All over school, people were talking about Fred West being arrested and Ayrton Senna's death and other names I'd never heard of. Not that they were talking to me, anyway. By September 1994, the beginning of year nine, I was the most isolated I'd ever been. Starr still avoided me. My teachers had all reached breaking point with me, apart from Mr Hicks and my biology teacher, who thought I was enthusiastic and average. My father had spent a few days with me at my grandmother's that summer, where they both pretty much ignored me, although my grandmother had at least bothered to haul me up for slouching. My father's communication was confined to when we weren't in the same town – brief letters about the hospital and Mr Tickles and the weather in London.

Dear Tallie,

I'm sure you don't need filling in on everything, he wrote, *so I'll be quick. They've dug up the street to mend a broken water-pipe and the old sycamore tree outside the house had to go. Kathy and her parents are moving – she said it's a shame she won't get to say goodbye to you – apparently they've accepted an offer and the buyer's quite keen to move in soon. They're going out to Dubai to stay with an aunt until they decide what to do next. I passed on your regards – hope that was alright. I didn't know if you two were still close – you haven't seen her much since you left Primary, have you? People move on, I suppose.*

Hospital's busy, as usual. The cat is being bullied by

another tom. I keep hearing them fighting at night. If they keep it up I might have to start shutting him in – the noise is awful.

Hope everything's going well for you.

Best,

Dad

I started to write a letter for Kathy, then gave up. I hovered between tearing up my father's letter and keeping it as proof of how little he understood or cared about me. I tore it up in the end, and flushed it down the loo. Afterwards, I stood looking at my eyes in the mirror, amazed at how dry they were. No more mother, no more Kathy. My father would probably kill off Mr Tickles next.

In the second week of term I was held back after a textiles class for not having my hair tied up. Edith had had to go in to lunch without me, so I was standing in a queue at the canteen by myself. Groups of older kids were jostling around me, shouting insults and in-jokes above my head. I saw Toby Gates and his friends just in front of me in the queue, flirting with some girls in the year above. The girls were all giggling and tossing their hair around; I tried not to be noticed. Someone behind me stumbled, and pushed me into the group ahead. I caught one of them with my elbow, and held on to someone's shirt to stop myself from falling.

"Watch it," the girl said. She jerked away from me, making me stumble again.

"Fucking Juniors," someone else said, and everyone laughed.

"It wasn't my fault," I said, my face burning.

"Don't speak until you're spoken to," the first girl said, and pinched my arm. They all laughed again.

"Don't do that," I said. I glared at the pincher. Out of the corner of my eye I noticed Toby half-turn away, grinning awkwardly.

"She's gonna cry," one of Toby's friends said. "Look at her… "

"I'm not," I said, but now that everyone was saying it, I felt like I might. I left the queue. I heard one of the girls call something after me, then more laughter.

I got to my next class hungry and in a bad mood; Edith tried to talk to me when we were sitting down, but I ignored her, and she descended into a hurt silence. Our maths teacher arrived with a mug of coffee and a pile of marked homework sheets. "My hands are full, so everyone line up at the front to collect your homework," she said.

I stood up too quickly, catching my foot on the leg of my chair, which clattered backwards, making everyone turn their heads to look at me.

"Tallulah," the teacher said, frowning. "Pick up that chair at once."

I'd been halfway down to pick it up already, but when she told me to do it I stood up again.

"Tallulah, I said pick it up."

"No," I said.

The teacher gave me a hard stare; I returned it and she looked away first. "Fine," she said. "If you're going to act like a child you can be treated like a child." She tore a detention slip from her register and started scribbling on it.

"No," I said again, and flipped my desk over.

Pens and pieces of paper rained down around me. Someone screamed, then laughed and everyone drew back.

"Jonathan, go and get the Headmaster *immediately*," my teacher shouted.

"See ya," I said, strolling towards the door. I watched my hand turn the knob and my feet carry me outside, but my brain wasn't connecting with what was happening.

After a moment, I heard footsteps run after me, and then Edith was at my elbow. "Tallie, what are you *doing*?"

"They're gonna expel me anyway."

"They won't," she said, unconvincingly.

"I'm not going back." I pushed through the doors of the school entrance and started off down the driveway towards the school gates, my pulse gradually slowing.

"I'm coming with you then," Edith said. She linked arms with me. "Where are we going?"

"Who cares," I said. "We could join the circus, I guess."

Edith stopped.

"I think there's one in town," I said. "I'll be a trapeze artist, you be one of the clowns."

"I don't want to be a clown," Edith said. She was nibbling the pendant of St Christopher nervously.

"Clean up after the elephants then, or something."

"You're being mean."

"Sorry, Ed," I said. "You can't run away though – your parents would kill you."

"Your dad will too."

"He won't even notice."

Edith started crying. I walked away.

"Tallie please don't go," she called after me.

"I have to," I said.

They found me an hour later, sitting by the side of the road, waiting. There was no point carrying on – I knew Edith would have told them which direction I'd gone in.

∗ ∗ ∗

"I'm going to Georgia's for dinner," Aunt Gillian says. "I'm sure she'd love to see you too."

"Maybe next time," I say. My head's too full of my father and Jack and Toby right now.

We take the lift down together, hug outside the hospital, and she steps into the road, hailing a taxi. "See you tomorrow, darling."

"See you."

As soon as she's out of sight I check my phone, although

I already know Malkie hasn't called yet, I would have felt it vibrate. Slow down, I tell myself, he said a couple of days. At least it'll give me time to work out what I'm going to say.

I don't know if he'll want to tell me anything though. I don't even know if he'll show up – the Uncle Jack I remember never seemed to do anyone any favours, he was too angry all the time. Which I guess is how I could have been described back then, too.

∗ ∗ ∗

The school wanted to call my father.

"Don't bother," I told them.

"Who should we call instead?" the school secretary asked. She was standing with a neatly squared fingernail pressed down on the telephone hook, the handset cradled between her chin and shoulder and gold bangles clinking on her wrist. "We have to call *someone*."

My grandmother blew into school. From the window I saw her stop the headmaster on his way from the car park to his office; we could all hear snatches of her shouting at him. The headmaster must have realised this, because he tried to steer her inside, taking hold of her elbow. My grandmother shook him off and started thrusting her finger into his chest. The school secretary tutted behind me. "What on earth does she think she's doing?" she asked.

"He shouldn't have tried to grab her," I said.

She gave me a dark look.

It was agreed that I could spend some time living with my grandmother, and that she would get a private tutor for me.

"Tallulah's grades have never been very impressive," Mr Purvis said, flicking through my academic reports. "She's failing maths and physics, and she's only just scraping by in French. I don't even have a Latin report for her... " He looked at me over the rims of his glasses. "Tallulah, have you attended Latin at all this year?"

"No," I said.

He faced me for a moment, then cleared his throat and shot a look at my grandmother. My grandmother stared back at him. "Moving on then," he said. "Just about the only subjects she does okay in are biology and art."

"Art," my grandmother snorted.

Mr Purvis stood, came around the front of his desk, and leaned back against it. "The way things are going... " He rearranged his tie. "We have an academic reputation to uphold, and she has a lot of catching up to do in these next two years before she sits her exams. Perhaps you can persuade her to apply herself. Now, if you'll excuse me, I have a meeting to get to." He ushered us out of his office and closed the door.

My grandmother pursed her lips at me, and told the secretary to order us a taxi.

We didn't speak on the ride back to her house. My grandmother hummed something under her breath, I had the window rolled down and the wind blew my hair across my face. Already I felt my shoulders lifting.

When we arrived, I turned left at the top of the staircase out of habit and walked towards my old bedroom. Then I stopped, and went back. I put my suitcase in the room that my parents had always shared, showered in the en-suite then unpacked my clothes into the dresser and went downstairs to find my grandmother.

She was sitting in the living-room, drinking. "Gin and tonic." She waved it at me. "Want one?"

"Alright," I said. I hadn't drunk gin before. At school we'd had vodka a couple of times, straight, after the lights were out and the Housemistress' footsteps had died away. It had burned my throat and my insides, and the hairs in my nose had felt like they were curling up in protest. My first cigarette had been just as unpleasant, but after a while I'd stopped noticing how harsh the smoke felt and enjoyed the rhythm of the inhale, exhale.

My grandmother poured me a small measure of gin and a lot of tonic, and dropped two ice-cubes and a slice of lemon into the glass. "For beginners," she said.

"Thanks."

I sipped my drink. It tasted much nicer than the vodka, which hadn't even had a label on the bottle. My grandmother was humming again, not looking at me. "How old are you?" she asked suddenly.

"Thirteen and a half."

"It's a wonder it took you so long to run off, really." She took another sip. "Well, you're here for a few months. See if I can't straighten you out, or something along those lines."

I took another slurp of my drink. My grandmother raised an eyebrow. "May I ask, however, why you called me and not your father?"

"Dunno," I lied.

"Hruh," she said, looking at her glass. "I forgot how life for young people is merely a series of spontaneous decisions."

There was a silence.

"Are you gonna call my father?"

"Don't worry about that," she said, waving her hand. "I'll smooth things out with Edward." She got up and headed for the door. "You can amuse yourself now."

* * *

If I'd found my grandmother's house shabby before, the few years that had passed had turned it into more of a decaying shell. Window panes had fallen out in several bedrooms, plaster was crumbling from the ceiling. Instead of tackling the problems, my grandmother had shut off large areas; in a house of well over twenty rooms, we lived in the kitchen, the living-room, my bedroom and hers. The whole place creaked in the cold. Gusts of wind prised themselves through cracks and vents to hug us as we went about our business indoors. The ceilings were too high, and except for in the hallway, there were no carpets. Every morning, after my shower, I felt steam rise from my skin when I stepped out of the bathtub; no matter how frantically I rubbed myself with my towel, my body was goose-pimpled within seconds. My teeth chattered constantly. My grandmother didn't believe in central heating – she drew the green velvet drapes in the living-room and told me to put another jumper on.

We ate every meal together, and aside from the noises made by the house, we ate in silence. A few days after I'd arrived, I cracked during breakfast. My grandmother had been snapping the pages of the newspaper open and I'd been staring at the ceiling, which was developing a large brown stain, like a dirty tributary across the white.

"Don't you think it's kind of unsafe living like this?" I asked.

"When I want your opinion," my grandmother said, acidly, "I'll send you to structural engineering school."

I bent over my bowl, playing with my cereal, splashing milk around to mask the burning I felt in my cheeks. My grandmother watched me for a moment before saying, "If you don't want it now, you can finish it for lunch."

I shoved the bowl in the fridge and stomped upstairs. "I hope you find something dead in yours," I said, as soon as I was out of earshot.

I decided to carry out a survey of the rooms. Whatever my grandmother thought, my father and Aunt Gillian would probably agree that some upkeep was needed. That was how I came across the library – most of the rooms I'd seen before, but once, poking at a door I'd previously assumed to lead to a cupboard, I felt it swing open, dislodging a ton of dust. Books covered three of the four walls; the fourth wall had a bay window with red and gold curtains tied up with red velvet ropes, and there was a fireplace with a poker, coal scuttle, shovel and brush arranged neatly in one corner. The air inside smelled odd – maybe mould – but it was in surprisingly good shape in comparison to the other rooms.

A few afternoons later, when the tutor had left for the day, I was flicking through *Gulliver's Travels*. I'd chosen it because it had a cool picture of a ship on the front, half submerged beneath cartoon waves. I was only a couple of chapters in when my grandmother burst into the room, looking thunderous.

"What are you doing in here?"

"Reading. I found it on the shelf."

"Leave," she snapped.

"But… "

"Get out of here immediately."

"Aren't I allowed to read?"

She snatched the book away from me.

"You can't do that."

Her face was red and her eyes were shimmering, as if she was about to cry, but she didn't, and she didn't speak again.

"Sorry." I said after a moment. "I didn't know… "

After a moment I left. I skulked upstairs for most of the afternoon before going to find her. She was sitting on the sofa in the living-room, her eyes closed and her legs stretched out and crossed at the ankles.

"I'm sorry for doing something I shouldn't," I said.

"You weren't to know."

"Are you still angry with me?"

She opened her eyes. "No, I'm not," she said, finally. "But I don't want you snooping around in there."

"Why?"

"I have my reasons."

Like – you're crazy? I lingered. "Can I sit down here with you?"

"I'm going to watch television," she said. "You can stay or you can go, but you have to be quiet."

My grandmother watched *Murder, She Wrote* regularly. She liked Angela Lansbury's perm and disapproving looks. I didn't want to go back to my parents' old room and lie on the bed by myself, so I stayed. We watched as Angela's character, the mystery writer, tramped all around the murder scene, interrupting police, shaking her head and picking up clues. My grandmother waved her drink around and shouted at the screen: "No, not there… Why don't you *think*, woman? It's not going to be the schoolteacher is it?"

When it was over she turned the TV off and leaned back into the sofa, lighting a cigarette. "What did you think of it?"

"Does that happen every episode?" I asked.

"Does what happen?"

"Does she always find dead bodies?"

"There has to be a murder, doesn't there?" She took a long drag.

"But that's not even realistic," I said. "How many episodes have there been? How many dead bodies has she found?"

"There are more dead people in the world now than living," my grandmother said, blowing out smoke.

"Hhmm."

"Are worried you've shacked up with a madwoman?"

"No," I lied.

"Go on, I know you brats used to make up stories about me," she said, waving the smoke away.

"No we didn't."

"I suppose I deserved them. I was always standoff-ish."

"I guess you were a little bit."

She smiled wryly. "That's better. Your mother always said honesty came naturally to you."

I blinked, surprised by the mention of my mother.

"I'm going to start on lunch," my grandmother said. "Are you coming?"

I looked at the cobwebs drooping from the ceiling, and the dust-streaked windows. My mother had been here; she'd sat underneath the cobwebs, and talked about me to my grandmother, apparently.

"I'm going outside for a bit."

"As you wish."

I went out and played badminton in the garden, ducking underneath the net I'd set up between two hawthorn trees the day before, trying to reach the shuttlecock's downward swoop before it hit the ground. Maybe my grandmother was the only person who was actually nice to my mother, then, I thought, although I couldn't really remember them talking, except during the picnic.

I hit a particularly mean overhand, scrambled across, and the shuttlecock sailed over my outstretched racquet and into the water behind me. "Shit."

I parted the reeds along the edge of the lake with my racquet; if the shuttlecock was there, I'd never find it. I scuffed my shoe along the cracked wood of the jetty, trailing my racquet in the water. Just beyond the edge of the landing stage, something was glinting in the water, blurred by the ripples. I lay on my stomach and tried to focus on it; it seemed to be round and small and shiny. I tried to scoop it up with my racquet, but the water was already way too deep. I stood up and kicked off my shoes, closing my eyes as I jumped.

The cold made my heart stumble. I opened my eyes – everything was soft and muted, shimmering in the waves I'd created. Below me I saw our rowing boat shift then settle again in the shadows; we'd sunk it a few summers before, trying to drive a mast into it. Something slimy wrapped itself around my wrist and I struggled frantically, until I realised it was just a reed. I doggy-paddled in one spot. I could hear the wood of the jetty groaning, and a faint buzzing that I couldn't identify.

I dived towards the shiny object. Down there, it didn't look so shiny. My fingers closed around it and I swam upwards, kicking until I broke the surface.

Now I could make out what the other noise had been. My grandmother was running down the lawn, her long legs eating up the grass and wisps of grey hair tumbling out of her bun. "I'm coming," she was yelling. "I'm coming."

I heaved myself up and out of the water and stood there shivering until she reached me.

"What happened? Did you fall?"

"I jumped."

Her mouth fell open, then she stretched out her hand and gripped me by the upper arm. "Let's get you inside."

"What on earth were you doing, diving into the lake at this time of year?" she asked, when I was changed and sitting in the living-room. Just this once, she'd allowed a fire to be lit, hauling logs from the gardening shed into the house. "Are you ill?" She clamped her hand against my forehead.

"No," I said, pushing her away. "I'm fine." I took a gulp of my tea. "I thought I saw something."

"What did you see?"

"Nothing."

"So help me, my girl, if this is your way of paying me back… "

"It's got nothing to do with you," I said, and I was taken aback to find tears coursing down my face. I opened my palm and showed her the aluminium ring pull I'd dredged up.

My grandmother shook her head at me.

"I thought it was my mum's wedding ring."

"Why would your mother's wedding ring be in the lake?"

"I don't know, no reason," I said, sniffing and sipping at my tea. I just wanted it to be, I thought, and then I'd have something of hers for myself.

"Tallulah, you can't dive into the lake in the middle of winter – you could make yourself sick."

I brushed my cheeks with the heel of my hand. "I won't do it again."

"Good."

"Thanks for not being angry."

"Of course I'm not angry."

It's how my father would have dealt with it though.

"Thanks anyway," I said.

She stroked a lock of hair away from my face. "Anytime."

∗ ∗ ∗

A week later, I was leaning out of my bedroom window, smoking a cigarette I'd stolen from my grandmother, when I heard the doorbell. My grandmother answered the door and a man's voice filled the hallway.

"Tallulah," she called.

I sprayed deodorant on myself generously then went downstairs, praying it wasn't my father. My heart did a funny dance when I saw Malkie standing in front of the door. We smiled awkwardly at each other.

"What's wrong with the two of you?" my grandmother asked. "Cat got your tongues?"

"What've you done with your hair, doll?" Malkie asked.

Earlier that day my grandmother had marched me into the bathroom, pushed me onto the toilet lid and taken her scissors to my hair, rapping me on the head when I swore. Now I was fringe-less and sleek locks fell in waves around my face.

I ran my fingers through my new cut. "It's gone," I said.

"I can see that," he said.

"Don't you like it?"

"It's nice. Just makes you look a little… older."

"Hruh," my grandmother said. "I think you'll find the word you're searching for, Malcolm, is *feminine*. And Tallulah, don't stand chatting on the stairs. Come down and greet our guest properly."

"Hi, *Malcolm*," I said, offering him my hand. "How do you do?"

"Very well, thank you," Malkie said, taking my hand in his. I giggled. My grandmother gave us a cold look. "Malcolm is going to be teaching you piano," she said. "Apparently this was a long-standing agreement." She looked at her watch. "You know where the piano is, Tallulah."

I took Malkie through to the dining-room and sat on the piano stool; he drew up a chair next to me. "First," he said, "we gotta get your posture right." He placed one hand on my shoulder, and the other on my lower back. "Drop your shoulders," he said. "And straighten your back."

I tried to drop my shoulders. Across the hallway we could hear my grandmother shouting at the TV: "What's this nonsense about ghosts – come on, woman, it's not going to be a ghost, is it?"

"Why are you really here?" I asked.

"I'm a friendly face, and Matilda thinks you need one right now." He took a penny out of his pocket. "So here I am, if you ever need to talk. On the other hand, as we're sitting at the piano, why don't we give it a whirl?"

He took my right hand and placed it on the keys with the penny on top of it. "Move your fingers," he said. "Play some notes."

I played a few notes. The penny slipped off my hand. Malkie picked it up and put it back. I played again; he caught it this time before it hit the floor.

"The trick," he said, "is to move your fingers without moving your hands too much. It should come from your wrists and arms."

I stared at him. "How can I move my fingers and wrists without moving my hands?"

"You gotta use gravity."

"What?"

"It's all about control," he said. "You gotta control your fingers, but you gotta let other stuff help you."

"Riiiiight," I said.

He poked my back again. "Don't slouch. Why don't you practise single notes with the penny on your hand? We can start with middle C."

I took him to the front door when he left. "Can I ask you a question?"

"Sure."

"Did you meet Uncle Jack in prison?"

"Nope," Malkie said. "And that's not a very polite question to ask, young lady."

"Sorry," I said, squirming inside.

"I met him in about 1974," Malkie said. "Your aunt too. She was wearing flared trousers back then, and neat little waistcoats."

I tried to picture Aunt Vivienne in flares and a waistcoat, but I couldn't.

194

"And your mom – she looked like a blonder Raquel Welch. Jeez she was pretty."

"Who was that?"

"Look her up, doll."

I paused. "Why did you all stop... being friends?"

"What makes you say that?"

"I didn't know you when I was younger. Or Uncle Jack."

Malkie shook his head. "Life gets in the way."

"But why?"

"It happens. Make sure you do your practice."

When the front door closed my grandmother came out into the hallway. "How was it?" she asked.

"Playing the piano hurts," I said.

"Hruh," she said, and went back into the living-room.

∗ ∗ ∗

My grandmother liked soups, and since the cook had left to run a nearby pub kitchen just before I came to stay, I was drafted in to help. I peeled the vegetables, and she chopped them up, her hands moving fast, like water running out of a tap. We had pea soup, carrot soup, ham and lentil soup, chicken broth and Irish stew, although they all tasted mostly of salt, which my grandmother used liberally.

The night after my first piano lesson, we were making carrot soup. I was peeling the carrots and my grandmother was drumming her fingers on the counter. I never peeled fast enough for her.

"I heard you asking Malkie some questions," she said.

"Yeah," I said. "I wanted to know stuff about my mum." I scraped my finger with the peeler. "Shit."

"If you must swear," my grandmother said, "say fuck. No one likes to think about excrement."

"Fuck," I said. "That hurts."

"You want to know anything else?"

"About Aunt Vivienne and Uncle Jack too, I guess."

"Ach, those two." She coughed.

"Why did you say it like that?"

"How exactly did I say it?"

"Like *those two*, like you were annoyed with them."

"Because they were troublesome when they were younger."

"Why?"

"It was in their nature I suppose." She put her hands on her hips. "Edward and Gillian were quiet, Vivienne and Jack were not. Much like someone else I could mention."

"But what did they do?"

"All manner of things."

"Like *what*?"

My grandmother looked at me out of the corner of her eye. "Albert used to say they were too close," she said eventually.

I pushed a pile of gleaming-bright carrots towards her; she brought the knife down hard on the first one, slicing off an end, and carried on until they were all done. She swept the carrot slices into the pan. "Garlic."

I brought over two cloves from the fridge and she crushed them with the side of her chopping knife. Her fingers picked the waxy yellow pieces out of their wrapping and threw them in the pan with the carrots.

"They spent all their time together. Thick as thieves – that's what their teachers used to call them. Just a euphemism for bullies, as far as I could make out."

"Who did they bully?"

"Anyone who wasn't in their little twosome. Edward, for one." She drizzled some olive oil into the pan and started to heat it up. "You know," she said, stirring the onions, "this soup might actually work."

"What about Dad then?" I asked.

She pointed her wooden spoon at me. "Well go on – ask."

"What was he like when he was the same age as me?" Or, why does he have such a problem with me?

"He was a very good boy."

"Is that it?"

196

"What do you mean, is that it? That's what he was," she said. "He was a very devoted child. Never left my side."

"That's not very interesting."

"Don't be such a fool, Tallulah," my grandmother said. "You don't have to be bad to be interesting." She turned the heat down. "We'll let that simmer for a while."

We ate in the kitchen that evening as we did every night. It was the only warm room in the house.

My grandmother poured herself a drink, laid the butter out and sliced a loaf of bread. I dipped a thick piece in my soup, weighing up a question in my mind. "Do you know where Uncle Jack is?" I asked eventually.

"I most certainly do not."

"You said at Mum's funeral that he was still in the country."

"Did I?"

"Is he?"

"I don't know, Tallulah. I haven't seen him in years."

"Because you don't like him?"

"Why on earth would you think that?"

"You don't sound like you do."

"What people say, and what they mean, are often two completely different things," she said, taking a spoonful of soup. "Pass the salt, please."

I fetched the salt and pepper from their place next to the cooker. "Aunt Vivienne never comes to visit by herself, does she?" I asked.

"No," my grandmother said.

"Don't you miss her?"

"She and I haven't spoken properly since she was sixteen." Her hand shook a little when she next lifted the spoon to her mouth.

"What happened?"

"She thinks I betrayed her," she said after a while. "My children had a tough childhood, I suppose, and Vivienne's never forgiven me for it. I would never have done it on purpose, though. It's a terrible thing to have to do, to let your

197

children walk away."

"Why does she think you betrayed her?"

"You can't always tell the true intentions behind a person's actions. And you don't always get on with the people who are most similar to yourself."

"Did you get on with Grandad?" I asked, wondering if that was what she meant by the children having a 'tough childhood'.

My grandmother pursed her lips. "He was crazy," she said. "He used to ride past my mother's farm at six in the morning on his horse and take me off with him." She looked down at her wedding ring. "I had to cling on for dear life."

I couldn't imagine my grandmother clinging on to anybody. "Do you miss *him*?" I asked.

"It's certainly different around here without him." She touched her face, just below the eye, and I pictured the children watching as my grandfather hit her there until she was bleeding and half-blind. "He was so strong-willed, your grandfather, like a hurricane – blowing in and out and taking what he wanted. I'd never met anyone like him."

"Do my dad and the others miss him? They never talk about him."

"I really wouldn't know how they feel," she said, and her voice had gotten harder.

∗ ∗ ∗

I call my boss to swap shifts the next day. He grumbles, but I don't give him time to say no. When I hang up, I sit in bed for a moment, trying to work up some energy. I'd rather risk looking like a stalker and go back to Gray's Inn than the hospital. But if Toby *does* agree to see me, it'll be better to wait until all this is over.

I sit underneath the open window with my father's old medical textbook propped up in my lap. I run my finger down the index page, and find it – *Atelectasis: where alveoli may collapse or close, with the consequence of reduced or absent gas exchange.* In other words, it becomes difficult to breathe. *If left untreated, atelectasis can be fatal,* I read. *Smokers and the elderly are particularly vulnerable.*

I don't know how my grandmother escaped that particular fate; she was already wheezing heavily a month after I went to live with her. Although after our talk over the soup she started spending more time with me, so maybe I just hadn't noticed it before.

She started to ask me more about my father, and my relationship with him, lecturing me about his responsibility, and how much he needed my support as well. I thought about trying to explain what my father had been like – how he was always away. And how he'd changed after Uncle Jack showed up. And then that day. But I could never tell her that I'd thought he killed my mother. And by that point, the effort of talking for too long made her face turn a weird shade of purple, and something warned me never to get her riled up.

It was a relief sometimes to escape to a different room with my tutor, where she couldn't interrupt, and even more of a relief when Malkie turned up one Saturday morning, car keys jangling in his hand.

"I came to see if you wanted to run an errand with me?" he said. "I need to go into London, pick up my car from Dennis, my mechanic."

"What do you want me to do?"

"I'd enjoy the company. I could drive you back this evening."

"Yeah, cool."

"Don't you need to ask Matilda?"

My grandmother appeared behind me. "Ask me what?"

"It's really creepy when you do that," I told her.

"Thank you, Tallulah, I'll bear that in mind. Ask me what?"

"Can I go to London with Malkie to pick his car up?"

"That depends," my grandmother said. "When will you be back Malkie?"

"Not too late – scout's honour."

"As if I'd believe you were ever in the scouts," she said, but she nodded.

"Thanks, Grams," I said, and kissed her cheek.

We waited thirty minutes for the train. I hooked my fingers over the top of the station sign and swung from it, showing off in front of Malkie.

"Don't break your neck, doll," he said.

Malkie smoked a cigarette and had a staring contest with one of the cows from the field the other side of the second platform. "Moo," he called to her.

We sat in a carriage that was as empty as the station had been. I breathed onto the window and wrote my initials in the condensation. Little towns slid past in grey and green blurs until the rain came and dirtied the windows, obscuring the view.

At Euston, Malkie strode purposefully ahead; I trotted to keep up with him, sidestepping families and backpackers sitting on the plastic green floor of the main hall and the concrete plaza outside. Dennis was in Shepherds Bush, a long tube-ride away. When we turned up he came out to meet us, wiping his fingers on a towel. Malkie showed me the car. "See that?" he said, running his hand over the bonnet. "Isn't she a beauty?"

It was pink and baby blue, with headlamps that looked like frogs' eyes.

"Isn't it a bit... girly?" I asked.

"Shows how much you know," Malkie said, and pretended to take a swipe at me.

Dennis said he'd be hours yet, so we found a bench in a nearby park to sit on. Malkie rolled another cigarette and lit it; it stuck to his lower lip as he spoke. "How's it going at Matilda's, doll?"

"She's pretty cool."

"She's a swell lady," he said.

"Do you know anything about her and my grandfather?"

I asked him.

"What do you mean?"

I wondered if he knew about my grandmother's eye. I didn't want to be the one to spill the beans if not. "I just... don't," I ended, lamely.

"From what I heard, they had a complicated relationship," he said, tapping ash onto the ground.

"Who told you that?"

"Jacky."

"What did he say?"

"Just once, when we were roomin' together after he got out of the joint, Jacky got a fever." Malkie stubbed his cigarette out. "He was saying all kinds of crazy things, getting frantic about her being left alone with him. Course, it was gibberish. It was after your grandpa passed away."

"He said he didn't want Grandma to be left alone with him?"

"That's what I thought at the time."

I thought about how angry my grandmother had been at finding me in the library. Maybe that was where he'd hurt her. Maybe he'd done more than just damage her cornea. None of the family ever spent time in that room, and maybe that was why. I felt sick.

"Penny for them," Malkie said.

"Was Uncle Jack *afraid* of Grandad?"

"Well it sounds like your grandpa had a nasty temper."

"How nasty?"

"I'll tell you a story Viv told me," he said, lacing his fingers together. "When she was fourteen she had a fight with her old man. He knocked her out – broke her arm, two ribs and her jaw. They found three teeth in the fireplace." He coughed. "So sounds 'bout as nasty as it gets."

"Oh."

"You okay, hon? You're looking a little pale."

"I thought it was just Grandma he hit." I tried to picture Vivienne as a fourteen-year-old, but I could only see Starr,

201

and I felt something inside me go out to my adolescent aunt. "I'm glad I never met him."

"That's 'cos you're smart."

I made a face at him, but I didn't feel sick anymore.

"Your aunt was a little high when she told me that story," Malkie said. "So she could have been confused, I guess. But I got the sense it was true. And my old man knocked us around too – maybe that's why she felt she could talk about it with me."

"What happened to *your* dad?"

Malkie chuckled. "One day I realised I was nearly twice his size, and I stopped being scared. Then he died. And I will say this – you remember people differently after they're gone."

Dennis wasn't finished until ten o'clock that night, and it was nearly eleven by the time we made it onto the motorway.

"Matilda's gonna skin me," Malkie said, peering through the windshield.

"I'll stick up for you."

"Thanks, sugar." He turned the heating up and fiddled with the knob on the glovebox, then slammed his fist against it and it sprang open. "Here, wanna mint?"

"No thanks."

"You can go to sleep, if you want."

"I'm not sleepy," I said, yawning again. "Tell me about yourself."

"What about me?"

"Where do you live?"

"I've got a few places I crash at," he said. "Nothing fancy like Matilda's."

"Where *have* you lived?"

"Canada, obviously," Malkie said. "Birmingham. Glasgow. I've lived in Spain – I was there for five years or so. I went there after Paris, and I went to Paris around the time that your mom and Vivienne were moving in together, just after their flat-warming party." He grinned to himself. "I seem to remember waking up in the bath."

"Did my mum and Vivienne… suit each other?"

"Sure. Evie was real good at cheering Viv up when she was in one of her moods."

"Oh." I thought about teenage, mistreated Vivienne hardening into moody, adult Vivienne, and wondered how my mother had been able to ever cheer her up.

"They were pretty tight. It's a shame they fell out later."

"Why did they?"

"Dunno, doll. I wasn't around by that point."

I laid my head against the passenger window and watched colours appear and disappear in the rain drops on the side-door mirror. Malkie switched on the radio and started crooning along to some country classics; within five minutes, I was fast asleep.

✳ ✳ ✳

'They're not all real, you know.'

It's no wonder Aunt Vivienne is temperamental, really.

I flick through a few more pages in the book, reading a paragraph here and there, then shut it. I suppose by definition a medical textbook has to be about all the things that can go wrong with our bodies, but it's bringing back bad memories. Why wouldn't my grandmother trust me enough to tell me about my grandfather – was she ashamed she'd let it happen? Then again, I never told her how I felt about my father. If I'd been open with her, maybe she could have made it better. Or maybe not – she hadn't managed to mend her relationship with Aunt Vivienne, after all.

After a moment of hesitation, I put the textbook on my bedside table and go into the kitchen to turn the shower on.

Eleven

I make my way to the hospital early. It's busier and brighter than yesterday. A young nurse is being shouted at by a doctor as I walk past the Intensive Care desk. I'm comfortable enough to sit alone in my father's room now, reading the notices on the wall – fire safety instructions, a reminder to wash hands regularly and a newspaper clipping pinned directly above my father's bed. I stand up to peer at it more closely and realise it's a clipping about him, some grateful journalist had a relative in my father's hands, and has written about the calm, professional care received by both patient and visiting family. Why was he so strong for everyone else and so utterly useless with me?

It's a relief to go to the bathroom, away from the beeps and the whirring and all the hospital gear; I dawdle in there, rinsing my hands for ages. On the way back, I stop at the open door to another ward. A doctor is doing the rounds with two nurses. One of them must be in training. She looks young and nervous and when the doctor asks her to take blood from one of the patients, I think she's going to faint.

"You've done it before, haven't you?" the doctor asks.

"Yes," she says.

"Good." He hands the chart to the older nurse, gives the room another quick scan and walks out, smiling cheerfully at me as he passes.

"Sister?" the patient says. "One of you's a sister, right?"

The junior nurse is opening the bag with a fresh needle inside; her hands are shaking. The older nurse puts her hand on the younger one's back and leaves it there. "Are you ready?" she asks.

The younger one pulls herself up and sets her jaw. "Yes," she says.

"No," the patient says, he looks terrified.

"Now," the older nurse says to him, "this isn't going to hurt. Nurse Salter is very competent, I promise. Top of her year at uni."

"Christ," he says.

Nurse Salter sits next to him. "Hold your arm out, please," she says. He looks away as she ties the tourniquet and sterilises the area with an alcohol wipe. "There'll be a very little sting as the needle goes in," she says. "But it'll be over soon."

He whimpers softly when she inserts the needle, then she's pushing a tube into the hub, filling it, and the needle's out. She puts a cotton pad against the puncture, applying pressure to hold it to the arm, and tape to keep it in place, then discards the needle and labels the tube.

"Very nice work," the older nurse says. "Both of you."

"Thanks," Nurse Salter says, shakily. She and the patient have both gone grey again.

"We'll get you some water," the older nurse says.

"What about a whisky?" he asks.

They all laugh, and I'm strangely jealous. I do a lot of the same jobs as nurses already: listening to complaints, making small jokes, cleaning up puke. But nurses connect with people, they make a difference.

The two leave the room, noticing me like the doctor did earlier.

"You're Dr Park's daughter, aren't you?" the older nurse says.

"Yep."

"You're on the wrong floor I'm afraid – he's one below us."

"I know," I say. "The toilets down there weren't working."

"This building," the older nurse says, clicking her tongue. "Give your father my love, won't you?"

"Yeah," I say. "No problem."

I walk with them to the lift and then go down one floor. No one else has arrived yet. I take a seat next to my father's bed again; I wonder whether he knows the doctor I saw upstairs, whether he'd approve of his briskness, if that's what people mean when they say calm, professional care. I look down at him, at the blond hairs on the backs of his hands, and the dopey expression people get when they're asleep. You're easier to deal with when you're unconscious, Dad, I tell him silently, then my inner Gillian says, don't think like that in here. Even if I don't want my father in my life, that doesn't mean he deserves to die, or stay comatose permanently. I straighten the hem of my skirt.

"I used to want to work in a hospital, you know?" I say out loud, feeling stupid. "That didn't work out, obviously."

He takes a sudden, shuddering breath, and I'm sure I catch his eyelids flickering.

I cross the room and yank the door open, my heart pounding. "Can someone come in here please?"

Down the hall the nurse who was being chewed out earlier looks up, sulkily, from her clipboard.

"I think he opened his eyes," I say. Her expression isn't very encouraging, but I keep talking. "I think he looked at me."

"I'll come and check on him," she says, and starts walking slowly in my direction.

"Are you his nurse?"

"For today."

"Are there loads of you?"

"Loads of us?"

"I've seen someone different each day."

"Well… we're all very fond of your dad," she says. She's

nearly reached the doorway and she smiles at me for the first time. "We all wanted to help out."

"Thanks," I say, trying to smile back.

She leans in close. "He's the only doctor that all the staff like, actually."

"Really?" Really?

"Dr Park's never too busy, doesn't push people if there's a decision to be made."

"Yeah?"

She nods at him. "I don't need to tell you what he's like though, do I?"

I smile inwardly. Well yes, you do actually. He spent all day patiently letting other people make decisions, then came home and refused to let his own daughter do the same.

She goes over to the bed and checks the monitor. "What did you say happened?"

"He took a deep breath, then I thought he opened his eyes." My voice kind of squeaks when I say the last bit.

She hums as she checks his chart and peers at his monitor. I wonder if Gillian's on her way.

"His heart rate's gone down," the nurse says, straightening up. "I'll get the doctor to come by and have a look."

"Is he okay?"

"I'm sure everything's fine," she says, but she looks worried.

I go back to the toilet and lock myself in a cubicle. I sit on the loo, bending forwards so my face is almost touching the knees of my jeans, hands clapped onto either ear; I try to control my breathing. If there's a problem, it'll be my fault. I didn't want him to wake up before Malkie brought Jack round, and now he's getting worse.

Eventually I sit up. I pee, wash my hands and face and pat myself dry with some flimsy blue paper towels. Strange that I was here less than an hour ago; it seems longer now.

✳ ✳ ✳

207

Malkie's story about my grandfather made me feel weird for a while, but I mostly forgot about it after the bike incident.

It was muffled voices that woke me and took me to the top of the stairs. I looked down and saw the bike in the hallway. The door to the living-room was closed and there was a slash of light underneath it. I couldn't hear who was talking, or what they were saying and I wondered about the cyclist. Apart from the tutor and Malkie, no one came to see us at my grandmother's. We were at least a fifteen-minute walk from the village and it was late. A sudden panic took hold of me, and I rushed to my grandmother's room to check whether she was asleep and we were being burgled. Her bed was still made up. I looked at the clock on her bedside table – two in the morning.

I went back to the top of the stairs and called out. The voices paused; a floorboard along the corridor from me creaked and night air rustled through cracks in the walls. I felt all the hairs on my arms stand up, then I heard quick footsteps and light flooded the hallway. Someone was standing framed in the living-room doorway.

"What is it, Tallulah?" my grandmother asked.

"I heard voices."

"So you decided to get out of bed at two in the morning on a school night?"

"I heard voices," I said, stubbornly.

"Yes, well now you know – I sleep badly. I'm old. Go back to bed."

"Who are you talking to?"

There was a pause.

"I'm talking to an old acquaintance. Now go back to bed."

My bed was cold when I got back into it. I wished I had Mr Tickles there to sleep on my feet. I curled up into a ball and tried to stay awake, listening out for the cyclist leaving, but I fell asleep straight away.

✳ ✳ ✳

Malkie came to teach me once a week. I was picking it up fast, he said. It must be in my blood. "Your mother was musical," he said.

"I didn't know that," I said. There was a small squeezing feeling inside my chest at the thought that I didn't know everything about her. "What did she play?"

"She played the piano too. Didn't she ever tell you?"

"No."

Malkie shifted in the seat beside me. "She wanted to be a concert pianist when I knew her," he said. "She was practising loads until she was 'bout twenty-five, then something happened to distract her, or so I hear."

"She was twenty-five when I was born."

Malkie grinned. "Yup."

I tried to imagine my life in twelve years time. "Do you think twenty-five is young to have a baby?"

"Depends on the person," he said. "Your grandma was twenty when your Aunt Gillian was born."

"Really?"

"Really. Young and beautiful, or so I hear."

"My grandma was beautiful?"

"Oh yeah. Good-looking family, the Parks. Especially your Aunt Vivienne." He jiggled his eyebrows.

"She's not as beautiful as she thinks she is," I said, feeling jealous.

"Oh, she is, and more," Malkie said. "Don't worry, doll. You'll outshine her one of these days." He clapped me on the back and checked the clock on the wall. "Speaking of family – I'll be going back to Canada for a little while. See my mom while she's still up and running."

I hadn't thought that his mum might still be alive. "How long will you be gone for?"

"Hopefully not too long. I'll bring you something nice."

"You won't come and see me."

He shook his head at me. "You have a lot of attitude for someone with fancy new hair and clothes."

"Well, it's true," I said. "You never came to see me before."

He ruffled my hair. "I'll definitely write – I promise. Now, I better get, you have studying to do."

I pulled a face.

He stood up and shrugged his jacket on; it was beige, with a white sheepskin lining. He was wearing cowboy boots too, and a woollen hat with ear flaps. He looked like an Eskimo brought up on Clint Eastwood films.

"Malkie," I said, pulling the black keys of the piano up until they stuck there. "Did *you* like my mum?"

"Course I did."

"Why?"

"I dunno – why do you like anyone? 'Cos she was kind and funny."

"When her and Vivienne fell out," I said. "It wasn't… "

"Wasn't what?"

"My mum didn't do anything wrong? Vivienne was just being Vivienne, right?"

He started to say something but I cut him off.

"I mean – I get why she'd be angry with Grandma, even if it's not really her fault my grandad was horrible to her. But my mum couldn't have done anything bad to her."

"No," Malkie said. "Your mum would never have done something bad to Viv. She didn't have a bad bone in her body. She was just a sweet kid."

"She wasn't really a kid."

"Not a kid then," Malkie said. "But there was something about Evie that made you want to look after her. I guess 'cos she'd had to bring herself up, after her parents died. You kind of wanted to give her a break."

"Oh."

"You'll grow up, princess," Malkie said. "And you'll see we all just want the same things, really."

When he'd gone I went to find my grandmother in the kitchen.

"When did you grow up?" I asked her.

"Is that a joke, young lady?" She was unscrewing a bottle of arthritis pills and counting them out carefully onto the kitchen table.

"How do you *know* you've grown up, then?"

She carried on counting the pills, heaping them into small neat piles. "Growing up is just about feeling comfortable in your own skin," she said. "Some people never manage it." She looked up. "Are you going to bother me, or are you going to do your homework?"

"I'm bothering."

"Silly question, I suppose." She put her bottle down and looked at me. "There's nothing wrong with it. People are just scared of change."

I eyed her pills. "I'm not scared," I said.

"Good girl," she said. "Be brave in everything, even things you don't want to do."

She rested her hand on my forehead. I closed my eyes and concentrated on feeling her fingers as solid, things that wouldn't fall away, but they were as dry and as light as paper.

∗ ∗ ∗

The whole three months I stayed there, the house and grounds felt like they were always on the verge of snow although it didn't in fact arrive until early December. When I finally woke up to see the world covered in a frozen white blanket, I ran outside with boots and an overcoat on, breathing in air that was so crisp it burned my throat on its way down.

Underneath the snow, the garden looked like it rolled on and on forever. I lay on my back and made a snow angel, like my mother had taught me when I was younger, enjoying the feel of my skin go numb then hot again. Eventually I sat up and went to explore the rest of the garden. The lake was solid, and a lonely bird was chirping mournfully in the middle of it, eyes fixed on the food swimming underneath the ice. When he was still there after dinner, I brought him some bread, and left it on the jetty.

My grandmother stopped working in the garden when she slipped on a fine layer of frost and hurt her hip, so I had to do the planting, preparing the beds for onions and digging up the rosemary and winter radishes. My grandmother watched from the living-room and banged on the window if she thought I wasn't treating her vegetables carefully enough.

"What took you so long?" she'd say when I came inside, my fingers swollen and red from the cold and the work. "When I was younger I had to do this, the washing, the cooking and the scrubbing all in one afternoon. You would never make it."

"Yeah, but we have technology now," I said.

"Hruh," came the reply.

I was planting rhubarb when the first attack came.

I heard the crash and ran indoors, not stopping to take off my muddy shoes.

My grandmother was lying face-down on the rug. Her walking stick was stretched out in one hand; she'd knocked over the bottle of port on the table.

"Grams... " I put my arms around her waist and turned her to face me. Her eyes were wide and her mouth kept falling open.

"I'm going to call an ambulance," I said. "I'll be back in one minute." My tongue felt thick with fear.

My grandmother's eyes narrowed and colour started to come back into her face. "Don't... " she said. She closed her eyes and breathed in deeply.

I put my face closer to her to hear better. She opened her eyes wide. "Don't be ridiculous. Call Edward," she said. "And don't move someone who's fallen over – my neck could have been broken."

"I'll remember," I said.

"You won't need to," she grumbled. "Just call Edward."

I called my father, my hands shaking as I dialled the number. He came on the line after what seemed like ages. "Yes?"

"Dad, it's me. Grandma's had an attack, or something."

"What happened?"

"She fell over, and then her face looked funny. Oh, and her mouth was open."

"I can hear you, you know," she called from the other room.

"Tallulah, stay there," my father said. "Don't do anything. I'll call an ambulance."

See, I told my grandmother silently.

"I'll get a train up and be with you in a few hours."

My grandmother complained about the noise of the siren the whole journey to the hospital.

"Well," one of the paramedics said, "the good news is you don't seem to be slurring your words."

The doctor who looked her over was called Dr Philips and he wore a red polka-dot tie. I sat next to the bed, trying to slow my heartbeat down. Everything's going to be okay. Everything's going to be okay.

"You seem to have had a mild stroke," Dr Philips said when he finished. "But with the right medication, there should be no long-term effects. We'll have to keep you in for a few nights."

"My son's coming," my grandmother said, drawing the blanket around her. "He can take care of me."

"I wish my mother had the same trust in me," Dr Philips said, cheerfully. I wondered about his mother – he looked about ninety years old himself.

"Do you want some water?" I asked my grandmother.

"No," she said. She pushed the blanket away and tried to stand up.

"Now, now, Matilda," Dr Philips said. "What's all this? You can't move, you know. You have to stay right here and get our little nurse to look after you."

"I can't stay in bed all day," she said. "Get out of my way."

Her hand groped for her walking stick; I picked it up and took it outside the ward.

"Tallulah," she said. "Bring me my stick at once."

213

"No," I said. I came back in and replaced the blanket. "You can't go anywhere. Not until Dad gets here at least."

"She's quite right, you know," Dr Philips said. "Just get some rest. Snug as a bug in a rug, that's what you'll be."

My grandmother looked at him as if he'd farted. "Are you retarded?" she asked.

"I'll go get you some water," I said, trying not to laugh.

Dr Philips followed me out.

"Ignore Grandma," I said. "She's just mad she can't do things for herself."

"Of course," Dr Philips said; he didn't seem especially offended. "Tell your father I'll be around if he'd like to discuss the patient."

I found a water cooler and filled a plastic cup. My grandmother drank half of it, then passed it back. "I'm tired," she said.

"Do you want me to close the curtains?"

"That would be nice."

I closed the curtains and brought her an extra blanket from one of the other beds. "Let me know if you need anything," I said, perching back on my chair.

"You're a good girl, Tallulah," she said, turning over. "And you'd make a good nurse."

It was already dark when my father arrived. After some wrangling with Dr Philips, my grandmother was told she'd be discharged the next morning.

"Tell the staff to leave me in peace," she said, and fell back asleep.

I slept too, in the taxi on the way back to the house. My father woke me up at the front door. I climbed out, foggy and aching from being slumped against the window.

"You don't snore anymore," my father said. "You used to when you were little, did you know that?"

"No."

The taxi pulled away and left us in the pitch black. My father spent a few minutes trying to locate his key; I shifted awkwardly from one foot to another, aware that this was the first time we'd been alone together since I went to school.

We went straight to bed.

The next morning my grandmother's mood was even worse. She hadn't liked the food or the hospital bed and she didn't like the broken heater in the taxi. My father and the taxi driver helped her upstairs and into her own bed, and I could hear her complaining that now she wouldn't be able to watch her TV programme.

My father paid the driver and came to join me in the kitchen, looking exhausted. "I'm going to get a district nurse to come in and check on her," he said, yawning. "I think that's the safest thing to do. She's ready for some soup now."

"I'll take it," I said. I put a tray together, soup, bread, a jug of ice water and an orange. My father watched me expressionlessly.

I stumbled going up the stairs.

"Careful," my grandmother called, "I only have good china."

I placed the tray on the bedside table and sat down at the foot of the bed. "How are you feeling?" I asked.

"A little foolish," she said. "How are you feeling?"

"Scared," I said.

"Yes," my grandmother said. She patted my hand. "Well, you didn't lose your head. That's something to be proud of."

We smiled at each other.

"Dad says he's going to get a district nurse to come and look in on us."

My grandmother raised her eyebrows. "Us?"

"I'm not going to leave now you really need me."

My grandmother tightened her grip on my hand. "You're a very loving girl, Tallulah."

"Let's try this soup," I said.

I stayed with her until she fell asleep. Her head rolled forwards and she started mumbling,

"Not like that, careful – you'll fall, Albert – put me down – I can't breathe – "

I ran a sink full of hot water in the kitchen and dropped the dirty dishes into it. My father came in. Out of the corner of my eye I could see that he was standing there, hands resting on the back of a chair. "I haven't perhaps said," he started, then cleared his throat. "Thank you for taking care of Mother today. I know it's a lot of responsibility for someone your age."

I wiped my hands on a dishtowel, and turned to face him. "Have you told Aunt Gillian or Aunt Vivienne yet?"

"Gillian's coming up tomorrow."

"What about Aunt Vivienne?"

He shook his head. "I'll do the dishes."

I dropped the dishcloth onto the table and went upstairs.

∗ ∗ ∗

I could see Aunt Gillian's suitcase in the hallway. I was sitting halfway up the stairs, listening to her conversation with my father in the kitchen.

"Of course she's not coming," she said.

"Did you tell her what happened?" my father asked.

"Yes, yes. You know what she's like. She has other 'engagements', Edward. Too busy to see her own mother."

"Don't be too hard on her, Gillian."

"*No one's* too hard on her." Aunt Gillian's voice was rising. "She likes to play the victim, and you know it."

I felt a stab of irritation. If Vivienne's story about being knocked out was true, she *was* a victim.

"She has no thought for others," Aunt Gillian said.

I walked slowly upstairs. My grandmother was sitting up in bed, spooning porridge into her mouth. "How are you today?" she asked.

"Gillian's here."

She grimaced. "I see."

"How's your porridge?"

"Disgusting, without salt. Salt is the only good thing in this world."

"Other than gin," I said, sitting down on the end of her bed.

"Hruh," she said. "You'll never settle down with a tongue like that."

"I don't want to settle down."

"We all need somebody, my darling."

"Even you?"

"I have somebody," she said, nodding her head at me.

"But really, did you need Grandad?"

"What's with the questions all the time?" she asked. She flung the bedcovers back. "Open the window, I need some fresh air."

"Okay, okay," I said, getting up quickly. "I'll do it. You're meant to be resting."

"I'll rest when I'm dead," she said, gritting her teeth.

I opened the window, and went back over to the bed. "Don't use that word."

"Dead?"

"Don't say it."

"There's nothing to be afraid of," she said. "It's what we're born to do."

"Can we please not talk about it?" I said, biting the inside of my cheek.

"Tallulah," my grandmother said gently. "You have to let go at some point. Look at me – I've buried both parents *and* a husband. Sometimes it helps to talk about it. And sometimes it helps to throw away their things so they're completely invisible everywhere but in here." She tapped her chest. "That's what I did with your grandfather."

"Why?"

"When he died, it was almost as if I died too." She sighed. "I went through the house ripping all the telephone cords out of the wall, so I would never have to hear more bad news."

"So you *did* love him?"

"It's complicated, darling."

"If dying is so horrible for other people, then why do you want to do it?"

217

She held her arms out to me. "But there might come a time when I'm in a lot of pain, sweetheart." She held up her hand as I turned to leave and I went back to her. She smiled at me and brushed a lock of hair away from my face. "We won't talk about it then. But I'm not afraid." I twisted away from her. "Fine, go downstairs. Tell Gillian I'm ready to receive her now."

"Yes, Your Majesty."

"That's my girl."

* * *

The next few days Aunt Gillian cooked and cleaned for us while we played cards upstairs on my grandmother's bed. I was in charge of taping *Murder, She Wrote* and looking after the garden. My grandmother watched from her bedroom window now, screaming orders at me from there. She also let me smoke her cigarettes, until Aunt Gillian caught me behind the rose garden. "What would your father say?" she cried.

"Not much," I said.

My father had left the day Aunt Gillian arrived, threatening to come back and take me home for Christmas. I tried to make my grandmother let me stay but she sided with him.

"But I don't want to leave you," I said, frustrated.

"Edward would be lonely if you didn't go," she said, stroking my arm, and I tried not to look too sceptical.

"*You'll* be lonely if I do."

"I'll enjoy the peace and quiet." She saw the look on my face. "Of course I'll miss you, silly girl. But I'm getting too old to keep an eye on you."

I rolled my eyes. "Okay."

The night before I left, my grandmother showed me where the champagne was kept and I opened a bottle, under her direction, and served it in two glasses that had been chilling in the fridge. I sipped at the drink, not sure about the dry, sharp taste.

"Here's to us," she said.

The taxi driver taking me to the station the next morning was cheerful, but I didn't want to talk. I still felt guilty for leaving. The district nurse had wheeled my grandmother out to say goodbye, although she'd tried to walk. "I don't care," the nurse said, when my grandmother waved her arms indignantly. "You go in the wheelchair or you don't go at all."

"Well, then I'll go in the chair," my grandmother said, disgustedly. "I suppose you'd like to start breathing for me next, would you?"

The view outside the window of the train seemed to be getting greyer the closer we got to London, matching my thoughts. I wasn't looking forward to Christmas alone with my father. We'd gone to Gillian's every year since my mother's death.

At home, my father opened the front door wearing a dark blue jumper with leather elbow patches; I'd never seen it before. "Come in," he said. "How was the journey?"

"Fine."

I dragged my suitcase to the foot of the stairs and ran into the kitchen. Mr Tickles was lying underneath the table; he looked even more battered than before. I scooped him up and hugged him. "Miss me?" I asked him. I stroked him underneath his chin and he started his rattling.

"I'll take your suitcase upstairs," my father said, appearing behind me.

"No, I'll do it. And I promised I'd phone Grandma."

"Yes, of course. Fine. How is she?"

"She's probably lonely."

"Well, Gillian and the children will spend Christmas with her, so you don't have to worry so much."

I looked down at Mr Tickles who was drooling onto my hand. "She'll be complaining when I go back then," I said. "Gillian fusses too much for her."

My father frowned. "You're talking about the Easter holidays, I take it."

"No," I said, feeling a flush rising up my neck. "I'm going

back after Christmas to look after her."

"I'm afraid not, Tallulah. You've spent too long away from school as it is," he said. "Your grandmother and I both think you need to rejoin your classmates."

"Grandma likes having me there."

"Of course she does."

"Then please let me stay with her. Just 'til she's better anyway."

"I don't know how long that'll be."

"I need to make sure she's okay."

"That's what the nurses are there for," he said. "And I'll be travelling up as often as I can. Too many people will just be in the way. Why don't you try to concentrate on school for now."

"I'm *not letting it happen again*."

My father looked taken aback. "Letting what... Ah. I see." He pinched the bridge of his nose.

Mr Tickles purred loudly in between us.

My father was the one who broke the silence. "We'll discuss this later," he said. "In any case, it's nice to have you back." He smiled grimly, then went into his study and shut the door.

I went upstairs. Mr Tickles trotted behind me, rubbing his gums on any sharp corners that were easy to reach. The house was hot compared to my grandmother's. I took off my jumper and jeans, unzipped my suitcase and pulled out a dress she'd given me, a black halter neck from the fifties with a full skirt, fitted bodice and red polka dots. She'd made it herself, she said, for a Christmas party one year. My grandfather was only interested in racing and she hadn't always got enough money from him to buy food for the week, let alone clothes. But my grandmother had been a farm girl. She planted a vegetable garden, kept chickens, walked to town to buy fabric cheaply. When my grandfather fell off his horse one winter and broke his leg, she convinced him to set up an account for her and make regular payments into it.

"How did you convince him?" I asked.

"I wouldn't bring him anything to eat or drink until he'd done it," she said.

I pulled the dress on, smoothing the fabric down and looking in the mirror. I didn't fill the bodice out – my grandmother had warned me about my weight.

"No one likes a skinny girl," she said.

"Why?" I asked.

"You look like you couldn't bear children."

"I don't think that's what boys my age are looking for."

I telephoned her from my bedroom, sitting on the floor with Mr Tickles passed out in front of me. "How are you?" I asked her.

"Hungry," she complained. "That Nazi woman won't let me have any dinner."

"Are you sure?"

"Well, she won't let me have what I want."

"Eat what she makes you, Grams. You can't starve yourself."

"Don't you start."

"Eat."

"Fine," she said. "You left a sketchbook here. Would you like me to send it on?"

"No," I said. "That's for you."

I could hear pages rustling on the other end.

"They're very good," she said. "Hruh, when did you do that one?"

"Which one?"

"The last one."

"A few days ago," I said. "When you were asleep." It was a pencil sketch of her, dozing in bed. Her hair had come unpinned and the light coming through the window had made her look fuzzy and transparent.

"It's lovely," she said. "I'll frame it."

"Okay," I said. "Grams?"

"Yes?"

"Dad told me I'm not coming back to see you until Easter."

"He shouldn't have. I was going to do that myself."

"It's alright."

"I still want you around, very much."

"Yeah, I know."

"Don't be angry with your father."

"I'm not," I lied.

"I'd better go," she said. "I need to get that Nazi woman to take me to the toilet."

"I'll call you soon."

"Goodbye, sweetheart."

"Bye Grams."

I hung up and went downstairs. My father was making stew and potatoes in the kitchen.

"I recognise that dress," he said.

"Grandma gave it to me."

"You two seem to be very close these days."

"Yeah."

"That's good. You certainly seem to have brought her out of her shell." He was looking down at the pots on the stove; he still seemed angry from our conversation earlier. "I gather Malkie's been teaching you the piano."

"Yeah."

"Have you enjoyed that?"

"Yeah."

"Maybe we can see about getting you some lessons at school as well."

"Mm-hmm."

"I know you don't want to go back," he said. "But Mother is really too frail to take care of you any longer."

"She'll get better."

"She'll be fine, Tallulah, but she's tired and weak."

"She'll want someone she knows around the house."

"It's a nice thought," my father said. "But you have to go back to school."

"It's not just a thought," I said.

I turned around to leave. My father called my name.

"What?"

"I tried to take some time off work this week, but it wasn't possible."

I knew Grandma was wrong, I wanted to say. I knew you wouldn't be lonely without me. I knew you'd just be at work anyway.

"I don't care."

"I'm sure you don't," he said. "I just thought I should let you know."

"Well now I know."

I slammed the door behind me.

✳ ✳ ✳

I spent the holidays trying to read *Romeo and Juliet*, our set text, although every time I thought about going back to school my spine felt cold.

As far as I could see, the tragedy depended on Friar Lawrence's message not reaching Romeo on time, which seemed pretty unlucky. And Romeo made me feel uneasy, falling in love with Juliet in about a minute. He made me think of my mother and Uncle Jack in fact – now I was older, looking back, I could feel the crackle of tension between them, and I didn't want to think about it.

I bought the Christmas tree myself that year, haggling with the man who was selling them by the side of the road, then dragging it home. I put it up in a giant pot in the living-room and started decorating it. Mr Tickles came to watch, and tried to kill all the baubles.

My father was off work on Christmas Day and up early, sitting at the kitchen table when I came down. I'd spent Christmas Eve alone, watching re-runs of old comedy shows.

"Merry Christmas," he said, awkwardly.

"Merry Christmas," I mumbled. The sky was bright outside, but colourless, like salt. My father was already dressed.

"Would you like some pancakes?" he asked.

"Sure."

He started moving about and opening drawers, hunting for a whisk. I flopped down on a chair. "What's that noise?"

"I don't know," my father said, egg in one hand.

We went into the living-room. The tree was swaying in the corner of the room. Purple bows and gold bells were clashing into each other and bouncing across the floor. In the middle of the tree, two big eyes stared out at us.

"That bloody cat," my father said.

I reached into the branches and pulled Mr Tickles out, kissing his nose. "What are we going to do with you?" I asked.

My father looked around the living-room. "Would you like to open your presents now?"

I shrugged. "Do you want to?"

"For goodness' sake."

"Alright," I said. "Let's open them now."

We sat by the tree. I had five presents: *Tom Sawyer* from my father – 'it was my favourite when I was a boy,' he said – money from Aunt Vivienne, a fountain pen from Aunt Gillian, a music-box from Georgia and some pearl-drop earrings from my grandmother.

"They're Mother's," my father said when I opened the box. "An anniversary gift from my father."

"I thought Grandad didn't buy Grandma presents."

"Not often," he said. "On very… special occasions. I don't know why she's giving them to you."

"She says they'll suit my hair," I said, reading the note she'd written. "What's wrong with me having them?"

"Your ears aren't pierced are they?"

"No, but I could get them pierced."

"And you're only thirteen."

"I'm nearly fourteen." I wondered what he meant by 'special occasions'. Occasions like when my grandfather beat his wife, or her daughter? My father's face was stony; he could have been thinking about those times too. Maybe he'd been afraid for my grandmother like Uncle Jack had been.

He stretched his hand out for the box. I handed it over silently, then gave my father his present. I'd bought him *Birdsong*, by Sebastian Faulks. It was the biggest thing I could find at the bookshop, and the woman at the till had praised my choice. "It's very moving," she'd said. "And sexual."

Outside, I'd flicked through a couple of pages, but it didn't seem too graphic to me.

My father unwrapped the book slowly. "Thank you, Tallulah," he said. "This will certainly go on the to-read pile."

"Thanks for my book too," I said, politely.

"Yes, well," he said. "How about those pancakes now?"

We ate for the rest of the day: pancakes, chocolate coins from my father's nursing staff, satsumas, nuts, turkey, roast potatoes, stuffing, carrots, Christmas pudding with brandy cream. I called my grandmother to say thank you for the earrings, but Aunt Gillian answered and told me she was sleeping. After I'd hung up, I curled up on the sofa and watched films. I used to do that with my mother, my head in her lap, one of her hands stroking my hair, the other writing thank you cards. She liked to get them posted off quickly.

During an ad break, I realised that the raised voice I'd been hearing for the past five minutes wasn't the background soundtrack for the film; it was coming from my father's study. He had an extension line in there so calls could come through without disturbing the rest of the house, but this didn't sound like the voice he used for patients. I tiptoed down the hall, avoiding floorboards that I knew creaked or groaned.

"It's really irrelevant now," he was saying. "It's not the money. We *have* money… I don't see why I should… I had every right to interfere… "

I tried to creep closer. Mr Tickles came up behind me and rubbed himself against my ankles, purring loudly. I nudged him away with my foot. "Meeooooowww," he said, displeased.

"Of course I didn't trust him," my father said. "He wanted

225

to take her away from me. He told me."

There was a pause – the person on the other end must have started talking.

"I know it could never happen," my father said, sounding angry. "But I wanted to avoid any trouble. *You* of all people should understand."

Pause.

"Who knows what he would have done if I hadn't? He certainly threatened to… As I said, it's irrelevant now. What's done is done. I'm quite sure we won't hear from him again. No, don't make excuses for him, Mother, Jack wants to punish me. I don't want to talk about it. And I don't want those earrings in my house. Yes, Merry Christmas. Goodbye."

I heard the sound of the receiver being replaced and footsteps coming towards the door of the study. I scrambled back to the living-room and lay down quickly on the sofa, my throat pulsing in time with my heartbeat, trying to make sense of what I'd just heard. My grandmother had been right when she implied Uncle Jack was still around, then.

'He wanted to take her away from me.'

I realised something that I must have known all along: Uncle Jack had loved my mother, and he'd wanted her to go away with him.

I concentrated on breathing slowly.

Would she have gone?

Maybe she'd really loved him back. Even if she'd warned him off that time in the rose garden, she could have changed her mind. She'd only got depressed after he left, after all. And my father knew it too.

'I should have known… I pushed her away.'

Had he been talking at cross-purposes to Kathy's mum? I'd never considered that he could have been talking about pushing her away emotionally – he certainly did that after Uncle Jack appeared.

He knew that there was something between them. That's why he'd been angry and cold to her. And then he'd come home early and found them talking. He *could* have let her die on purpose.

The footsteps were getting heavier now. The film had started up again and I forced myself to look at the screen. The TV showed the reflection of my father standing in the doorway, looking in at me, but he didn't say anything. He was in bed by the time I switched it off.

Twelve

When 1995 came, my second stint at boarding school came with it. Having had free run of my grandmother's house and garden made me chafe even more against the rules, the curfews, the separation of the girls and boys, the exact measurements specified in the uniform code. But I was determined to make her proud. I'd promised her I wouldn't act up. It was hard, though, when the teachers were unsympathetic, and even Edith was off with me. I was glad to get to my first art class. I arrived early and found Mr Hicks setting up the desks. "Hey," I said, feeling shy.

"Hi there, Tallulah," he said, turning around. He looked like he was going to say something else, but then stopped, and gave a short laugh. "Wow."

I flushed.

"You look very different."

"My hair's shorter."

"I can see that."

"My grandma did it."

"Do you want to help me finish setting up?"

"Okay."

He looked at me again, then his eyes slid away, then back. "Sorry, I'm half asleep – here, put a sheet of tracing paper out for everyone."

"Okay."

"Thank you," he said, formally.

He didn't look at me properly for the rest of the afternoon or comment on my work. I wondered if he was annoyed at me for some reason.

I had maths after art. I slunk in and took a place at the back. Cressida sat diagonally in front of me, across the aisle from Edith. Halfway through the class she reached across and poked Edith with her pen. "I think you might have lost something," she said, quietly, and brought something out of her school shirt.

"My necklace," Edith said, sounding like she was going to cry. "Where did you get that?"

"I found it." Cressida looked back and smiled at me nastily.

"It's Edith's," I said.

"I don't see her name on it."

"It's her St Christopher necklace."

Cressida smirked. "Maybe next time she won't keep her valuables underneath her bed like a retard."

I stood up. "I think Cressida's confused," I said, loudly. "She thinks the necklace she's wearing is hers but it's actually Edith's."

"We'll discuss this after class," our maths teacher said.

"*I* think we should discuss it now," I said, even louder.

"I think we should see what Mr Purvis has to say about your behaviour," she said, but she looked at Cressida. "*Is* that your necklace, Cressida?"

"It *looks* like it," Cressida said, simpering. "I could have picked up the wrong one though."

"Edith?"

"I probably left it lying around," Edith said.

"Give it to me," the teacher said. "You're not meant to be wearing jewellery anyway. Edith, you can collect it after class."

I was sent to the Headmaster's office and escorted

immediately back by the secretary. "Tallulah is having some adjustment issues," she said to my maths teacher. She had pink acrylic nails that day. She spoke in a stage-whisper, so the whole classroom could hear her. "Herbert feels that she should be allowed to settle back in at her own pace, for now."

"Who's Herbert?" I asked, and the other students sniggered.

"Mr Purvis, of course," the secretary said. Her face had gone the same colour as her nails.

"Alright then, thank you for bringing her back, Miss Duvall," the teacher said. "Tallulah, work with Edith for now. We've moved on to trigonometry problems. And no more interruptions."

I slid into a chair next to Edith, who stared at me. "Thanks," she said, shyly.

"It's okay," I said.

* * *

I circle the waiting-room while a group of medical students check on my father. I brush past the fronds of overly-green synthetic plants, underneath neon strip-lighting. The air seems stale and I wonder, fleetingly, how my father found the strength to walk through the hospital doors day after day for the last twenty-five years.

The aunts arrive. I tell them what the hospital has told me – he's been in and out of consciousness since his eyes opened, and they're monitoring him closely.

"They say no need to panic," I say, "but they'd prefer us in here for now."

"Of course. Come sit down," Aunt Gillian says, soothingly, although I think I see her lower lip tremble.

The chairs are hard, plastic, orange versions of the ones you find in schools. I always hated sitting still on them. In summertime, when you stood up, sweat slicks showed where the backs of your thighs and knees had been. Much better to keep moving.

Maybe I never felt comfortable inside my skin. My grandmother would have a lot to say about that.

I flick through the magazines. Someone called Lady Helen Taylor is on the front of *Vogue*, showing a lot of even white teeth and striking greenish-blue eyes. They're the same colour as my mother's; the same colour as Toby's.

My mother would be turning forty-six this month if she'd lived. Uncle Jack, out there somewhere in the world, must be forty-nine, if he's five and a half years younger than my father. Toby was about eighteen the last time I saw him.

My father's birthday is the fifth of May, born three and a half years after the end of the Second World War when my grandmother was still twenty-one. The same age I am now. I don't know how she did it; there's no way I could cope. Clearly my father felt the same way – he was in his early thirties when I came along, but he and my mother must have decided not to have any more children after me. He probably realised he wasn't cut out for fatherhood.

"I haven't seen a soul since we got here," Aunt Vivienne says, standing up. "No wonder people die of neglect in these places."

"Where are you going?" Aunt Gillian asks.

"If you must know, I'm going to the bathroom," Aunt Vivienne says over her shoulder.

"What if he goes back into a coma?" Aunt Gillian asks, when she's gone. "How are they going to wake him up?"

"They normally reverse the cause of the coma," I say. "Like, they'll give someone a glucose shock if they had low sugar, or medicate them to reduce swelling on the brain, things like that. Sometimes they induce hypothermia for cardiac patients."

"Isn't that dangerous?"

"Apparently it works," I say. "They cool them down to two or three degrees lower than body temperature for about a day, externally or intravascularly."

"This isn't some experimental treatment they do in the East?"

"I read about it this morning," I say. "In a British medical textbook."

"I still don't like the sound of it," Aunt Gillian says.

"It's probably to reduce the risk of ischemic injury," I say.

"That sounds familiar," Aunt Gillian says; she looks half-placated.

"It's a restriction of blood supply to tissues," I say. "After a heart attack, the blood flow's insufficient and... "

Someone runs past the waiting-room door, screaming, and we both freeze, but it's just a kid in a Spiderman outfit.

"Mac, get *back* here," a woman calls after him.

We exchange looks – Aunt Gillian releases her breath and I wipe away the trickle of sweat that's started down my face.

"Now where's Vivienne got to?" Aunt Gillian murmurs.

∗ ∗ ∗

Exams came. I sat in the stuffy room with two hundred and twenty-three other students and stared at the questions in front of me. Someone had left their coffee mug on the original paper, the photocopier reproducing two hundred and twenty-four faint smudgy rings. I bit my lip in frustration, I cursed my private tutor. I tried working on several problems, but gave up halfway through each. I looked at the clock – only fifteen minutes in. We weren't allowed to leave before half an hour was up, but after ten minutes more of tapping my pen on the desk, a teacher came and told me I could go.

After that, Mr Purvis summoned me to his office and told me I was on a final warning. Mr Hicks had volunteered to take over as my personal mentor, he said, and we would meet once a week to work through the assignments I was struggling with most. If I still didn't improve... He looked bored, shuffled his papers and I was dismissed.

Mr Hicks was in the corridor outside, chatting to some female students. When he saw me come out of the office he waved me over.

"Walk with me to the studio," he said.

I carried his register for him and he made small-talk until we were out of earshot.

"Did Mr Purvis tell you the plan?"

"Yep."

"You're going to have to pull your socks up, you know."

"I guess."

"Look, Tallulah, I honestly think you're a talented student."

I kept quiet, but I felt my skin heat up.

He put his hand on my shoulder. "Let's say we meet lunchtime every Friday – we can have thirty-minute progress sessions. And, of course I'll be available if you have any problems during the rest of the week. But you'll have to trust me, and work hard even when you don't like the subjects."

"Okay."

"Promise?"

"Promise."

"Friday, then," he said. "Come find me in my office."

∗ ∗ ∗

When I failed all my exams, Mr Hicks got the teachers to give me extra essays to get me in practice, and catch-up notes for the last term. He was still positive in art class. I was very good at shading and perspective, he said. Edith elbowed me in the ribs.

"You're his favourite," she said. "He never says anything about *my* work."

I looked at her drawing. Bright balls of colour stuck rigidly out of a vase, which was sitting on a perfectly square table.

"That's because you don't have any perspective," I said, taking her pencil. "Draw the table like this – the lines should get closer to each other here to show that they're further off in the distance, see? Things nearer your eye are bigger, things further away are smaller."

"If only you could apply some of that knowledge to your physics homework," Mr Hicks murmured behind me.

I jumped.

"I'm sorry, I thought you knew I was here." He winked at me. "Well carry on with the good work. But don't put me out of a job." He smiled and strolled off.

"You like him back," Edith hissed.

"I don't."

"You do. You've gone red."

"I don't. I was just surprised," I said lamely.

"He's cute. He's got dimples."

"Do you want me to help you or not?"

"Yes, help me. Teacher's Pet."

My first session with Mr Hicks was scheduled for three weeks into the term, after I was 'settled', he said. I was five minutes late, so I ran; I was out of breath by the time I reached his office.

"Come in," he called.

I pushed the door open and stopped there. None of us had ever seen the inside – Mr Hicks called it his sanctuary. A rumour had gone around that he'd been seen going into the room with nothing but a towel on once, and a few girls in my year had tried to look through the keyhole after that, but it'd been too dark to make anything out. As far as I could see, the room was basically a cupboard, with shelves lining three of the four walls, and a deep, wooden desk piled high with paper in the middle of the floor. The one unusual item I could see was a futon mattress shoved behind one of the shelving units, and I wondered if Mr Hicks lived here.

"Take a seat," he said. He was sitting on the other side of the desk, so all I could see of what he was wearing was a white linen shirt, and a dark leather bracelet. He could have had a towel wrapped around him instead of trousers. I blushed when I thought of this.

He put away a cigarette he'd been rolling and smiled at me. "Look, I know exams seem pointless. But everyone has to do them, so what we'll be discussing here is how you get through them with minimum fuss, okay?"

"Okay."

"As well as anything else that's been on your mind." His smile dropped for a moment. "So, if you don't mind me asking... "

"What?"

"Last September," he said. "When you went to live with your grandmother. Miss Duvall tells me you asked to telephone her rather than your father."

"Did she?" I muttered.

"I was just wondering if there was a problem between you and your father?" He smiled encouragingly.

"Like what?"

"I'm sorry," he said. "I don't like to pry, but obviously I care about your welfare... " He pulled a face. "I'm trying to be delicate here, but I'll just come out and ask. Does your father in any way mistreat you?"

I felt myself flushing. "Like touching me?"

Mr Hicks looked awkward. "Or put you down, verbally. Or even hit you. They're all forms of abuse."

"No," I said, louder than I'd intended.

"I'm sorry, Tallulah. I didn't want to put you on the defensive. I want you to feel that you can talk to me about anything."

"Yeah, fine."

He drummed his fingers on the desk. "We've obviously hit a nerve," he said. "Let's start again. How about I tell you something about myself and *my* relationship with my parents, and then you can see I'm not judging you."

I shrugged.

"Well." He cleared his throat. "Take my father, for instance. He had a thing about art being only for girls and homosexuals."

Mr Hicks wasn't looking in my direction, but I thought I saw his jaw tighten. "By the end of my time in that house we only spoke to each other through my mother. And then she died over Christmas, and we haven't spoken since. So you

235

see, I understand completely not getting along with a parent."

He looked sad, and I wondered how close he'd been to his mum. I wanted to comfort him, but that thought made me blush as well.

"Sorry your mum died."

He sighed. "People can't possibly understand until they go through it."

"Everyone thinks they know best," I said. "They either want to forget it, or talk about her. Especially if they didn't know her, they want to talk about her."

Mr Hicks gave me a half-smile. He'd taken the cigarette out again and was pinching it at both ends. "I'll take that as a hint. But back to what we were saying. It's stupid, but my father will never change his mind."

"He sounds like an idiot."

"Well… Some people just can't get along. Does this sound familiar?"

"Yeah, kind of."

In my head I saw my father's disinterested face. Whenever I thought of him, he did the same thing: he looked blank, then he turned away. I could see him turning away from me in the hall, going into his study, turning away from me and walking back to the car when he dropped me off at school. I pushed the images away.

Mr Hicks nodded. "It's perfectly normal," he said. "And I'm sure your dad's very fond of you, really. But you do deserve to be told how special you are. Which is why you've got me. And now the important thing is to get you to start socialising, showing some team spirit – it'll go down well with Mr Purvis, if nothing else. How about a sport? How are you at netball?"

I was okay at netball it turned out, and my PE teacher said they needed someone tall to stand by the goal and hit the ball away when it came near. It was easy, she said. After the first few games, I started to enjoy it. It *was* easy, and in the summer it was nice to be outside, the sun baking the tarmac.

"I've heard you're practically an Olympian," my grandmother said during our next telephone conversation.

"What does that mean?"

"That you're doing very well for yourself."

"Oh." I wondered who could have mentioned it.

She gave a hacking cough.

"What did the tests show?" I asked.

"Nothing."

I sighed. "I know you're keeping things from me."

"Such as?"

Such as strange visitors in the night.

"Coughing means the nerves leading to your lungs are irritated," I said. "It can be a symptom of pneumonia."

"The tests are fine. You shouldn't worry so much."

"I can't help it."

"I know," she said. Her voice changed. "You're as hard as nails, my girl, but you've got a soft centre."

"I'm not a very good nail, then."

"You're a perfect granddaughter and that's what counts." She wheezed slightly as she said it. "My head's splitting in two. Hruh. Just hope they've invented the cure for everything by the time you're old."

"Mr Hicks says they already have but the drug companies are holding us to ransom."

"Well, if Mr Hicks says so. Who is this Mr Hicks anyway?"

"He's my art teacher. He's really nice."

"Your uncle fractured his leg twice when he was on the hockey team," she said, from nowhere.

"I didn't know Uncle Jack played hockey."

"Oh yes, he was very good at sports. He was the school's fastest long-distance runner."

"Weird," I said.

"You're your own person," my grandmother said, as if she could hear my thoughts. "You're not like Jack, if that's what's worrying you."

"Yeah." Although who knows what he's like since you

237

guys never talk about him.

"I have to go, Tallulah. Be careful now."

"Love you."

"I love you too."

✳ ✳ ✳

Eventually, 1995 turned into 1996. Russian soldiers and rebel fighters engaged in Chechnya, the O.J. Simpson civil trial started, Dolly the sheep was born, and *Braveheart* won best picture at the Oscars. I stayed on the netball team, I hung out with Edith, I went to my sessions with Mr Hicks. As much as I hated to admit it, I found myself developing a grudging respect for my father's academic ability. But after a few weeks of Mr Hicks' help, I started to get into the routine of schoolwork. Some of our studying must have even got through, because my grades got better, even if I wasn't going to win any awards. I wasn't reading my father's textbook as often, but biology was still easily my best subject apart from art. In others I trudged through weeks of individual assignments that turned into months of class projects; at least in art I was really enjoying myself. I made sketch after sketch of any subject I could find on the school grounds and sent them to my grandmother – a magpie, a discarded prefect's badge, the empty swimming pool early in the morning. When I stayed at hers over the holidays I saw she'd framed all of them and hung them in her bedroom and on the staircase.

"Hruh," she said, one summer, "I thought school was to educate and refine you, not turn you into a farmhand.

"Says the woman who grew up on a farm."

But it was true. I was toning up from all the netball – my muscles had hardened and the skin covering them had bronzed nicely from being outdoors. My fingers were constantly stained and flaking with paint and I smoked like a chimney.

My grandmother muttered something about femininity as a lost art and beat me soundly at Monopoly.

Sometimes my father joined me at my grandmother's. He sat in his chair in the living-room, reading medical journals while I spread my homework out on the coffee table. Ever since I'd taken his textbook, I'd wondered whether I should say something. There were questions I wanted to ask him about his work, and how easy he thought it would be to get into the medical world. Not necessarily to be a doctor – my grades weren't good enough for that – but maybe I could be a nurse. Maybe we'd finally be able to break through and have a proper conversation, I thought, or maybe he'd be angry with me for 'borrowing' something of his. Instinctively, I held back each time there was an opportunity to speak about it.

Otherwise I spent my vacation time alone with my grandmother. The rest of the family seemed to have retreated a little too – if Uncle Jack had been the mysterious cyclist, he hadn't shown up for a while, and he wasn't calling my father either, as far as I could tell. I hadn't seen Michael, Georgia or James for ages, although I heard that Michael had aced his A-Levels and had a place at Cambridge to read Italian and French. Aunt Gillian had reported this to my grandmother on one of her rare visits. My grandmother had banned her for a while because she said there was no point paying for home help if Aunt Gillian was going to redo everything herself, and unfortunately she preferred the home help.

Occasionally, I'd hear Starr's name in passing at school, or see her across the canteen. Apparently she'd signed up to the drama group, and was busy breaking the hearts of all the theatrical boys. I envied her easy manner with them. I still hadn't had a real conversation with a boy, unless you counted Stuart – who sat next to me in maths and once left an obscene note in my pencil case – and I didn't. My relationship with Mr Hicks was the closest one I had with a Y chromosome. I thought about it at night, when the lights were out, and wondered if maybe I did have a crush on him. My skin always felt clammy when we were in his office, especially my palms. I lived in fear that he would touch my hands for some reason and discover how disgusting they were, but, at least at first, he wouldn't even leave his side of the desk. He was friendly and entertaining; he acted like I was a little sister, rather than a student, but definitely not like we were equals. In the beginning, he made notes while I was talking; later on he sat making a steeple with his fingers. I started off shy, looking at the floor when I had to describe something I couldn't understand in lessons; after a while, I felt relaxed enough to sprawl in my chair, or rest my elbows on the desk in front of me. He liked using props to demonstrate the answers to maths questions. He made me laugh. He always offered me tea or squash and he always listened carefully to me, and never made me feel like I was being petty or stupid. After the first session, he never pushed me to talk about my parents. A couple of times I mentioned my mother, how she was a pianist, like me, and the stories she used to make up for me when I was younger, how she'd written a few of them out, and illustrated them with pencil drawings of me and my sidekicks in our adventures. Mr Hicks said she sounded like a real artist, and he'd like to see the books if I could find them. I didn't tell him my father had hidden all her stuff away. My father's weird behaviour and indifference didn't seem to matter when I was with Mr Hicks.

After two years, I was turning up a few minutes early to each session, and lingering for a few minutes after the bell for afternoon classes had gone. I really looked forward to Fridays.

***

I throw down *Vogue* and pick up *Cosmopolitan*. Sarah Michelle Geller is wearing a red, lacy dress for the 'Hot Issue'. Toby used to have a crush on her, I remember. *Buffy* had just started when I left school, and he watched it religiously. I throw that down too.

Aunt Vivienne comes back in. "I didn't see any nurses," she says, "but I did meet a charming young man who asked after my younger sister." She sits down. "I assume he meant you, Tallulah, and not Gillian. He didn't seem to need glasses."

"Where exactly did you meet this young man?" Aunt Gillian asks, icily. "In the ladies' toilets?"

"At the café," Aunt Vivienne says. "He said he remembered us sitting together the other day."

"Hmmph," Aunt Gillian says.

"I told him you were engaged," Aunt Vivienne says. "Cheekbones like yours should not be thrown away on spotty adolescents."

I stay quiet. It must be because I'd just thought of him, but for a moment I was sure she meant Toby, and my heart is still hammering.

It was the start of my GCSE year when some boys from the Upper Sixth came over to mine and Edith's table in the canteen. Edith was trying to persuade me to come into town with her when she stopped halfway through a sentence; one of the boys who'd been walking past had peeled off from the others and was standing next to us. I turned around and caught his eye.

"I'm Toby," Toby Gates said to me.

"Hi," I said.

"You play on the netball team, right?" he said.

"Uh-huh." Toby Gates had nice eyebrows, I noticed. And good skin.

"I've seen you – you're pretty good."

"Thanks."

"Can we sit with you guys?"

"It's a free country."

The other two came over reluctantly. I recognised them from when they'd come to watch Melinda play netball – she had long blonde hair and big boobs and they got this funny look on their faces every time she ran.

"This is John and Francis," Toby said.

I could feel Edith shaking beside me. "This is Edith," I

said.

"Cool to meet you, Edith," Toby said. The other boys muttered something under their breath.

"We've already met," Edith said, turning pink. "In the library. You asked me for a pen."

"Well, cool to see you again." Toby turned to me. "When's your next match?"

"Next week."

"We're coming along to watch."

"Okay."

"What you eating?"

"School dinner."

"Yeah, but – did you go for the vegetarian or the meat option?"

"Oh. The meat, I guess." I poked my dinner with a fork; it wasn't giving me any clues.

"Yeah, me too. I like meat."

"Um, me too."

"I like chicken," Edith said.

The boys at the other end rolled their eyes. The one called John mouthed something to the other. He had curly hair and a turned-up nose that made me want to punch it. I glared at him; his friend nudged him and he shut up.

"Anyway," I said. "We should go. See you at the match."

"See you," Toby said.

Edith lay face-down on the bed for an hour, with her head underneath her pillow.

"Come on," I said. "It wasn't that bad."

"Toby Gates," she said. "*Toby Gates sat with us.*"

I flopped onto the bed. "He's just a boy."

For some reason, the story of how my parents got together was in my head – how she was there with a friend, and how my father appeared out of nowhere.

"He's seventeen," Edith said, sitting up. "Do you know what girls in our year would do for a seventeen-year-old boy?"

"Take their clothes off?"

242

"He's an Adonis," Edith said. She looked wild.

"You're such a geek," I said. I rolled over and picked my Discman off the floor. I turned it on and started listening to David Bowie; I could see Edith's lips moving and she looked annoyed. I stood up on the bed and started swaying to the music, pretending to sing into an imaginary microphone. Now she looked horrified and shrank away from me. I took the earphones out.

"You can't do that in front of the boys," she said. "Everyone will think you're nuts."

"What about this?" I asked. I did my best Michael Jackson 'Thriller' impersonation, which wasn't very good.

"I mean it," Edith said. "If we sit with them again we have to act grown up."

"They sound fun," I said, rolling my eyes.

"Tal, please," Edith begged. "I *really* like Toby."

"Okay, okay."

"Do you think he thought I was stupid?"

"No."

"His friends did."

"His friends are idiots," I said. "Who cares what they think?"

"Toby probably does."

"Then he's an idiot too."

"Most people care what others think about them," Edith said. "It's kind of weird that you don't, you know."

I picked some dirt out from under my nail and tried to shrug that off.

✳ ✳ ✳

Toby stood with Edith at the next match, while his friends sat at the back and threw things at each other.

Mr Hicks was there too. He waved when I looked over, and I nearly missed a ball. Otherwise, I had a good game. By the time the whistle blew, the goal attack I'd been marking was red-faced and out of breath.

"Nicely played," one of the older girls called after me as I jogged off the court.

Mr Hicks walked over to meet me. I caught a whiff of his smell – sharp and sweet at the same time – and felt suddenly light-headed. "Good game, Tallulah," he said. "You look like you're getting into it now."

"I'm okay at it," I said. I wondered, briefly, if I was better than Uncle Jack had been at hockey.

"You're better than okay," Mr Hicks said, smiling at me. "I'm really proud of you, you know?"

"Thanks," I said, feeling like the world could end right then and I'd still have a big grin on my face.

Mr Hicks left when Edith and Toby came over.

"Why was Mr Hicks talking to you?" Toby asked.

"He's my art teacher."

"Tallulah has a crush on him," Edith said, batting her eyelashes at Toby.

"Don't you think he's too old for you?" Toby asked.

"What are you, my dad?"

Toby went red. "I'm just looking out for you."

"I can look out for myself," I said. "And like I said, he's just my art teacher."

"Fine," Toby said.

"Don't be angry, Tal," Edith said. "We thought you were really good out there today."

"*Great*," I said. "Thanks *so much* for coming to watch."

Toby was shaking his head. I thought he was going to walk away from us, and I felt a weird prickle of disappointment, but he just looked me in the eye, "Are you always such a bitch?"

I felt my mouth turning up into a smile, in spite of myself. "Yes."

"Good to know," Toby said. He was grinning back.

Edith was still waiting outside when I finished changing. "You *do* have a crush on Mr Hicks," she said. "Why won't you admit it?"

"Shut up," I told her.

We walked back to our building in silence. I thought about how Edith always came to cheer me on at matches; I thought about how she never ate her treacle tart whenever it was on the dinner menu so I could have double because it was my favourite pudding, and got a heavy feeling in my stomach. "Sorry, Ed," I said. "You don't have to shut up."

She gave me a look out of the corner of her eye. "I tell you whenever I like a boy."

"Well, I don't like one, so I can't tell you about it."

She was quiet again for a while. "I don't think Toby likes me," she said, eventually.

"Of course he does."

"I mean like, like."

"What's so great about him anyway?"

"He's sooooooooooo good-looking. Can't you tell?"

"He's alright."

"He's *beautiful.*"

"Fine," I said, sighing. "He's beautiful."

✳✳✳

My grandmother lost her voice for a week. When I spoke to her afterwards, she sounded deep and raspy.

"It's like talking to a robot," I said.

"Robots can't talk," she said.

"They can in *Star Wars.*"

"What's that?"

"A film, or a cultural movement, depending on who you talk to."

"Hruh," she said. "It's quiet here without you."

"No wild parties?"

"Certainly not now," my grandmother said.

"Did you *used* to have parties there?"

"A few."

"What were they like?"

"Champagne, expensive clothes. Boring people. Vivienne invariably made a scene."

I grinned. "Have you always been this grumpy?"

"No," she said. "Not always." She was silent for a moment, apart from her breathing.

"How are you feeling?"

"Oh, you know. My feet hurt. You young people. You don't know how good you've got it."

"Homework's not good."

"You wait until you get out there in the real world."

"Are you eating?"

"Yes, yes."

"And drinking lots of fluids?"

"You're almost as bad as Gillian. Now tell me about school."

I told her about the netball championships, and the day the boiler had shut down. I told her about my science project – growing tomatoes in different environments – and how Mr Hicks had helped me get my first ever B in maths. I didn't tell her about Toby.

"It's good to keep busy," she said.

"It's school," I told her. "They *make* you do things. How's Dad?"

"Same as always. They work him too hard at that hospital."

"Uh-huh."

"It's time for my medication."

"I'm calling again tomorrow. You have to tell me what happens in *Murder, She Wrote*. And take some hot water and honey for your throat."

"Yes, yes, stop pestering me," she said, but she sounded pleased.

A few evenings later, on my way back to my dorm after a late netball practise, I saw Toby and his friends walking ahead. I slowed down. I hadn't told my grandmother about him because I didn't know how to feel anymore. Edith talking about him constantly must have been rubbing off on me; recently I'd caught myself thinking about him during class.

He went into the boys' dorm without seeing me. That

246

night he turned up in my dream. He was wearing his rugby kit and he was muddy and out of breath. He tried to hold my hand and brush my hair away from my face. I woke up feeling restless and couldn't get back to sleep.

Thirteen

I cross and re-cross my legs.

"How long have we been here?" Aunt Gillian asks.

"A few hours," I say.

She fidgets.

Outside, a doctor is talking to the parents of a teenager who has just been admitted. They look like they're in shock – chalk-white, not really saying anything. I wonder if he's telling them the prognosis isn't good, and how often my father had to do that. Whether it ever got any easier. The father has his back to me, but suddenly he turns and I see his profile. For a moment my heart stops; it's Mr Hicks, his black curly hair sticking to his head in damp swirls like he ran here. I'm rooted to my chair although I want to disappear. I can practically smell the cigarette smoke and turpentine on him, and when he opens his mouth, I stare at his teeth to see if they are Hollywood-white, like I remember them. Then I hear his voice. It's not Mr Hicks. Not even close. The man searches for his wife's hand and they hold on to each other like life-buoys.

I remember feeling that close to the real Mr Hicks once, feeling like – apart from my grandmother – he was the only one who supported me. "You understand everything better than you give yourself credit for," he said.

"You explain it better," I said.

"You're very sweet, you know?" he said. "You can't teach that."

I feel sick. At how corny I sounded, the way I behaved around him. That was the lesson I asked him for a cigarette, and he looked at me like he was wavering.

"I shouldn't really encourage you – how old are you?"

"I'm sixteen in a month."

"On your sixteenth birthday then. And not before."

"What's the difference between now and then?"

"The law, I'm afraid."

"You sound like my dad."

"Why?"

"He thinks I'm a kid too."

"That's ridiculous. No one could mistake you for a child."

My whole body feels like it's burning up now.

Stupid. What did you talk about then? How your father made all your decisions? How he wouldn't let you look after your grandmother because you were too young? And Mr Hicks looking sympathetic, saying, "Well I think you're very mature, I really do."

Aunt Gillian's phone buzzes and for a second I think it's Malkie calling and I jump to my feet. She looks guilty. "I'll call you back in a minute," she whispers into the receiver.

I rub my eyes, trying to get rid of the past. That might have been the day we discussed career options, too. The day I first told someone I wanted to be a nurse. He was collecting little clay pots that had been drying on ledges and placing them on a tray, I remember, and he turned around and said that was a great idea. We'd have to work on my maths and chemistry, of course, but my biology was already good.

"Cool," I'd said.

"Cool," he'd said, and laughed. "Okay, good. Good. Nothing else you want to discuss?"

"No," I said. "Don't forget my birthday present, though."

He winked at me. "I hope you're good at keeping secrets."

* * *

"I'm going downstairs," I say. "See if the café's still open."

"Don't be too long," Aunt Gillian says.

It feels like my life has been a low-budget family drama lately, with only enough money for three sets – hospital, café, home – and my father playing the lead role, even if he's out of sight.

I dial my voicemail number – nothing. I pocket my phone and buy a herbal tea; my nod to being healthy. It's more of a pretence than a nod, and I suddenly want to talk to someone who I've never been able to fool, someone who really knows me. Maybe that's why I've been missing Toby over the last few days.

I cup my hands around the tea and breathe it in: lemon and ginger. It reminds me of a teashop in town Edith and I sometimes hung out in at the weekends. After a while, Toby started joining us, even though it was always full of girls and female teachers and he always looked too big and gangly for the crockery. Some of the teachers would come up and talk to him, laugh at how out of place he looked, and I thought about telling him how I thought the place was twee and ridiculous and that I only went because Edith liked it, but I never did. I kind of liked that he'd take being laughed at so he could hang out with us.

I remember it was easy to find things to talk about, even though we saw each other every day. Toby discovered I barely knew any current TV shows and tried to educate me on *Baywatch* and *Xena*, while I described the joys of *Murder, She Wrote*.

I take my first sip of the lemon and ginger. He even came shopping with us. Every Saturday there was a market in town, mostly, by that point, for the tourists. They came and took photos of the Saxon-era church and the yellow irises along the banks of the canal and the shopkeepers who stood in their doorways wearing aprons, squinting in the sunlight. The old

250

men who sat on the benches in the main square for the rest of the week were swept away, along with the sweet wrappers and coke cans that littered the cobblestones. Instead the place was full of stalls selling tat: antique bowls and oranges and children's books. The three of us would do a slow circuit, and each of us had to name the item we'd least like to own. Then we played rock, paper, scissors, and the loser had to buy their item. That was how I ended up with the hand mirror in the shape of a bear's head, and Edith bought a VHS of *A Nymphoid Barbarian in Dinosaur Hell*. Toby paid three pounds for a jar of buttons.

The other boys wouldn't join us; we used to meet them out on the playing fields instead. After that first lunch, they were okay. John was on the swimming team. Francis was Toby's best friend, they played rugby together. He had four female fans in the first year who turned red whenever he walked into a room; I liked how crinkly his eyes were already, and his big, slow smile. If he'd been older and had longer hair, he might have been Malkie's brother.

The boys scared Edith. She didn't like it when they farted around her, or had arm wrestling matches, but she acted game in front of them so she could spend time with Toby. Lunchtime was the same every day – Toby and Francis messed around, showing off their muscles, and Edith swooned.

One time we agreed to break out at night and meet on the playing fields. Me and Edith climbed out of the window and shimmied down the drainpipe. The boys were waiting for us on the grass, tussling with each other, snorting with laughter. I lit a cigarette and sat watching them, thinking how much fun it looked to be a boy. Edith crouched down next to me.

I pointed up at the stars. "Check them out. You can't see them in London."

"That's Ursa Major," she said, indicating. "The Great Bear."

"You know stars?" Toby asked, flopping down onto the grass beside us.

"A little," Edith said, and I could tell she was turning pink.

251

"What about star signs?" John asked, joining us.

"That's not the same thing."

"Course it is. They're all up there. I'm a Scorpio, which means I'm a fantastic fuck." He waggled his eyebrows.

"John, can you just stop thinking about your dick for one second?" Toby said.

John picked his nose and flicked snot in Toby's direction. "Can't," he said. "It's too big to ignore."

"Up yours."

"That's mature," John said.

"You can talk about being mature when they finally let you finish nursery," I said.

Toby looked at me. "What star sign are you?"

"Aries, I think."

"Stubborn and headstrong," Edith said.

"Actually, that's kind of a good fit," Toby said, laughing.

"Shut up," I said, grinning. I looked at Toby out of the corner of my eye. Everything about him was exactly as it should be, I realised: his eyes, his nose, his eyelashes, which were dark and long, but still not girly. His hands, which were usually rammed in his pockets, were smooth and tanned and long, with blue veins that stood out a little from the surface. His stomach, which I caught a glimpse of when he yawned and stretched in front of me, was completely flat, and there was a dark trail of hair that led from his belly button down to the elastic of his boxer shorts.

"Wanna play catch or something?" I asked.

"What are we, five?" John said.

"We're playing catch," Toby stage-whispered to Francis, and he bounded over towards us.

"Francis is It," I said, and ran as fast as I could in the direction of the gym. Out in the middle of the field, the night was black as ink. I jarred my ankle several times where the ground was higher or lower than I expected it to be. I heard footsteps thumping after me, then Francis shoved me and I lost my footing completely, dropping onto my knees.

"You're It," he said, and I heard footsteps retreating.

I tagged John, who got Toby, who came after me. I tried to run in zig-zags. He chased me around half the field until we were far enough away from the others that I couldn't hear them at all. I couldn't hear anything except the blood in my ears, but I could feel the damp grass and the fresh wind, and everything seemed better than it had for a long time.

Toby lunged at me, his body knocking into mine, and we went down. We were tangled up on the ground, and I could feel the heat of his breath on my neck, and his hands on my shoulder blades, then they were gliding lightly over my skin. I turned onto my back and his hands stopped, fingers splayed at the edge of my ribcage. I was aware of the mud and turf beneath me, and Toby above me, and past him, the sky, which was so far away it almost didn't exist.

We looked at each other and I felt the blood drain from my ears and rush around my body. "What are you doing?" I asked.

"Nothing," he said, sliding off quickly. "I mean – nothing." He sounded hoarse.

I started to feel stupid, sitting on the ground while he was standing with his hands back in his pockets. I got up slowly, brushing myself off.

"Hurry the fuck up," John yelled across the field.

"I'm It, I guess," I said. I felt flat all of a sudden and something made me afraid to catch Toby's eye.

"Yeah," he said, jogging back towards the rest of them. I followed him, trying not to let my feet drag too much.

"Are we fucking playing or what?" John called, when I was closer.

I tagged Edith, who was only making a half-hearted effort at running away. She went after Toby – I could hear her giggling and panting, while Toby dodged her outstretched hand, then she gave a little scream and fell in a heap.

"Fucking girls," John said in disgust.

Toby stopped and went back for her and the rest of us moved vaguely in their direction. I felt bad for Edith, falling over in front of her one true love. I started to say something to brush over it, then I got close enough to see her gazing up at him, showing all her teeth in a smile.

"You okay?" Toby asked.

"I think so."

"Want a hand?"

"Yes please."

Toby slipped her arm around his shoulders, then straightened up slowly, bringing her with him. They started limping in my direction. Edith was deliberately hanging off him, letting him take all of her weight, and giggling again. "You're really strong," she said.

Francis and John made noises like they were being sick. I felt my stomach twist inside me. It's just Edith being Edith, I told myself. It wasn't like Edith though. She was being girlier than normal, and Toby wasn't even looking at me anymore.

"Can we stop now?" she asked, shivering melodramatically. "I'm cold."

Toby took off his jacket and put it around her.

We gave up after that, and lay on the ground, sharing my last cigarette. Edith nearly choked on it when it was her turn, and Francis gave her a hefty whack around her shoulders.

"Ouch," she said, her eyes streaming. Toby and John hid their grins, and I felt affection for her again.

"It's a really strong one," I said, and she looked at me gratefully.

* * *

Thinking about that night must have drawn Aunt Vivienne somehow, because she comes past the café and waves a cigarette in my direction. "Smoke? I need to do something wicked."

Outside, I light up and pass Aunt Vivienne my matches. She smokes Gauloises, I notice. I'm sure it fits in with her image of herself.

"It's a filthy habit, you know," she says.

"I can still quit."

"The folly of youth." I can't read her expression. She reaches over and takes my chin in her hand, tipping my face up. Her fingers start to dig in to me, but she just squeezes and lets go. "Did you ever hear how we met? Me and your mother?"

I shake my head.

"It was Edward who introduced us. He brought her round one evening for dinner. I used to throw very decadent dinner parties." She makes a face. "I thought your mother was the most divine being I'd ever seen. She was wearing some hideous floaty nonsense, and her hair was huge. Such a 70s cliché, but absolutely beautiful."

I stay quiet. She might be trying to make up for what she said at dinner the other night. But even now she can't bring herself to be straightforwardly nice about my mother.

"Eddie had a night shift at the hospital, so he left first." She pulls on her cigarette. "We were getting on well – I invited Evie to stay the night. Malkie and Jack and Guillaume were due to stay that night too." She sees my expression. "No, not Starr's father."

"I didn't ask," I mumble.

"Anyway, that's how your mother became one of the gang." She inclines her head. "She fit in very nicely, so we looked after her when your father went off on his little trip to Africa."

"Dad went to Africa?"

"Oh yes – some tiny country down in the south, somewhere."

"Lesotho?"

"That's the one."

I wonder how I didn't know this.

"He was the only doctor in the whole country, from the sounds of it," Aunt Vivienne says. "Which suited him just fine, I'm sure."

"How long was he there for?"

255

"Oh, a year or so." She looks amused. "I don't think Edward thought being on two separate continents necessarily meant they were on a break, but I warned him – girls don't take kindly to being left alone."

"Don't be such a bitch about it," I say. It tastes like metal in my mouth, the idea that my mother had been abandoned like that, after she'd lost her parents as well.

"A bitch?"

"Yes," I say. "A bitch. Don't be a bitch. I know you can be decent sometimes."

"Quite the mouth on you, darling."

I close my eyes and hold my breath, keeping the smoke inside for a moment. I can feel Aunt Vivienne watching me still.

So Dad thought you were going to wait for him, Mum? I'm guessing you didn't, exactly, or Aunt Vivienne wouldn't be telling me this.

I can see the parallels between them and me and Toby already. None of us managed to come out and talk about our feelings properly, avoid any confusion. It makes me feel closer to my father in a strange way, and sorry for him.

"I've never had many female friends," Aunt Vivienne says. "But your mother… "

I open my eyes, exhaling. "Can we not, please?"

Aunt Vivienne shrugs.

"I wonder if someone's come to see us yet," I say.

She looks away. "This place is a shambles," she says. She brings her cigarette up quickly and pulls hard on it. She doesn't get nervous, I tell myself. You're imagining things now.

I finish my cigarette and stretch, placing my hands on the small of my back and twisting until I hear a crack. I can't get too angry with her. I understand what it's like to be friendless.

'They're not all real, you know… '

Was it Grandad who messed you up like this, Aunt Vivienne? Do any of the others have friends? I can't think of any of my father's. He never seemed to want them, but maybe he didn't trust anyone enough.

That's where the damage started, isn't it, with good old Albert Park?

I feel another buzz of adrenalin. "Let's go back in," I say.

"Whatever you say," Aunt Vivienne says, and blows smoke out through her nose.

✳✳✳

Mr Henderson, my fifth-year biology teacher, had a hooked nose and a limp and thinning white hair and reminded me of Mr Tickles.

We were learning about genetic inheritance – dominant and recessive alleles. "Brown eyes are dominant," Mr Henderson told us, beaming. "And blue eyes are recessive. Can you tell me why two blue-eyed parents can't produce a brown-eyed baby... Tallulah?"

"You need the alleles to be present in both chromosomes in the pair," I said. I'd read about this in my father's textbook. It'd confused me at first – my father had blue eyes, and my mother had green, but mine were brown. Hazel was a recessive colour too though, and in certain lights my eyes were hazel.

"Great." Mr Henderson wrote 'alleles to be present in both' on the board. "But can two brown-eyed parents produce a blue-eyed child?"

Everyone else looked bored, even Edith.

"Yeah," I said. "The parents might have heterozygous chromosomes, where they carry the alleles for both blue and brown eyes."

"*Exactly right*. That would give these parents a twenty-five percent chance of conceiving a blue-eyed baby." He sat down heavily behind the desk at the front. "Fifteen minutes until the bell. First person to finish the multiple-choice questions on page sixty-three gets a prize."

I sped through the questions and raised my hand. Mr

Henderson made a note of my name just before the bell rang, then motioned for me to stay behind.

He rummaged around in his drawers while everyone else filed out, and finally produced a black and grey rectangular object. "Your prize – a mini, illuminated microscope."

I went up to his desk and took it from him. "Thanks."

"You deserve it," he said, shutting the drawer again. "You obviously share your father's love for science."

I felt a bump of surprise in my stomach. "You know him?"

"I taught him in my first few years here." Mr Henderson started rubbing the lesson off the whiteboard. "Actually, although I never had him as a pupil, I coached the hockey team and came across your Uncle Jack, too."

"Oh yeah, my grandma said he played."

"He was our star," Mr Henderson said, wrinkling his forehead. "Haven't you seen the photos along the fourth-floor corridor?"

"No."

"I was very fond of both those boys," he said. "Although I can imagine Jack would have been a handful in class. Very bright and interested, your uncle, but only on his own terms." He shook his head. "I know your father's in the medical world now, but I rather lost sight of Jack. What exactly did he do after school?"

My mouth felt dry all of a sudden. I put the microscope away in my schoolbag, fumbling with the straps. "He went away."

"Well. Pass on my regards to both of them," Mr Henderson said.

I left the classroom and was walking to my session with Mr Hicks when I heard someone call my name.

"Tallie."

"Starr?"

She was wearing ripped tights that day, and slinky little fur-lined boots. I noticed, with envy, that she'd put on thick black eye makeup and it made her eyes look huge. When I tried I always ended up looking like I'd been punched.

"Tallie, are you hanging around with Toby Gates?" she asked.

"Yeah. Why?"

"Watch yourself."

"What do you mean?"

"I mean... Don't bite my head off again, but one of the girls in my year started a rumour that he only likes you because you're blowing him."

"What?"

"You know... oral sex."

"I know what it means," I said, my face flushing. "I haven't done it."

"Right," she said, "well, she's just jealous. He dumped her and she thinks she's got more right to him because you're so young, blah, blah." She waved her hand. "But people talk. Especially about Toby – he's hot, you know? But he's been around. Just don't get too close to him."

"Why not?"

"You'll get a reputation."

My heart was thudding angrily. "I'm meant to be afraid of what people are going to say?" I asked as two girls walking past stared at us. "You know they used to talk about me all the time, right?"

"You always were a stubborn little brat," Starr said. "Just don't say I didn't warn you."

"Thanks for the warning," I said. "It's been fun."

Starr rolled her eyes and walked off. I watched her go. I felt sick about Toby, that he could have liked other girls before me, maybe more than me. In fact, I didn't even know if he *did* like me.

I barely paid attention to what Mr Hicks was saying in the session. I finally came around and realised he was waiting for an answer from me.

"What?"

"How's netball?" he repeated. "I hear we're on course for

the gold in the county championships?"

"Yeah, good."

"I like your top, by the way – green's a good colour on you."

"Thanks," I said, confused.

"Are you alright, Tallulah? You seem a little distracted."

"I'm fine."

"Are you worried about going home for the holidays?"

"No, my dad's away. I'm staying with my cousins."

"It probably makes it harder – getting to know each other – if he's not around?"

"I guess." My father seemed to only use his study and his bedroom now anyway. Days could go by with both of us living there and not running into each other.

"It's difficult, being a teenager," Mr Hicks said. "Adults forget that, but it's a real period of change, both within and without. It helps if you have a stable environment." He pushed his chair back, "Which is why I'm so pleased that we've been having these mentoring sessions. I really feel like you're coming along. And I hope you feel the same way?"

"Yeah. I like coming here."

"Good," he said, rummaging among the papers on his desk. "I'm going to give you my mobile number. I'm not really supposed to, so best if you don't tell anyone, but I don't want the good influence of these sessions to stop just because you're outside school grounds. Okay?" He handed me a scrap of paper with a number printed carefully onto it. I put it in my pocket, furtively. I could imagine what Edith would say if she found it.

* * *

I turned up on Aunt Gillian's doorstep, rucksack over one shoulder, a stack of required reading in one hand and a cat-carrier in the other.

"Come in, come in," Aunt Gillian said. "Let me take those books off you." She led the way down the corridor. "I've put you in Michael's room, he's in Cambridge and they don't get a half-term."

"Cool."

"The other two are off next week. I just don't know where the time goes – James in his final year, and you and Georgia doing your GCSEs." She put the books down, hugged me then stepped back.

"Now," she said. "You'll have to excuse me, I'm in the middle of dinner. Make yourself comfortable and come join me in the kitchen whenever you're ready."

I went upstairs and let Mr Tickles out of the carrier. He shook himself and jumped onto the bed, then curled up and went to sleep.

"Fine," I said to him, and went downstairs.

Aunt Gillian was pouring glugs of wine into a pan. The radio was on, a pop station, and she snapped it off when I came in then laughed guiltily. "Force of habit – George doesn't like me to listen to that kind of music. He says it rots my brain."

"I don't mind," I said, sitting down. "Who's your favourite, then?"

She blushed. "That nice Australian man, I like him. Very thin, dark hair."

"Nick Cave?"

"You're laughing at me." She switched the radio on again. The DJ was talking now about Ireland's recent decision to legalise divorce, and Aunt Gillian pulled a face. "People are too quick to give up on marriage these days, that's the problem," she said.

I tried to clear my throat noncommittally. "Can I help with dinner?"

"Absolutely not."

"How's Michael?"

"He's doing very well. He'll be living in Rome next year as part of his year abroad."

"Cool."

"And how's everything going for you?"

"Yeah, good."

"Really?"

"Yeah. I guess I'm on track for the exams."

"Oh, how *wonderful*," she said, beaming at me. "You've found your feet, then." She ground some salt and pepper into the pan. "I always knew you would. It just takes some of us longer than others."

"Mm-hmm."

"And what do you think you'll do after the exams? Any celebration plans?"

"Dunno. There'll probably be some parties I'll go to with my friends."

"That sounds *terribly* exciting," Aunt Gillian said. "You must be very popular then." I winced a little at how enthusiastic she seemed to be about my having friends. I must have been almost given up as a lost cause. "I'm going to take Georgia to Milan for a week on a little shopping trip, a reward. You'd be very welcome to join us. We could make it a real girls' holiday." She beamed at me again.

"Thanks," I said. "I might go see Grandma, though."

"Oh, you're too nice for your own good, Tallulah. You're allowed to do something for yourself you know."

"It's a nice offer," I said, smiling at her.

She came around to give me a hug. "I'm very proud of you."

"Thanks."

"We all are, you know that? Especially Edward. He's *so* proud."

"I'm... " I started to say, before I heard the front door open.

"Mummy, something smells delicious," Georgia called out.

"Oh good – they're home," Aunt Gillian said to me. "I'm making lamb, sweetheart," she called to Georgia. "Come and say hello to your cousin, then set the table."

Georgia bounded in. She hadn't changed that much, I thought. She was plump and pretty, her uniform straining around her chest, and her shoelaces undone. "Hi Tallie," she said, throwing her arms around me.

James came and stood in the doorway behind her. He looked different – he was pale and his nose and chin seemed sharper. "Hi, Tallie," he said, his voice was surprisingly low. "Get me a beer, Mum."

"Oh, alright then." She brought over a can of Heineken. "But not too many before dinner – you must have homework."

"Whatever."

Georgia went to the far drawer of the kitchen dresser and took out cutlery and napkins, then sneezed loudly, turning her face away from the things in her hands.

"Are you *still* coming down with something, sweetheart?"

"I think so."

"Well, you better not touch those, then."

Aunt Gillian finished setting the table, while Georgia coughed and blew her nose into a handful of tissues and I tried to turn my face away without being rude.

For most of that week, I lurked in the music room, reading, or feeding Mr Tickles leftovers, while Georgia stayed in bed.

The Saturday before I was due back at school, I took the tray up for her. The room was stuffy and Georgia was propped up on about four pillows. She waved and looked glad to see me.

"Dinnertime," I said, putting the broth down on the bedside table. "This reminds me of Grandma's."

Georgia widened her eyes. "Oh I never asked – how *was* it? Living with her?"

"I wanted to stay longer, but she got ill."

"Yeah, Mum was upset about Grandma chucking her out," Georgia said. She pulled a face. "She really likes looking after people."

"How come it was my dad that became the doctor then?"

"Mum doesn't think women should work. Not after having kids, anyway." She blew her nose and pulled the bedcovers up to her chest.

"What about Vivienne? Is she a secret call-girl or something?"

"Oh," Georgia giggled, "Mum says Starr's dad is really rich and famous. And married. I think he sends them money so they stay out the picture. Kind of sordid, right?"

"Yeah," I said, and I felt sorry for Aunt Vivienne, and for Starr. "And Uncle Jack – do you know what he did after…?"

"No idea," Georgia said. "I'm so sorry I missed your visit." She plucked at the bedcovers.

"Your mum invited me to Milan."

"Oh God, you have to come. She's so excited about it, but nothing's going to fit me out there, it'll just be super expensive clothes for skinny Italians."

"I might."

"Are you coming back over Easter at least?"

"I'll be at Grandma's. And the boys are in their last year, so I guess they might wanna go on holiday before uni."

She clutched my wrist. "You hang out with older boys? How did I not know this?"

"They're exactly the same as boys our age," I said, but I could feel my skin warming.

"Tallie, do you have a boyfriend?" Georgia asked, suspiciously.

"No."

"I can't believe you've been here this whole time and you never said anything."

"I don't have a boyfriend," I protested. "Seriously."

"Do you *like* a boy, then?"

"I dunno."

Georgia threw her hands up. "You're so secretive! You're as bad as Michael."

"There's nothing to tell."

"Do you have any good-looking friends?"

"Toby's kind of hot."

"Who does he look like?"

"Like, have you ever seen *Boy Meets World*?"

"Yeah, you mean like the main guy? The one with curly hair?"

"No, his best friend – the one with the big eyebrows."

"Oh… He's *cute*," she said.

"I thought he was going to kiss me this one time. But, we haven't done anything."

"I bet he likes you," she said. "Is he nice?"

I didn't meet her eye. "I don't know – he's cool, yeah."

"How does he make you feel?"

"Confused," I said. "Like I'm tongue-tied, I guess. He's funny, and I can never think of anything funny to say back." I dug some dirt out from underneath one thumbnail with the other. "He smells nice, as well. And he can bend his thumbs all the way back to touch his arm." I tried to show her.

"It sounds like you like him," Georgia said, lying back in bed. "But I don't know – Mummy says I'm too young for a boyfriend, anyway. You have to tell me what happens. *Call me.*"

* * *

A few days after I got back to school, I came down with whatever Georgia had. I was in the San for four days then they moved me back to the dorm when I wasn't infectious any more. Toby brought me pink roses that made me glow inside, until he admitted they were Edith's idea. Being alone with him felt even more confusing than before – I couldn't work out if he was being flirty or shifty. He offered to read *Tom Sawyer* to me, which I'd only gone back to after Aunt Gillian had gone on about how proud of me my father was, but then seemed tongue-tied when Edith arrived with a new hairstyle and plucked eyebrows, and couldn't get out of the room fast enough.

"Did I disturb something?" she asked.

"No."

"Oh, I nearly forgot, Mr Hicks said to give you this." She held out a pink card.

I propped myself up on my elbows. There was a quick thumbnail sketch on the front, a girl lying in bed and a doctor checking her chart. Underneath he'd written:

What is it, Doctor?
I'm afraid you have a bad case of nothing much.
Then why are you afraid?
It's contagious.

"I don't get it," Edith said. "But don't you think it's cute?"

"Yeah, it's nice. He's nice," I flopped back onto the pillow. "I need to sleep."

She pottered around for a few moments. "Do you mind if I go find Toby then?"

"Go ahead."

"Are you sure?"

"Jesus… "

"Okay, I'm going."

She skipped out the door. I tried to sleep, but I kept thinking about how pleased Toby had seemed to see me. I felt sure it was real.

My flu didn't last much longer. When Edith saw me polish off a bowlful of jelly she let the school nurse know I was better.

"Thanks a lot," I said.

"I can't live with the windows open anymore," she said apologetically. "*I'm* probably getting ill now."

I had to go around collecting assignments from all the classes I'd missed. Mr Hicks was the only one to let me off.

"Thanks for the card," I said, feeling awkward.

"Glad to have you back," he said, squeezing my shoulder.

I took a detour back from the studio, past the fourth floor. The corridor was lined with framed photos, and eventually, I came to the hockey team, 1971-2. My heart sped up as I looked at it, and at the guy in the middle of the front row. His hair was longer than I remembered, and fell over one eye, but the other eye looked directly at the camera, creased up in a smile. Uncle Jack was happy in the photo, in a way I'd never seen him happy before.

✳✳✳

April came. My father rang me up early on my birthday to send me his wishes. I could almost see him checking it off in his diary. "How's everything going over there?" he asked.

"Good. Dad, I can go stay with Grandma this Easter, right?"

"If that's what you want. Will you be coming to London at all?"

"For the first few days."

"I'll see if I can take the time off," my father said. "The cat sends his – hmm – love."

"Can you put him on the phone?"

There was a short pause, then I could hear a strange metallic rasping on the other end. "Hi, Mr Tickles," I said.

"He washed the receiver," my father said, coming back on.

"I miss him," I said. "I'll call about when I'm coming home."

"Well, happy returns, Tallulah."

We rang off. I wished Malkie would appear to take me out for the day, but I hadn't heard from him since he left for Canada.

Edith gave me a bracelet while we were standing in the lunch queue. I was touched when I unwrapped it. I'd seen it in a jewellery shop in the village, and I knew it cost a lot.

"Do you like it?" she asked anxiously.

"Yeah, Ed," I told her. "It's beautiful."

She beamed.

Starr found me in the hallway and gave me a card from Aunt Vivienne and a book voucher. "Spend it wisely," she said, and grinned at me. "Mum's no good at presents, sorry about that."

I grinned back. "Thanks. And sorry for… "

"No worries."

"Tell your mum thanks, too."

"If I must." She gave me a quick hug and jogged off.

Toby and the guys were waiting on our usual bench when me and Edith took our lunch trays outside. They cheered when they saw us.

"You told them?" I asked her.

"Yeah, come on," she said, giggling.

I followed her over. "Guys… " I said, putting my tray down. "I don't want to make a big fuss."

"It's not a big fuss," Toby said.

"Sweet sixteen," John said. "Now you can smoke after sex."

"Cool," I said. "I think."

Toby was sitting next to me and he laid a present down in front of us carefully.

"What is it?" I asked.

"Unwrap it."

It was a paint brush set, in a black, canvas case, with individual pockets for each brush. The brushes were shiny and clean. I took one out and slipped the protective plastic off, stroking the head across the back of my hand.

"How much was that?" John said suspiciously.

"I thought you'd like them," Toby said. "You said you like art class." I found myself noticing a small brown mole, just beneath his left ear, and then his ears themselves, which were pink and curly like question marks, and then I was looking into his eyes, which really were very green. He looked back at me, and I felt a warmth in my abdomen that spread downwards.

"Thanks," I said, looking down at the brushes. "I love them."

Fourteen

If I could freeze my life at a single point and say – this is where I could have been happy, if it'd stayed like this – would I have chosen that moment? Or would I go back much earlier, to before my mother died?

I buy a coffee this time – maybe I really am an addict – and take it to out into the corridor to drink. I lean back against the wall. If I'd never gone to boarding school, I'd never have met Toby. Maybe I'd have met someone else, maybe it would have been more straightforward. But maybe not.

I close my eyes and let my head connect with the wall. You're pathetic, I tell myself. As if your teenage crush was all you needed to be happy. Even if it felt like much more than a teenage crush at the time.

I remember Easter being late that year, so school broke up a few days after my birthday. In the end my father had to work throughout the holiday, so after days of roaming around the house by myself, I invited Toby over.

"Nice place," he said when I answered the door.

"Thanks."

We grinned at each other, nervously. I'd been looking forward to meeting up with him, but now that he was on my doorstep, it felt weird to see him outside of school. He looked like he felt the same way; he kept ducking his eyes away from mine. His hands were deep in the pockets of a pair of baggy brown cargo trousers; he wore an orange t-shirt and, over that, an open denim shirt. His trainers were scruffy and suede and wide, making me wonder how big his feet were. I looked down at my outfit – black drainpipe jeans and a cropped lace cardigan.

"This isn't going to work," I said. "I went for Michael Jackson and you turn up as Snoop Dogg?"

"I swear I *always* wear sequins and gloves at home."

"Come in," I said. "I'll give you the grand tour."

I led him into the kitchen and brought some beers up from the cellar. "I hope you don't need a glass," I said. "I haven't been washing up."

"I can tell."

"Well, this is the kitchen," I said. "We eat here."

I walked him to the dining-room. "There's a big table in here for when guests come, except I can't remember when we ever had any… and this is the hallway." We trooped through. "This is where my dad hangs his hat and coat."

"Where's he?"

"At the hospital."

"He works long days?"

"Yeah, pretty much."

We went through the rest of the house, ending up in my bedroom.

"It's nice," Toby said. He picked up one of my records. "Pretty old-school, aren't you?"

"Yeah," I said. "Put one on, if you want."

Toby flicked through them. I shooed Mr Tickles off the bed, and tried to wipe away all the fur he'd left behind.

"No Nirvana then? No Red Hot Chili Peppers?"

"Why?"

"You always seemed like a grunge chick to me."

"I'm not sure you can pull off 'chick'."

"I was hoping you wouldn't notice," he said. "What about this one?" He held up a Fleetwood Mac album. "And who's Evelyn?"

270

"My mum. They were hers."

"Oh."

We sat on the bed together. Halfway through the first track, Toby shifted away.

"Do I stink?" I asked him.

"What?"

"You moved." I cringed at hearing myself making weird jokes.

"No." He looked at me again. "You smell... good."

His face was close to mine. I swallowed, suddenly feeling the need for moisture in my mouth. The needle started skipping and Toby jumped up to fix it.

"Want something to eat?" I asked.

"Yeah." He sounded relieved.

I made us cheese sandwiches and we sat on the floor to eat them, listening to The Beatles.

"Have you used your paint brushes yet?" Toby asked.

"I will this week."

"Well," Toby said. "When you do, the girl in the shop said they were good for oils, especially."

I pictured him flirting with her – an art-student type, tiny and pretty, big-eyed and wearing black – then tried to put it out of my mind. "Maybe I'll finally get As in art," I said, "thanks to you." I poked him in the ribs, but he wasn't smiling.

"Don't you get As already?" he asked.

"Maybe once."

"So why's Mr Hicks your mentor?"

"What's your problem with him, anyway?"

"It's not me," Toby said. "It's the girls who always get obsessed with him. His last favourite got expelled. Apparently she had a showdown with him in class, asking why he didn't love her."

I shrugged. "Well I'm not really the showdown type."

Afterwards we played snap and pairs and I won both games. I hoped Toby wasn't finding the afternoon lame, but

271

he seemed to be having fun. Mr Tickles came and lay on the cards and Toby stroked him under his chin, which made my toes tingle and Mr Tickles purr in ecstasy.

We made pasta together for dinner. I added everything from the fridge, which was only garlic paste, basil leaves and salami. I left it too long without stirring and everything burnt, so there was a layer of flaky black carbon on the bottom.

"It's *interesting*," Toby said.

I fed the salami to Mr Tickles, and scraped the rest into the bin. "I get a lot of takeaway," I said. "My mum was a really good cook – guess it's not genetic."

"How did she…?"

"Hit and run," I said. "My dad was there. I wasn't."

"Shit," Toby said.

I tried to shrug, but my whole body had stiffened up. Toby came and sat next to me, "You don't have to talk about it if you don't want," he said.

"I was at a friend's," I said, "and when I got back he was all bloody and stuff. At first I thought he'd killed her… You know, beaten her up."

"Really?"

"Yeah, crazy, huh?"

"Why?"

"Dunno," I said. "Maybe I was delirious. And my dad's brother was there, and they don't get on. But then they said she'd been hit by a car. They said she ran out in front of it."

"Well… " Toby looked uncomfortable. "At least it wasn't your dad, I guess."

"He told the police it was his fault."

Toby's eyebrows shot up. "Did he mean it?"

"I don't really know."

He looked at his hands in his lap. "Tal, I don't know what to say."

"He was probably in shock too," I said. Now that I'd started talking about it, I didn't seem able to stop. "It was horrible, seeing her like that." I felt sick when I remembered it.

I wandered into the dining-room after that and picked out a few notes on the piano. If Toby had come and put his arms around me then, maybe everything would have been different. I know I wanted him to so badly it felt like I was going to break myself into tiny pieces wishing it.

Instead, he came to the doorway and gave me a tight smile. "I better go."

I shut the piano lid with a bang and walked past him to the front door. I opened it and stood back. So Toby wanted nothing to do with my crazy family, I told myself. Fine by me. I could have told him more – about my mother really being in love with her husband's brother, about my grandfather abusing my grandmother and my aunt. Or how my own dad couldn't look me in the eye. That would really have freaked him out.

"Sorry," he said, avoiding my eye. "I just have to get back."

"I get it."

"I'll see you when you're back from your grandma's?"

"Yeah."

He looked at me then and bent down to kiss my cheek. I could feel him trembling. "See you."

"See you."

✳✳✳

I was clipping Mr Tickles' claws when the phone rang the next day.

"Hi, it's Toby."

"Yes?"

"Look, I'm sorry about last night. I shouldn't have run away like that."

I lay back on my bed. "Don't worry about it." I tried to make my voice sound dismissive, but it caught halfway through.

"I just… freaked out."

"You think?"

"I'm sorry. It kind of brought back memories of my brother. He died when I was younger."

He'd gone quiet, and for a moment I thought I hadn't heard him right. "I thought you were an only child?"

"I am now."

"Shit," I said. Which wasn't exactly the most sympathetic I could have been. "I'm so, so sorry. What happened?"

"He hanged himself. Apparently I found the body, but I don't remember it at all."

"*Jesus.*"

"Yeah, no one at school knows about it; it's kind of grim. My parents won't talk about it."

We didn't speak for a moment while I tried to think of what to say. "That's awful."

"Yeah."

"Did they try to make you see a counsellor?"

"Course. Finding the body – they loved that. I went twice. You?"

"Yeah. For a while."

"Don't tell anyone. I just wanted you to know."

"Course I won't." I felt a sudden thrill inside me – he trusts me – then felt guilty again.

"Anyway," he said, "enough family crap. Do you want to come camping with us next week?"

"Who's us?"

"The guys. We go to Broadwater Forest every year."

"I'll be at my Gran's."

"Leave early. You're seeing her over the summer."

"Well… " I rolled onto my stomach and got the phone cord tangled up in my armpit. I unwrapped it from myself in time to hear Toby say, "We've never asked a girl before – think of it as an honour."

I felt a smile growing on my face. "I'm flattered."

"You should be. So is that a yes?"

"Is Edith coming?"

"I haven't asked her."

"You going to?"

"Yeah," he said, "course."

"Okay," I said. "Gimme details later."

I gave him my grandmother's telephone number and we hung up.

I thought about Toby a lot over the next few days, when I was packing for my grandmother's, or tidying my room or showering, or doing anything. Maybe that was why we liked each other so much, I thought, because we'd both seen people we'd loved die. Except Toby hadn't seen his brother die – he'd found him already dead. And it must have been worse than I could even imagine if his mind had wiped the image. But he was so together, no one would know. No one *did* know. I felt proud, in a weird way, that he'd been able to handle it so well.

But he must have been supported by his family, too, I told myself. If my father had been more like them, I probably wouldn't be so messed up. If I'd gone to live with my grandmother from the start…

On the other hand, I told myself, maybe I would have frozen to death if I'd lived with my grandmother for any longer. The house was only slightly less icy in the spring than in the winter.

"You shouldn't be in the cold, it's not good for you," I said, pushing her into the sunshine. She dozed off while I did my homework nearby. Occasionally she woke up and demanded water. "I'm burning," she said. "Are you trying to finish me off?"

I rummaged around in her things until I found a floppy hat for her to wear. "It's not even that sunny," I told her. "You must be cold-blooded or something."

"I've heard that one before," she said.

"Who from?" I asked, but she waved the question away. "So, has Aunt Vivienne come to visit yet?" I asked, casually, arranging the hat on her head.

"You're not as dumb as you look, Tallulah."

"I'll take that as a compliment."

She seemed much better now; her cheeks were pinker and

her eyes looked clearer. She was impatient being confined to her wheelchair; she followed me around more, poking her nose into everything I did. Toby called every day and it was hard to hide the conversations from her.

"What's with the heavy breathing?" he asked once.

"Shut up, I'm jogging."

"Now?"

"I'm going to the bottom of the garden."

"Why?"

"Privacy."

"Who exactly are you hiding from?"

"My grandma – she's turned into a spy."

"Where's your dad?"

"London."

"Sorry – should I not have asked that?"

I shrugged.

"Tal?"

"I shrugged."

"You know I can't see that down the phone, right?"

"It's okay. We can talk about my dad being in London."

"How often do you see him?"

"Maybe a few weeks a year."

"You're lucky," Toby said. "My dad's around all the time – he took voluntary redundancy a few years ago."

"What did he do?"

"Construction foreman." He cleared his throat. "I got a scholarship."

"Oh." I'd never even considered how other people paid their fees. "So he's used to being in charge?"

"Yeah," Toby said. "But he's cool. He kind of wanted Danny – my brother – to get into the business with him, but after he died, Dad said I should do whatever I wanted. He got a t-shirt saying *I'm with Genius* when I got the scholarship."

"You don't want to be a foreman?"

"I want to make a lot of money so my mum can retire."

"What does she do?"

"She's a teaching assistant."

"My mum used to be a waitress," I said. "She was good with people."

"How come you're so terrible, then?"

"Har-dee-har-har."

"I'll be quiet."

"She *was* nice," I said. "Everyone liked her." I thought of Aunt Vivienne. "Nearly everyone. And she was really beautiful."

"Yeah? Did she look like you?"

"No," I said, trying not to smirk. "She had really amazing hair – she used baby shampoo."

"You sound like you really got on."

"Yeah," I said. "At least I had an amazing mum, right?"

"True."

"What was your brother like?"

"He was really sweet – the quiet type. He used to look out for me at school."

"What do you mean?"

"I used to be really tiny, and he was quite big for his age – he used to scare off all the kids who picked on me, even though he'd never have actually done anything."

"He sounds cool."

"You'd have liked him. You'd like my dad, too."

"You'd like my Grandma."

"Oh yeah?"

"I should go check on her," I said.

"Talk tomorrow?"

"Talk tomorrow."

"Who was that?" my grandmother asked when I went back up the lawn.

"I thought you were asleep."

"Who was it?" she asked again, ignoring me.

"Toby."

"A boy from school?"

I looked at her; she'd closed her eyes and was smiling to herself.

"Just a friend."

"Of course he is."

"Can we drop this?"

"If it's bothering you," she said, still smiling. "But he's got you mooning all over the place, my girl."

"I'm *not*."

"You are."

I chewed my fingernail for a moment. "What did you do when you liked a boy?"

"It's been too long for me to remember."

"How long?"

"I was sixteen when I met your grandfather – towards the end of the war."

"Did you have a boyfriend before Grandad?"

She gave me a look.

"What?"

"In my day, young women were encouraged not to spread themselves too thinly."

"So no?"

"No."

"How did you two meet?"

"He was a pilot," she said. "He was a neighbour too, but I'd never really noticed him until a barn dance I went to on my birthday… I remember we danced the first dance together, and he wouldn't let me partner anyone else afterwards."

"Was he handsome?"

"The handsomest."

"And then what?"

"I let him chase me for two years," my grandmother said.

"Why?"

"Hruh," she said. "I was young, but I knew what marriage meant for women. You think I wanted to cook and iron shirts all day?"

"But you did marry him."

"He wore me down," she said. "He was very persuasive."

I wondered if violence had been part of his persuasion.

"I remember the day I said yes," she said. "He disappeared, and came back with a suitcase full of roses. He said if I wanted, he'd bring me roses every day."

"Did he?"

"Of course not," she said, putting her hand over mine. "But don't look so despondent about it, my darling."

"I don't even know how to spell that." I leaned over and kissed her cheek.

"My smart-aleck granddaughter."

∗ ∗ ∗

The next time Toby called, my grandmother made a point of wheeling back and forth past the telephone. After four trips, I grabbed one of the handles of her chair, pulling her up short.

"What?" she asked, trying to look innocent.

"Why are you spying on me?"

"I'm making myself a drink."

"Go away," I said. "Now."

She gave me another innocent look and wheeled away, stopping just inside the living-room.

"Go further than that," I called.

"I'm a prisoner in my own home," she shouted back.

"Sorry," I said into the receiver. "She's got nothing better to do." I leaned back against the wall and slid down it until I was sitting on the carpet. "So, how's tricks?"

"Alright. What you up to?"

"Hanging out with Grams." I wove the fingers of my free hand into the wine-coloured shag-pile. "I feel bad leaving her."

"You don't have to come," Toby said. He cleared his throat. "I mean, obviously, it would be cool but... "

"I want to come," I said. "It's just, it's not like my dad will come see how she is, or anything."

"Don't they get on?"

"I don't know. One of my aunts – the younger one – doesn't speak to her, and *she* doesn't like spending too much time with the other aunt."

"Is she just an older version of you?"

"And then there's my uncle, who turned up out of the blue, and pissed everyone off for some reason, then disappeared again. Then her and my dad – they don't talk much, but they don't fight either."

"You have an interesting family," Toby said.

"You mean weird."

"I didn't say that."

I paused; I could feel my stomach knotting up at what I was thinking of saying. "Uncle Jack was definitely the highest point of weirdness. My dad really changed afterwards."

"How so?"

"Him and my mum started fighting. I don't remember them fighting before – that could have had something to do with her getting depressed. And he didn't look after her at all, he got my aunt to do it. And he seemed really annoyed with me."

"With you?"

"Yeah."

"Why would he be annoyed with you?"

"I dunno," I said. "We don't talk either. It got worse after my mum died."

"What happened?"

"Well – he sent me to boarding school for one thing."

"My parents sent me, too."

"But I didn't want to go, and it was only a week or two after it'd happened." I swallowed, trying not to let any tears out. "And... I can't explain it... He looks at me like he doesn't know me. Just after the accident, I felt like... " I suddenly realised exactly how he'd made me feel, something I hadn't been able to admit even to myself. "I felt like he wished it was me who died."

Toby was quiet for a moment. I could hear my breathing down the line. I tried to stifle it and made a sobbing sound instead.

"I'm so sorry, Tal," he said eventually. "That sounds shit." He paused again, and I finally got myself under control. "I'm sure he doesn't feel like that."

"Maybe not."

"I wish I was there with you."

I rubbed my cheek with the heel of my hand. "We kind of just leave each other alone now."

"Do you mind?"

"I – " I stopped. "We've never even *talked* about it. Other than the medical details – he never asked how I was. Not once."

"Tallulah," my grandmother called. "Are you still on the telephone?"

I took a deep breath. "Gotta go," I said.

"Don't."

"I have to."

"Are you okay?"

"Yeah."

"You sure?"

"Yeah, sure. I don't mind telling you these things."

"I don't mind telling you things either."

"See you in two days, then."

∗ ∗ ∗

Edith was hyper-excited about the camping trip, but the day before it was scheduled she got mumps from her younger brother and couldn't come. "I *hate* him," she moaned. "This was my best chance of getting with Toby."

I made sympathetic noises, but I was secretly pleased about not having to share him. Then I felt guilty and wondered if I should tell Edith that I liked him – but nothing's going to happen anyway, I told myself.

When the train pulled into Worthing platform, Toby was standing alone. He was carrying a backpack, his hat pulled down over his ears. Seeing him there without the others took me by surprise. I waited for a moment, scuffing my shoes before I went over.

"Hey," he said, looking terrified.

"Hey yourself. Where's everyone else?"

"Francis had to go visit his cousin – new baby or something," he said. "And John's on holiday with his folks."

"So it's just us two?"

"Yeah. Is that okay?"

My mouth was dry. "Sure, why not?"

The woods the boys had chosen were dense and tangled, with berries growing in splashes of red. They smelled like smoke and wet dog.

"What do you think of it?" Toby asked, gesturing around.

"It's nice."

He took my hand shyly, brought it up to his mouth and kissed it. "I wanted to show it to you," he said. "It's kind of an escape for me – from home and Danny, and my parents… "

I squeezed his hand.

"Come on," he said.

We walked until we got to a clearing that sloped down to a pond. Two lone ducks circled the edges of the water, calling mournfully to each other. The trees were tall enough to block out most of the light.

We worked silently, driving the pegs into the ground and stretching the material over the poles. Toby surveyed it when we'd finished. "Not bad for a girl."

"Watch it."

We threw our bags inside, then sat down facing each other on two nearby logs.

"Did you bring a sleeping bag?"

"Yeah," I said. "But I think it might be kind of moth-eaten."

"You can share with me if you want?"

"Okay." I could feel my stomach flutter. Play it cool.

"I've got another blanket too. Oh, and I brought these." He reached into his pockets and brought out two squashed peanut-butter sandwiches, wrapped in cling-film.

"What do you guys do around here, anyway?" I asked, as we ate.

"Drink," he said. "Talk about stuff. Sports mostly."

"I'll drink."

Toby grinned. "I've got beers." He rummaged around in his bag and pulled out two six-packs. I noticed again how strong and smooth his hands looked.

"If we keep them in the pond they'll be colder," he said.

"Okay."

It took three beers each for the sun to go down. We sat, knees touching, playing poker with matches that I'd found in my jacket pocket.

"So a straight flush wins?" I asked.

"Yeah."

I laid down a jack, and a queen of diamonds, next to the ten, king and nine on the ground.

"You're like a cards fiend," Toby said, shaking his head.

"Beginner's luck," I said, trying to not grin from ear to ear.

"I'm going to win those matches back, you know that, right?"

"You can try."

"How about winner gets both sleeping bags?"

We played a few more hands and Toby took nearly all the matches back off me. I finished my beer and lay back along the log, looking up at the silhouettes of the treetops and beyond, at all the warm, daylight colours that were pooling at the bottom of the sky. There was a loosening inside me, like everything I'd been able to talk to Toby about didn't matter anymore – my father's coldness, losing my mother, worrying about my grandmother. Maybe the woods could be an escape for me too.

I felt a sudden pang over Edith, ill at home. But I hadn't done anything wrong, I reassured myself.

Toby went and fetched us more beers. He passed me one, brushing my hand with his fingertips, and sat beside me on my log.

"I'm cold already," I said.

"Here, have my jacket." He wrapped it around me, then huddled closer. "We should make a fire."

"We should definitely not do that," I said, hiccupping. "You're drunk. *I'm* drunk."

He put his arm around me, making me jump. "What do you wanna do, then?"

"I dunno," I said. Starr's words came back to me. I wondered if he'd done this with other girls, too, the arm pulling them closer as he worked up towards a kiss. I tried to take another swig. Maybe he wasn't going to try to kiss me. Maybe I didn't measure up to the others.

"Truth or dare?" he asked, after a moment or two of silence.

"Alright. You start."

"Truth."

"Is… it really true you pulled Melissa Albrecht?"

Melissa Albrecht was famous at our school for being bigger than most of the rugby boys.

"Yeah," Toby said. "But I was wasted."

"How was it?"

"Scary."

"Uh-huh."

"Your turn."

"Truth."

"Okay." Toby cracked open another can for himself. "What about you – kissed anyone you shouldn't have?"

"Nope."

"What d'you mean?"

"I mean nope," I said. "I haven't kissed anyone." I took a long drink, trying to hide my flaming cheeks.

"What, like, ever?"

"I guess there was Tom at primary school," I said. "But he slobbered all over me."

"Wow, really?"

"Really."

"How did that happen?"

"Isn't it your turn again?"

"I can't believe you've never kissed anyone."

"Well I haven't. I must be hideous – case solved."

Toby grinned.

"What?"

"Remember the first time we sat with you guys, and you gave John a dirty look 'cos he was laughing at Edith? You kind of look like that now."

"Like what?"

"Like you're gonna rip my head off."

"Yeah, well… "

"I like that I can't impress you, which is kind of weird, I guess. But you're actually kind of sweet to other people." He twisted the ring-pull on his can backwards and forwards until it snapped off. "Like when you found a clump of hair in your cake in that stupid café, and you didn't tell them because you thought the owner would be embarrassed."

"And I'm not sweet to you?"

"Not always." He took my hand in his, drawing circles with his finger on the back of my wrist, and up my arm. "You've got really soft hands."

"Mm-hmm."

"Not really helping with the moment, are you?"

"I don't know what to say."

"Nice things."

"Like what?"

"Like – you're so sexy," Toby said.

"You want me to tell you you're sexy?"

"No *you* are. You're the sexiest person I know."

"Okay. I mean, thanks. What's so funny?"

"Nothing, it's just… I think I'm in love with you," he said.

I saw his mouth coming towards me; his breath smelled like peanuts. Then his lips were on mine, and I opened my mouth instinctively. My hands were hanging at my side, being useless, and I shifted on the log to find the right position. Toby pulled away, and looked at me with such a weird expression that I almost laughed.

"Is this okay?" he asked.

"I dunno," I said, feeling my cheeks flare up again. "I've never been kissed before, remember?"

"I didn't mean that," he said. "I meant… do you want to keep on kissing?"

"Yeah. It's nice."

We kissed again, and this time I tried to copy Toby's movements, the way he bit me gently, or ran his tongue along the inside of my lip. He let out a kind of sigh, like he'd been holding himself together, and a tickling feeling ran up my spine and exploded at the base of my brain. I put my arms around him and dug my fingers in, enjoying the heat underneath his clothes, but I still didn't feel close enough, and I pressed myself forwards until there was no space left between us and I was touching him with the whole length of my body. He was cupping his hands around the back of my head, holding me to him as the kisses got harder, almost painful, and I realised I'd wanted this since the moment he came over to my table and sat down next to me.

Toby pulled away again. "Fuck," he said. "I want you."

I caught my breath.

"Is that too fast?"

I shook my head, not trusting myself to speak. I crawled into the tent ahead of him, feeling the cool material of the sleeping bag beneath my hands in the dark, and the thump of my heart in my chest and my throat. Toby flicked on his torch and tied it to the zip dangling from the ceiling, so a small spotlight bobbed gently in the middle of the space. When he turned around on his knees I could see the bulge in his jeans. I reached out and put my hand against the swelling. I could feel the blood thundering through me. I shook my head to get rid of the buzz in my ears, and everything in front of me slid to one side, then returned to its original place.

He took my jumper off me, and my t-shirt, kissing me the whole time, his lips warm and dry. "I'm sorry about the other day," he said, in between kisses. "I really want to take care of you, you know?"

286

"Can we not talk about that now?"

A picture of my mother appeared uninvited in my mind, then, even worse, Uncle Jack and my mother that day in the rose garden. I pulled back from Toby, but he didn't seem to notice. "Hey," I mumbled.

He was fumbling with the clasps on my bra, swearing under his breath. I felt like I couldn't breathe. I kept hearing Uncle Jack's voice in my head: 'not what nice girls do', and the sound of my mother's hand across his face. I closed my eyes and saw my mother at her birthday party now, white-faced and grieving, Uncle Jack vanished again.

"Stop," I said. "*Stop*."

"What's wrong?" he said; he was still trying to unhook my bra.

I felt a bubble of panic rise inside me. "Fucking *stop*," I said, twisting away and lashing out. My knuckles cracked against his nose and upper lip and I felt the jolt run up my arm to my shoulder. Toby grabbed at my wrist with one hand and brought the other up to his nose.

"*Jesus*," he yelled. "What was that for? That fucking hurt."

"*Get off me*." I tried to wrench my wrist away, and it came dangerously close to his face again.

"What's your fucking problem?"

"Don't *touch* me."

He sat and stared at me. "Why?"

"Why do I have to explain?"

He looked disgusted. "Everyone in my year laughs at me, you know. They say I'm your love-sick puppy."

"I didn't *ask* you to love me."

"You don't have to treat me like shit, either. If you like me too, you don't have to hide it."

"I *don't* like you," I said. "You follow me around like a fucking creep – I feel sorry for you, that's all."

Toby recoiled like I'd hit him again. "Fine," he said. He sighed loudly. "We can go to sleep, if you want. Then tomorrow you can go home and you don't have to see me again. How does that sound to you?"

"Why wait until tomorrow?"

"What?"

I grabbed my t-shirt and crawled towards the opening of the tent.

"Where are you going?"

"Don't speak to me like I'm your kid."

"Don't fucking act like one, then."

"Fuck you, Toby."

"That's fine, then. Fuck off."

I pulled my top on and walked into the woods, deliberately not putting my hands out to clear a path so by the time I stopped I was covered in scratches. I leant against a tree trunk and lit a cigarette, wrapping my free arm around myself and cupping my shoulder to try to stay warm. Half of me was frustrated that I hadn't been able to go through with it, and the other half was furious with Toby for not understanding why I couldn't. I pulled on the cigarette. If he loved me, then he'd come after me.

I finished two cigarettes, stamping them out in the roots of the tree. There were no stars out up beyond the tree-tops. My heart hurt.

"Fucking fuck you, then," I said.

I waited for what felt like over an hour before I went back. I was shivering, and my body felt flushed with the cold. I crawled in. Toby was inside his sleeping bag, facing away from me. My sleeping bag was out. I rolled myself up inside it and faced the side of the tent, trying to hold my limbs tight so they stopped convulsing. I could hear Toby's breathing nearby; after about another hour, it became more regular and I knew he was asleep.

The next morning we packed up without a word. Images from the night before kept swimming before me: Toby kissing me, Toby taking my top off, Toby seeing my body. We'd gone so quickly from that intimacy to this heavy silence that I felt ashamed it had happened at all. Every time I remembered the moment I'd punched him, my insides shrivelled in humiliation. In daylight, and hungover, I couldn't be sure I hadn't overreacted.

In London we walked into the underground together.

"Tal, I… " Toby started.

"I've gotta go," I said.

"I'm sorry. I shouldn't have kissed you."

"Yeah." I felt my eyes well up. I looked down at the floor and willed the tears not to spill over. "I don't think we should tell anyone about it."

"Bye then," he said, and left me at the barrier.

I spent the rest of the week clearing out my room. My father left me to it; he didn't ask about the camping trip.

I phoned my grandmother every afternoon. Mr Tickles jumped onto my lap and pawed at me while I spoke to her, asking for affection. Toby called four or five times, but I couldn't face him. The second-to-last time he left a short message, which I deleted, saying he wanted to talk. The last time, he sighed and then hung up.

∗∗∗

I take my cup back to the boy on the till.

"Thanks," he says, uncomfortably, and looks away. Maybe he thinks I'll report him to my 'fiancé' if he talks to me. It's pathetic that when I think of my imaginary fiancé, I think of Toby, isn't it?

I go outside, breathing in the fresh air in big gulps. I check my phone again. Still nothing from Malkie.

"Hurry up," I say out loud.

The lift on the way back up is packed: two nurses chatting, an elderly woman in a wheelchair and a porter to push it, and a family with young kids. They all get out before me, the kids dropping crisps everywhere as their mum tries to surreptitiously take the packets back.

Aunt Gillian and Aunt Vivienne are exactly where I left them, both looking off into the distance. Aunt Gillian is rubbing her right thumb back and forth over the fleshy bit between left thumb and left palm. Aunt Vivienne is tapping a pen against the magazine lying open on her lap. If ever I've seen two people trying to keep hold of their anxiety, this is it. I guess it's been a long time since I was told to wait in here; anything could be happening right now.

"Hi," I say.

They both start.

"A shrub or small tree," Aunt Vivienne says. "Anagram of 'camus'."

"Sumac."

"I think you're right," she says, scribbling it down.

"How did you know that, dear?" Aunt Gillian asks.

"Grandma had one."

"How clever."

"How was he?" Aunt Vivienne asks.

"Who?"

"The boy in the café."

"Fine," I say, sitting down. "I think I've scared him off for good now."

It's what I do, guys.

Toby was probably the most persistent, but I was stubborn, and eventually even he gave up.

I'd avoided him for the first week of summer term, but he managed to catch me once, grabbing my shoulder.

"Tal… Can you stop running off, please?"

If I hadn't been so dumb, I would have talked to him then. I should have remembered that his childhood trauma was almost worse than mine, that he'd freaked in front of me too, but at the time all I could think was that I couldn't listen to him tell me how much he liked me as a friend, or worse, how he didn't want to be friends anymore because I was damaged and mental.

"Just get out of my way. Please."

I remember he moved out of the way and sighed again, like I was the most irritating person in the world. "Off you go then."

"Whatever," I said, and walked past him.

Aunt Vivienne's tapping the pen again. It sounds much louder in my brain than it really can be. I start to bite my thumbnail, then think better of it.

If I'd listened to Toby…

I hadn't told Edith about what had happened on the camping trip, but she started acting jumpy around me anyway. The day after I ran into Toby, I saw her giving me little looks out of the corner of my eye, until I asked her what was up.

She giggled. "Nothing really."

"Please stop staring at me then."

We were probably going to gym class when we were having the conversation. I remember we were outside. Edith stopped walking suddenly, and said, "I have to tell you something."

I heard footsteps behind us, they got faster, then someone tapped me on my right shoulder. "Hey," Starr said. She'd dyed her hair blonde, with dark roots, making her look like Debbie Harry. The school had recently voted to scrap uniforms for the sixth-formers and she was wearing a tight striped top, a denim miniskirt and a bomber jacket with the sleeves rolled up. I remember looking down at myself, tugging at the hem of my too-short netball skirt, trying to make it seem less scandalous. Next to Starr, I looked like a child prostitute.

"Hey," I said.

"Good holiday?"

"Yeah, alright. You?"

"Great. We went sailing for two weeks," Starr said. She inspected her arm. "Think the tan's wearing off already. Bloody weather." I looked down at her beautiful honey-brown colour. "Look, I've got to run, but I came to tell you about this party the Drama Group's having, for the end of our play. You coming?"

"The play or the party?"

"You don't have to come to the play. It's some weird Russian shit about an albatross or something."

"*The Seagull*," Edith said quietly.

291

"What?" Starr asked.

"It's a play by Chekhov," Edith said.

"Maybe," Starr said. "I just do backstage."

"Where's the party?" I asked.

"It's at the drama teacher's house, on campus," Starr said. "It'll be crazy. She's some weird hippy who makes us call her by her first name. Apparently she gets really drunk and cries at these things."

"Oh?"

"It's after the last night; two Fridays from now."

"Cool."

"Anyway," Starr said. "See you there." She started to jog in the other direction. Edith stared after her.

"Your cousin's really pretty," she said.

"What did you have to tell me?"

"Oh – nothing," she said. "It can wait."

I felt a strange sense of relief. Afterwards, I realised I knew all along what she was trying to tell me.

"I hope your boss understands about all of this," Aunt Gillian's saying.

"What?"

"Wasn't it him you were calling earlier?"

I try not to meet her eye. "He doesn't really have human emotions," I say. "But he hasn't fired me yet."

"Oh."

I want to tell her that, actually, I'm trying to get in touch with her errant brother – the one who went to jail and the whole family stopped mentioning. I need to ask him a few questions about my mother, and whether or not they were in love. And whether my father knew and that's why he went so weird.

I stand up and walk around the room once, pretending to be looking for something. No one's even talking about why we're here anymore.

"Last one," Aunt Vivienne says. "Six letters, beginning with 'd'. At great cost."

✳✳✳

Another week passed before I saw Toby again. I knew Edith had been hanging out with the boys, but she was vague when I asked her what they'd been up to. Then, on Friday, Toby was waiting outside after my biology class. I felt a half-embarrassed grin spread over my face – I hadn't completely driven him away then. "Hey," I said.

"Hey yourself. Where you going now?"

"French."

"Can I walk with you?"

"Sure."

"Look – I just wanna say I'm sorry," he said. "For what happened. You know, on the trip. That's what I was trying to tell you last time."

"It's fine. I'm sorry too."

"Okay, good." He looked relieved.

We fell into step. Toby was cracking his knuckles. I looked at him properly; he was wearing a white t-shirt that made his eyes seem greener, navy blue shorts that he'd rolled up at the bottom so they stopped just above the knee and grey plimsolls. I tried not to think of his body underneath, how warm it had been when we were kissing.

"What's wrong?"

"What do you mean?" he asked.

"You seem kinda nervous."

Toby shook his head. "Tal, we're friends right?" he said. "Nothing's going to come between us, yeah?"

"Yeah," I said.

We reached the door of my French class, and he stood in front of it so I couldn't go in. "Cool," he said. "Have lunch with us?"

"Yeah, alright."

French class felt longer than usual; I ran out of the door when the bell rang, heading to our old spot outside. John and Francis were kicking a football around.

293

"Hi," I said, sitting down on the picnic bench. "You okay?"

"Hey, Tal," Francis said, coming over. "You're looking… nice."

"Thanks," I said, surprised.

"Hey, Tal." John joined us. "I didn't expect to see you here."

"I haven't been kicked out yet."

"No, I meant, about Toby."

"What about him?"

Francis shoved John. "Nothing," he said.

"I mean about Toby and Edith," John said.

"What?"

"You didn't know?" John asked.

Francis gave him a dirty look; John smirked. "Was I not supposed to say anything?" he asked. "Shame. Oh well, Toby's coming now. You can ask him about it."

"Yo," Toby said, dropping his bag on the floor. He saw our faces. "What happened?"

"John told Tal," Francis said. He shrugged helplessly. John was still grinning. Toby looked at them and then at me. "You prick," he said to John.

$$* * *$$

I called my grandmother, but she was sleeping. The nurse was on her way out.

"It's my afternoon off," she said. "I'll wake her up this evening and tell her you called."

"Can you leave a note at least?"

"Fine."

I kicked the phone-booth when I hung up.

I went to bed early and lay there staring at the ceiling, wondering if my insomnia was back. I must have fallen asleep though, because I woke in the middle of the night, arms and legs strangely heavy. I heard the telephone ring downstairs in the Housemistress' office, and footsteps shuffling out to answer it; it must have been the phone that woke me.

I got out of bed to pee. On the way back, I stopped at the top of the stairs. The Housemistress was sitting on the bottom step, rabbit-faced slippers on her feet. Normally the sight would have made me laugh, but this time something made me lean over the banister and call down to her quietly. "Who was that?"

She started and turned to face me. "Tallulah. How long have you been there?"

"Not long."

"Oh, goodness. It's so strange that it should be you up." She seemed flustered.

"What is it?"

She hesitated.

"What?"

"That was your father on the telephone. It's your grandmother."

I sat down too, on the top step, with my knees pressed together. "What about her?" I asked, as the Housemistress started climbing up towards me. "Is she okay?"

"She had a nasty fall," she said, kneeling in front of me. "You know, maybe we should get you a hot drink or something."

I clutched the banister. "Why?"

"The nursing company just called your father," she said. "The nurse found your grandmother when she got back this evening."

"How is she?" I asked, but even before I asked I knew what was coming next.

"I'm sorry, Tallulah. She's dead."

∗∗∗

We hear voices suddenly coming from my father's room. Someone shouts "Check the monitor", and then footsteps are slapping along the corridor floor, much too heavy for a child this time.

"Doctor," the voices start up again. "You're needed."

We're frozen, all turning towards the sounds but none of

us daring to go out into the hallway to see what's happening. No one looks shocked. I feel like we knew this was coming.

"Oh fuck," Aunt Gillian says in a whisper; I think it must be the first time I've heard her swear.

A surgeon comes into the waiting-room, dressed in full operating gear. "Miss Park?" he says, looking straight at me. "I'm afraid your father's situation is deteriorating. He's being prepped for surgery now."

"What happened?"

"He's tamponading – an artery must have been punctured during the PCI. It's not uncommon. We'll do everything we can."

We follow him into the hallway. They wheel my father out and into the operating room.

"He'll be alright," Aunt Gillian says, putting her hand on my shoulder. I can feel her shaking.

"Ladies, if you don't mind waiting in the room down the hall," a nurse says, her arms full of bandages.

"But… " Aunt Gillian starts.

The nurse goes into the theatre, and we catch a glimpse of tubes and instruments and people moving around, with my father in the middle, before the door swings shut.

Fifteen

The night before the funeral, we stayed at Aunt Gillian's house, me, my father, Aunt Gillian, Uncle George, Michael and Georgia. James was away on a school trip, and no one was talking about Vivienne. I'd heard Aunt Gillian pleading with her down the telephone. "Of course we tried. No one knows how to get in touch with him, Viv. Anyway, it's *Mother's funeral*. It's not the time for grudges… "

Uncle George had burst in on Aunt Gillian then. He was out of sight, but I'd heard him demanding the telephone, waving aside her objections. "It's bloody work, Gillian."

We drove to my grandmother's the next day. The church was just around the corner from the house; it was cold and the minister droned on, without ever saying my grandmother's name. I stared at the back of Uncle George's head in the pew in front of me and noticed how little flecks of white skin kept dropping from his hair onto his shoulders. He seemed even more irritable than normal; halfway through the service he got a phone call and went outside. I heard his voice raising over the minister's from time to time, shouting about 'liability', 'betrayal', and once, 'little shit'.

As soon as we got back to the house, my cousins were sent upstairs to pack my grandmother's things into boxes. Uncle George had brought some over in the boot of the car.

"No sense in wasting time," he said. "We'll have to recuperate the cost of the funeral anyway."

"George," Aunt Gillian said, looking scandalised.

"Well it's true. You said the old bird was down to her last penny, so that rules out a nice big inheritance." He looked gloomy.

"This is hardly the time to discuss it."

"Oh yes, I forgot how close you all were."

"She was my *mother*."

"Grow up, Gillian. If you're going to get hormonal maybe I'll go for a walk."

"Perhaps you should walk off a cliff," I suggested.

"*Tallulah*," Aunt Gillian said.

"Sorry, Aunt Gillian. I didn't mean you."

"This isn't getting us anywhere," my father said. "We've all had a stressful morning. Gillian, if you want to put the kettle on, I'll go up and see how the packing is coming along." He adjusted a shirt cuff.

"You don't seem that broken up, either," I said. For some reason, looking at my father's blank face made me angrier than looking at Uncle George's red one.

"Why doesn't someone just put her down?" Uncle George said.

"*George*."

"She's pretty much a wild animal anyway."

He didn't see the plate leave my hand and fly towards him. It happened so quickly, I wasn't sure I'd seen it either. The sound of his glasses, knocked off his ears and cracking on the floor, woke me up and I turned on my heels and ran.

"You're just proving my point," he yelled after me. I heard a scuffle, and saw over my shoulder that my father and Aunt Gillian were physically restraining him. "You need a bloody psychiatrist, girl."

I went outside and sat in the rose garden, my thoughts even blacker than my dress. I heard Georgia and Michael calling to each other from upstairs, through open windows.

"Look at this spaniel-clock! Isn't it *cute*?"

"It's bloody hideous. Put it in the bin-bag to throw out."

"I'm keeping it. *I* love it."

I clenched my fists. I felt a weird hatred for Georgia, claiming things that had belonged to our grandmother when she hadn't even really known her.

My father found me and started trying to give me a lecture, polishing his glasses on his sleeve.

"Save it," I told him. "I'm not in the mood." I went to walk off but he caught my arm.

"Try to think of others, Tallulah," he said. "We're all going through this together."

"Please don't touch me," I said, shaking him off.

∗ ∗ ∗

We troop back into the waiting-room. I feel disconnected from my body, and wonder if that's how my father feels too – if he's conscious somehow, but not within himself.

I was so angry with him it's hard to believe. Yesterday, the day before. Most of my life. I left the day after my grandmother's funeral; I couldn't bear to stay in the house if my grandmother wasn't there anymore.

I remember my father already being gone – due back at work – and Michael dropping me off at the station. I remember he gave me a plastic bag and said, "We found these. Georgia thought you might want them."

"Thanks. And thanks for the lift."

"Aren't you going to see what they are?"

"Okay." Inside the bag was every picture I'd ever drawn or painted for my grandmother.

"They're good," he'd said. "Especially that one of the landscape, you know... the cliff-top and the beach. That somewhere you've been?"

"It was a photo I found in a magazine. Somewhere in South America."

I remember him turning the engine off and shifting to face

299

me. He was wearing jeans and a tight red jumper that clung to the muscles on his arms; he looked so much older. "Smoke?"

"Cheers."

I slump back into one of the waiting-room chairs. What then? Smoking, stubbing out the cigarette, shaking the plastic bag. "Thanks for these, again." Opening the door.

"It was Georgia's idea. She's the sweet one."

"Say thanks to her too."

"Yeah. Take care, Tallie."

Was it really only a few days ago that I got the telephone call about my father? It feels like I've been here forever. But that memory in the car feels like yesterday. I can almost smell the dusty upholstery, Michael, the wet paint of the benches along the station platform. The car fumes as I walked back to our house, mingling with the flowers spilling through the park railings. The windows of the houses I passed were going gold and burnt orange in the setting sun. Then our house, gloomy with all the lights off. I stood outside, wishing my father was dead, wishing I could speak to Toby, or Edith, imagining them together as I stood there, rage building up inside me.

As soon as I opened the door I knew that something was wrong. Same hallway – dark, parquet flooring and deep red runner. Same steady tick of the Great Western Railway clock that hung in my father's study, coming muffled through the wall. There was a smell that I couldn't put my finger on, though. Something musty and sweet at the same time, and I kicked off my shoes, running through the house to look for Mr Tickles, who would normally have been at my feet by now.

I know exactly where I went looking for him. All his favourite places first: sofa, washing-machine, under my bed. Then my wardrobe, calling him, getting more and more frantic.

Did you not notice he was gone, Dad? Were you more shaken by Grandma's death than I realised? At the time I thought you just didn't care.

I rest my face in my hands. Even now it makes my stomach drop, thinking of how I found him, eventually, in my laundry basket. He must have been dead for a while, because his body was stiff and his eyes looked flat. I cradled him to me. I let my tears fall onto his coat, already greasy and matted from old age and showing patches of greyish skin underneath. For a second I thought I saw his chest rise and fall, and I had a sudden crazy thought that my tears had brought him back to life, but it must have been some air escaping, because his heart never started beating again.

✳ ✳ ✳

My sessions with Mr Hicks continued the week after the funeral. He was wearing a green jumper when I opened his office door, and he must have had a shower not long before, because he looked and smelled minty-fresh. Seeing him made my heart-rate jack up.

"How are you doing, Tallulah?" he asked.

"Not so good."

He pulled a sympathetic face. "I hope you know I'm here if you want to talk about your grandmother. Anytime."

It was Toby I really wanted to talk to though, and I felt my throat start to close up.

"Don't cry. Here – have a tissue." Mr Hicks scrabbled around on the desk and handed me a piece of off-white cloth.

"It's kind of dirty," I said, holding it between my thumb and forefinger. Mr Hicks spread his arms and grinned ruefully. The cloth smelled like turpentine when I blew my nose in it.

"I like it when you smile, you know?"

"What *is* this?" I asked, scrunching it up.

"A sketch I was working on earlier."

"Sorry I snotted all over it."

"I'll take it as a veiled critical reaction." He picked up the bin and held it out to me. "Would you like a glass of water?"

"Thanks."

He went off and came back with a glass. The water in it was warm and cloudy; I took a sip and thought about spitting it back out, but Mr Hicks was leaning against the desk on my side now, right next to me. "I hope your friends are looking after you properly."

I tried to make a non-committal noise.

"Well, if you don't mind me asking, how's your relationship with your dad, then? Maybe this is a time for you both to get to know each other."

"It's alright."

"Are you sure?"

"It's the same as always." I put down my glass, trying not to meet his eye.

"Of course, of course," Mr Hicks said. He put his hand on mine; it felt warm and dry. An image of him holding me, tilting my face upwards, came into my mind, and I blushed so hard it felt like pins and needles. He picked my hand off the table and held it in both of his. I thought of Toby again, and the camping trip, and now Toby and Edith together. Him kissing her instead of me. Edith looking up at him adoringly. I pressed my fingers into the heel of Mr Hicks' palm; I thought I could feel his pulse underneath the skin. I kept looking into his eyes; he didn't flinch, didn't move his hand away. My heart was knocking about in my chest so hard I thought my ribs might break. All I could think about was how much Toby would hate it if I kissed Mr Hicks.

"I really like seeing you," I said. "I mean… you're cool."

He kept looking at me; the corners of his mouth twitched. "You're pretty cool yourself."

"No I'm not."

"You're beautiful, you're independent, you're smart. You're not a fake, Tallulah, like a lot of the other girls your age." He squeezed my hand back, and let go of it. "Sorry, I shouldn't have said that. You wouldn't see it. You don't have to try to force some semblance of creativity into these useless lumps." He laughed. "I'm joking, of course. But you

302

have a special way of looking at things." He jerked his head in the direction of the door. "And you're better than them. Especially your friends, from the sounds of it. They should be really taking care of you at this stage, and instead you're being neglected."

"They're busy."

"Too busy for grief?"

"I guess."

He turned my chair so I was facing him head-on, and leaned towards me, looking right into my eyes. "Well, remember you always have a friend here. Just use discretion. Always consider whether it's in our best interests to draw negative attention to ourselves, especially in your position here, which is... " – he looked like he was searching for the right word – "... tenuous. Does that make sense?"

"Okay," I said. I could feel the heat of his breath on my face, and my own was coming too fast. Mr Hicks looked so serious – I didn't know if I was in trouble for what I'd said earlier.

He straightened up and smiled. "Are you done with the water?"

"Yeah."

He moved around to the other side of the desk and sat down, looking back to his old self. "Well – we should talk about your academic progress. How do you feel about the summer exams?"

* * *

"So, come to the party," I said. "My cousin invited me – it's for all the Drama Group and their teacher."

"Yeah, I've heard about her," John said. "Batty." He nudged Toby with his foot. "Maybe you'll get lucky. Oh wait – "

"Have you ever even spoken to a girl and not made her throw up?" I asked him.

"Ouch," John said. "Just because... "

"Shut up, John," Toby said.

"You haven't even heard what I was going to say."

"*No one* wants to hear what you've got to say," Francis said.

None of us had discussed Toby and Edith's relationship since John had told me. Toby had been avoiding me and Edith was away on a language trip with her German class that wouldn't get back until later that afternoon.

"Anyway," I said. "I have to go." Toby started to say something but I picked up my bag and slung it over my shoulder. "See you lot later. The party's at nine."

"See you there," Francis said.

Edith was back by the time I finished my last class, waiting in the dorm for me. "Tal," she said. "The trip was *amazing*. We drank beer out of a giant mug, although then the teacher caught us and we weren't allowed out of the hostel again at night, but Amy met this German boy and snuck out and then we had to cover for her."

"I thought you hated Amy," I said.

"She's not so bad," Edith said. She was unpacking. "She was really nice to me the whole time – she thinks Toby's really handsome, she said."

"Good for her," I said. I lay down on my bed, and stared up at the ceiling.

"Tal, are you mad at me?" Edith asked. She stopped unpacking and came and sat on the end of my bed. "Toby said that nothing was happening between you."

Oh did he? "Nothing was."

"Yeah, but," Edith said. "I just feel bad that it happened behind your back."

I shrugged and gritted my teeth.

Edith got up. "As long as you're okay with it," she said.

"Whatever. Are you coming to the party?"

"Oh yeah, Toby invited me," she said.

"No he didn't," I said. "I did. After my cousin invited me, remember?"

"Are you *sure* you're not mad at me?" Edith asked.

"Sure," I said and felt like pushing her down the stairs. "I'm gonna have a shower."

"Okay," Edith said. "I'll have one after you. I've got so much to tell you about the trip. And this one thing that Amy did... " She started laughing.

I picked up my towel and left the room.

✳ ✳ ✳

We met the boys behind the gym. The two of us got there first and crouched down by the grey wheelie bin, waiting for the others. I lit a cigarette while Edith fussed with her tights. She stopped and watched me inhale. "Does your dad know you smoke?" she asked.

"I don't know. Maybe," I said. I'd had a four or five beers before we left the dorm and I could feel the blood starting to build up at the base of my neck; I was going to have a massive headache tomorrow.

Edith was running her fingers through her hair with a worried expression. "How do I look?" she asked.

"Fine."

"Really, how do I look?"

I looked at her properly. Her lips were smeared with orange lipstick, and her eyelashes were very long, making her eyes look huge.

"Very pretty," I said. She did look kind of pretty, in a really messy way.

"Tal, you here?" Francis' voice hissed.

"Yeah."

We stood and walked around the bin. The boys were huddled together on the other side, looking unsure of themselves.

"What now?" Francis asked. He was carrying cans of lager in his trouser and coat pockets; all of them were, I could hear sloshing and clinking coming from everyone.

"I'll see if I can find my cousin."

The bungalow was twenty metres or so from the gym. We

305

could hear music coming from inside, and light pooled on the grass by our feet through a chink in the curtains. I walked up to the front door and knocked; a girl in a yellow tutu opened it. She had a plastic cup full of clear liquid in one hand, and a cigarette in the other. I knew her name – Bailey – she was one of the prefects in the A-Level year; last month she'd given a reading at assembly on the dangers of getting into strangers' cars. "Yeah?" she said. "What do you want?"

"Is Starr around?"

She bent forwards; her breath was sickly sweet and her makeup was running. "Come in," she said. "I'll try to find her for you."

I followed her in, leaving the others outside. There was a narrow, packed corridor with five rooms leading off it, two on each side and one at the end. Through the first left-side door, kids were dancing in the living-room. On the right, in the kitchen, more were mixing cocktails. As I looked in, one boy was drinking out of a ladle.

"Not in here," Bailey said, poking her head into the living-room. "Let's try the back."

We picked our way down the corridor. She pointed to the second door on the left. "Judith's bedroom. It's out of bounds." She pushed open the door on the right. I could see a small bathroom with yellowish tiles on the walls. A boy was asleep in the bath; another was sitting on the toilet with his hand up the top of the girl in front of him. His face was ecstatic. The girl turned towards us. Her eyes were glassy and she was clutching a bottle of tequila at her side. "'Sup Bailey," she said.

"Someone's gonna puke," Bailey whispered to me. We backed out.

"Only one room left," she said. "This is where we have workshops sometimes."

She pushed open the door to a conservatory. The drama teacher was in the middle of the room, playing the bongos. Starr was sitting on the piano, rolling a cigarette. One of her followers was standing next to her, mimicking the drama teacher's eyes-closed, head-back pose. Two boys were flicking through a copy of *Lady Chatterley's Lover*, laughing at something about halfway through.

"Tallulah," someone called. I turned on my heel and felt sick all of a sudden. Mr Hicks and a tall, horsey woman were standing over by the window, looking at the room with raised eyebrows. He beckoned me over. I thought he was going to tell me to go home, but he just nudged the woman and nodded at me. "This is one of my art students from year eleven." He was being normal with me again.

The woman looked me up and down. "She looks very young." She wore a large gold cuff on her left wrist and a short red dress that she kept tugging down at the hem. "Gary." She put her hand on his arm. "Do we have to stay here? Watching Judith do her whole ethnic thing is making me feel nauseous."

"I'm finding it quite amusing," Mr Hicks said. "What do you think, Tallulah?"

They both looked at me. I shrugged.

The woman sneered. "Don't pick on her, Gary, she's just a baby."

I felt my face heat up. "Later," I said, and turned away, catching Starr's eye.

"Tallie, you made it," she called, waving at me and nearly falling off the piano.

I walked over to her.

"This is my cousin Tallie," Starr said, nodding towards me. "This is Melia."

"Melia?"

"Short for Amelia," the girl said. She tossed her hair over her shoulder.

"Sorry about that," I said; Starr took a sip to hide her grin. "I went to Grandma's funeral," I told her.

"Bummer," she said.

"Your mum wasn't there again."

307

Starr shrugged. "Don't look at me – she never explains herself."

I looked down at the ground, feeling really tired all of a sudden. Starr gave me a gentle prod with her foot. "Sorry... You know," she said. "I think she was genuinely shocked, though. Me too. I always thought Grandma would outlive everyone."

"Thanks."

"Speaking of family, did you hear about Aunt Gillian and that creep?" she asked.

"You mean Uncle George?"

"Yeah. The pervert." Starr wiggled on the piano, trying to pull her dress down.

"What happened?"

"They're getting a divorce."

"Oh?"

"Yeah. Big shock, 'cos it's the first in the family or something. My mum's hysterical."

"She's upset?"

"Are you kidding? She's so happy she nearly soiled herself. Anything that Gillian does wrong makes her feel all warm and fuzzy." Starr took another sip of her drink.

"Why are they getting divorced?"

"He's a criminal," Starr said. "I know – like, duh. But it's just embezzling, or something boring like that. So it's bye bye Georgie."

"Yeah, I can't see Aunt Gillian visiting him in prison."

"Maybe for conjugal visits," Starr said, and snorted. "Not."

"So, you here by yourself, Tallie?" Melia interrupted.

"My friends are outside."

"Who'd you bring?" Starr asked.

"Toby and that lot."

"Oh God, not that idiot, John too?" Starr pulled a face. "He's always trying to get into everyone's pants. And what's up with you and Toby?"

"Nothing," I said, studying my fingernails. "He's going out with Edith."

"The ginger?" Starr threw her head back and laughed. Melia copied her. "Good for her." She stopped when she saw my face. "How do you feel about it?"

"I don't own him."

"That's not how the rumours went."

"Whatever," I said. "They can do what they want. I'm gonna go get them."

"I'm gonna smoke this," Starr said. She hopped off the piano and opened a window. "Help yourself to alcohol. Someone brought vodka – it's in the freezer."

"Cool," I said.

"Who opened a window?" the drama teacher asked shrilly. "It's ruining my concentration."

I went back outside. The others were standing around awkwardly. It was windy and Edith was only wearing a thin dress – her lips had turned blue and she was shivering, although no one had thought to offer her a jacket, or she'd refused one.

"Come in," I said. "There's some vodka in the freezer, apparently." I held the door open and stepped to the side.

"Dude," Francis said, coming past me. "The drama group. They're mental." I looked at where he was pointing; four boys in the kitchen were shaking salt out onto the counter and snorting it.

"I'm gonna find some girl who's wasted," John said, pushing his way into the living-room.

Toby and Edith came inside. I shut the door after them. Edith's eyes looked bigger than ever.

"Let's go find this vodka," I said to her.

The boys in the kitchen made a path for us to walk to the freezer. I opened it and started pulling out drawers. There were two bottles of vodka in the second drawer, and next to them a bag of frozen peas, a pair of boxer shorts and a wooden spoon.

309

"I put those there," one of the boys said. "Nice surprise for Judith tomorrow morning."

His friends high-fived him.

"Great," I said. "You seem really funny." I took a nearly-empty vodka bottle out and picked two plastic cups off the side. "Let's go, Ed."

"Don't you want me, baby?" the boy called after us. His friends laughed and I heard slapping sounds, like they were high-fiving again.

"Jerks," I said.

"Yeah," Edith said, quietly.

We found the others in the living-room. John was dancing in the middle of the floor and the other two were sitting in a corner. Some girl was in Francis' lap and he looked at me, embarrassed. I grinned at him.

"Hold these," I said to Edith. I poured us two half-cups of vodka to finish the bottle. We lifted them up and knocked them together.

"Cheers," I said. I drank a mouthful; the vodka tasted disgusting, but it was warm on the way down. Edith retched.

"That's so *strong*," she said.

"I'll find you some juice," Toby said, getting up and leaving the room.

"Want any?" I asked Francis.

He held his can up.

"Okay," I said. I drank another mouthful and could feel my stomach heaving already.

"Are you alright?" Francis asked me. The girl in his lap hiccupped.

I nodded. My head felt light, it must have been the spirit interacting with the beers. I downed the vodka and jumped up, nearly falling over; someone on my right put a hand out to prop me up.

"I'm getting some more," I said.

I walked into the kitchen; the back of my head was thumping and the room was spinning.

"Tal," I heard Toby say. "You don't look good, you should have some water."

"I'm fine."

I couldn't see him until he put his hand out to close the freezer drawer. "You don't look fine," he said. "You should go back to the dorm. I'll take you."

"I don't think Edith would like that."

"Listen," he said. His fingers were digging into my wrist. "I'm sorry about the camping trip, and I'm sorry that I got with Edith. I know you said you were cool with it but I don't think you are."

"Get over yourself."

"Look, if you're *not* cool with it… " He leaned in closer, until our foreheads were almost touching. "If you're not… If you just said that… "

"What?"

"I would end it with her."

"How nice of you," I said.

He drew back and looked at me. "I mean it. I would break up with her right now if you asked me to."

My wrist hurt from where he was squeezing it. I looked at his face, floating in the middle of the fug of alcohol. Him and Edith made no sense, I thought. They were opposites. Does Edith know about your brother? I wanted to ask. I looked at his eyebrows, which were thick and black, and his eyelashes too. They made me want to reach out and tug them. It was strange, I thought, how some people looked so good you wanted to be around them. Like Toby. Like my mother.

"Just go back to your girlfriend," I said. I could hear myself slurring.

"Fine." Toby kicked a cupboard door and left the room.

"*He's* not very happy," someone said and everyone laughed again. This room found everything funny. A boy put his arm around my waist and tried to kiss me. I elbowed him in the stomach, picked up the bottle and left.

I stood in the living-room doorway and poured myself

some more alcohol. I saw Toby and Edith kissing in one corner, his hands in her hair. I sat down on the sofa arm, spilling half my drink. Another couple were kissing next to me; I tried to focus on them and realised it was two boys.

Starr was dancing in the middle of the room now with Melia and two other girls. John was hanging around them with his mouth open. One of the girls said something to Starr and pointed at me. They stopped dancing and came over.

"Your cousin looks smashed," one of them said, giggling.

"Tallie, are you wasted?" Starr asked.

"No," I said. I drank some more.

Starr eyed me. I belched; the girls made faces and backed away.

"Tallie was never very refined, were you?" Starr said.

"Can't make a silk purse out of a sow's ear," I said.

"What does that even mean?"

"Dunno," I said. "Grams used to say it all the time." I felt tears building up behind my eyelids. "She's dead now."

"Jeez, Tallie, what a downer," Starr said. She took my shoulders. "Sort yourself out, go drink some water in the bathroom until you feel better." She reached for the vodka. "I'll take this."

"I'm fine," I said. I fell backwards onto the two boys, who swore at me and left.

Starr gave me a pitying look and pulled me upright. "Pace yourself, Cuz. I'm not gonna rub your back while you spew."

They went back to the dance floor. I stayed on the sofa, drinking and avoiding looking at Toby and Edith.

"Why did you leave?" someone said quietly in my ear. I turned my face upwards. Mr Hicks looked down at me, his head tilted to one side.

"I don't like your friend," I said.

"Nicola?" he said. "She's just having a bitchy day." He sat down next to me.

"Oh yeah?" I said. "Me too."

"Why?"

"I don't want to discuss it."

"If you can't tell your mentor… "

"Why don't you just be a guy tonight, and not my mentor?" He smiled.

"I'd much rather hang out with you than any of these kids here." I put my hand on his knee. I tried to see out of the corner of my eye if Toby was watching us. Everything was kind of blurred, except Mr Hicks, when I turned back. His face was perfectly neutral.

"Come and talk to me outside, Tallulah."

I got up and followed him out the room. I thought I saw Toby and Francis exchange looks as I left.

Mr Hicks found a spot in the corridor to lean against the wall. He was drinking orange juice. "I should report you, you know," he said. "Unless that's lemonade you've got in your hand."

"It's lemonade."

Mr Hicks put his hand over mine and brought it and the cup up to his face. "It doesn't smell like lemonade."

"So, report me," I said, feeling annoyed at how uptight he was being. I twisted my hand out of his. "Is that why you brought me out here?"

"You know you're not allowed to drink until you're eighteen," Mr Hicks said. "As a matter of fact, I don't believe any of your friends are eighteen yet either."

I shrugged.

"The boys I'm willing to overlook because they're in the sixth-form and they're not my pupils," he said, looking at me out of the corner of his eye. "But I'm your personal tutor. I'm responsible for you. And I'm very fond of you Tallulah, you know." He took a sip of his orange juice.

My head was too clogged up to follow the conversation, but Mr Hicks was pausing like he expected me to say something.

"Really?" I asked.

"Yes." He looked at me from under his lashes. "I'm aware

we have a – connection. That's why I agreed to take you on as my personal student. It's why I can't just let you run amok tonight."

I downed the vodka. "It's all gone now," I said. Breathing and talking at the same time was becoming difficult. "You can just pretend you never saw it." I threw my empty cup on the floor and put my hand on his chest, partly to keep my balance, partly to feel him. I took a deep breath in and tilted my face up towards him, like I'd imagined in our last session, but he didn't kiss me.

"If I pretended I hadn't seen you," Mr Hicks said, and put his arm around my shoulders, pulling me towards him. "If I pretended that, then you would owe me a big favour."

Someone walked past and he shifted slightly, so that I was leaning into him, like I couldn't stand.

"Stupid kids," he said to the person passing us.

I looked up. It was the girl from earlier, Bailey. I felt like telling him he didn't need to put on this show, that she was already smashed, but something was wrong, although I couldn't quite work out what it was.

Mr Hicks was squeezing my shoulder. I felt like I was going to be sick. I dropped the vodka bottle I'd been clutching in one hand and he yelled and jumped backwards. I looked down. The lid hadn't been screwed tight and the bottoms of his cream chinos were soaking wet.

"Bloody mess," he muttered.

"Sorry, sir," I said. The ceiling started to slide down towards me and the floor slid upwards; I closed my eyes and felt myself falling, but something stopped me. I just wanted to rest my head, which was getting heavy.

"Timber," someone yelled.

"What's going on out here?" another voice asked; it sounded upset. I felt myself shuffled along, then heard a door click.

"One of the younger students appears to be intoxicated," a man's voice said.

"Oh dear," the upset voice said. "A lower-school student? How did she get in?"

"There isn't exactly a strict door policy," the man said. "You know, Judith, I think it's probably best if we don't mention to any of the staff that she was here."

"Of course, oh dear. Herbert has always been against these parties – oh dear. I never thought anyone *underage* would be drinking."

"Half these kids are underage."

I opened my eyes and tried to focus. I was being held upright; my head was hanging down and I could see a pair of shoes and two bare feet. The feet were bony, with freckles all over; the toenails were yellowish at the ends and curling inwards. Looking at them made me start to feel sick again.

"Socks," I said.

"What did she just say?" the feet asked.

"I can't tell," the shoes said. They were brown loafers with tassels on.

"Socks," I said louder.

"Are you alright?" shoes asked me. "What are you trying to tell us?"

"Perhaps we should take her to the sick bay?" feet suggested.

"Yes, don't worry. I'll do that," the shoes said. "You stay here and keep an eye on the rest of them."

"Oh, thank you so much. You're such a wonderful help." The feet were fluttering their eyelashes. I felt myself being picked up.

"We'll go out the back way," shoes said. "Don't want to draw unnecessary attention here."

"Of course, of course." The feet moved in front of us, opening the back door and shooing us out. "Thank you, again. I knew I could count on you."

I felt sleep fighting me, trying to make me let go of everything. I didn't have the strength to hold out. I closed my eyes – I couldn't hear anything but buzzing, and a

315

strange panting noise. I couldn't see anything. I couldn't feel anything, not even the sickness anymore.

The shoes were carrying me away from the party. They weren't being very careful with me. I was being bumped and shaken about. We stopped and I heard the scratch of metal on metal, and then a door open.

"Nearly there," the shoes said. There was a click and I felt a pink burning inside my eyelids. I could smell turpentine. The shoes laid me down on something soft. They were soothing me, stroking my hair and taking my cardigan off. I moaned and tried to turn over. The shoes took my shoulders and pushed me back.

"I'm looking after you now," they said. "You're okay."

I groaned.

"You've been very bad tonight," they said. "Drinking, sneaking into parties, answering back. You're a very wild child."

"No," I said, but it was muffled.

"Yes," the shoes said. I felt them undoing the buttons on my shirt. I tried to stop them. I pushed fingers away, struck out wildly in all directions. The fingers came back and caught my wrists, holding them, tightly at first, then softer as I felt my strength flowing out of me. I could hear shushing sounds.

"No," I said. "Don't."

"You want this just as much as I do," the shoes said. "You've been playing games with me all year. Pretending you're shy and sweet, watching me in class, blushing when I talk to you. Then swearing you're not the kid everyone thinks you are. And the other day, when you gave me the signal. I knew what you were doing. You're not an innocent, are you, Tallulah? You know how you make me feel."

"I didn't," I said. The words felt like they were being dredged up from somewhere deep inside me.

"Oh yes, you've been very bad," the shoes said. "Be a good girl now."

Water gathered beneath my eyelids in frustration. I tried

to open my eyes, but it was too much. I felt something scrabbling around at the buckle of my belt and then my jeans being pulled down to my knees.

"No," I said again. This time I couldn't gather enough breath to speak out loud. A heaviness was on top of me, then I felt something slippery thrust inside my mouth. I coughed and retched. Whatever was on top of me shuddered, making my head rattle and a wave of pain wash over me. I heard grunting noises; they seemed to be coming from inside my mouth, but I wasn't making them. Then the weight lifted off of me, and I could feel hot blasts down near my crotch.

"Pink. Very unexpected," the shoes said. "Did you wear these especially?" I heard the sound of someone sniffing, long breaths drawn in. "I can't tell you how good you smell."

Then my knickers were being pulled down. I tried to hold on to them, keep them up, but my head was getting heavier and heavier. That was the last thing I knew.

∗ ∗ ∗

"Tallie?" a voice said.

Slowly, light was beginning to come back to me. Shapes shifted in front of my face, blurred at first, then they cleared.

Starr was sitting at the end of my bed. She was rubbing my leg; her eyes were pink and puffy. "Tallie, are you okay?" she asked.

"Yeah," I said. Starr leant forwards and I realised I hadn't spoken. "Yeah," I tried again. Again my voice wouldn't come out.

"Tallie, what happened?"

I sank back onto my pillows, exhausted.

"Mr Hicks said he tried to take you to the sick bay," Starr said. "But you broke away from him and ran off. We found you a couple of hours later. You had all these cuts and… "

I looked down at my body; there were two red marks around my left wrist, and a long scratch on my arm. My jaw felt tender, too. I rubbed it.

"Did you get them from falling over?" Starr asked.

I shrugged – I don't remember.

"Did someone hurt you?" she asked, her voice lowered.

I shrugged again. Images swam messily in front of me.

"Oh, Tallie." She sounded like she was going to say something more, but then held back.

I tried to drag my voice up to the surface. "Water," I finally croaked.

"Of course." Starr jumped up and went to get me some water. I lay in bed, hands clenching the duvet until they got weak. "Don't think about it," I muttered.

"What was that?" Starr came back.

"Nothing." I sat up, took the glass from her and drained it. I lay back down and rolled over. My whole body ached.

"Are you going to talk to me?" Starr asked.

I closed my eyes, but that made me feel dizzy.

"They're not going to call your father," Starr said. "Mr Hicks persuaded the other teachers not to tell Mr Purvis. He said you're under enough stress already, and he'd keep an eye on you."

I stayed on my side, with my back to her.

"I'll let you sleep," Starr whispered. "I'll be in the common room if you need me."

* * *

I got up and showered when Starr left. I went over every inch of my body with the soap, scrubbing between my legs especially hard. When I turned the water on myself, I saw it had gone pink. After I turned off the tap, I stayed in the cubicle for a moment, leaning my head against the wall, eyes closed tightly.

Out of the cubicle I looked at myself in the mirror. I seemed the same – same hair, same face, same breasts, although now there were little purple bruises around my nipples and on my cheek. I wrapped a towel tightly around myself. "Don't think about it," I said to my reflection.

"Tal?" Edith called.

She was standing in the middle of our room; Toby was behind her. "Are you okay?" she asked. "We were just wondering if you needed anything?"

"Nope," I said. I forced a smile for them and adjusted my towel.

"Can I talk to Tal alone?" Toby asked Edith.

"Yeah, sure," Edith said. She turned on her way out and gave me a worried look. "Tal, you shouldn't *drink* so much."

"Right," I said.

Edith left. Toby faced me, hands in his pockets.

"Turn around," I said. "I need to put something on."

He turned away; I saw his face screw up as he did. I went back into the bathroom and took my robe from its hook. I'd never used it. It felt soft, like it had when my grandmother had given it to me the previous year. I pulled it on and tied the belt in a double-knot around the waist.

Toby was facing away from me when I re-entered the dorm. I cleared my throat and he turned; his face was blank now.

"Cigarette?" I asked him.

"Yeah," he said.

We went back into the bathroom and opened the window. I sat on the toilet cistern and Toby stood in front of me. I lit two cigarettes and passed one to him.

"How did you get in?" I asked.

"Francis and John are distracting the Housemistress," he said.

"I see," I said. I crossed my legs; Toby looked away.

"What did you do last night?" he asked me.

I inhaled deeply. "I went to the party with you guys," I said. "I had too much to drink. Then I don't know. I don't remember."

"Do you really not remember?" Toby asked.

"Really."

Toby sucked on his cigarette and looked down at the floor.

319

"I was the one who found you," he said, eventually. "You were moaning and you were pretty scratched – you kept saying something over and over again."

I inhaled again and looked out the window.

"Don't you wanna know what you were saying?" Toby asked.

"No," I said. My voice shook. "And I don't want to talk about last night."

"Why, if you don't remember?" Toby asked.

I hopped off the cistern and stubbed the butt out in the sink. "I don't want to talk about it," I said. I opened the toilet lid and dropped the butt down into the water. Toby watched me carefully.

"You're not going to get suspended," he said. "You're not even being reported for drinking underage."

"Yeah, I know," I said. "Starr already told me."

"Mr Hicks sorted that out."

"I know."

"Don't you think that's nice of him?" Toby asked. "He didn't have to go out of his way for you."

I looked out of the window again. Plump white clouds drifted in the sky; the sun poured itself through the open space.

"I don't want to talk about it," I said. I reached over and flushed the toilet and watched as my cigarette was sucked out of sight.

PART THREE

Bones

Sixteen

There were five weeks left of term after the drama party and the summer was rolling out before us. Windows were left permanently open in the classrooms and from where I sat in English I could see the front lawn. On Fridays, the gardeners cut it, and the smell of fresh grass mixed with the trails of honeysuckle, jasmine and lavender that grew beneath the classroom windows. Ladybirds traipsed across the doodles in my exercise books, legs and wings akimbo, like they were coming apart in the heat. One time I saw a crow with a worm in its beak hopping around on the gravel outside, the worm wriggling desperately like some dull pink ribbon caught in the wind.

Sometimes I felt my eyes fill up for no reason, in the middle of a class. Sometimes I missed my mother so much I hated her.

I stopped hanging out with the others, stopped eating lunch. I showered three or four times a day, and sometimes at night.

"Tallulah, don't you have a private tuition session now?" my maths teacher asked me when I showed up to a lunchtime revision class.

"I don't need them anymore," I said.

"Right," she said, and went back to her marking.

One Monday we were called into an emergency assembly.

Mr Purvis stood on stage, his face the colour of beetroot. A serious crime had been committed on school property. Mr Hicks' office had been broken in to and defiled, he said.

"And to make matters worse, this same student left a threatening note for Mr Hicks. And he tells me this has been going on for *weeks*." His voice crescendoed; I thought I could see spit forming at the corners of his mouth. "This school will not tolerate the bullying of its staff by pupils, or *anyone*. I suggest that if you have any information about the perpetrator you come forward with it now. Otherwise, if this behaviour does not stop immediately, we will be forced to question *everyone*."

Whispers broke out as he swept off the stage. I looked around for Toby. He was sitting two rows behind me with his arm around Edith's shoulder. Her face was white. Toby looked utterly calm.

Edith tried to speak to me after the assembly; I saw her pushing through people and turned away quickly. I didn't feel like talking.

I nicked an apple from the canteen and went to the far side of the playing fields. I took my shoes and socks off and dug my toes into the soil. I could hear someone calling my name in the distance but I ignored it; I lay back, shielding my eyes from the sun with one arm, and bit into the apple.

"Jeez, are you deaf or something?"

Starr flopped down next to me.

"Selectively."

"Well, thanks for making me run after you like an idiot."

"I didn't make you run after me."

I threw my apple core into a bush and lit a cigarette. I tried to make the clouds above me into something interesting, but they just looked like clouds. 'Lack of imagination', my grandmother would have said. I blew smoke rings out above my head.

"What's wrong with you anyway? You've been really quiet recently."

"When's recently?"

"Don't be annoying," Starr said. "I know something's wrong. You can tell me."

"I'm late."

I watched her face, waiting for the realisation to hit her. Her mouth dropped open. "How late?"

"I don't know," I said, running my fingers through my hair. "A few weeks, maybe. I was never regular."

She grabbed my arm. "Who's the father?"

"Does it matter?"

"Yes," she said. She looked uneasy. "Maybe not right now."

"It's not important."

"Tallie… "

"Yes?"

"You've got to tell him."

"No way. You know how it is."

"Tallie, come on," Starr said. "Stop being such a fucking hero and ask for help."

"I'm not being a hero," I said. I looked back up at the clouds. "My dad won't want to deal with this."

"If you don't tell him then I will."

"You can't," I said, gripping her hand. "You can't grass on me."

"It's not grassing if you need help."

"You can't tell or it's grassing," I said.

Starr smacked her forehead with her free hand. "We're not ten anymore, Tallie," she said.

"Fuck off, Starr," I said. "You can't tell him, and you can't make me either."

"You can't just ignore it and think it'll go away."

I stubbed out my cigarette and rested my hands on my lower abdomen. It still felt tight; nothing moved. I drummed my fingers on the skin. "It's fine," I said. "Everything's fine."

I wiped my nose on the back of my hand. An ant or something was crawling up my back. Sweat trickled from my armpit; time for another shower. I put my shoes and socks back on and jumped up, too fast. Everything started to go grainy for a moment, then black. I reached out and my hand touched hedge. I held on to the branches until my eyes started to clear. "Help… "

"What is it, hon?" Starr asked, jumping up too. That's why I liked her – she forgave everything so easily. "You changed your mind?"

"No," I said. "But I'm gonna go to the nurse. Can you come with me?"

"Yeah, sure," Starr said. "Now?"

"I guess," I said.

"Okay," she said, and put her arm around my shoulder, then stopped. "Shoot, I have a careers interview in five minutes. Can we go after that?"

"No, it's okay," I said. "I can go by myself."

"You don't have to do that. Just wait for me. Or I'll cancel."

"I'll wait," I said. "Don't cancel."

"Are you sure?"

"Yeah. I'll go have a shower first."

"Okay, come find me afterwards yeah? I'll be in my common room."

"Yeah."

"Promise?"

"Promise."

"I've gotta run," she said. "You okay getting back to the dorm by yourself?"

I rolled my eyes. "Yes."

"I'm a worrier." She was grinning and I grinned back. "See you later, idiot."

She jogged off and I straightened up and looked around; my hands were itchy from the prickles on the bush. Boys had gathered in the field next to me while I was lying down and a rugby game had started. I saw a group of girls waving handmade flags – Francis must be there.

I tried to follow Starr and jog around the outskirts of the field, keeping away from everyone. It felt harder than normal, like I was seriously out of shape. I hadn't been playing netball recently; my PE teacher had threatened to haul me up before Mr Purvis, but I'd still refused. I couldn't face changing in front of everyone.

I slowed down when I reached my dorm building and went inside. Edith was in our room, making notes from her Latin textbook. "Oh." She tried to smile. "Hi."

"Hi."

"You forget something?"

"Nope," I said. "This is my room too."

I shut the door. Edith put her book down.

"Why are you reading in here during lunch?"

"I had a fight with Toby," she said. "What have *you* been doing?"

I shrugged. "Eating lunch."

She fidgeted. "Tal, do you know anything about... "

"I didn't do it, if that's what you're asking," I said. I peeled off my shirt. Edith looked away.

"No, I didn't think you did," she said. "That's not what I'm asking."

"I haven't spoken to anyone about it either," I said. I felt exposed standing there, with the black of my bra showing through my white vest. Maybe my breasts were bigger, I thought. They felt sore around the nipples and fuller, somehow. I picked up my towel from where I'd left it, draped across my bed.

"Okay, whatever," Edith said.

"Okay, whatever," I mimicked.

"You've been really weird recently," Edith said, frowning. She looked at me closely. "How many showers have you had today?"

I shrugged.

Edith pursed her mouth. "You know, sometimes I think you actually have issues, Tal. Like, serious issues."

"Jesus Edith, pot calling kettle black much?"

She jumped up. "I'm going to go find Toby." She paused

at the door. "You know, if you're mad at me for going out with him, it'd be better if you just admitted it."

"Stick it up your arse," I replied.

She slammed the door behind her. I uncurled my fists; my hands were shaking.

I padded into the bathroom and turned the light on, looked at myself in the mirror, and turned it back off. I couldn't understand why Edith never said anything about how I looked like a pile of crap – my family certainly would have.

I showered in the dark and dried myself for a few minutes. I felt my breasts; they definitely felt heavier and more fleshy.

"Shit," I said.

✳ ✳ ✳

The nurse was temporarily away from her office. The notice said she'd be back in fifteen minutes, but it didn't say when she'd written it. I rested my head on the door, breathed fog onto its glass, then rubbed it off with my sleeve.

"Bloody NHS," Starr said, sitting down on one of the orange chairs outside the office.

I sat next to her.

"Chewing gum?" she asked, offering me a stick. I took one and put it in my mouth, scrunching the wrapping up and pitching it into the bin on the other side of the corridor.

"I had to come here once," she said. "That fucking Melissa Albrecht hit me in the face during a hockey match." She rubbed her nose like she was remembering the pain. "I thought she broke it, but the nurse said she couldn't see any difference."

Starr's nose was as perfect as it always had been.

"Yeah," I said. "I think Melissa might have cracked your head at some point, too."

"Ha-ha. Only two more weeks of school left then."

"Yep."

"What are you doing this summer?"

"Dunno." I chewed my lip. "I thought I might go away with

the boys, but that doesn't seem like a great idea anymore."

"Hon," she said, looking sympathetic. "Do you want me to put a hit out on that Edith girl?"

I grinned.

"Try not to care about guys," she said. "If you don't care, you're never disappointed."

"You're pretty bleak."

She grinned. "Mum's homespun wisdom – not mine."

We were silent for a minute. I wondered if she knew about what our grandfather had done to Aunt Vivienne. Hey, so, funny story…

I stretched my legs out, then shifted in my seat; an ache had started down in my pelvis. I felt fuzzy, like I was in pain, but it was too far away to judge properly.

"You look kinda spaced out, you know."

"I don't feel great," I said. I rested my head between my legs. "I think I'm gonna puke." I felt my stomach contracting and something rushing up inside me, towards my throat and then out of my mouth.

"Holy shit," Starr said.

I gasped, drawing air in with shaky breaths. I was on my hands and knees, a pool of vomit in front of me. Starr was standing on her chair. "What the fuck just happened?" she asked.

"I puked, arsehole."

"Fuck," Starr said. "That fucking stinks."

My throat was burning. I wanted water and my bed. I felt something sticky in my knickers. "I think I'm gonna lie down," I said.

"Here?" Starr asked.

"Yes," I said. "Right here." I tried to give her a sarcastic look, but I was finding it hard to focus.

"Okay, okay," Starr said. She climbed off her chair carefully and took me under the armpits, pulling me slowly to my feet. When I was upright I leant on her shoulder, trying to regain my balance.

"It's okay," she said. She patted my back. "I'll take you to the San."

"No," I croaked. "My room."

"I can't take you there," she said, her forehead creasing. "Someone's gotta see you first, check you're okay."

"I'm okay," I said, even as everything around me started to go black.

✳ ✳ ✳

When I woke up my father was sitting by the bed. My eyes took a moment to focus on our surroundings: a white room with light-green curtains. It wasn't the San, definitely a hospital ward.

My father had his head cradled in his hands; he jumped when I shifted in the bed, and looked up. "Tallulah," he said. He seemed angry. "You're fine."

"Oh," I said. It seemed weird that he was mad at me for being fine. I felt like giggling, but something inside me said it wasn't the time. My mouth felt like I'd been sucking on cotton wool balls. "Where am I?"

"In the local hospital," he said, and I wondered vaguely if it was the same one my grandmother had been in after her stroke. "The school called for an ambulance after you wouldn't stop bleeding."

"What happened?"

"They think, from the symptoms – and a useful piece of information provided by your cousin – that you may have experienced a miscarriage."

Thanks for that, Starr.

"You'll have to have a D-and-C, but that's routine." He stood and started pacing up and down at the end of my bed. "You're extremely lucky."

"Okay."

His anger was almost physical, pinning me down. I felt exhausted already, although I'd only just woken up.

"How could you have done it, Tallulah?"

"What?"

"How could you have kept this to yourself?"

He stopped pacing and gripped the rail at the end of the bed. "It was *incredibly* dangerous, especially with the symptoms you had. You could have had some serious complications."

I closed my eyes. "But I didn't?"

"No."

"Okay then."

"It's *not* okay, Tallulah."

"Can we just forget it?"

"*Forget* it?"

"Please don't do the parenting routine now," I said, opening my eyes. "You can pretend you care when we've got witnesses."

My father shook his head at me, his mouth puckered in disapproval. "Don't *you* pull the teenage abandonment routine," he said. "I sent you to a school where you should have been stimulated and encouraged and kept safe, but it's clearly not worked out that way."

"She needs rest, Dr Park," a nurse said from the doorway. "Perhaps you should wait outside."

"I'll just be a minute," my father said. He looked back at me, calmer now. "What you did was very irresponsible," he said. "Frankly, I'm disappointed in you, Tallulah. But I'm more disappointed in the school for not keeping a better eye on you."

"I guess they didn't want me any more than you did."

"After all the trouble you've caused you should be grateful they haven't expelled you. That would look much worse on your record."

"Grateful?"

"Yes, Tallulah, grateful. A lot of people have put themselves out for you over the years; gratitude should be much easier for you than it seems to be."

I swallowed, and felt the urge to giggle again. I'm losing my mind. Going cuckoo.

He sat down, looking tired. "Nevertheless. It's obviously quite a shock, what you've just been through – that's why I've decided to withdraw you from school and place you in a remedial college."

"You're joking, right?"

My father frowned. "No."

"I don't get a say in this at all?"

"I thought you'd be glad to leave. You always wanted to before."

"I wanted to go home," I said. "To Grandma's or somewhere." I felt my eyes fill in frustration and I swallowed again. "I don't want to go to a remedial school."

"Well, I'm afraid the Headmaster is in agreement with me on this one," my father said. "You don't have a choice." He passed his hand over his eyes. "I'm taking you home for a week to recuperate. But then you'll be starting at your new college."

"Can't I just get a tutor?"

"I'm sorry, Tallulah," he said. "If you're to have any chance of passing your exams you'll need an intensive learning environment over the next month or two."

"They're just GCSEs," I said. "They don't mean anything."

"They're important," he said. "So we'll see how you do this summer and take it from there."

"Please," I said, gripping my blanket.

"You're only sixteen," he said eventually. "I know it's hard to understand. I know you think I'm pushing you on this. But it's for the best. It's really the most important thing you can do – educate yourself."

"Mum left school at sixteen."

"Your mother lost both her parents and had no support network."

"Where's *my* support network?"

"*I'm* here," my father said. "Looking out for your welfare, as I always have done. Frankly, I think I deserve to be treated with more respect. I know your mother would have been sad to see you turn out so self-centred."

I snorted. "Don't talk about Mum like you knew anything about her."

"Pardon me?"

"You probably never cared about her either, did you?"

"You're clearly feverish," my father said, coldly. "I'll get the nurse to come and take your temperature."

"Why can't you do it?" I said. My skull felt like someone had it in a clamp. I dug the heel of my palm into my temple. "You spend all your time at work, looking after other people, but you've never looked after us. I can't work out whether you're a shitty doctor, or just a shitty dad."

My father was shaking his head. "I know what you're really talking about here, Tallulah, but you're wrong."

"How am I wrong?"

"You were a child. And you didn't see how it happened."

"I heard you talking about it."

"There was nothing I could do to save her. Believe me, Tallulah, you can be as unpleasant as you want, but it can't make me feel worse than I already do."

"Because you know it was your fault."

"Because I couldn't do anything."

"You didn't want us around, you were so mean to us. I know you were fighting with each other. You could probably have done something and you just pretended you couldn't."

My father went purple. "You can't honestly believe that."

"And as soon as she was dead, you packed me off to boarding school."

"Tallulah. That isn't funny."

"And now you pull me out of school and send me to some remedial college where I have *no* friends."

"I'm taking you out of the extremely expensive and desirable boarding school I sent you to because you're failing at your subjects and you… " He stopped, looking at me.

I wanted to punch him. "I what?"

"You got yourself into trouble," he finished, and paused

again. "I thought you were smarter than that."

"I was *raped*."

Now he went white. "You're making it up."

"You think I'd *lie* about that?"

He jumped up and started pacing again. "When did it happen?"

"About a month ago."

"Why would you wait until now to tell me? Why wouldn't you tell the police or the school?"

"Why is it always my fault?"

"I don't understand," my father was saying. "I don't understand how that could have happened. It's impossible." He came forward and gripped my shoulders. "Tallulah, if you're lying you have to stop it *right now*."

"I was raped," I yelled at him. "Some arsehole raped me and then I was pregnant, and now I've had a miscarriage *and you were never there for me*." I sat up and tried to swing my legs out of the bed. "And it wasn't my fault, Dad. It wasn't *my* fault."

My heart monitor was bleeping like crazy. I sensed, rather than saw, nurses hurrying in and trying to get me to lie down again. One of them hissed at my father, "You should know better than to get the patient riled up like this, Doctor."

"Tallulah," he said, "you're trying to pay me back for putting you in the school in the first place, but it won't work, do you understand me? I don't blame you, but... "

"*Get him out of here*," I screamed. I carried on screaming until another of the nurses grabbed my father by the elbow and steered him to the door.

The first one who had looked in was shushing me. "It's alright, calm down now. This isn't helping matters."

I looked back at him as he was jostled out of the room, his face still white.

"I don't want to see him," I shouted. "Don't let him in."

"Alright, Tallulah. Just calm down."

I didn't see him again.

334

The nurse who gave me a check-up after the procedure told me briskly that I'd be able to leave that afternoon. "Who shall we inform?" she asked, clipboard in hand.

"I'm taking a taxi," I said. "Back to school. Someone's meeting me there."

"Your father?"

"No."

"I see. Is it the young gentleman waiting outside?"

My heart thumped painfully. "Who's waiting outside?"

"I don't know. He's at reception now."

"Did he say his name was Toby Gates?"

"I didn't get his name."

"Tell him I'm asleep," I said.

"We're going to need the bed soon," she said, and moved off.

I opened the door to my room a crack and peered down the hall to my left. I could see Toby sitting in a chair opposite the reception desk, his head tilted back. To my right the corridor marched onwards. I could see a sign for toilets and baby changing, and a payphone in the distance. I closed the door and got dressed quickly. I called a cab and then hung up and dialled reception.

"Can you pass on a message to Toby Gates?" I asked. "He's at reception now. Tell him he needs to call Edith immediately at Honeysuckle House – it's important."

I opened the door again and saw Toby sit up, like someone was talking to him. He looked in my direction, and pointed towards the pay phone sign. I gave it a minute; when I next looked out, he was gone.

I checked myself out of the hospital and got into the taxi. At school I asked the driver to wait for me. The Housemistress started out of her seat when I walked in, but I called to her, "My dad's waiting outside. I just need to collect my things."

She nodded and sat back down, looking awkward.

No one was in the dorm, luckily. I didn't know what I would say to Edith if I saw her, or anyone else. I grabbed my suitcase and shoved my clothes inside, my shoes, towel, the medical textbook, a packet of digestive biscuits I'd been stashing underneath the bed, my wallet, my toothbrush and two framed photographs: one of my mother, the other of my grandmother and me. I left the bracelet Edith had given me and Tom Sawyer – I still hadn't finished it.

I dragged my suitcase down the stairs and waved to the Housemistress. "Bye."

"Goodbye, Tallulah," she said, looking like she was about to burst into tears. "Don't forget us."

The driver helped me manoeuvre my case into the taxi, climbed back in and started the meter. "Where to, love?"

"Shrewsbury train station," I said. As we drove off I looked straight ahead, but I heard the bell go for lunch break, and out of the corner of my eye, I thought I saw red hair among the heads bobbing between buildings on their way to the canteen.

I moved to a youth hostel in London. I didn't leave a forwarding address.

*** * ***

The sky outside the window is angry; the wind's picked up and is chasing dark clouds our way. They're chafing above the hospital, and I can almost feel the thunder building up inside them.

Amid the chaos, the city is winding down; cars choke into life then rumble off, cats spit at each other and people click off light-switches and computer screens. I have a sudden craving for chips, fat yellow ones in paper twists with a mountain of salt on top. Malkie bought some like those for me when we came in to London to visit the mechanic. We found a wall somewhere to sit on, with a streetlight nearby, and ate them, picking them up with hands encased in fingerless gloves, letting the vinegar seep through the bottom of the wrapping and onto our jeans. We probably looked like a couple of tramps.

"Tallulah, love, you'll catch a cold like that," Aunt Gillian says.

I move my forehead from the windowpane.

I wonder, if my mother was right about damaged people, how's it affected Aunt Gillian. I guess she worries too much and that keeps people at a distance. Aunt Vivienne doesn't trust anyone, Uncle Jack went to jail, my father…

"Did Grandad ever hit Dad?" I ask.

"Now, really," Aunt Gillian says. "Where did that come from?"

Aunt Vivienne gives a short bark. "He hit all of us," she says.

"Let's not talk about this now," Aunt Gillian says.

"Though it was Jack he really had it in for." Aunt Vivienne inspects her nails.

"Why?"

"Jack was the youngest, the baby. And he was naughty. Our father used to say the beating was to teach him discipline."

"Jack wasn't just naughty," Aunt Gillian says. "You were both naughty. But Jack was *bad*. He was selfish and mean. He stole, Vivienne, and he wouldn't say sorry, ever. No one could handle him. He used to punch us. Bite us. He was *wild*."

"He was a *little boy*," Vivienne says, and I think I catch her eyes glistening. "Not an animal. Don't speak of him like he was that. He's had a shitty life, Gillian, and you know it. The bastard used him as a punching bag and no one ever stepped in to help him. And Jack was the one who provoked Albert if he seemed to be focusing on me, don't forget that." She wheels around to look at me. "The last time he came for me, Jack bit through his finger. He left me alone after that."

I'm stunned. I guess Uncle Jack was nice to one person, at least.

"There's only been one person who ever loved Jack in his entire life," Aunt Vivienne continues. "How do you think that must feel?"

"Well, he's difficult to love," Aunt Gillian snaps.

They glare at each other, then Aunt Gillian throws her

hands up in the air. "For goodness's sake, you'd think we were invisible," she says.

"Not much chance of that," Aunt Vivienne says.

"I want to know what they're *doing*."

"They're probably doing a pericardiocentesis," I say, mechanically. "They need to get rid of the fluid that's built up in the sac around the heart, so they put a needle inside and cut open a window to drain it."

"Oh," Aunt Gillian says; she looks green, then seems to make an effort to pull herself together. "You *have* been a mine of information today."

"I didn't realise we had a second doctor in the family," Aunt Vivienne says. Her chest is still heaving. "Pity we're not Jewish."

"They had to do it for my mum," I say, looking her in the eye.

"Ah," she says, and looks away first.

There's a momentary silence.

"I'm going to find someone," Aunt Gillian says.

Aunt Vivienne shrugs, and we follow her into the corridor.

"No one's around," Aunt Gillian is saying. "What kind of hospital is this, anyway?"

"Please," someone says, and we turn as one. It's the nurse I spoke to this morning. "We can't have you blocking the hall like this. There might be an emergency." She looks sympathetic. "Why don't you all go home for a few hours? Get some rest. I'm sure we won't be able to tell you anything definitive until later this evening. We'll call you as soon as we have any news."

"I don't see why we have to leave," Aunt Gillian says, querulously, "we haven't been causing any trouble."

"I'm not saying you're a trouble," the nurse says, gently.

"Why then?" Aunt Gillian asks, but Aunt Vivienne interrupts her – "Yes, thank you, Nurse. We'll go home and wait for a phone call."

"I'll call you myself," she says.

"I'm not going," Aunt Gillian says, as soon as the nurse is out of earshot.

"You heard what the nice lady said, Gillian."

"Viv, he's our *brother*. You don't go home when your brother is being operated on."

"You do when you're told to."

"Just think how it would look."

"For God's sake, Gillian. We're not being followed by the national newspapers."

"I know, I *know*," Aunt Gillian says. She looks frantic, and I'm not sure she really heard Aunt Vivienne at all. "There must be somewhere we can be out of the way. He's a *doctor* here for goodness sake. You'd think they'd bend the rules a little for his family. We're almost one of them."

Aunt Vivienne looks pointedly at Aunt Gillian's Cartier watch.

"They said they'll call as soon as anything happens," I say. "There's nothing else we can do." I'm tired. I want a smoke and a sandwich and to curl up under my duvet and sort through everything that's going on in my head.

"What about a café in the area?"

"They're *closing*, Gillian."

"Well, why don't you stay over, Tallulah? That way we can be together when the news comes through."

"Don't you think he'll make it?" I ask. I feel dumb for not realising it sooner; there are beads of sweat gathering at the roots of her hair and her mouth looks almost bloodless under the lipstick. Maybe she only gets through things by pretending they're not happening, but now she can't pretend anymore. Or maybe I'm in shock – I vaguely remember being anxious a while ago but now I'm definitely not, a little buzzy, maybe. The other two waver in front of me, like shapes in the desert. It couldn't happen, a voice inside me keeps saying. He couldn't die before I understood everything, not now I've actually started asking questions.

"Oh no," Aunt Gillian says, hurriedly. "No, of course

that's not it."

Aunt Vivienne blows air out through her mouth, noisily. "So we can leave?"

"Yes, I suppose so."

We gather our things and head over to the lift.

"Will you be going back to yours?" Aunt Gillian asks; she looks like she's trying to be casual.

"I think I should."

We reach my bus stop.

"I'm going to call a cab," Aunt Gillian says. "Would you like me to drop you off?"

"No thanks. I like the bus."

"I'll get in with you, Gillian," Aunt Vivienne says.

"Oh, alright," Aunt Gillian says. She takes my hand in hers and squeezes it. "I'll see you soon," she says, uncertainly.

"Soon," I say.

She kisses me on the cheek and they move off.

The bus takes ages to arrive. I smoke two cigarettes and organise my purse, throwing out old ticket stubs and chewing-gum wrappers and a two-pence coin that seems to be growing mould.

When I board the bus I sit at the front of the top deck again, leaning against the yellow rail nearly all the way home. Some man comes and sits next to me, tries to strike up a conversation. He's about twenty years older than me. "How long have you lived here?" he asks.

"All my life."

"I love London," he says. "So busy, so metropolitan."

"Sure."

"I'm from Montreal, originally. Lived in Paris for a few years. Paris is more *chic* than London, but not as lively, don't you think?" His accent is different to Malkie's, but there's something about the way he looks, the way he's slouching forwards in his seat that reminds me of him. I feel like crying. "I've never been to Paris," I say.

"It's not possible," he says in mock horror. "So close!"

340

I try to smile at him, but I can feel my eyelids starting to close.

"I'm sorry, am I bothering you?"

"No," I say. "I'm just tired. Excuse me."

I go and sit on the lower deck. I can feel his eyes on my back as I make my way down the stairs, clutching on tightly in case I lose my balance.

It's late when I get home. I pee as soon as I get in, and wash my hands thoroughly, scrubbing underneath my nails. Looking at Aunt Vivienne's perfect manicure all day has made me feel grubby. I let myself into my flat, boil the kettle and scrape my hair back into a ponytail, then try to find a face-wipe to clean away some of the dirt and grease that I've picked up. Now the water's ready, I fancy a beer instead. On the table my phone bleeps pathetically, the battery is almost dead. I have to be available for the hospital, I think. Fucking shit. Maybe Aunt Gillian's right. Maybe I should be more worried. Maybe we shouldn't have left. What if he wakes up and no one's there and he dies of neglect? Or he might never wake up, and I'll never get to see him alive again.

I need to distract myself, do something positive. I grab a beer, get out a notepad and pen and sit on my bed, tallying up my monthly outgoings. I could move to a smaller flat, if that's possible. I could stop eating.

I draw a cat at the bottom of the page, with a collar. I've done the research. I could start off as a healthcare assistant – I don't know how well they get paid, though, or if they get paid at all.

I can cope with the long hours, the heavy lifting, the sadness. As long as it's not my own family. I remember how my father felt in my hands the other day.

I write *Mr Tickles* underneath my doodle and shut the notepad. I take a swig of the beer. I can ask at the hospital about work experience. I don't know if I can stand another vigil in the waiting-room though. Maybe I'll go to work tomorrow – just until I hear about the operation.

I go to bed with my phone plugged in to the socket a few feet away; the green charging light makes me feel better.

$* * *$

I chose the youth hostel in Kings Cross because of its distance from my family, rather than its standard of hygiene. The bathrooms were windowless, the stairs always smelled like pee, and the tables and chairs in the kitchen were nailed to the floor.

'Charming,' I imagined my grandmother saying, 'but beggars can't be choosers,' I reminded her.

The manager took a week's payment up front and pushed the register across the desk for me to sign. I scribbled something down – the first name I could think of.

"Lauryn Hill," he read.

"Yep."

"That's not your real name."

"Why would you think that?"

"Not my business," the manager said, deadpan.

I took the key from his outstretched hand.

I sent a letter to my father, telling him not to look for me. I told him I wasn't interested in seeing any of them ever again. I walked halfway across London to post it from a different address, and if he was trying to find me, I didn't hear about it.

Kings Cross in 1997 was supposedly in the middle of a regeneration project, but it looked pretty grotty to me. The building façades were peeling or blackened by pollution; every other shop was a kebab takeaway or a casino, and traffic blared past at all hours of the day and night.

"I thought this was meant to be a red-light district," one of the backpackers from my dorm said. "I've only met one prozzy. She had a kid with her and he'd shat all down his leg."

I was sharing a mixed dormitory with only one other girl. It felt strange after the strictness of school dorms, and I never got used to walking in on boys changing.

Sometimes new faces would appear in the place of old

ones, but however enthusiastic they started out, they all ended up lying in bed fully clothed in the middle of the day. Me and the other girl went about our business, both job-hunting, although she was also taking evening classes; seeing her scuttling off at seven in the evening, textbooks clutched to her chest, made me feel ashamed.

I applied for the waitressing job after she showed me the advert. 'Needed: female 16-25 years, good memory, flexible hours.'

"I have fixed hours for lessons," she said. "Otherwise I'd apply – it's about twenty minutes on the bus."

"I'll give it a go," I said.

I disliked my boss from the beginning. I was wearing black woolly tights, a black, high-waisted cotton skirt and cropped black jumper when I turned up for the interview. He took one look at me and sneered. I felt my stomach drop. I handed him my CV and waited while he flicked his eyes over it.

He gestured to two grubby chairs in the middle of the floor. We sat down. "How old are you, then?"

"Sixteen."

"And you went to a fancy school?"

"Yes."

"Ever waitressed before?"

"Yes," I lied. "Private events." What I mean is I carried a cake out from the kitchen at my mother's birthday party.

He held his hands up. "Well, I hope we won't be too low-class for you."

I ground my teeth. "I hope so too."

He scowled at me. "I guess we need someone who can speak the bloody language," he said. "Can you start nine a.m Monday?"

"Yes."

"You're hired." He pushed himself up and scratched his giant belly. "Cash in hand – come fifteen minutes early so I can show you the ropes. After that, it's a rota system."

I went back to the hostel. One of the boys was in the dorm,

343

reading *On the Road*.

"Hey," he said.

"Hey."

"How did your interview go?"

"I got the job."

"Cool."

"Not really. The owner's a knob."

"Fuck the establishment," he said. "What's it for, anyway?"

"Waitressing."

"That's alright, right? Good tips."

"I guess."

"What do you wanna do?"

"I used to wanna be a nurse."

"Changed your mind?"

"I didn't do my exams."

"You probably don't need to," he said. He went back to his book. I lay on my bed for a few hours, trying to work out how I could get into medicine without qualifications. I didn't know if I even wanted to anymore. I couldn't think of anyone in the healthcare profession that seemed nice; the nurses who'd looked after my grandmother hadn't been great. The nurses in the hospital after the miscarriage had been worse. And then my father.

Do I just stay at a café forever, then? I asked myself. I tried to see past next week, but I couldn't.

I steeled myself to the life that followed, although working at the café was worse than I'd thought. My boss didn't bother trying to hide how much I got on his nerves from the start. The work was long and left me with aches in my feet and arms and back and neck. One of the boys in the dorm offered to give me a massage once, and used the opportunity to start kissing me; hot, wet kisses that felt greasy on my skin. I let him do it. I didn't try to stop him when he wanted to go further, even. Afterwards, I gathered my clothes up and took a shower. He was waiting on his bed for me to come to him again, but I went to my own and turned onto my side to face the wall. I could hear him breathing uncertainly, then the springs in his mattress squeak as he lay back down.

After a few months, I was close to snapping. I joined the public library and checked out all the books I could find on chemistry, biology, medicine, nursing and career opportunities. I read them in the park if it wasn't raining, or on the staircase at the hostel if it was. I took notes. I answered questions and looked up the answers, marking myself like a teacher would have done. I even wrote essays. I thought about taking evening classes; I got as far as walking into the building of the local adult education centre before I realised I wasn't an adult yet. Maybe they'd find it suspicious, how young I was, and turn me in to the police. My palms felt clammy. I turned and pushed my way out the front door again.

I didn't want to present myself at a GP surgery, or the local hospital for the same reason. I couldn't lie my way into work experience there as easily as into being a waitress. Maybe my father could have helped me get work experience – if I'd stayed on, taken the exams. If he hadn't withdrawn me from the school and let me know he blamed me for everything that happened. I convinced myself it was for the best; I didn't want to be like him – I didn't want anything to do with him. At least as a waitress I could pretend I was following in my mother's footsteps instead.

After a while, I took most of the books back. A couple I'd lost in the dorm room, among my other stuff. I paid the fines on those and never went to the library again.

Seventeen

Four years or so after I went to live at the hostel, I was unloading my tips into my locker in the hallway of the hostel. Someone grabbed my arm and I shook it off instinctively, my body taut and poised to run.

"*Tallie?*"

I hadn't seen Starr since I'd left school.

"Is it really you?" she asked. "You're here?" She looked like she was ready to cry.

I felt my stomach flip, and my toes and fingers prick with something. I couldn't work out if it was terror or relief. "Yeah, it's me," I said, slamming the locker shut and turning to face her. "What are you doing here? How did you find me?"

"Nice, that's real nice, Tal." She looked pissed now. "No one's heard from you in years and that's the hello I get."

"I'm sorry," I said, feeling shamed. "I didn't expect to see you here, that's all."

"Dick," Starr said, but she smiled at me.

"So, what *are* you doing here?"

"I followed you in," she said. "I thought I saw you on the street outside but you were too far away to hear me call." She stepped back and took all of me in.

"I've been working," I said, suddenly embarrassed by my appearance. "Gimme a minute to shower, then we can talk."

Starr sat on my bed while I showered. I came back fully clothed; she was perched on the edge of the mattress, her nose wrinkled up. There was no one else in the dorm. "Thank fuck for that," she said when she saw me. "Let's get out of here."

We grabbed a six-pack of beer from the fridge and walked with it to a church garden in nearby Islington. It'd been raining, but the sun was out, making little rainbows in the puddles, and in the drops clinging to the poplar trees that grew in the church and the park opposite. I spread my parka out on a bench almost completely hidden by the rose bush behind it.

"So," Starr said, as soon as we sat down. "Why'd you run away?"

"I didn't run away."

"You, like, totally disappeared, Tal."

"My dad took me out of school anyway, enrolled me in a remedial college. I just left early, before the exams."

"Don't you think that's a little immature?"

"Look," I said. "I've never been good in school. And me and my dad never got on. I don't wanna see him."

"Well… "

"Seriously. I'm not going back."

She looked at me for a moment, then shrugged. "Your call. What have you been up to, then?"

"Not much. Working," I said. I lit a cigarette and took a drag. "What about you?"

"Yeah, I'm fine, fine," she said. She tucked her hair back behind her ear, looking around the churchyard. "Is this where you hang?"

"It's not so bad," I said. "I generally work at night. I sleep. I don't go out much."

"What *do* you do?"

"Save my money. I want to get somewhere of my own."

"Pretty grown up of you, Little Cuz."

"Yeah, I'm living the dream."

Across the road we could hear dog owners exchanging

347

pleasantries, and mothers telling their toddlers to be careful on the swings. The churchyard was completely empty except for an old man sweeping autumn leaves off the path a few yards away, and a cat stalking a pigeon.

"What happened to your moggy?" Starr asked, pointing at the cat.

"He died," I said. I wiped my nose with the sleeve of my jumper; I still got a sinking feeling whenever I thought about Mr Tickles.

"Sorry, man," Starr said. "He was like, your best friend, or something lame, wasn't he?"

"What if he was?"

Starr looked at me out of the corner of her eye. "You almost had me there, you know?"

I grinned, and rammed my hands into my pockets.

"Even *you're* not that much of a loner."

"Don't be mean about my cat," I said. "He was better company than most people."

"Sucks," Starr said. She gave me a friendly punch. "Anyway, enough of being depressing. I've got a riddle for you. Which of our family members is obsessed with The Beatles?"

"I don't know. None of them?"

"Aunt Gillian." Starr grinned.

"Why?"

"'Cos of her husbands."

"What?"

"Think about it... I just picked up on it the other day. John, George, Paul." She tapped the top of the beer can.

"Who's Paul?"

"The latest one. Oh yeah, of course. He was after your little invisibility trick."

"Drop it."

Starr gave me an innocent look. "Alright, touchy. I was just gonna say Gillian goes out of her way to find the creep-o-lahs."

"What was John like?"

"Don't remember him, really. I was only two. But, I mean, George – yuck." She shuddered theatrically.

I wondered about Michael. He must have been five when John died, old enough to remember him. We'd never talked about it though, even after my mother.

Starr was still talking, "I saw this programme on TV last night… Did you know men get boners after they're dead?" She cracked her can open and took a swig. The cat in front of us looked around, hissing at the noise. "Scat," Starr said.

The pigeon took off. The cat glared at us then curled up in a nearby flowerbed.

"Yeah," I said. "Angel lust."

"Of course," Starr said. "You always knew the weirdest things."

I opened my can. "Grandma told me that," I said.

"You guys talked about sex?" Starr mimed sticking her fingers down her throat. "I can't think of anything more hideous. Even my mother has more sense."

"It came up during a programme we were watching."

"It came up?" She waggled her eyebrows.

"You're not funny," I told her.

She cackled. The cat opened one eye and glared at us again.

"So what about you?" she said, keeping the can to her mouth. "Have you… since?"

"No." I took a swig of beer; I'd brought approximately seven guys back to the hostel since I'd been living there.

"Me either then."

I gave her a look. "Everyone at school knew about you and Pierre. And you and David, or whatever his name was."

"It doesn't count if it's less than two minutes."

"Right," I said. "Hope that philosophy works out for you. And the staff at your nearest STI clinic."

"It does," Starr said, serenely.

I yawned.

The cat lifted its head and started washing its paw vigorously.

"I need to go back," I said. "I'm knackered."

"Fine," Starr said. "I'll walk you."

In the street she linked her arm through mine and started talking about art college; I concentrated on staying awake. "One of the maintenance guys is super hot – Ricardo or Rodrigo or something like that. I'm thinking of giving him my number. Anyway, my bus stops here. See you soon, yeah? You're not gonna move again, now I know where you are?"

"Probably not."

"You're a piece of work, Tal."

"Love you too."

∗∗∗

I hear from the hospital that the operation was successful. My father's under again, though.

Any chance he'll come round before the apocalypse? I want to ask, but I just thank them and hang up.

Work is a bad idea. I've got a headache that won't go away even after two Nurofen, and my boss is in a rotten mood; I'm barely through the door before he's yelling.

"Go take a cold shower," I mutter, while I'm tying the apron strings behind my back.

He glares at me.

It's almost as bad as the other day. I forget orders, undercharge two tables, snap at the guy who's asking for Dijon mustard.

"Look around," I tell him. "Does it look like we've got Dijon mustard?"

"It's not fancy or anything," he says, hurt. "It's just not as strong. I can't have anything too strong."

I feel like throwing my notepad at him. "I'll see if we have any in the kitchen," I say.

I push through the kitchen doors. "Any Dijon mustard in here?" I ask.

350

Tony, the other chef, doesn't even look at me. "That's stuff's too expensive for Tight-Wad."

I sit down on the stool that's shoved up against the wall in between the huge fridge and the dishwasher.

"Please don't make me go back out there," I say. "Please don't make me tell Table Four there's no Dijon."

Now he looks at me; he grins and takes a cigarette out of his pocket. "Have one on me," he says.

I take it. "I'm not due a break for another two hours."

"I won't tell," he says. "Tight-Wad's on the phone – he won't notice."

"Thanks."

The cigarette goes a little way towards repairing my frayed nerves, but the headache's worse now. I go back to Table Four with a sorry look on my face. "No Dijon," I say.

He sniffs. "Guess I'll make do. Can you scrape these onions out, too?"

I sigh. I pick up his plate and carry it over to the kitchen. I scrape the onions off the burger into the bin.

"Stop wasting good onions," my boss yells at me.

"He doesn't want any."

"Well, he should have said before he ordered. That onion comes out of your pay."

I put the plate down on the microwave. "Shut up," I say.

"What did you just say?" he asks, squinting at me. He's chewing a toothpick and a strand of saliva dangles out of his mouth when he speaks.

"Shut *up*."

He goes purple. "Final warning, missy."

I go to the kitchen door. I look out the porthole and see Table Four tapping his foot. I think about my father, back in his coma, sleeping his life away. "I can't do this," I say. "I quit."

"You can't fucking quit," he yells. "We've got no one else until six p.m."

"I don't give a shit," I say. "Why don't you serve them yourself?"

Tony turns away, delicately; he's still chopping, but I think his shoulders are shaking.

"Rot in fucking hell."

"Right back at you."

I tear the apron off and throw it at my boss' feet. He takes the toothpick out and points it at me; for a crazy second, I think he's going to throw it at me, like a mini javelin.

"You'll come crawling back," he says. "And just so you know – you'll never get a job here again. Or a fucking reference."

"Fine by me," I say. "You probably can't write anyway."

He advances towards me, and I slip away and out the back door. I can hear him screaming abuse after me all the way down the alley. Then I'm out on the street and cars are pouring past me. The sky's cloudy and I've got nowhere to be and no money. I should have at least made him pay for my last few shifts. But I don't care, I can't stop grinning. I start out in the direction of the tube.

∗ ∗ ∗

"So, you're okay for money, right?"

Starr stubbed her cigarette out in the pint glass I'd given her for her orange squash and dropped the butt in the bin behind her.

I ran a hand through my hair and gestured around. "I'm fine," I said. "Check out the palace."

She wrinkled her nose. Dirty laundry was strewn over every surface and there were dirty dishes piled up in the sink. The posters the last tenants had put up had left darker patches on walls that were sun-bleached around them. The only trouble I took was over the plants growing on the window-sill; I watered them every night, and clipped them like my grandmother had taught me.

"You've been here one month?"

"Yeah."

"You haven't done much with it."

"What's wrong with it?"

"It smells weird."

"Yeah." I took a drag of my cigarette. "Something's rotten in the fridge, but I can't find it."

"Jesus, Tallie." Starr looked disgusted.

"It's fine," I said. "Rent's low. There are no rats this time. The loo flushes." I shrugged. "What more do I need? It's better than the hostel, anyway."

"Yeah, well." She tugged her skirt down, inching the hem to just above her knees. "So you're still at the café?"

I took a gulp of coffee – the mug had a crack in it, I noticed. "Yeah," I said. "It's okay. I know the customers – who tips well, that kind of shit."

"Right."

Starr let go of the hem of the skirt, and ran her fingers over the front of it, smoothing the leather down. It looked like it had cost her well over a hundred quid, and made me feel even plainer in my denim shorts and oversized grey jumper. Her t-shirt was white, with some sort of punk logo on the front, and her gloves were fingerless and matched her skirt.

"What are you up to then?" I asked her. "Still with that maintenance guy?"

"Ricardo?" she purred. "I'm living with him now." She stretched her improbably long legs and gave me a sly smile. "Mum's furious." She opened the handbag slung across the back of her chair and took out some purple lipstick, rolling it around the table in front of her. "He has a motorbike." She leaned forward. "And he's very good with his hands."

"Yeah, you said." I dragged on my cigarette again and stubbed it out. "Probably lucky, given his job."

"You're such a Park."

"It's your name too."

"Not for much longer." She pulled a face. "I'm thinking of changing my name – I might marry Ricardo."

"What would you be then?"

"Garcia."

"Starr Garcia?"

"Yep."

"Sounds kinda stupid, don't you think?"

"Not as stupid as Tallulah," she said, drawing out the looooh syllable.

"Granted."

"Mum said my name came to her in a dream." Starr shook her head. "If I'd been a boy she was going to call me Leopold."

"Bet you're glad you weren't."

"Amen."

I finished my coffee. "More squash?"

"Nope. I should head soon." She swung around in her chair to watch me while I got up to boil the kettle. "Gotta pack – I'm going on holiday to Spain with Ric. It's gonna be heaven."

"Good for you."

"What about you? What would your name have been if you'd been a boy?"

"I dunno."

"Probably something boring like Edward or Jack. Speaking of… "

"Yeah, why d'you think he left?" I asked.

"What?"

"Uncle Jack. Why d'you think he left?"

"I wasn't going to talk about Uncle Jack, I was going to talk about Uncle Edward." Starr leaned forwards, resting her elbows on the tabletop. "He asked about you recently," she said.

"And?" I could feel my breath catch in my throat.

"And nothing. I didn't tell him we meet." She was watching me closely. I turned away and ran the tap, filling the kettle.

"Tallie, are you seriously never gonna go back home?"

"What's the point?"

"Because he misses you," Starr said. She tapped out a beat with the scuffed toes of her black Doctor Martins. "And you're being a little bitch by staying away."

"You don't know anything about it."

"I know how he feels," Starr said. She stood up. Even without heels she was three inches taller than me. I switched the kettle on.

"I don't feel great about lying to Uncle Edward."

"You lie all the time."

"Yeah, but he's a nice guy."

"He doesn't really miss me."

She shook her head. "You're wrong."

"I know him better than you."

She gave up, throwing her hands in the air. "So what was it you were asking?"

"Why Uncle Jack left. Do you know?"

"He was on the run, wasn't he?"

"From what?"

"Drug lords, I heard."

"Don't you think that's a little bit dramatic?"

"What do I know? Why are you so interested, anyway?"

I shrugged. "I guess I see it more from his perspective now, I guess."

Starr raised her eyebrows. "Your situation is totally different, Tal. You have a dad who wants you around. Uncle Jack was a loner already. You're an idiot if you think he's any kind of a role model."

"Your mum wanted him around."

Starr screwed her face up like she was remembering something. "She did try to track him down, I think. But she forgets people pretty quickly."

"I don't think she'd forget him," I said. "Do you remember her at my mum's birthday? The one just before she died. Your mum had a fight with Gillian about him."

"My mum used to pull hissy fits all the time, Tal." Starr smeared lipstick onto her forefinger and patted it onto her lips. "I stopped paying them attention when I was, like, seven."

"Oh."

She saw the look on my face. "Don't feel bad for me, doofus. I'm not asking for sympathy. I'm fine, Mum's fine."

"So she really never talked about Uncle Jack? Did everyone just pretend he'd never been there, or something?"

She gave a world-weary sigh. "Forget it, chick, that's my advice. If you start thinking about all the weird shit that goes on in this family you'll be here all day." She checked her reflection in a pocket mirror. "You ever see any of the old gang?"

"No," I said.

"Why not?"

"I told you, I haven't spoken to anyone since I left."

"You know I bumped into Toby the other day?"

My heart gave a thump so hard I felt it in my fingertips. "How would I know that?"

"Well, I did. He's a lawyer." She put her lipstick and mirror away. "I asked about everyone – do you wanna hear?"

"Okay," I said. Now my heart was beating triple-time.

"Edith's doing some costume design course, can you believe that? The hunky one, Francis, did biology at uni, forget what he's up to now. That little creepy one… "

"John?"

"Yeah, him. He's training as an accountant, go figure."

"Is Toby still with Edith?"

"Nah. She found herself and broke up with him." Starr shut the clasp on her handbag. "You should get in touch with him. He's pretty hot stuff. I'd have a crack if I didn't have a psychotic cousin to worry about."

"And a boyfriend."

"And a boyfriend. Like you could soon." She blew me a kiss. "I should be going."

∗ ∗ ∗

I see Toby straight away. He's leaning against a bike stand, talking to a leggy blonde girl. She keeps flicking her hair over her shoulder and tipping her head from side to side like a bird. As I get nearer she reaches out and hits him,

356

playfully, saying: "Stop it."

Oh come on, I think.

Toby looks up and sees me. "Jesus," he says.

It takes me a moment to hear him through the blood pounding in my ears. "Nope, just me."

"Tal?"

"Yeah." Then, because I don't know what to say, and the blonde is giving me a dirty look: "How are you?"

"How am I? How are *you*? No one's seen you for ages."

"Well, I've been around."

The blonde girl giggles. I can't help hating her.

"What are you *doing* here?"

"I was trying to find you."

"How… " he starts, then stops. "Sally, this is Tallulah." He nods at me and the blonde. "Tal, this is Sally."

"Hi," Sally says, sniffing.

"Did you wanna go for a drink?" Toby asks.

"Sure."

"Now?"

"Sure."

Sally pouts. "Tobbeeeee – you promised you'd take *me* for a drink," she says, linking her arm through his.

"Sorry," Toby says. "Another time. I haven't seen Tal in ages." He disengages himself and comes to stand next to me.

I smirk at her.

The pub is packed and Toby sloshes beer all over himself on the way back to our table. He carefully sets the pints and a packet of crisps down in front of me and inspects his shirt. "Fucking shit," he says, under his breath.

"It's just a shirt," I say, ripping open the crisps. I stuff three in my mouth; I haven't eaten all day and I'm starving.

"Just a shirt that I paid a lot of money for," Toby says.

"Just a shirt."

"You're still annoying, I see," Toby says.

"You're still uptight, I see."

He sits down and gulps his beer. "So, what did you want

to see me about?" He gives me a quick once-over. "You look different."

"It's been five years."

"Right, yeah." He's almost finished the pint. I can't tell if he's nervous. "So where have you been?"

"Here in London. I lived in a hostel for a while, now I'm renting a bedsit. I hear you're a lawyer these days."

He shrugs. "I'm still a junior."

"Were you always this prickly?"

"What did you expect, Tal? You disappeared off the face of the earth one day. You didn't even say goodbye."

It's not nerves then. In a weird way, his anger makes me feel better about tracking him down. He cares enough to be pissed at you, I tell myself.

"I wasn't really in the mood for a send-off."

Toby winces. "Sorry."

"It wasn't your fault."

"No, I know that. I'm just saying I'm sorry."

"Forget it."

"I came to the hospital," he says. "The nurse said you weren't seeing anyone, but I thought you'd see me. Then I got a phantom phone call from Edith and by the time I got back, you'd vanished."

"Yeah," I say. "I couldn't face you."

"I thought you hated me."

"No."

"I thought that was why you never got in touch."

We drink our beer in silence. Finally, Toby puts his glass down and sighs. "Seriously, what made you come back now? There must be some reason."

"Starr found me about six months ago," I say, sneaking a look at him; he doesn't blink. "She visits me occasionally. Last week she said she'd run into you." I shrug. "I dunno. It made me think about you guys. I wanted to see you again."

Toby looks at his hands. "Well, I'm sorry about being aggro. My feelings were hurt. I thought we were friends."

358

"We were."

"It didn't feel like it, when you ran off. That's all I'm saying."

"Yeah, well. It didn't feel like it when you secretly got with my best friend."

"Did you actually care?"

"You're the genius now. What do you think?"

Toby half-grins. "I've always been a genius," he says.

"And modest."

"And good-looking."

"And shy, and retiring."

"So why didn't you want me?" His tone's light, but he keeps his eyes on me as I take another gulp of beer.

"It wasn't that easy, Toby."

"It seemed pretty easy to me." He takes a sip. "I was crazy about you. You know that, right?"

"I liked you too," I say. "But it felt like everyone I liked died. So no, not that easy for me. And then Edith… "

"Yeah," Toby says. "We don't really talk anymore."

"Oh."

We're silent for a moment. At the table next to us, two men in business suits are laughing hard about something; one of them has the red face that comes with a lack of oxygen. He leans into the wall, slaps it and takes a deep, juddering breath. "You've got to be *kidding me*," he says.

"There's another reason I wanted to see you," I say. My mouth feels dry and my tongue seems to be swollen, so I have to stop and swallow a few times before I carry on. "My dad's in hospital – he had a heart attack."

"Oh my God," Toby says; he scrapes his chair around the table until he's next to me. "Is he okay?"

"Yeah," I say, "maybe, I don't know."

"What do you mean?"

"He was in a coma," I say. "He kind of woke up the other day, but he kept drifting in and out, and then he had to have an emergency operation. They said they'll let us know when

359

he's awake properly."

"How are you doing?"

"I'm okay," I say. "I hadn't seen him since I left school either."

Toby draws back to look at me. "*What*?"

"I told you – I've been living in a hostel."

He looks angry again. "So you went off completely by yourself?"

"Yeah."

"You *always* shut people out," he says. "You should have called me. I would've looked out for you."

I scratch at the varnish on the table. "I know," I say, eventually. "And I know you were the one who trashed the art room by the way."

"How?"

I put my hands in my lap. "I worked it out," I say.

"Are you pissed off?"

"No." I should have fucking killed Mr Hicks.

I want to say thank you. I want to tell him how knowing that someone was standing up for me made me feel grateful and ashamed of my own behaviour at the same time. That I should have looked out for him too, instead of leaving him to deal with his brother's death alone.

Tell him everything, inner me says. Tell him you feel guilty and glad and resentful and defiant and vulnerable and he's the only one who can navigate his way around all that.

"I'm really, really sorry," I say. "For everything."

"I'm sorry too," Toby says. "The whole time you were away I was thinking about how I made all those mistakes with you, and how I'd make it up to you if I ever saw you again." He gives me a half-smile. "I probably should have started with that. And it *is* really good to see you."

There's another silence, then he drains his beer and stands up. "I've got an exam coming up – I should go revise."

"Oh."

"What's your number?"

I hesitate.

"I'm not letting you disappear again."

I write the number down on the back of an old receipt I find in my bag and push it towards him. He picks it up and puts it in his pocket without looking at my scrawl. "See you," he says. He bends down and kisses me on the lips. It's a long kiss, forceful. At first I feel nothing, then suddenly my whole body is throbbing and my head is buzzing, and I just want to keep on doing this forever. He pulls back, straightens up and walks out of the pub.

I sit and finish my beer, taking time over each sip.

When I leave it's dark and surprisingly chilly for a summer evening. The recent heat has broken, and the streets are slick with the sheen of rain. My phone rings and I fumble in my bag for it; it keeps slipping out of my fingers.

"Fuck exams," he says. "Can I come over and see you?"

"No," I say. "I have to go to bed."

"That's not putting me off."

I find myself grinning.

"What did you say?"

"I didn't say anything. I'm smiling."

"I can't tell that over the phone, you know."

"I know."

"So, can I come over?"

"Yes."

∗ ∗ ∗

We kiss, we talk. We talk for half the night at each other and over each other. Toby's brought a bottle of whisky around, and we drink that, neat, from plastic cups. We start out in the kitchen, and somehow we end up in the bedroom, although I'm not too clear on how we get there. I take a pillow off the bed and lie on the floor and he sits next to me, his hand in my hair.

"What are you thinking?" he asks.

"I'm thinking about something I read earlier," I say.

"Oh good."

"Shut up, it's interesting. There's this thing in physiology called 'Dead Space', where a third or so of every resting breath is exhaled unchanged."

"Come again?"

"It means the oxygen hasn't been diffused in the alveoli from the alveolar gas into the blood passing by in the lung capillaries. That's the Dead Space – the portion of air where no useful transaction has taken place."

He strokes my face with his free hand. "You sound like a doctor."

"Maybe a nurse."

He tells me about his law conversion, and uni, and travelling around Europe for three months. I feel sad that I never did any of this, and he says, "You're still young", and then I laugh at him again for looking so serious, like twenty-three is old and he grins and says his family are worried he might turn into a prick, and I think I might have loved him all this time, or maybe it's the whisky.

Then we're kissing again, and I'm not scared this time. He takes his clothes off first, and then mine; each time he takes a layer off his hands tremble. When we're completely naked he lies on top of me, very gently, just skin-on-skin. I finally feel comfortable in mine, maybe it's being next to his. He's hard, underneath me, and I want him. I move my hips up and then it's happening and, this time, it's right.

Afterwards, he talks some more. I half-see him get up to open the window then come over to me and I feel him gently shaking my shoulder.

"I'm not asleep," I say, "I'm listening. I heard everything you said."

"Sure," he says. "You've been snoring for half an hour."

"I was in a sex coma," I say. I wrap myself around him, not minding the stickiness from earlier. He bends his head down to kiss my collarbone, then my neck, then my chin, my mouth, and we start again.

Eighteen

Bones are made up of marrow, nerves, blood vessels, epithelium and various tissues. When there is a break in the continuity of the bone, it is called a bone fracture, or more colloquially, a broken bone. Fractures are mostly commonly caused when the bone comes into contact with another body (such as the ground, a wall, even another person) and the force of this contact is too high, but sometimes they can happen after a period of accumulated trauma to a particular area (such as the legs if you run too much); these fractures are known as *stress fractures*. On average, you will suffer two fractures in your lifetime.

The development of the human skeleton can be said to start at the end of the third month after conception, when your bones begin to calcify inside your mother's womb. When we are born, we have over two hundred and seventy of them, but as we grow some fuse together, and the tissue hardens.

It takes twenty years to fully grow, one year less than the age I am today. As I dream next to Toby, I have two hundred and six bones, and they're as strong as they'll ever be.

✳ ✳ ✳

Toby leaves early the next morning to pick up clean clothes before work.

"Call me," he mumbles into my ear, and I roll over and grab his chin.

"Stay," I say, eyes still closed.

"How about I come round tonight? I get the feeling you're not a morning person anyway."

"Less talk, more sleep."

I vaguely hear the click of the door being closed, then it's four hours later and I'm sitting up blurrily, not quite sure if what happened really happened.

I shower and stand in front of the mirror, running my fingers through my hair. I should get a cut – a proper one. I've been butchering it myself for the last few years and it shows. I crack my joints, knuckles, neck, shoulders, lower back. I text Aunt Gillian, checking in. I read. I go out and buy tea bags and lemons and make myself some iced tea. I do almost anything other than think about my father, and how worried I should be right now.

On the table my phone beeps angrily at me.

Princess – found Jack. Coming round this afternoon about three o'clock. Malkie.

I check my watch. Two fifteen p.m.

I put on a lacy white dress, then take it off; it makes me look like I'm taking my Holy Communion. I put on a white, sleeveless, v-necked shirt instead, and bright green shorts. I tie my hair back and dab the skin under my eyes with concealer – don't want Malkie to notice how tired I look. And maybe Uncle Jack?

At five to three the buzzer goes; he's early.

"Oh God," I whisper to myself. "Oh fuck oh God." I don't know if I'm ready to see him now. I still haven't decided what to ask him, got things straight in my head.

I let him in and he clomps up the stairs. I leave my front door open and put some glasses in the freezer to chill so we can have iced tea.

"Hey."

I turn around. "Hey yourself."

He comes in and hugs me.

"Want a drink?"

"No thanks. You sure you want to see him?"

I try to swallow.

"You sounded pretty urgent the other day, doll."

"I am," I say. "It is."

"I don't know what you want with him," Malkie says. "But like I said before, you gotta be prepared for him to be changed, okay?"

"Yeah," I say. "I'm fine."

Malkie sighs. He looks at the clock on the oven and gestures to the door. "Shall we?"

My heart's in my mouth. I grab my purse and lead him out of the flat, double-locking the door behind us.

"So where are we going?" I ask.

"You know a pub called The North Star on New North Road?"

"Yeah."

"Okay. We're going there."

What if it turns out it wasn't an accident, after all? What then? I try to distract myself with thinking about Toby.

"Tallulah, you okay?"

"Yeah."

"You just looked a little flushed. You got a fever?"

"No, I'm fine."

We cut through the estates, and then the nice residential roads, with cute three-storey houses and windowboxes and well-mannered teenagers learning to drive in quiet squares.

The dry-cleaners comes into sight, and the Golden Jade – Chinese food and fish & chips – and then we're opposite the pub. There are a few bollards in front of the building; someone's leaning against one now, smoking and coughing a lot, bending over to spit into the gutter.

A drunk, I think, until Malkie crosses the road and stops in front of him. "Here we are," he says. I don't know who he's addressing; the man in front of us is still bent over. I look at him properly and feel like I've been punched in the stomach.

"Uncle Jack?"

He looks up and grimaces at me, coughing some more. Even standing straight up he looks bent over. His arms are hanging loosely by his sides. He's lost weight and his hair is dirty. "Hi, kiddo," he says. "Malk said you wanted to see me."

Beside me, Malkie shifts uncomfortably again. "I thought maybe it would be better to meet out here – neutral ground."

"Okay," I say. I can hear my voice, a pitch or so higher than normal. I'm looking at Uncle Jack's eyes – they're bloodshot and dead flat. "Is he alright?"

"Jacky's not going to cause any trouble, are you?"

"Nope," Uncle Jack croaks. "Cross my heart and hope to die." He grins at me.

Malkie's looking even more worried than before. "You *sure* you're ready for this?" he asks.

"Yes," I say, at the same time as Uncle Jack.

Malkie hugs me and steps backwards. "I'll be on my way then," he says. "But you have my number now. Call me if there's any problem. Any problem at all."

Uncle Jack pulls a face.

We watch Malkie shamble off; when he reaches the corner he turns around and raises his hand to me. I wave back at him. *Call me*, he mouths and vanishes from sight.

"You've got even friendlier since we first met," Uncle Jack says.

"I'm in shock," I say. "I didn't think Malkie would find you. You disappeared, remember?"

"Yeah, I guess I did."

I bite my lip. "How *did* he find you?"

"He knew where to look for me."

I remember Starr saying that Aunt Vivienne tried to track Jack down too, and wonder, briefly, how she went about it. And why she didn't try harder.

"It's funny, actually – you think we're so different when

366

we're really the same person. Guess Malk's just cuddlier." He coughs again, retching at the end of this fit.

I dig out a bottle of water from my bag and hand it to him, silently. He drinks thirstily, spilling half around his mouth and chin, then tries to give it back.

"You keep it."

"What did you want to talk about?"

He's shivering uncontrollably. The afternoon's as cloudy as the morning, and I can feel goosebumps starting. I wrap my arms around myself. I don't want to be alone with Uncle Jack, but I can't take him into the pub. He's clearly in a bad shape, and the last thing I need is a public drama.

"Look," I say. "We can go to my flat. But no funny business."

"What do you think of me?" Uncle Jack asks, then holds up his hand. "Don't answer that."

We walk back together without speaking, Uncle Jack coughing next to me. The noise reminds me of my grandmother and I wish she was there with us. 'Be brave,' I hear her saying.

Inside, I throw the keys on the kitchen table and turn to Uncle Jack. "Does anyone else know you're around?" I ask.

"Nope."

"Didn't you ever want to see them? Vivienne at least?"

Uncle Jack shrugs. "Maybe it was best I stayed away," he says. He looks sick and clammy. "So?"

"I asked Malkie to find you," I say, "because I want to know some stuff."

"Yes?"

Breathe, then launch. "About my mum. About when I was younger. Lots of shit happened that I don't really understand, and I feel like you were the reason it happened."

"Always the villain with you, huh?" He sits down in a chair, letting his head fall forwards until I can't see his face anymore. "I haven't slept since she died you know."

"Who?"

"Who do you think?"

I shake my head, although I know what's coming.

"Evie," he says. "I haven't slept since Evie died."

Hearing my mother's name is exactly like that feeling on a rollercoaster; the feeling of my insides plummeting. "You haven't slept for eleven years?" I say.

"You know what I mean. Were you always this pedantic, Tallulah?"

"Pretty much."

Uncle Jack laughs and shrugs his shoulders. There are dark circles around his eyes and his cheekbones jut out like little cliffs overhanging the dark fleshy pool of his mouth. Outside I'd thought that he was just unhealthy, but now I recognise the look from people at the hostel.

"You on heroin?" I ask.

"There – that's my smart little niece," he says, rubbing the back of his hand against his cheek. Skin rasps against beard and sets my teeth on edge. Uncle Jack laughs again; he's starting to annoy me. "So what did you want to ask me about your mum?"

"Do you know what happened the day she died?"

"No," he says. "I left when Eddie came home early."

"Oh." I feel deflated suddenly, like I've been waiting for his answer for a really long time, and now it's never coming.

"Sorry I can't help," he says. He does look sorry, or at least that's what I think his face is doing. He squints at me. "Why are you asking now, anyway?"

"Dunno," I say. "I guess when Starr was the only person I saw, it didn't seem as important." I shrug. I don't know how to explain what I've been thinking – how suddenly it felt like the right time to clear up unanswered questions, confront things from the past that I've never understood.

Dear Uncle Jack, if you hadn't shown up, my mother might still be alive. Then I might have finished school and gone to university. But I think I've let that possible life stop me from living this one.

I cross over to the sink and lean back against it, facing him again. "What *can* you tell me about my mum, then?"

He looks sly. "What do you mean?"

"Why was she so upset when you turned up?"

"She obviously didn't want to see me, wouldn't you say?"

I think back to the conversation in the rose garden, remembering what my mother had said: 'Don't you dare say anything. I've worked so hard to build a life for my family. I won't – I won't let you come between us, you hear me?'

"What did you have over her?"

Uncle Jack slams his fist down onto the table. "You were always so strong, weren't you, Tallulah?" he says. "So unable to forgive weaknesses in anyone else, huh? You had it so fucking *easy*, that's why."

My heart's going a million miles a minute, but I keep my voice steady when I answer him. "Apart from everyone dying, I guess I had it okay."

I start clearing up the crockery from the draining board, shoving bowls and mugs into cupboards, rattling and slamming, half to get away from him, half to let myself calm down. Uncle Jack comes to stand next to me, holding his hands up in mock surrender. "Sorry," he says. "This isn't going well, is it?" He leans back against the counter. "Has anyone ever told you you look nothing like your mother?"

"I've got eyes don't I?"

"You're too defensive, kid."

"Don't call me kid. Or kiddo."

"Here." He pulls an envelope from the inside pocket of his jacket. "I put this together after Malkie got in touch. This is for you. Don't say I didn't try to look out for you."

He's baring his teeth in the wolf smile I remember from our first meeting. I take the envelope; it feels heavy. I slide the flap open and look at, then run my finger over the giant wad of notes inside. They're dirty and creased, lined up neatly in order of value. Fives, tens, twenties.

"Is this drug money?"

"So suspicious."

"Can you blame me?"

He pulls a face.

"Excuse me for not falling at your feet," I say. "I thought junkies were pretty tight."

"Don't you worry about me," he says. "I've got my own little stash."

"I don't worry about you," I say. "I don't want your money, either." I put the envelope down next to the sink, between us. Uncle Jack licks his lips.

"It's yours," he says. "Take it."

"Nope."

I walk to the fridge and open the door, pulling out milk and a packet of coffee.

"I'm not taking the money back," Uncle Jack says. "I mean, Christ… " He runs his fingers through his hair. "I'm trying to do the right thing, here, ki – Tallulah. Can you just let me, for once?"

"I don't want to be mixed up in something dodgy."

"It's not dodgy."

"How can I believe that?"

"It's not," he says, trying to look sincere. "It's from Edward. A more upright man than my brother has yet to be born."

At the mention of my father's name I feel a pang; I haven't thought about him once since Malkie turned up, even though he's the reason I needed to work all this out. I haven't even mentioned his condition to Uncle Jack, although I can't be sure he'd care.

"Why would you have my dad's money?"

"A coffee would be good," Uncle Jack says.

"Tell me about the money first."

"Edward gave it to me."

"So you said. Why would my dad give you money?"

"Your dad didn't give it to me. Not exactly."

"So you stole it off him?"

"No."

I roll my eyes. "I think your brain's been fried by all those drugs. Did he give it to you or not?"

"Yes, Edward gave me the money." He looks up then, trying to catch my eye. "But not your *dad*."

"What?"

"My brother," Uncle Jack pauses, "is not your dad. I am."

For a moment I feel like I'm falling, not my stomach this time, but my brain. I put a hand out to steady myself. "I'm sorry?" I croak.

"I'm your father."

"You can't be."

"I know, I know; it was a surprise to me too. But Evie wouldn't have done the dirty on me." He sees my expression. "I'm sorry, I didn't mean that. That was low." He bites his lip. "What I was trying to say was – we were an item. We were in *love*, for fuck's sake."

"You and my mum?"

"Now don't tell me you hadn't guessed that."

"I knew something had happened," I say, even though a voice inside is saying you did. You always knew. Even if there had never been that weirdness going on, you look exactly the same as Uncle Jack. "… She was always so scared of you."

Uncle Jack laughs again. "That's a good one."

"When did you get together? Where was my d – where was Edward?"

"Away in Africa." He tugs at his ear-lobe. "I'd worshipped her from the moment I met her. And then, one night, I walked her home – this is before she lived with Viv – and she asked me to come up." He spreads his hands in a shrug. "I didn't need asking twice."

Please, no more, I think, but he's carrying on.

"She was so gorgeous, your mother. And we were happy, you know, really fucking happy. We spent all our time together, didn't need anyone else. I remember when she told me she was pregnant – I couldn't stop kissing her."

I shift from one foot to the other; it feels strange, jarring,

371

to hear myself mentioned like that.

"Is this why she had the fight with Vivienne?" I ask.

Uncle Jack smiles his wolf smile again. "My sister can be a tad possessive," he says. "She said Evie was just using me while Ed was away. That she didn't love me as much as I loved her."

"Nice friend."

He laughs.

I clear a space on the sofa and sit down. A million questions are crowding my brain, but I can't work out which are the important ones right now. "Then what happened – how come she ended back up with Edward?"

For a second I think I chose the wrong question – he looks angry again, really angry, and I don't understand what he says next. "I'd have given my life for Evie, you know? And you too. I *did* give my life."

"What are you talking about?"

"Protecting you."

"What do you mean?"

"Why do you *think* me and Evie didn't work out?"

"Drugs?"

"Nope."

"You went to jail?"

"I did." He has his arms wrapped around his body, hugging himself. "And she waited a whole three months before moving in with my brother."

There's something else in the room now, something big. Uncle Jack's blinking at the floor. I feel my voice sitting at the bottom of my stomach, and I have to clear my throat twice before I can get the next question out. "Why?"

"Because I killed him," he says. "I killed my father."

Part Four

Blood

Nineteen

"*What?*"

Nothing I ask seems enough of a reaction. "How? *Why?*"

We look at each other properly for the first time.

"My father was a bully," Uncle Jack says, "Everyone in the village was scared of him. His kids walked around with black eyes, permanently, and no one said anything." He scratches his face; if not for the tremor in his hand, I'd assume he was completely calm right now. "He never liked Evie because she had no money. When he found out we were going to have a baby he lost it, told me he'd disinherit me before he let me squander the family savings on some gold-digging whore."

"What did he do?"

"We'd gone to see Mother. Albert was meant to be away that weekend – meeting someone who was trying to sell him a horse. Our flat in London was pretty dingy, and Evie ended up looking after Starr more than Viv did. She needed a break. You were nearly due and she used to fall asleep all the time."

"Was he there?"

"I'd gone to the pub. Mother was upstairs, reading. Evie was in the library, just sitting, thinking about you, apparently. She liked doing that." He takes a deep, ragged breath. "We found out afterwards the meeting hadn't gone as planned. The man was asking too much for the horse, and Albert didn't like to be taken for a ride. He came home early. When he walked in on Evie, he was three sheets to the wind and in a foul mood. He started on her, saying she'd never get a penny out of him. Accusing her of lying about who the father was." Uncle Jack looks at me quickly, then away again. "She stood up to him, and then he got violent."

I feel faint.

"That's the scene I came home to, my father pushing Evelyn around." He splays his fingers open. "He put his hand on her face, like this, and shoved her backwards onto the floor. She was crying, she was alone and scared and the bastard could have killed her. Or you. Then, when I come in, he starts on me. Shouting about how worthless I am."

"What did you do?"

"I hit him."

"That's it?"

He shakes his head. "He fell over and cut his face pretty bad – he was lying there bleeding and I couldn't stop." He gives me a funny smile. "I hit him enough for his heart to give out."

"Then what?"

"Your mother was horrified – couldn't understand that the man had had it coming." He's working himself up into a rage, and now he points a shaky finger in my direction, "After everything he'd done to me."

For a moment I feel trapped. If he'd wanted to hurt you, he would have done it by now, I tell myself. He wants you to understand him, that's all. I focus on breathing slowly. "So. You went to prison."

"Yes I went to prison."

"And?"

"For manslaughter. Twelve years. Out in ten." He laughs. "That's when I started taking heroin – I'd only ever done cannabis before, believe it or not." He looks at the floor. "There was a mix-up. I asked for gear, but it was a heroin-tobacco blend. They said it would be less likely to show up on drug tests. And the rest is history."

I let myself fall backwards on the sofa. The tap is dripping onto the dirty mugs and empty beer bottles in the kitchen sink; it's easy to let myself get distracted by the noise. Drip, *your father killed your grandfather*, drip, *your mother never told you*, drip, *and then she married his brother…* drip, *while your real father turned into a junkie.*

"Why," I start, and then I don't know where to go with the question. "Why… didn't you stay in touch? Why didn't I know you existed?"

Uncle Jack lets out a sigh. "I *killed* him, Tallulah," he says. "As much as I hated the bastard, I'd crossed a line even he'd never crossed. And your mother wouldn't look at me anymore, let me touch her."

"So she wouldn't come and see you?"

"She did – once or twice. She felt guilty, like it was her fault we'd been at Mother's in the first place. But she didn't want to visit, I could tell."

"Then?"

"I stopped coming out of my cell. I just wanted to smoke H. Visitors can't get in if you don't want them. That's the one thing you have control over."

"And my mum?"

"Edward told me he found her in a hostel."

I feel my heart give a little thud. My father – Edward – my uncle. I think of him in surgery, surrounded by tubes and green gowns and shiny instruments, and somehow he seems even more vulnerable now I know the truth. If he'd died on the table, there'd be nothing left, I think. When my mother died, I was proof that she'd existed, but he doesn't even have that.

"I don't blame her for going back to him," Uncle Jack is saying. "Not really. She was scared and alone, and, out of all of us, Eddie's the nicest. And maybe Viv was right, maybe she never stopped loving him anyway, the whole time we were together." He stops and takes a cigarette out. "And then she watched me… " He's trying to light the cigarette but he's shaking again. "Sorry, kiddo," he says. "Guess I'm not as hard as I look. I just… " He closes his eyes and a tear squeezes out, "I fucking adored her. And you. Or at least, the idea of you. I just keep thinking it was going to be so different. That's all I think about, really. How my life was meant to be so different."

He takes a long, harsh breath, then he's quiet and all I can hear is a hum in my ears.

"I wanted to tell you a long time ago, but… " He gestures to himself. "… Evie told me I'd ruin it for you two, then Eddie said he wanted to look after you, he said I'd do a shitty job. They gave me the money to disappear, and I guess I couldn't really say no, the state I was in."

I feel a rush of conflicting feelings when he says this – so Edward actively chose to keep me, after all, even if he did a terrible job of making me *feel* wanted.

Uncle Jack wipes his cheek with the back of his hand. And he wanted me too. "But Malkie… When he said he knew where you were… He said you wanted to see me… "

"Jack," I say, and then I can't go on.

✳ ✳ ✳

I can hear Toby running up the stairs as soon as I've buzzed him in, then he's pounding on the flat door. I open it so suddenly he falls in, then has to grab me to stop me from falling too.

"What happened?" he asks. His face is inches from mine; I feel calmer suddenly, in the face of his panic. My dad is not my real dad, I tell him, and watch him try to process it.

"*What?*"

"Yep."

"Is this… The one who had a heart attack?"

"He's my uncle," I say, "but he was actually with my mum before she and my other uncle – my real dad – went out."

"Wait," Toby says. He sits down at the kitchen table and pulls me in front of him. "Start again."

"I just saw him."

"Your…?"

"Uncle Jack. My real dad."

"Where's he now?"

"I told him I had to go to work, I couldn't deal with any more revelations. And then I texted you."

"It's a pretty big fucking revelation." He circles his arms around me. "How are you feeling? Do you think you've taken it in yet?"

"Wait, it gets better." I can feel myself grinning, stupidly. Don't fall apart now. "I *also* found out that Uncle Jack got into a fight with my grandad and my grandad had a heart attack and died and Uncle Jack – my dad – went to prison for manslaughter." I drop my face into my hands. He's going to run away if you tell him any more of this shit, I think. "It's just a fucking mess," I say, and then I start crying.

"Tal," Toby says, softly. He pulls me onto his knee. I press my face into his chest, letting the sobs break and subside. The cotton of his shirt is sucked away from his skin and towards my mouth with every deep breath inwards; I can hear his heartbeat.

"No wonder you're so fucking crazy," he mumbles into my hair.

"*Hey*."

"I'm joking."

I blow my nose on a napkin. "Sorry, I got mascara all over your shirt."

"I really need to stop wearing them around you," he says, and I grin for real. "So, do you wanna talk about it?"

"Where do I start?"

"Wherever you want."

I blow my nose again. "What do I say to him now I know? If he wakes up. Do I bring it up? Do I wait for him to tell me?"

"Bring it up."

"But he clearly didn't *want* me to find out."

"Well maybe it was your mum's idea to keep it a secret."

"Maybe." I dunno how I feel about that, either.

"And this was why your dad was weird with you when you were younger – is that what you think?"

"Yeah," I say. "Actually, he *was* fine until Jack showed up."

"And then what?"

"Maybe when Uncle Jack turned up, he thought my mum was going to leave with him and he was so scared of losing us he was horrible to us. Or maybe he was angry… I don't know."

He pushed us away, I think, like he told Kathy's mum. But he must have loved my mother a lot. He took her back even though it meant raising me; he must have really adored her.

Toby's frowning. "Did your mum still like Jack then?"

I lean my head against his shoulder. "There was definitely something between them. Even I could tell and I was ten."

"Okay."

"*God*," I say. I wipe my eyes and take a deep breath. "I feel bad for all of them. I mean – one guy kills his abusive father and goes to prison, loses his girlfriend and daughter, and the other one's stuck bringing up his brother's child, wondering if his wife is pining away for the father-killer."

Toby shakes his head. "When you put it like that… "

"I *know*."

We catch each other's eye, and suddenly we're both laughing. I feel weirdly better already, I feel my mind and body stretching forwards, unfurling themselves. I feel hopeful, I think.

Toby squeezes me. "What are you going to do now?" he asks.

"I guess I'll see him again," I say, and I have a sudden tug of sadness again. "I should hear more about it, I *want* to hear more about it. He's just… I'm not sure I can do it straight away."

"Understandable."

Maybe I'll get Malkie to keep an eye on Jack, make sure everything's okay. I give a silent prayer of thanks that he came back from Canada.

Another thought strikes me, and I sit up again. "I just can't believe all the adults knew what Jack did," I say. "When he first turned up at my grandma's, I thought everyone was tense because he hadn't told them he was coming."

"How did your grandma react?" Toby asks.

"She didn't really."

Why not, Grandma? Did you feel responsible? For the first time since I went to live with her, I can't imagine what she'd say in this situation. I remember Vivienne, that summer back in 1991, saying 'she did what she always did, nothing.' Maybe my grandmother was so worn down she could only go along with her circumstances. Not act for herself, not make decisions. She couldn't have been so crazy for my grandfather she sacrificed her kids for him, I try to tell myself, not when she was so loving to me.

I realise Toby's been talking. "What was that?"

"Could I wash myself in your kitchen?" He nods at the shower, "I ran all the way from the station."

"Sure," I say. I try to pull myself together; I look at him like I'm seeing him for the first time, run my finger along his jawline. "You don't have a beard."

"Nope."

"But you've got more manly-looking since I knew you."

"I should hope so."

"You were so cute back then," I say. "What happened?"

I lean forwards for a kiss, then we're interrupted by the telephone. It sounds shriller than normal, and louder, and it brings me back to what's going on around me. I'm up and across the floor before it rings for a third time, the receiver in my hand.

"Miss Park?"

"Yes."

"I'm calling from the hospital." Down the line she clears her throat. I look at Toby, we both seem frozen exactly as we are. Outside, the evening is still, hanging perfectly in the air.

"He's awake," she says.

*** ***

Aunt Gillian and Aunt Vivienne are in the reception area when I arrive. They're both in yellow, strangely – Aunt Vivienne in a Grace Kelly-style lemon dress with a nipped-in waist, and Aunt Gillian in an apricot chiffon shirt and black trousers.

"There you are," Aunt Gillian says. "What took you so long?"

"Taxi got stuck in traffic," I say, peeling my jacket off. I left Toby at the flat when I went out to hail one; it feels nice to know I'll be going home to someone tonight.

We file into my father's room. He's staring at something on the ceiling and doesn't seem to hear us.

"Don't get him too excited," the nurse says. She looks suspiciously at Aunt Vivienne, who looks back at her, all innocence.

We stand over him. Aunt Gillian is crying already and Aunt Vivienne looks wary.

"Hi Dad," I say.

My father tears his eyes very slowly away from the ceiling. "Who's that?" he asks.

"It's me, Tallulah."

"Tallulah?" My father seems to think about the name for a minute.

"Your *daughter*," Aunt Gillian bursts out. "And Gillian and Viv. Your sisters."

"Sisters?" my father asks.

"Oh *God*," Aunt Gillian wails.

We stand awkwardly in front of him, not knowing what to say next. I look at Aunt Vivienne; she shrugs.

My father sighs. His face looks funny, unfocused. I lean closer so he can take a look at me. My throat is pulsing in time with my heartbeat.

"Evelyn," he says, very quietly.

"No, it's Tallulah," I say. "Mum was Evelyn."

My father's face clears. It hits me, now that our eyes are

382

locked, how there are little flecks of gold in his irises.

"It's Tallulah," I say again.

"I know," my father says. "Tallulah."

* * *

The technical term for bleeding is 'hæmorrhaging', meaning the loss or leaking of blood either outwardly, such as through an orifice or break (cut) in the skin, or inwardly, when the blood escapes from blood vessels within the body.

As an adult in good health, you can lose up to twenty percent of your total blood volume with no long-term damage done. After that your skin might become clammy, your fingernails and lips bluish, your head dizzy. After a loss of forty percent, your body goes into shock, and immediate treatment becomes critical. However, if incompatible blood is transfused the new cells are perceived as 'foreign invaders' and the body's immune system will attack them, causing shock, kidney failure and even death.

It is the red blood cells that determine the blood type for each person. These contain a variety of antigens (substances that trigger the production of antibodies), which divides them into types: A, B, AB and O. Each child inherits one antigen from the mother and one from the father, which is why it is common for children to have the same blood type as at least one parent.

I've always known my blood type, it's the same as my father's: O negative, the universal donor. Anyone can receive a transfusion of our blood, but we can only receive from another O negative individual. If I start hæmorrhaging, it will be my father who can save me.

* * *

"Edward," Aunt Gillian says, dabbing at her eyes with a handkerchief. "You gave us such a fright."

"How are you feeling?" I ask my father.

"I've been better," he says.

"Yeah, probably," I say, and I try to smile.

"How have *you* been?" he asks, looking at me. His face is as blank as it always was, except that now his eyes are bigger, and purplish underneath.

"Okay," I say. "Worried about you."

"I didn't mean that," he says.

"I know."

"Don't talk in code, you two," Aunt Gillian says, automatically. "It's rude."

I'm looking at my father, drinking him in. I guess he does look a little bit like Omar Sharif – not the smiley, horse-betting, card-playing Omar Sharif in real life, more like his character in *Doctor Zhivago*, the tortured, honourable medic.

"Always enjoy sticking your nose in, don't you?" Aunt Vivienne's saying now. "People don't need to tell you absolutely *everything* that's going on, Gillian."

"Oh for goodness's sake, Vivienne," Aunt Gillian says. "Would it really hurt so much to be civil?"

My father closes his eyes.

"Both of you shut up," I say. "Dad's awake, so let's try and get on for half an hour. Just half a fucking hour."

I see my father smile quickly; just a flash, then it's gone.

"I swear," Aunt Vivienne says grimly. "*Someone* in this room is going to die of high blood pressure, and it might just be me."

Twenty

Aunt Vivienne comes to stand next to me by the window. We watch Gillian plump my father's pillow for him.

"My daughter's been updating me on your whereabouts, your health, you know," she says. "Little details like that."

"I thought so," I say. "It feels funny."

She folds her arms. "I'm not a mind-reader, Tallulah."

"Knowing that you two were thinking about me, I mean." I rock back on my heels, resting my hands against the windowsill behind me. "I always assumed that everyone just went on with their lives without me."

"Well, we did struggle on," Aunt Vivienne says; her mouth twitches. "But you don't forget family. Even when they seem to have forgotten you." She cocks her head at me. "Why did you come back?"

I chew my lip. "My mum said something when I was younger," I say. "About damaged people."

"Yes, well," Aunt Vivienne says. "If anyone knows damaged people it would be this family."

"But not just that they're damaged."

"No?"

"She said it's a cycle. So when you're damaged, you're damaged for life."

Aunt Gillian looks up from my father's side. "Tallulah,

darling. Must you talk about that here?"

"She can talk about whatever she pleases," Aunt Vivienne says. "It's one of the great things about our democratic society."

"This is not a democracy, this is a hospital," Aunt Gillian says, but she turns back to my father.

"And what was the conclusion?" Aunt Vivienne asks.

I shrug. "She was saying that when you're damaged, you damage others, and you put yourself in situations where you're going to be damaged again because it's the only way you know how to be." I shrug again. "But I didn't get it. And then I was so angry that she left me… " I stop. She wasn't just talking about the Parks, I realise. She needed security because she'd lost it after her parents died. And then when my father went away too she needed reassurance, and she turned to Uncle Jack. She just fell for him harder than she expected. But that was why she blamed herself – she thought that her neediness had caused all the trouble.

Aunt Vivienne looks impatient. "And now you want to prove her wrong?"

"I guess."

"Your mother was very smart, you know," she says. "I wasn't her biggest fan, obviously, but she was no ball of fluff."

"I know you don't hate us as much as you pretend to," I say, and she smiles at me. I think about telling her that Jack is back – that I know everything. That I understand now why she might have felt my mother betrayed her brothers, why she resented her. It wasn't her fault though, Aunt Vivienne. That was the way she was damaged.

I squeeze my eyes shut and think of Jack as he was in my flat, half strung-out and high, and I can't bring myself to say any of it. Aunt Vivienne loves Jack I know, really loves him, and it'll be much worse for her to see him in that condition than it was for me. He knew that too – that's why he wouldn't let her visit him in prison.

"Starr's flying home tonight," I say. "She said she'll come visit."

"As long as she doesn't bring that ape with her."

"Have you met him?"

"You know Starr – she never brings them home if she likes them. She's afraid I'll scare them off."

"He's probably really nice," I say. "She wouldn't like him otherwise."

"I did something right, then," Aunt Vivienne says. "It's a terrible bore loving men who don't give a hoot for you."

I think of a fourteen-year-old Vivienne, unconscious with her teeth in the fireplace; I think of Uncle Jack trying to rile my grandfather himself so Vivienne would be left alone. I think of the scene between her and Malkie after my mother's party – 'I'd die for him, you know.' I think of Aunt Vivienne at the prison, being turned away by the guards, sitting in her car in case Uncle Jack changed his mind. Waiting for hours, then driving home and checking the calendar to see when the next visitation day was.

I lean in quickly to kiss her cheek. She puts her hand up to the spot I've just pecked, blushing; it makes her look like a little girl.

"What was that for?"

"For being you," I say.

She blushes deeper, then calls over to Aunt Gillian, "Gillian, just be quiet for a minute, will you? Let's leave these two alone."

"We've only just got here," Aunt Gillian says, but Aunt Vivienne takes her by the elbow.

"You owe me," she says over her shoulder.

I sit next to my father again when they've gone, leaning forwards and resting my hands on the bed. "I'm sorry," I say.

"You've nothing to be sorry about." He coughs. It sounds like a smoker's cough – a proper hacking noise, with plenty of phlegm behind it.

"I thought you were going to die."

My father leans back onto his pillows. He pats my hand. I take his in mine; it's very cold.

"I went over what you said for a very long time," he says, slowly. "I suppose I was in denial. I didn't want to face up to the guilt of having put you in that situation. I tried to talk to the school about it and have action taken against the person who… But without you there, and I didn't even know if it was a teacher or a student." He grips his bedsheets.

"It was a teacher."

I think I see his eyes glisten. "I'm so sorry that it happened to you."

"It's fine," I say. "I mean, it's not fine, but it's in the past."

He looks guilty. "And I suppose I did seem cold when you were younger, but that wasn't because I didn't love you… Don't love you." He trails off.

"Dad… "

"And as for your mother… "

"Dad, it's okay. We can talk about this later."

"No," he says. "I want to talk about it now, while we still have time."

"Okay."

"I loved your mother."

"Of course."

"It's important for you to know that although she… she probably married me to secure a future for you," he says, "that doesn't mean you should think less of her."

"She didn't… " I start, but he holds his hand up to stop me.

"She never did a single thing without thinking of you first." He squeezes my hand tightly. "Your mother loved you very, very much, Tallulah. Don't think that she didn't love you more than anyone has ever loved anyone, because she did."

"I know," I say. "And I'm sorry I blamed you for her dying." I clear my throat. "I saw Jack earlier. I know…" I try to figure out how to phrase it delicately. "Everything, I guess."

"He told you about your mother?"

"Yeah."

"Did he explain?"

"Grandad? Yeah. And he gave me some money – he said he got it from you."

"Ah." My father passes his free hand over his face. He's silent for a moment. "I have to admit, I didn't give him enough credit. I thought he just wanted to come between me and your mother, to punish us. But he said he still loved her. And you."

"What happened at Grandma's that time? Why were him and Mum fighting?"

"He'd threatened to tell you everything."

"Oh." And then what? Was she scared I'd think badly of her? Is that why she got depressed? Or did she still feel guilty for everything that happened?

"So we paid him to go away." My father coughs again. "I thought he'd take the money and run."

"He did."

"But he came back again, after Evie died, with some idea about claiming his own back. He said he'd take me to court." He frowns. "I know – legally speaking – he had no leg to stand on, but by then it was too important for you not to find out. You were so devastated about your mother, I was afraid."

I have a sudden flashback to the telephone conversation I'd overheard that Christmas – so it was me Uncle Jack had tried to get back, not my mother.

"And you paid him off again?"

My father bites his lip. "I did. I'm sorry. I know it was wrong of me. Mother said I shouldn't interfere with someone trying to right the wrongs they did their children. And she was… " This time the coughing fit wipes out the end of the sentence.

"Take it easy, Dad."

"I truly believed," my father says, hand to his mouth, "he couldn't give you a stable, loving home. And I managed to persuade him, finally."

I lean back in my chair. "I always thought Mum was keeping a secret from you," I say. "That *that* was why she was scared when he turned up."

"She was nearly eight months pregnant when she moved in with me," my father says. "It would have been quite hard to keep that a secret, believe me, even without my medical training."

I can't hold back my laugh, in spite of the situation.

He shakes his head. "Your mother did keep secrets," he says, slowly. "But not very well. I could tell she still had feelings for Jack. And then he called that afternoon – he said she'd told him to. I didn't know they were speaking behind my back. It made me realise that perhaps she still wanted to be with him. Confirmed my fears, I suppose I should say. But I should never have confronted her." He stares at the ceiling.

"Hey," I say. "You didn't know what was going to happen."

I've been blaming him for the wrong thing, I realise. It wasn't his fault my mother died – he didn't push her, he couldn't have fixed her. It *was* his fault I felt abandoned afterwards, but then he was traumatised too.

"I'm sure you'll have plenty of time to get to know Jack better now?"

"I don't know."

"I know we had a falling out," he says, letting out a pent-up breath. "And you seem to have done a pretty good job of growing up without me – but I'd like to spend some father-daughter time together, if you'll let me call it that. Getting to know each other again."

I hesitate. I still have questions.

Then again – maybe she did still have feelings for Jack, after everything, but I think my mother loved my father too. He was the stable, caring one. He's who she chose to raise her child with. That means something to me.

"What do you think?" my father asks; he looks anxious.

"I'd like that too," I say.

"Good," he says.

"But slowly."

"I really am so sorry, Tallulah."

"Dad," I say. "Just concentrate on getting better. We can

390

talk about everything else later, okay?"

"Okay."

"Good."

He smiles weakly, then puts a hand up to his face, and pats his right eye.

"Something wrong?"

"It's twitching," he says. "Just a little annoying." He coughs again.

"Do you want some water?"

He nods.

Another nurse comes in. "I'm afraid visiting hours are over," she says.

"Let me get him a drink," I say. I pour him a cup, and stand next to him while he sips at it.

"I'll come back tomorrow," I say.

He looks up. "That would be nice."

I bend down and kiss him on the forehead and he puts his hand up, catching my hair, tugging it.

"It took a heart attack to bring you back," he says.

"No," I say. "It wasn't that." I want to shake my head, but he seems to be using my hair as support.

"Good," he says. "Because I don't think I could survive another one."

The nurse gives me a sympathetic smile as I leave the room.

"They're all a bit groggy for a while after they wake up," she whispers to me. "He'll get better, don't worry."

"He's fine already," I say.

She gives me one of those pitying looks they keep for relatives in denial, and closes the door behind me. Outside my father's room a cleaner is mopping the floor. My shoes squeak as I pick my way around the bucket, and everything smells waxy, fresh and new.

PART FIVE

Heart Again

Twenty one

Did you know the heart is the only organ not completely in thrall to the brain? Specialised pacemaker cells at the entrance to the right atrium are myogenic, meaning they will contract without an outside influence – such as the electrical impulse coming from the central nervous system. In fact your heart forms two weeks after fertilisation, and beats in the fifth week of the gestation period, before it is first fed by this impulse.

In other words, if you cut your heart out it could – in theory – continue beating.

* * *

When I was younger we went on a day trip to the museum. I don't know which museum; it was dark and had waxwork figures re-enacting scenes from Anglo-Saxon life. Men carrying shields and spears, women stirring huge cauldrons. My mother held my hand around the exhibitions and let me have an ice-cream in the café afterwards.

I remember sitting in the museum grounds with my face turned up towards the sun, my mother and father opposite me. My father wasn't wearing a tie that day, and he took his shoes and socks off to feel the grass with his bare feet. The two of them exchanged looks and laughed when I asked about the sandy hair growing on his toes. Years later, I realised that we must have looked like an odd little trio, the two full-bodied, blond parents with their skinny, dark-haired daughter.

I remember it being a national holiday, or something like that, because the place was crowded with people. Some boys – they must have been teenagers, although at the time they seemed old to me, and I hid behind my mother's legs when they came near – were kicking a football around, and my father kicked it back at them when it landed on our picnic blanket. He kicked it quite hard, and one of the boys, the closest one, clapped him and said something complimentary. My mother raised her eyebrows, "I didn't know you played football," she said, and my father laughed again.

We must have gone somewhere else, although I don't remember that, because it was late when we came home, my mother carrying me in her arms. I fell asleep up there, my cheek nestled in the crook of her neck, my father walking next to her on the kerb side. Just before I dropped off I felt his hand reach up and ruffle my hair. I heard him murmur something, and a car whoosh past. Then my mother's heartbeat pumping blood around her body, warm and safe and full of love for me.

Acknowledgements

There are countless people I would like to thank, but I should start with Ruth Salter and Jenny Slattery (two friends who happen to be great nurses). During my MA I practically lived at their flat and the week before I had to hand in my first piece of writing they were talking about the heart; this started me thinking about the metaphorical possibilities inherent in medicine, and the novel took off from there. I'm also eternally grateful for the existence of Wikipedia, and Orijit Banerji, another friend and a brilliant doctor, who kindly read through the medical sections for accuracy.

My agents, Natalie Butlin and Christine Green at Christine Green Authors' Agent, have been wonderful, working tirelessly on the manuscript and still finding time to prepare delicious lunches for me. Also Claire Anderson-Wheeler, who gave me my first invaluable feedback on the novel before jetting off to New York. I will definitely be taking you up on your offer of a drink out there someday.

My editor, Lauren Parsons, and the rest of the brilliant staff at Legend Press. Having someone fall in love with your book and get behind it as they have done has been the most incredible feeling.

My tutors, Fiona Stafford, Annie Sutherland and Philip West at Somerville College, who were fascinating and encouraging and made Austen, *Beowulf* and Shakespeare even more enjoyable, if that's possible.

I owe a huge debt to Susanna Jones at Royal Holloway, who always believed in this book, and Andrew Motion, who led me gently to the conclusion that I would make a terrible master criminal.

John Robertson and Charles Milnes, two of the nicest, most understanding bosses I could have hoped for.

For their patience and for all the drinks, the following writers: Emma Chapman; Liz Gifford; Carolina Gonzalez-

Carvajal; Lucy Hounsom; Liza Klaussmann; and Rebecca Lloyd-James. No one makes gin more fun.

My amazing friends, whose excitement about my becoming an author has been so moving. My favourite family, Janet, Alex and Hannah Gordon; Tallie might be a lot like me, but they made sure our lives were completely different. And my favourite cats, Daisy, Lucky and Maggie.

And last but not least, my boyfriend Tom Feltham. You're almost as brilliant a writer and editor as you are terrible at cleaning kitchen surfaces, and I love you very much.

Come and visit us at
www.legendpress.co.uk

Follow us
@legend_press